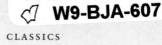

THE BLACK TULIP

ALEXANDRE DUMAS was born in 1802 at Villers-Cotterêts. His father, the illegitimate son of a marquis, was a general in the Revolutionary armies, and died when Dumas was only four. Dumas was brought up in straitened circumstances and received very little education. He joined the household of the future king, Louis-Philippe, and began reading voraciously. Later he entered the *cénacle* of Charles Nodier and started writing. In 1829 the production of his play, *Henri III et sa cour*, heralded twenty years of successful playwriting. In 1839 he turned his attention to writing historical novels, often using collaborators such as Auguste Maquet to suggest plots or historical background. His most successful novels are *The Count of Monte Cristo*, which appeared during 1844–5, and *The Three Musketeers*, published in 1844. Other novels deal with the wars of religion and the Revolution. Dumas wrote many of these for the newspapers, often in daily instalments, marshalling his formidable energies to produce ever more in order to pay off his debts. In addition, he wrote travel books, children's stories and his *Mémoires*, which describe most amusingly his early life, his entry into Parisian literary circles and the 1830 Revolution. He died in 1870.

ROBIN BUSS is a writer and translator who contributes regularly to *The Times Educational Supplement, The Times Literary Supplement* and other papers. He studied at the University of Paris, where he took a degree and a doctorate in French literature. He is part-author of the article 'French Literature' in *Encyclopaedia Britannica* and has published critical studies of works by Vigny and Cocteau, and three books on European cinema, *The French through Their Films* (1988), *Italian Films* (1989) and *French Film Noir* (1994). He is also part-author of a biography, in French, of King Edward VII (with Jean-Pierre Navailles, published by Payot, Paris, 1999). He has translated a number of other volumes for Penguin, including *The Count of Monte Cristo*, Jean Paul Sartre's *Modern Times*, Zola's *L'Assommoir* and *Au Bonheur des Dames*, and Albert Camus's *The Plague*.

ALEXANDRE DUMAS

The Black Tulip

Translated with an Introduction and Notes by
ROBIN BUSS

PENGUIN BOOKS

PENGUIN BOOKS

Published by the Penguin Group
Penguin Books Ltd, 80 Strand, London WC2R ORL, England
Penguin Putnam Inc., 375 Hudson Street, New York, New York 10014, USA
Penguin Books Australia Ltd, 250 Camberwell Road, Camberwell, Victoria 3124, Australia
Penguin Books Canada Ltd, 10 Alcorn Avenue, Toronto, Ontario, Canada M4V 3B2
Penguin Books India (P) Ltd, 11 Community Centre, Panchsheel Park, New Delhi – 110 017, India
Penguin Books (NZ) Ltd, Cnr Rosedale and Airborne Roads, Albany, Auckland, New Zealand
Penguin Books (South Africa) (Pty) Ltd, 24 Sturdee Avenue, Rosebank 2196, South Africa

Penguin Books Ltd, Registered Offices: 80 Strand, London WC2R ORL, England

www.penguin.com

First published as *La Tulipe noire* in Paris, 1865
Published in Penguin Classics 2003

6

This translation copyright © Robin Buss, 2003
All rights reserved

The moral right of the translator has been asserted

Set in 10.25/12.25 pt PostScript Adobe Sabon
Typeset by Rowland Phototypesetting Ltd, Bury St Edmunds, Suffolk
Printed in England by Clays Ltd, St Ives plc

Contents

Chronology

1802 Alexandre Dumas is born at Villers-Cotterêts, the third child of Thomas-Alexandre Dumas. His father, the illegitimate son of a marquis and a slave girl of San Domingo, had been a general in the Republican, then in the Napoleonic armies.

1806 General Dumas dies. Alexandre and his mother, Elisabeth Labouret, are left virtually penniless.

1822 Dumas takes a post as a clerk.

1823 Granted a sinecure on the staff of the Duc d'Orléans. Meets the actor Françoise Joseph Talma and starts to mix in artistic and literary circles, writing sketches for the popular theatre.

1824 Dumas's son, Alexandre, future author of *La Dame aux camélias*, is born as the result of an affair with a seamstress, Catherine Lebay.

1829 Dumas's historical drama, *Henri III et sa cour*, is produced at the Comédie-Française. It is an immediate success, marking Dumas out as a leading figure in the Romantic movement.

1830 Victor Hugo's drama *Hernani* becomes the focus of the struggle between the Romantics and the traditionalists in literature. In July, the Bourbon monarchy is overthrown and replaced by a new regime under the Orleanist King Louis-Philippe. Dumas actively supports the insurrection.

1831 Dumas's melodrama *Antony*, with its archetypal Romantic hero, triumphs at the Théâtre de la Porte-Saint-Martin.

1832 Dumas makes a journey to Switzerland which will form the basis of his first travel book, published the following year.

1835 Travels extensively in Italy.

1836 Triumph of Dumas's play *Kean*, based on the personality of the English actor whom he had seen performing in Shakespeare in 1828.

1839 *Mademoiselle de Belle-Isle*, Dumas's greatest success in the theatre, is staged.

1840 Dumas marries Ida Ferrier. Travels down the Rhine with Gérard de Nerval; they collaborate on the drama *Léo Burckart*. Nerval introduces Dumas to Auguste Maquet, who will become his collaborator on many subsequent works.

1844 *The Three Musketeers* begins to appear in serial form in March, the first episodes of *The Count of Monte Cristo* in August. Dumas starts to build his Château de Monte-Cristo at Saint-Germain-en-Laye. Separates from Ida Ferrier.

1845 *Twenty Years After*, the first sequel to *The Three Musketeers*, appears at the beginning of the year. In February Dumas wins a libel action against the author of a book accusing him of plagiarism. Publishes *La Reine Margot*.

1846 Travels in Spain and North Africa. Publishes *La Dame de Monsoreau*, *Les Deux Diane* and *Joseph Balsamo*.

1847 Dumas's theatre, the Théâtre Historique, opens. It will show several adaptations of his novels, including *The Three Musketeers* and *La Reine Margot*. Serialization of *The Vicomte de Bragelonne*, the final episode of the *The Three Musketeers*.

1848 A revolution in February brings in the Second Republic. Dumas stands unsuccessfully for Parliament and supports Louis-Napoléon, nephew of Napoleon I, who becomes President of the Republic.

1849 Publishes *The Queen's Necklace*. In May travels to Holland to attend the coronation of King William III.

1850 *The Black Tulip* is published. Dumas, declared bankrupt, sells the Château de Monte-Cristo and the Théâtre Historique.

1851 In December Louis-Napoleon seizes power in a *coup d'état*, effectively abolishing the Republic. Victor Hugo, joined by Dumas, goes into exile in Belgium.

1852 Second Empire proclaimed. Dumas publishes his memoirs.

1853 In November returns to Paris and founds a newspaper, *Le Mousquetaire*. Publishes *Ange Pitou*.

1858 Founds the literary weekly *Le Monte-Cristo*. Sets out on a nine-month journey to Russia.

1860 Meets Garibaldi and actively supports the Italian struggle against Austria. Founds *L'Independente*, a periodical in Italian and French. Garibaldi is godfather to Dumas's daughter by Emilie Cordier.

1861–70 Continues to travel throughout Europe. Writes six plays, thirteen novels, several shorter fictions, a historical work on the Bourbons in Naples and a good deal of journalism. Has a last love affair, with an American, Adah Menken.

1870 Dumas dies on 5 December.

Introduction

The Black Tulip, published in 1850, is the last of Alexandre Dumas's major historical novels. The premise is similar to that of *The Count of Monte Cristo*: a naive young man is caught up in the political upheavals of his time, after he has unwittingly aroused the envy of an unscrupulous rival, who plots to have him arrested and thrown into jail. But, unlike Edmond Dantès, who succeeds in escaping from captivity to take vengeance on those responsible for his imprisonment, the hero of this novel, Cornelius van Baerle, is saved partly by accident, partly by the efforts of a determined young woman and partly through the intervention of a benign ruler. Set in Holland, the novel is about justice triumphant and offers us an example of stoical resignation rather than implacable energy. Here, the solid virtues of the North replace the fiery temperament of the Mediterranean, which had been the setting for much of the earlier novel.

Dumas gives his readers their money's worth. In *The Black Tulip*, in the space of a mere 200 pages, he offers them a charming romance between his unjustly imprisoned hero and the jailer's beautiful daughter, framed in a narrative that involves real characters and events from history, as well as a brief tour of Holland, with excursions into some notable aspects of Dutch life, culture, horticulture and art. In a relatively brief historical romance, Dumas sets out to convey the essence of a whole society and culture.

'Do you want a sudden and complete feeling of foreignness?' asked a writer reviewing a Dutch novel in the *Revue des Deux Mondes* in that same year of 1850. 'Don't go to Constantinople, go to Rotterdam.'[1] Close though it was to France, Holland in the nineteenth century could seem quite remote, with its quaint customs, its Protestant ethos, its regional costumes and pictur-esque little houses. In the mental geography of the French Romantics, southern Europe had always loomed larger; Spain and Italy attracted them far more than the cold, puritanical North. In the second half of the nineteenth century, however, a few travellers, including Théophile Gautier, Gérard de Nerval and Dumas's friend, the art critic Arsène Houssaye, ventured beyond French-speaking Belgium and helped, in the books that they wrote on their return, to create a more positive image of the Low Countries. Cleanliness and prosperity were the basic constituents of this image, but it was not perhaps as well-ordered a society as this might suggest. As could be seen from their art, the Dutch had a sense of beauty and order, but also of the grotesque (something that appealed to the Romantic imagina-tion); they were associated with the Protestant values of sobriety and hard work, but at the same time with feasting and riotous excess.

Holland was seen, too, as an egalitarian society, the majority of its population belonging to a relatively affluent peasant class in the countryside or to the wealthy bourgeoisie in the towns. The Golden Age, when Holland had been the most prosperous country in Europe and a major naval power, might be over, but Dutch people still enjoyed a high standard of living. Some of this Dumas himself had the opportunity to observe, if only briefly, when he travelled to Holland in May 1849 for the coronation of King William III. It was on this occasion, appar-ently, that an acquaintance, the composer Friedrich von Flatow, told him about the history of the de Witt brothers, and their terrible fate at the hands of a mob in the Hague, in August 1672.

Dumas was, in the conventional sense, an uneducated man, with little knowledge of history. After the death of his father in 1806, when Alexandre was only four years old, he and his mother suffered a good deal of financial hardship. Dumas attended local schools until the age of fourteen, then went out to work. He came to write about history more by accident than by choice and always considered it, first and foremost, as a source of good stories. In other words, unlike most historical novelists, he did not intend to put his novelist's imagination to the service of the past, in order to throw light on events and the motivations of historical characters; rather, he drew on history because it provided good material for his imaginative fictions. Dumas always worked with collaborators, such as, in the case of *The Black Tulip*, Auguste Maquet, to whom he probably left the task of gathering the historical facts. The story of the de Witts – a gory tale of treachery and ingratitude – attracted his interest, but its purpose was to provide a peg on which to hang the entirely invented tale of Cornelius and Rosa. As for William of Orange, the one historical character who survives from start to finish, he appears in a totally different guise at either end of the book, firstly as the evil manipulator behind the murder of the de Witts, then as the wise ruler who sees justice done. There is nothing here that explains his motives or gives the basis for an informed judgement of his historical role. All we know is that he is reserved and inscrutable – and this could well be for no other reason than that Dumas is confusing William III with his great-grandfather, who was called 'The Silent'.

None the less, the novel does keep to the main facts in its account of the murder of the de Witts, and to understand its opening one must know a little about the earlier history of the region. Holland had been formed out of the seven northern provinces of the Spanish Netherlands (the ten southern provinces eventually coming together as Belgium). These United Provinces of the north had declared their independence from Spain in 1579, under the leadership of William the Silent, Prince of Orange. The war had not always gone their way, but by 1600 they were free of Spanish troops (though technically the war with Spain continued for another forty-eight years). The period that followed the achievement of independence was one of extraordinary prosperity for Holland, a time that is still known as *de Goude Eeuw*, or Golden Age, during which the Netherlands became the leading commercial power in Europe, and the country with the highest standard of living.

William the Silent was assassinated in 1584. He had not been a monarch in the conventional sense, but *Stadhouder*, a hereditary title for the head of state and military commander, who ruled in conjunction with the States-General, led by the *Raadpensionaris*, the elected Pensionary of the State of Holland. Inevitably, the division of functions in the States produced friction between the *Stadhouder* and the *Raadpensionaris*, which came to a head under William the Silent's grandson, William II. When William II died in 1650, leaving only a posthumous heir, the office of *Stadhouder* was left vacant. In 1653, the leader of the republican faction, Johan de Witt, became *Raadpensionaris* and eventually had the office of *Stadhouder* abolished in perpetuity.

De Witt was a brilliant statesman and diplomat, who devoted himself to maintaining his country's independence. He ended the first war with Holland's maritime rival, England, and managed to secure a favourable end to a second outbreak of war from 1665 to 1667. He also successfully formed the Triple Alliance against Louis XIV, who by his marriage had acquired a claim to the Dutch throne. But the chief threat to de Witt's power came from William II's son, William of Orange, whose pretention to the *Stadhouderat* was supported by a powerful faction within the country. In 1672, William was made *Stadhouder* and the Perpetual Edict abolishing the title was rescinded. De Witt resigned, but was exonerated when subsequently charged with treason.

This is more or less the point at which Dumas begins *The Black Tulip*, and the first four chapters are devoted to an account of what happened after Johan de Witt's brother, Cornelius, also an officer of state, was accused of plotting to assassinate William of Orange. There are several histories from which Dumas could have taken the facts that form the basis of his narrative; these include P. A. Samson's *Histoire de Guillaume III*,[2] the *Résumé de l'Histoire des Pays-Bas* by Frédéric, Baron de Reiffenberg,[3] and several biographies of Louis XIV. A number of other sources have been suggested, but it is impossible to be certain which, if any of them, Dumas (or Auguste Maquet) might have used. One version of the story, still recent at the time when the novel was written, was included in the sixth volume of a reference work called *Le Monde, histoire de tous les peuples*, which contains a history of the Netherlands contributed by Auguste Saint-

Prosper.[4] This is how Saint-Prosper describes the killing of the de Witt brothers:

A barber, no doubt bribed by some enemy, accused Cornelius of having offered him thirty-two thousand florins to assassinate the Prince of Orange. The people immediately rose up in indignation and threatened the magistrates who, giving way to fear, threw the accused man into irons and delivered him to the horrors of torture in order to make him confess an imaginary crime. Cornelius, in the midst of these torments, replied to his tormentors only by repeating the Ode of Horace which begins with the words: *Justum et tenacem propositis verum*, etc., an eloquent protest against injustice and tyranny. The Grand Pensionary had resigned his post and consoled Cornelius with his words and by his presence. The judges did not dare to condemn to death an innocent man; instead they ordered him into perpetual exile. But the mob considered this punishment too mild. It hurried to break down the doors of the prison, where the two brothers were to be found, cut their throats and began to drag their bodies through the streets. The murderers hacked the bodies of their victims into pieces which were sold around the town; a finger was worth fifteen Dutch *sous*, a thigh twenty-five . . . If he did not directly order these atrocities, William tolerated them and everything leads one to believe that he was the prime instigator of them, so much is it the case that ambition stifles feeling.

Many of the details here accord with what Dumas tells us: Cornelius de Witt's quoting Horace to his torturers, his brother Johan consoling him in prison, the dismembered bodies being sold (though Dumas mentions a price of 'ten *sous* a piece'; Reiffenberg, on the other hand, talks of the mob literally 'devouring' the corpses), and William's role behind the scenes as 'prime instigator' of the killings.

What Dumas does with the basic account is to elaborate it, embellish it and alter it to suit his purposes (for example, choosing to make the killing take place outside the prison, which agrees with some sources and allows him to invent a detail of his own, namely that William of Orange watched the murders as they happened). He also introduces two important fictional characters: the jailer Gryphus and his daughter, who form a bridge between this history and the real story, the one that begins in Chapter 5, with the modest Cornelius van Baerle and his tulips.

While many readers of Dumas's novel may have been unsure about the history of Holland two centuries earlier, they would certainly have made an association between that country and its national flower. The Dutch love affair with the tulip is in many ways more extraordinary than anything in Dumas's fiction; in fact, it may at first sight be surprising that he chose to build his novel around a competition to grow a particular variety of the flower, instead of involving his characters in the extraordinary financial dramas of what became known as tulipomania. The reason was that tulipomania reached its climax with the great crash of 1637, and Dumas wanted to peg his novel to the murder of the de Witt brothers, some thirty-five years later.

The tulip probably arrived in Europe from the Near East in the mid-sixteenth century and soon became popular with growers in France.[5] Among the first to introduce the flower into Holland was Charles de l'Escluse, or Clusius, who brought his tulip bulbs to Holland when he was appointed to a post at the University of Leyden in 1593. He set up a botanical garden at the university, which attracted the attention of enthusiasts in a country starting to enjoy the prosperity that came from its leadership in the realm of international trade.

It takes a long time, six or seven years, to grow tulips from seed, but once a plant has flowered, it produces outgrowths from its bulb, known as 'offsets', which can be removed and planted, to produce separate tulips that will themselves flower in a year or two. These 'offsets' play a central role in *The Black Tulip*.

The wild tulip is a flower of a single colour, but cross-pollination when flowers are grown together in gardens or nurseries has a tendency to produce hybrids, which in turn can be cross-pollinated to produce increasingly complex varieties. But the characteristic that most interested growers was the tendency of the tulip bulb to 'break': for a bulb from a tulip of a single colour to produce, quite unpredictably, a flower with a new, sometimes elaborate colour scheme – a white flower flecked or fringed with red, yellow or purple. Growers had no idea what caused 'breaking'; it was not until the twentieth century that it was discovered to be the effect of a virus (which explained a phenomenon that had already been observed, which was that broken tulips were weaker than others). Once broken, a bulb would remain broken; in other words, its seeds and offsets (unless they broke in their turn), would continue to exhibit the new patterns. The dazzling array of colours and new varieties produced by breaking was the reason for the tulip's unique popularity, while the unpredictability of the process and the length of time taken to grow the flowers explain the value that the bulbs rapidly came to acquire.

The market for tulip bulbs was in some respects comparable to that for paintings and other works of art, price being determined by the rarity of the object and the aesthetic value placed on it by the purchaser. Tulips were considered to exhibit the height of natural beauty; they were worshipped as evidence of God's artistry, and they were prized as objects displaying the taste and wealth of their owner. Very soon, the finest varieties were changing hands for astonishing sums of money and being given extravagant names in addition to their Latin ones: Admiral Pottebacker, General van Gouda and Semper Augustus. The last of these, apparently a variety that was slow to produce offsets, became the most famous and highly prized of all. By the 1630s, a single flower of a good variety could be worth many times the price of a painting of tulips by the finest artists in the field (who included Jan Brueghel and Ambrosius Bosschaert).

Once the market started to grow, there was no stopping it. By the mid-1630s, bulbs were changing hands for prices equivalent to the cost of a house – and in some cases to the cost of the finest town houses in the centre of Amsterdam. Bulbs and offsets were no longer sold as a piece, but by weight, using a goldsmith's measure, the ace, so that the buyer could have a better idea of the bulb's maturity. Once the most highly prized tulips had acquired such monetary value, their worth as aesthetic objects became less important; and since it took time for the bulbs themselves to flower, buyers often purchased bulbs which were left with the grower to mature in the ground. The bill of sale could then be sold on by the purchaser and might change hands several times, increasing in price as it did so. Each new buyer was in fact speculating on the eventual value of the flower and a sort of futures market in tulips came into being. Tulips were no longer valued as flowers, they had become a form of currency, an abstraction, traded for thousands of florins in taverns throughout Holland, by buyers and sellers who had never seen and probably never would see the property for which such huge sums of money were being exchanged. In this sense, they were comparable to those impressionist paintings that are bought as an investment by corporations and pension funds, then kept in a vault.

The crash came early in 1637, with terrifying suddenness. The price of tulips simply collapsed and those who were left with the vastly overvalued bulbs were often ruined. One of them was Jan van Goyen, a successful landscape artist who had given up painting altogether to spend the money he had earned with his brushes on speculating in bulbs. In January 1637 he purchased a total of fifty bulbs for the price of 912 florins (roughly the value of fifty tons of wheat or a hundred sheep) and two of his own paintings. Within days, the market crashed and he was bankrupt. He returned to painting and spent the rest of his life working to pay off his debts, but had still not done so when he died in 1656.

From being an example of God's artistry, the tulip became a symbol of human folly, the subject of sermons and caricatures. But instead of a speculator in bulbs caught up in the madness of the 1630s, Dumas shows us a man dedicated to breeding new varieties of the flower, whose passion, far from being a form of madness, is a shield against the kind of insanity that led to the assassination of the de Witt brothers. Cornelius van Baerle, in obedience to his godfather and namesake Cornelius de Witt, has experienced a naval battle; he has seen ships blown up and men perishing, and observed that, after all the destruction and slaughter, 'nothing had been settled either for or against, but that each side claimed victory, that everything had to be done all over again and that another name, that of Southwold Bay, had simply been added to the catalogue of battles' (Chapter 5) – so he decides to take literally Candide's advice in Voltaire's novel, and cultivate his garden.

Although there are similarities between the great tulipomania of the Dutch Golden Age and the modern art market, the source of the aesthetic super-value attached to the objects, which explains their apparently ridiculous price, is rather different. Mike Dash, whose book on the subject treats it primarily as an economic phenomenon, also points out that one reason why people in the seventeenth century attached such importance to the flower was that they saw it as the summit of creation in this particular sphere: 'The tulip was,' the French horticulturalist Monstereul wrote, 'supreme among flowers in the same way that humans were lords of the animals, diamonds eclipsed all other precious stones, and the sun ruled the stars.'6 The value that the Dutch placed on the flower was founded on the notion of flowers as the epitome of God's creation and their beauty as a means to glorify their Creator – a recurrent theme in the novel. Hence, too, the superiority of the natural flower over its representation by 'a painter, that is to say a kind of madman who tries to reproduce the wonders of Nature on canvas, disfiguring them' (Chapter 5).

This is the view that Dumas attributes to his villain, Isaac Boxtel, and it is not necessarily his own. Cornelius, though he may apply his genius to the creation of flowers, is still an artist, and behind this romance – charming or trivial, as you wish – is a reflection on Art. Since this is a novel by Dumas, there is nothing dull or heavy-handed in the way the subject is approached. But the tulip – 'that masterpiece of creation' (Chapter 5), 'a wonderful combination of nature and art' (Chapter 13) – is the other heroine of the novel, as Rosa realizes: she readily acknowledges the flower as her rival for Cornelius's love.

The tulip is central to the novel because of its role in the mechanism of the plot; but it also takes on a more symbolic function in the relationships between the main characters. It becomes the third party in the story of the relationship between Rosa and Cornelius, involving him in a struggle between his love for her and his art. It is the motive for Boxtel's jealousy of

Cornelius, a jealousy that is all the more intense since Boxtel is enough of a tulip grower himself to appreciate his rival's superior genius, just as Salieri is supposed to have been able to appreciate that of Mozart – 'for, underneath it all, he [Boxtel] was an artist and his rival's masterpiece meant a lot to him' (Chapter 6). The difference is that Boxtel has to struggle to achieve 'an art that he [Cornelius] seemed to be acquiring by instinct', so that in a mere two years he has 'covered his flowerbeds with such wonderful productions as no one, except perhaps Shakespeare and Rubens, had created after God' (Chapter 6).

Even though the exact nature of Cornelius's activity is problematic – Dumas most often refers to him as 'discovering' a new flower, only near the end describing him as 'the author of the tulip' (Chapter 31) – the novel can still be read as an allegory of artistic creation: in this sense, it describes, in Cornelius's imprisonment, the artist's solitary struggle to give birth to his masterpiece, with Rosa as his Muse. He has to struggle against the incomprehension of the ignorant (Gryphus) and the corruption and envy of those who wish to exploit it for money or fame (Boxtel), as well as against the inner temptations or distractions of politics and love, until his eventual triumph, when his creation is publicly hailed and given the recognition it deserves.

The Black Tulip is a novel about art, and it is also about a culture that was known chiefly to the French, and to Dumas, through its artists. Dutch painting had long been popular with collectors and patrons, but in the second quarter of the nineteenth century French critics started to accord it a new degree of respect and attention. Until then, apart from the work of Rubens and Van Dyck, that of Flemish and Dutch painters had not been easily visible abroad: 'Many Flemish and Dutch painters of the first rank were hardly known outside their own countries,' H. van der Tuin writes, in a monograph on the Netherlands masters and art criticism in France in the first half of the nineteenth century.[7] These virtual unknowns include Hobbema and, perhaps most surprising to us, Vermeer.

Painting in the Netherlands was broadly seen as a development of the German school, that of Dürer, and it tended to elicit admiration rather than enthusiasm. On the whole, travellers from France were more likely to head south, towards Italy. This had been particularly true of artists, under the influence of the Académie Royale des Beaux-Arts (later the École des Beaux-Arts), when conventional theory accorded the highest status to paintings of subjects derived from Greek and Roman mythology, and made the study of classical models an essential part of the artist's training. The annual Prix de Rome offered four years' free study at the Académie de France in Rome to the best students of the École des Beaux-Arts, who were required to make copies of classical sculpture and Italian Renaissance paintings.

None the less, the Louvre in the early nineteenth century had a reasonably representative collection of Flemish and Dutch paintings from the Golden Age, and the changes in perception that took place during the 1820s prepared the way for a new appreciation of their qualities. The Romantics valued truth above conventional notions of beauty; they could see the beauty in what might conventionally be dismissed as ugliness. They were not greatly interested in classical mythology or in grand generalizations; they sought local colour and the specifics that distinguish places and people, rather than universals.

As a result of this, characteristics of the painters of the Low Countries that had previously been considered as defects came to appear as strengths: there was a special kind of poetry in these pleasant, human landscapes and genre scenes. Indeed, the periodical *L'Artiste*, which did a great deal to promote appreciation of Dutch painters, with both articles and lithographs, actually suggested that they had benefited from staying at home, rather than travelling to Italy and copying classical statuary and Italian masters: 'The sedentary life of these admirable artists . . . is the quite natural explanation of the superiority of their manner of painting . . . the artists who travelled a lot are almost always superficial in what they observe.'[8]

One writer who contributed a great deal to this new assessment of Dutch and Flemish art was Dumas's friend Arsène Houssaye, a regular contributor to *L'Artiste* and *La Revue de Paris*, and the author of a two-volume history of Dutch and

Flemish painting.[9] Dumas was also acquainted with the Dutch painter Ary Scheffer, born in Dordrecht in 1795, who became drawing master to the children of King Louis-Philippe and, if only by his presence among them, helped to direct the attention of his French contemporaries to Dutch art.[10]

These writers were in no doubt as to the importance of art as a key to the Dutch soul. 'The true poets of Holland are above all her landscape painters,' Houssaye wrote,[11] having noted that in the Netherlands, painting took the place of literature: the history of the country, its customs, its scenery and so on, are in its painting – 'when one has that sort of poetry, can't one do without the other? Isn't Rembrandt equal to Molière and Ruysdael to La Fontaine?'[12] He admits, however, that Dutch painting is lacking in thought and feeling: 'more concerned with the living forces of Truth than with the high peaks of the Ideal, it has not been able to achieve the Beauty enshrined in the precious monuments of Greece and Rome'.[13]

It is not surprising, then, that in *The Black Tulip* Dumas makes repeated references to Dutch painting, both to support his argument on Art and Nature, and to conjure up a scene in the reader's mind. When, for example, he writes about the de Witts' servant Craeke riding through 'the winding meanders of the river which, with moist embrace, enfold those charming islands, fringed with willows, rushes and flowering grasses where fat flocks idly graze under the bright sun' (Chapter 5), he clearly has in his mind's eye a painting, perhaps by Paul Potter – 'friend of cows and cowherds, who so well understood the indolence of great oxen . . . sublimely naive'[14] – or by Ruysdael, who 'lived in familiarity with running water, rustling leaves, hedgerows, meadow grasses . . . the little boat asleep on the stream . . .',[15] or Berghem, who, Houssaye says, was 'the happiest man in the world, realizing that dream of all poetic souls: love and art'[16] – a phrase that could almost have been written to describe the hero of Dumas's novel, that supremely contented artist, doctor, tulip grower and lover, Cornelius van Baerle.

Dumas refers by name in the novel to seven painters: Gerrit Dow, Franz van Mieris, Rubens, Rembrandt, Gabriel Metsù, David Teniers the Elder and David Teniers the Younger. These allusions are not simply intended to embellish the text or exhibit the author's erudition. Each one has a specific purpose in its context and together they are intended to situate the novel in the cultural context of mid-seventeenth-century Holland.

The name of Peter Paul Rubens would have been familiar to all of Dumas's readers; the painter is the pivotal figure in Houssaye's history of Flemish and Dutch art, the first volume of which ends and the second begins with this 'genius of the first order'. In the seventeenth and eighteenth centuries, the Academy was divided over the merits of Rubens and Poussin, Rubens been seen as the great colourist and Poussin – 'the classic and virtuous Poussin'[17] – as the great exponent of form. Rubens's name appears only once in *The Black Tulip*, in a passage already quoted, coupled with that of Shakespeare, as second only to God in creative power (Chapter 6). Rembrandt, too, is mentioned in passing, his name suggested by the contrasts of light and dark in a scene on the prison stairs (Chapter 9).

Houssaye discusses both Gerrit Dow and Gabriel Metsù together under the general heading 'Painters of Private Life', emphasizing their qualities of meticulous observation, harmony and truthfulness. Dow, he says, would spend three days painting a single hand, which made him the despair of his patrons, his paintings reflecting the simplicity of his own life. As for Metsù, Houssaye says that 'no colourist ever possessed the gift of harmony to a higher degree'.[18] In the case of van Mieris, Dumas may be uncertain of the distinction between Franz van Mieris, who was a contemporary of Metsù and of the events of the novel, and his son Willem: it is the latter whose work corresponds more closely to the description of Rosa as being like 'those delightful women of Mieris and Metsù . . . framed in the first green shoots of the honeysuckle and wild vine' (Chapter 23).

The charm of the Dutch interior, with its Protestant bourgeois cleanliness and decency, contrasts with that other aspect of life in the Low Countries, the *kermesse*. The Dutch were famous for their drinking, carousing and merry-making: 'Never has more natural laziness produced more eagerness in shouting, singing and dancing than that shown by the good republicans of the Seven Provinces on the occasion of a fête' (Chapter 31),

Dumas tells us, citing as evidence the paintings of David Teniers the Elder and David Teniers the Younger, both specialists in themes of weddings, cabarets and peasant dances. Once again, there were examples in the Louvre, including the younger Teniers's paintings of a village wedding, a village fête, peasants dancing with bagpipes and the interior of a tavern.

By contrast to these apt references to Dutch painting, direct observation of Dutch scenery and towns is not especially evident in the novel. Dumas describes Dordrecht, Cornelius's home town, as hilly, when it is in fact a port built on reclaimed marshland, and paintings of the town by Cuyp, van Goyen and others show it as flat. What struck A. J. du Pays, one of Dumas's contemporaries, about Dutch towns was the uniformity of decoration on the façades of the houses and the tendency to use a single colour for all the houses in a given town,[14] Dordrecht's colour being yellow. It may be that in speaking of the bright red houses there, trimmed with white, bathing their feet in the water and with Oriental carpets hanging out at the windows (see Chapter 5), Dumas was thinking more of Amsterdam. But, as we know, he tended not to be meticulous about such details, as long as he had a good story to tell.

And Dumas had other things on his mind. *The Black Tulip* appeared at a moment of crisis in his affairs. In October 1850, the month before the book was published, one of his most cherished ventures, the Théâtre Historique, had gone bankrupt and his folly, the Château de Monte-Cristo, which he had built in Saint-Germain-en-Laye in 1844, had to be sold off at auction for 30,000 francs to pay his debts. He had fallen out, too, with his old collaborator Maquet, who had taken him to court over his failure to honour an agreement that Maquet would be paid an annual sum in exchange for the right to royalties in their joint works. There were to be other collaborators – Noël Parfait, Edmond Viellot – but none who suited Dumas as well as Maquet.

The loss of the house that he had named after one of his most successful novels together with that of the theatre was a terrible blow. If anything, he felt that of the theatre more keenly. He had built it four years earlier to produce not only his own works, but those of Shakespeare, Goethe, Schiller and Calderón. From his debut in 1825, Dumas had been associated with the Parisian theatre in its most exciting period. He had written *Antony*, one of the defining dramas of Romanticism. He had fought the battle against the old theatrical conventions alongside Victor Hugo, Théophile Gautier, Alfred de Musset and Alfred de Vigny. He had also been the lover of the actress Marie Dorval, who had played the heroine in *Antony*, sharing her with Vigny, and had wept at her graveside in May 1849, burying some of the best of his youth with her.

A year later, these personal disasters were to be followed by a disaster on a national scale. In December 1851, Louis-Napoleon, nephew of the Emperor Napoleon I and President of the Second Republic, seized power and established the regime that would eventually become the Second Empire. Dumas, like Hugo, was utterly opposed to this betrayal of the Republic. Together, they fled to Brussels, from where Hugo, with a price on his head, was eventually to retreat into exile on Guernsey. Dumas, for whom exile had been mainly an excuse to escape his creditors, returned to France, threw himself into journalism, planned to write a vast work encompassing the whole history of mankind, oversaw the publication of his collected works (eventually to number 301 volumes) and wrote his memoirs. Much of his time was taken up with editing and, to a great extent, writing his newspaper, *Le Mousquetaire*. His appetite for life remained, however; until his death in 1870 he continued to produce novels, plays, memoirs, histories, journalism and travel books at a prodigious rate, but the best of his work was behind him. *The Black Tulip*, the last of his great novels, is an unusually small-scale, intimate tale, not enjoying great favour with critics, but popular with Dumas's readers, who have been quicker to appreciate the merits of this story of a self-effacing artist, a brave girl and a mythical flower.

NOTES

1. J.-J. Ampère, in a review of Miss Toussant's *Leycester in Nederland, Revue des Deux Mondes*, Vol. VI, 1850, p. 864.
2. Three volumes, The Hague, 1703. The account of the murder of the de Witts, which differs in some respects from Dumas's narrative, is in Vol. II.
3. Two volumes, Brussels, no date (*c.*1815).
4. Six volumes, Paris, 1839. (My translation.)
5. I am indebted for the information that follows to two books on the tulip: Mike Dash's *Tulipomania* (London, 1999) and Anna Pavord's *The Tulip* (London, 1998).
6. Dash, *Tulipomania*, p. 73.
7. H. van der Tuin, *Les Vieux peintres des Pays-Bas et la critique artistique en France de la première moitié du XIXe siècle*, Paris, 1948.
8. *L'Artiste*, Vol. VIII, 1834, p. 133.
9. Arsène Houssaye, *Histoire de la peinture flamande et hollandaise*, 2 volumes, 2nd edition, Paris, 1848.
10. Scheffer's studio, at 16 rue Chaptal, in Paris, is now the Musée de la Vie Romantique.
11. Houssaye, *Histoire de la peinture flamande et hollandaise*, Vol. I, p. 40.
12. Ibid., Vol. I, p. 39.
13. Ibid., p. 6.
14. Ibid., Vol. II, pp. 268 and 274.
15. Ibid., p. 295.
16. Ibid., pp. 275–6.
17. J. S. Memes, *History of Sculpture, Painting and Architecture*, Edinburgh, 1829, p. 194.
18. Houssaye, *Histoire de la peinture flamande et hollandaise*, Vol. II, p. 202.
19. A. J. du Pays, *Itinéraire descriptif, historique et artistique de la Hollande*, Paris, 1862.

Further Reading

ON DUMAS

Hemmings, F. W. J., *The King of Romance* (London: Hamish Hamilton, 1979)

Maurois, André, *Three Musketeers. A Study of the Dumas Family*, translated by Gerard Hopkins (London: Jonathan Cape, 1957)

Schopp, Claude, *Alexandre Dumas. Genius of Life*, translated by A. J. Koch (New York: Franklin Watts, 1988)

Stowe, Richard, *Dumas* (Boston, 1976)

ON HOLLAND

Rowen, Herbert H., *John de Witt, Grand Pensionary of Holland, 1625–1672* (Princeton, NJ: Princeton University Press, 1978)

Schama, Simon, *The Embarrassment of Riches* (London: Collins, 1987)

ON TULIPS

Dash, Mike, *Tulipomania* (London: Indigo, 1999)

Pavord, Anna, *The Tulip* (London: Bloomsbury, 1998)

A Note on the Translation

La Tulipe noire was published in 1850, and almost immediately pirated in Belgium, with some cuts. The text used for this translation is the edition of the complete text published in Paris by Michel Lévy in 1865.

The first English-language translation, by Fayette Robinson, appeared in New York in 1850. A translation by Franz Demmler followed in England in 1854. As with most nineteenth-century translations of Dumas, Demmler's was quite heavily cut, though there was nothing in this novel to make a Victorian maiden blush. Instead, whole paragraphs of historical information, description, literary references and authorial asides were simply discarded, and a few errors introduced through misprints or spelling mistakes which have persisted in re-editions of this text up to the present day; these cuts include, for example, some two full pages about Haarlem at the start of Chapter 31. All this is a pity, because it reduces the novel to a mere story, a historical novel without any historical context. A full text, such as the one translated here, re-establishes that context.

The Black Tulip

CHAPTER I

A Grateful People

On 20 August 1672, the city of the Hague, so lively, so white and so trim that you would think every day was Sunday; the city of the Hague, with its shady park, its great trees rising above the Gothic houses and the broad mirrors of its canals reflecting the church towers with their almost Oriental cupolas; the city of the Hague, capital of the seven United Provinces,[1] was packed with a red and black stream of citizens in every one of its streets, hurrying, panting, anxious, running along with knives at their belts, muskets on their shoulders or sticks in their hands towards the Buitenhof,[2] that fearsome prison whose barred windows can still be seen today, where Cornelius de Witt,[3] brother of the former Grand Pensionary of Holland,[4] had been languishing ever since the accusation of murder was brought against him by the barber Tyckelaer.

If the history of that time – and, above all, of the year in the middle of which our story begins – were not so inseparably linked to the two names that we have just mentioned, the few lines of explanation that we are about to give might seem like an hors-d'oeuvre. But we must from the start advise the reader – that old friend to whom we always promise pleasure from the first page, and keep our word as best we may in those that follow – as I say, we advise the reader that this explanation is as indispensable to the lucidity of the story as to an understanding of the great political event within which the story is set.

Cornelius de Witt, *Ruaart* of Putten[5] (that is, inspector of the dykes of that country), ex-burgomaster of Dordrecht, his native town, and deputy in the States of Holland,[6] was forty-nine years old when the Dutch people, weary of the Republic as it was understood by Johan de Witt, Grand Pensionary of Holland, was taken with a great love for the Stadhouderat,[7] which Johan de Witt had for ever abolished in Holland under a Perpetual Edict imposed on the United Provinces.

Public opinion, in its capricious changes of heart, seldom fails to detect a person behind a principle, so, behind the Republic, the people saw the stern figures of the two de Witt brothers, those Romans of Holland, who would not stoop to flatter the national taste, but remained constantly on the side of freedom without licence, and prosperity without excess, while behind the Stadhouderat, they saw the grave, thoughtful, nodding head of young William of Orange, called the Silent[8] by his contemporaries and afterwards by posterity.

The two de Witts humoured Louis XIV,[9] feeling the growth of his moral ascendancy in Europe and having just witnessed his material ascendancy over Holland through the success of his brilliant campaign on the Rhine, made illustrious by the romantic figure known as the Comte de Guiche[10] and recorded in the verses of Boileau,[11] a campaign which in three months had crushed the power of the United Provinces.

Louis XIV had long been an enemy of the Dutch, who mocked and abused him as best they could,[12] almost always, it must be said, through the mouths of French refugees in Holland. National pride saw him as the Mithridates of the Republic.[13] As a result, the de Witts were confronted with the double animosity that comes from vigorous resistance to a power which is opposed to the feelings of the people, and from the weariness natural in any conquered nation when they hope that another leader might save them from ruin and shame.

This other leader, about to emerge and ready to measure himself against Louis XIV, however immense that French king's fortunes might promise to be, was William, Prince of Orange, son of William II and grandson, through Henrietta Stuart, of King Charles I of England – a silent young man whose shadow, as we have said, loomed over the Stadhouderat.

He was twenty-two years old in 1672. Johan de Witt had been his tutor and had brought him up with the intention of making a good citizen out of this former prince. With a love for his country that took precedence over his love for his pupil, he had removed the hope of obtaining the Stadhouderat from him by means of a perpetual decree. But God mocked this pretension of mankind that makes and unmakes the powers of the earth without consulting the King of Heaven: by means of the whim of the Dutch people and the terror inspired by Louis XIV, He had just reversed the policy of the Grand Pensionary and abolished the Perpetual Edict, re-restablishing the Stadhouderat for William of Orange, for whom He had designs of His own, still hidden in the mysterious depths of the future.

The Grand Pensionary bent before the will of his fellow citizens, but Cornelius de Witt was more recalcitrant and, despite the death threats uttered by the Orangeist mob which besieged him in his house in Dordrecht, he refused to sign the act to re-establish the Stadhouderat. Finally, at the insistence of his weeping wife, he did sign, merely adding after his name the two letters 'V. C.', or *vi coactus*, meaning, 'compelled by force'.

It was only by a miracle that he escaped the hands of his enemies that day.

As for Johan de Witt, he profited little better by his swifter and easier submission to the will of his fellow citizens. A few days later, he was the victim of an attempt at assassination. Though stabbed several times, he did not die of his wounds.

This was not at all what the Orangeists wanted. The life of the two brothers was an eternal obstacle to their plans, so they temporarily changed tactics, while remaining ready to accomplish one end by means of the other at a given moment, and tried to achieve through calumny what they had not been able to carry out with the dagger.

It is quite rare for God to provide a great man at the necessary moment to carry out some great deed, which is why when this unusual combination of circumstances does occur, history at once records the name of the chosen one and recommends him to the admiration of posterity. But when the devil takes a hand in human affairs, to ruin a life or overthrow an empire, it is very rare for him not to find some wretch immediately available, who only needs a word in his ear before at once setting to work.

The wretch who found himself in this case ready and willing

to act as the agent of the evil spirit was named Tyckelaer, as I
think we have mentioned, and was a barber by profession. He
came forward and declared that Cornelius de Witt – desperate,
as was proved by documents in his own hand, at the abrogation
of the Perpetual Edict, and consumed by hatred for William of
Orange – had charged an assassin with freeing the Republic
from the new Stadhouder; and that the assassin was himself,
Tyckelaer, who was so overcome by remorse at the very idea of
what he had been asked to do that he preferred to reveal the
crime rather than to commit it.

One may well imagine the indignation of the Orangeists at the
news of this plot. The procurator fiscal[14] had Cornelius arrested
in his house on 16 August 1672. And, in a room at the Buitenhof,
the *Ruaart* of Putten, the noble brother of Johan de Witt, like
one of the vilest of criminals, suffered the preliminary torture
intended to get him to confess his alleged plot against William.

But Cornelius had a great heart as well as a great mind. He
belonged to that group of martyrs whose political faith is as
strong as was the religious faith of their ancestors, and who
laugh at pain. During the torture, he recited the first stanza of
Horace's *Justum et tenacem*[15] in a firm voice, scanning the lines
properly, and confessed nothing, exhausting the strength and
fanaticism of his torturers.

Despite that, the judges acquitted Tyckelaer of all charges
and passed a sentence on Cornelius that relieved him of all his
offices and honours, made him liable for the costs of the trial
and banished him for ever from the territory of the Republic.

This judgment, against a man who was not only innocent,
but also a great citizen, went some way towards satisfying the
people, to whose interests Cornelius de Witt had constantly
devoted himself; but as we shall see, it was not enough.

Though history gives them a fine reputation for ingratitude,
the Athenians must admit that in this they come second to the
Dutch: they were satisfied with merely banishing Aristides.[16]

When Johan de Witt heard the first reports of the charges
against his brother, he resigned from his post as Grand Pensionary. He was equally well rewarded for his devotion to his
country. He took with him into private life his enemies and his

wounds, the only profits that generally accrue to honest people who are guilty of having worked for their country rather than for themselves.

Meanwhile, William of Orange, while doing everything in his power to bring this about, was waiting for the people, who idolized him, to make the bodies of the two brothers into the two stepping stones that he needed to ascend to the seat of the Stadhouderat.

So on 20 August 1672, as we said at the start of this chapter, the whole town flocked to the Buitenhof to witness Cornelius de Witt being released from prison, on his way into exile, and to see the marks that torture had left on the noble body of this man, who knew his Horace so well.

We should hasten to add that this crowd at the Buitenhof did not go there solely with the innocent intention of watching this spectacle, but that several in its ranks intended to play a part, or rather to take on an office that they considered had been inadequately carried out – namely, the office of executioner.

True, there were others who flocked there with less hostile intentions. For those, it was simply a matter of a sight which always pleases a mob by flattering its instinctive pride, namely, the sight of someone who has long been eminent being flung into the mud.

Had not this Cornelius de Witt, this fearless man, been imprisoned and weakened by torture? they wondered. Wouldn't they see him pale, bloodied and ashamed? Would it not be a fine triumph for the bourgeoisie – which was still more envious than the common people – in which every good townsperson of the Hague should take part?

And then, said the Orangeist agitators who had been cleverly mixed in this crowd and meant to wield it like a weapon, at once blunt and cutting, would there not be a little opportunity, between the Buitenhof and the town gate, to throw a spot of mud, or even a few stones, at this *Ruaart* of Putten, who had not only refused to accord the Stadhouderat to the Prince of Orange except *vi coactus*, but also wanted to have him assassinated?

Quite apart from which, the savage enemies of France added, if people acted rightly and were brave in the Hague, they would not let Cornelius de Witt leave to become an exile, knowing that once he was outside, he would resume all his intrigues with the French and live off the gold of the Marquis de Louvois,[17] with that great scoundrel, his brother Johan.

In this frame of mind, as one may imagine, people run rather than walk; and this is why the inhabitants of the Hague were proceeding so quickly towards the Buitenhof.

Among those who were running fastest came the honest Tyckelaer, his heart raging, but with no plan in his head, held up by the Orangeists as a hero of probity, national honour and Christian charity.

This fine scoundrel described the assaults that Cornelius de Witt had made on his virtue, embellishing the account with all the flowers of his wit and the resources of his imagination, quoting the sums which he had been promised and the infernal stratagems prepared in advance to make it easier for him, Tyckelaer, to carry out the assassination.

Every sentence of his speech, eagerly seized upon by the mob, aroused cries of ardent love for Prince William and shouts of blind rage against the de Witt brothers.

The crowd had even reached the point of cursing those iniquitous judges whose decree had allowed such an abominable criminal as that rogue Cornelius to get off scot free. And a few agitators muttered, 'He'll leave! He's going to escape!'

To which others replied, 'There's a boat waiting for him at Schweningen.[18] A French boat. Tyckelaer has seen it.'

'Good Tyckelaer! Honest Tyckelaer!' the crowd chanted.

'Apart from which,' said a voice, 'while Cornelius is fleeing, that Johan will also get away; and he's no less a traitor than his brother.'

'And the two scoundrels will go to France to eat our money, the money from our ships and munitions and dockyards, which were sold to Louis XIV.'

'We'll stop them leaving!' cried the voice of a patriot who was one step ahead of the rest.

'To prison! To prison!' the chorus replied.

Whereupon the citizens ran faster, muskets were charged, pikes shone and eyes flamed.

However, no violence had yet been perpetrated and the horsemen lined up to guard the approaches to the Buitenhof remained
calm, unmoved, silent and more threatening in their impassivity
than the whole of this mob with its cries, turmoil and threats,
motionless under the eyes of their chief, the captain of cavalry
of the Hague, who held his sword unsheathed but lowered, with
its point aligned with his stirrup.

The attitude of this troop, the only bulwark defending the
prison, contained not only the anarchic, noisy mob, but also the
detachment of town militia, placed in front of the Buitenhof to
support the guard in keeping order, but which was leading the
rioters with seditious cries of 'Long live Orange! Down with
traitors!'

The presence of Tilly and his horsemen was certainly a salut-
ary check on all these citizen soldiers, but shortly afterwards
they fired themselves up with their own cries and, since they did
not realize that one may have courage without shouting, they
put the silence of the horsemen down to fear and took a step
towards the prison, bringing the turbulent rabble in their
wake.

At this, Count Tilly rode forward alone in front of them and,
raising nothing more than his sword and his eyebrows, asked,
'Well, gentlemen, why are you marching and what do you
want?'

The militia waved their muskets, with further cries of 'Long
live Orange! Death to the traitors!'

'Long live Orange! Agreed!' said Tilly. 'Though I prefer happy
faces to sullen ones. Death to the traitors, if you will, as long as
you only desire it by your cries. Shout "Death to the traitors!"
as much as you like; but when it comes to actually putting them
to death, I am here to prevent it and I shall prevent it.' Then,
turning back to his soldiers, he shouted, 'Swords at the ready,
men!'

Tilly's soldiers obeyed this order with a calm precision that
immediately made the militia and the people retreat, amid a
certain degree of confusion that made the cavalry officer smile.

'There, there!' he said, in the jocular tone peculiar to men of
the sword. 'Calm down, gentlemen. My soldiers will not fire the

first shot, but you, meanwhile, will not take one step towards the prison.'

'Do you realize, officer, that we have muskets?' the commander of the militia said, in a fury.

'Heavens, I can see very well that you have muskets,' said Tilly. 'You keep brandishing them in front of me. But you, on the other hand, should realize that we have pistols, that a pistol has an easy range of fifty yards and that you are only twenty-five yards away.'

'Death to the traitors!' the town militia cried in exasperation.

'Huh!' grumbled the officer. 'You keep repeating the same thing; it's quite tedious.' And he went back to his place at the head of the troop, while the tumult continued to grow around the Buitenhof.

However, the inflamed rabble did not know that at the very moment when it could smell the blood of one of its victims, the other, as though hastening to anticipate his fate, was passing a hundred yards from them behind the crowd and the horsemen, on his way into the Buitenhof. For Johan de Witt had just got down from a coach with one of his servants and was calmly walking across the courtyard in front of the prison.

He had announced himself to the gatekeeper – who, in any case, knew him – by saying, 'Good day, Gryphus, I have come to fetch my brother Cornelius de Witt, who, as you know, has been condemned to exile, to take him away from the town.'

The gatekeeper, a sort of bear trained to open and shut the doors of the prison, greeted him and let him inside, closing the gates behind them.

Ten yards further on Johan met a beautiful young woman of between seventeen and eighteen in Frisian dress,[19] who gave him a charming curtsey. Chucking her under the chin, he said, 'Hello, my good and lovely Rosa. How is my brother?'

'Oh, Mijnheer Johan,' the girl replied, 'I am not afraid of the harm that will come from the ill they have done him, because that ill is past.'

'So what are you afraid of, dear?'

'Of the ill that they want to do him, Mijnheer Johan.'

'Ah,' said de Witt. 'You mean the mob?'

'Can you hear them?'

'They are very worked up, indeed. But when they see us, perhaps they'll calm down, since we have never done them anything but good.'

'Sadly, that's not a reason,' the girl murmured, before going away on an urgent sign from her father.

'No, my child, no. What you say is very true.' Then, continuing on his way, he muttered, 'There's a young girl who probably cannot read and who consequently has read nothing, but she has just summed up the history of the world in a single phrase.'

And, calm as ever, but sadder than when he entered, the Grand Pensionary went on towards his brother's cell.

CHAPTER 2

The Two Brothers

As the lovely Rosa had said, full of doubt and premonitions, while Johan de Witt was going up the stone stairway to his brother Cornelius's cell, the town militia did their best to get past Tilly's troop, which was standing in their way. And seeing this, the mob, which understood the good intentions of its militia, yelled at the top of its lungs, 'Long live the townsfolk!'

As for Monsieur de Tilly, he was as cautious as he was firm, and negotiated with the gentlemen of the militia under the cocked pistols of his troop, explaining as best he could that the States had instructed him to guard the prison square and its approaches with three companies of men.

'Why were you ordered? Why should you guard the prison?' the Orangeists shouted.

'Ah!' Monsieur de Tilly answered. 'Now here you are, asking me more than I can tell you. I was told "guard", so I am guarding. You are almost soldiers, gentlemen. You must know that orders are orders.'

'But you were given this one so that the traitors can leave town!'

'That may well be,' Tilly replied, 'since these traitors are condemned to be banished.'

'But who gave you the order?'

'The States, of course!'

'The States are committing treachery.'

'I don't know anything about that.'

'And you are committing treachery.'

'I am?'

'Yes, you.'

'Now, now, let's understand one another, gentlemen. Who am I betraying? The States? I cannot betray them since, being in their pay, I carry out their orders to the letter.'

The Count was so perfectly correct that there was nothing to argue about in his reply, so the shouts and threats doubled – frightful shouts and threats, to which the Count responded with complete civility.

'Now, gentlemen, I beg you to be so good as to disarm your muskets. One of them might go off by accident and, were it to wound one of my horsemen, we should lay out two hundred of your men, and that would displease us very much – but it would displease you even more, seeing that it is not what either you or I intend.'

'If you were to do that,' shouted the townsfolk, 'we should open fire on you.'

'Yes, but if you were to fire on us and kill us all, from first to last, those of you whom we should have killed would not be any the less dead.'

'So give way to us and you will be acting as a good citizen.'

'Firstly, I am not a citizen,' said Tilly. 'I am an officer, which is a very different thing. And then I am not Dutch, I am French, which is still more different. Consequently, I know only the States, which pay me. Bring me an order to give way, in the name of the States, and I shall instantly turn about, all the more gladly since I find it very irksome to be here.'

'Yes, yes!' cried a hundred voices, immediately joined by five hundred more. 'To the town hall! Let's go and find the deputies! Come on, come on!'

'That's right,' Tilly muttered as he watched the most fanatical of them hurry away. 'Go and ask the town hall for an act of cowardice and see where it gets you. Off you go, my friends, off you go.'

The worthy officer was counting on the honour of the magistrates who, for their part, were counting on his honour as a soldier.

'Listen, captain,' the first lieutenant whispered in the Count's ear. 'Let the deputies refuse these madmen here what they are asking for, but it would be no bad thing, in my opinion, if they were to send us some reinforcements.'

Meanwhile, Johan de Witt, whom we saw going up the staircase after his talk with the jailer Gryphus and his daughter Rosa, had reached the door of the room where his brother Cornelius was lying on a mattress, the procurator having, as we said, ordered the preliminary torture to be applied to him. The order of banishment had arrived and made it unnecessary to proceed to the extraordinary torture.

Cornelius, stretched out on the bed, his wrists shattered, his fingers shattered, had not in any way confessed to a crime that he had not committed and, after three days of suffering, had breathed again on learning that the judges whom he expected to condemn him to death had seen fit to sentence him only to exile. A man of sturdy body and invincible soul, he would have caused his enemies much disappointment if they could have seen, in the dark depths of the Buitenhof, the smile on his pale face, the smile of a martyr who has forgotten the mire of the earth after glimpsing the splendour of heaven.

By force of will rather than by any actual succour, the *Ruaart* had regained all his strength and was calculating how much longer the formalities of the law would keep him in prison.

It was at that moment that the voices of the town militia and those of the people were raised against the two brothers, threatening Captain Tilly, who was protecting them. The noise, breaking like a rising tide against the walls of the prison, reached the prisoner himself. But, threatening though it was, Cornelius did not bother to ask the cause of it or take the trouble to get up and look through the narrow barred window which allowed access to light and murmurs from outside.

He was so possessed by his unending pain that it had almost become a habit for him. Now, he experienced such delight at feeling his soul and his mind close to shuffling off the bonds of flesh that it seemed to him that mind and soul had escaped from matter and were hovering above it like the almost extinguished flame that hovers above the dying embers before leaving them to rise into the air.

He was also thinking about his brother.

Perhaps it was the other man's approach that, through the unknown, mysterious properties of magnetism,[1] discovered since that time, was making itself felt to him in this way. At the very moment when Johan was so present in Cornelius's mind that he almost spoke his name, the door opened, Johan came in and hurried over to the prisoner's bed, while the latter held out his injured arms and his hands wrapped in bandages towards this glorious brother whom he had managed to surpass, not in the service he had rendered his country, but in the hatred that the Dutch people felt for him.

Johan kissed his brother tenderly on the forehead and placed his stricken hands back on the mattress.

'Cornelius, my poor brother,' he said. 'You are in great pain, aren't you?'

'Not any longer, brother, since you are here.'

'Oh, poor, dear Cornelius! Believe me, I am suffering instead of you, then, at seeing you in this state.'

'Which is why I thought more of you than of myself and, while they were torturing me, I only pitied myself once when I thought, "My poor brother!" But you are here now, so let us forget that. You have come to fetch me, I think.'

'Yes.'

'I am healed. Help me to get up, brother, and you will see how well I can walk.'

'You will not have to walk far, my friend, because I have my carriage at the pond, protected by Tilly's dragoons.'

'Tilly's dragoons? Why are they at the pond?'

'Why, because it is thought that the people of the Hague would like to see you leave,' said the Grand Pensionary with his habitual sad smile. 'And they fear something of a riot.'

'Riot?' said Cornelius, staring at his brother, who did not know what to say. 'A riot?'

'Yes, Cornelius.'

'So that is what I heard just now,' said the prisoner, as though speaking to himself. Then, turning back to his brother, he said, 'There is a crowd on the Buitenhof, isn't there?'

'Yes, brother.'

'But, how did you manage . . . ?'

'What?'

'Why did they let you through?'

'You know that we are not greatly loved, Cornelius,' the Grand Pensionary said with sour melancholy. 'I took the back streets.'

'Did you hide, Johan?'

'I intended to reach you without wasting time and I did what one does in politics or at sea when there is a contrary wind: I tacked.'

At that moment, a still more furious sound rose from the town square to the prison. Tilly was arguing with the militia.

'Ah, Johan,' said Cornelius. 'You are a very fine pilot, but I do not know if you can steer your brother out of the Buitenhof, in this swell and over such waves of popular feeling, with the same success that you steered Tromp's fleet to Antwerp through the shoals of the Scheldt.'[2]

'With God's help, Cornelius, we shall at least try,' Johan replied. 'But one word, first.'

'Tell me.'

Another burst of noise reached them from outside.

'How angry those people are,' Cornelius went on. 'Is it against you or against me?'

'I think it's against both of us, Cornelius. As I was telling you, brother, what the Orangeists reproach us with, among all their silly slanders, is that we negotiated with France.'

'Poor fools!'

'Yes, but that is what they hold against us.'

'But if the negotiations had succeeded, they would have spared Holland the defeats of Rees, Orsay, Vesel and Rheinberg;[3] they would have saved Holland from the crossing of the Rhine and she could still think herself invincible in the midst of her marshes and canals.'

'All that is true, brother, but what is still more true is that if anyone were now to find our correspondence with Monsieur de Louvois, good pilot though I am, I could not save the skiff that is going to carry the de Witts and their fortune out of Holland. These letters, which would prove to all decent folk how much I love my country and what personal sacrifices I was prepared to make for her freedom, would be fatal to us as far as our conquerors, the Orangeists, are concerned. So, dear Cornelius, I hope that you burnt them before leaving Dordrecht to join me in the Hague.'

'Brother,' Cornelius replied, 'your correspondence with Monsieur de Louvois proves that you were recently the greatest, most generous and most clever citizen of the seven United Provinces. I love the glory of my country and above all I love your glory, my brother, so I was careful not to burn those letters.'

'Then we are lost to this earthly life,' the Grand Pensionary said calmly, going over to the window.

'No, on the contrary, Johan. We shall have the salvation of our bodies and the resurrection of our popularity.'

'So what did you do with the letters?'

'I gave them to my godson, Cornelius van Baerle, whom you know and who lives in Dordrecht.'

'Oh, the poor boy, the dear, innocent child! That learned youth who has the rare quality of knowing so much and thinking only of flowers that glorify God and of God who creates flowers! You gave him this fatal charge? But he is lost, my brother, poor dear Cornelius is lost!'

'Lost?'

'Yes, because he will either be strong or he will be weak. If he is strong, he will boast of us – because, however little he may know about what is happening here, however distant from it all he may be in Dordrecht and however absent-minded, he will, one day, learn what has become of us; and if he is weak, he will be afraid of being associated with us. If he is strong, he will shout forth the secret, if he is weak he will let it be forced out of him. So in either event, Cornelius, he is lost and we with him. We must flee, my brother, and quickly, while there is still time.'

Cornelius sat up on his bed and took his brother's hand, which shook at the touch of the bandages.

'Don't I know my godson?' he said. 'Have I not learned to read every thought in the mind of van Baerle and every feeling in his soul? You ask me if he is weak or if he is strong? He is neither one nor the other – but what does it matter what he is?

The main thing is that he will keep our secret, the more so since he does not know what this secret is.'

Johan turned his head in surprise.

'Ah!' Cornelius continued with his soft smile. 'The *Ruaart* of Putten is a politician who was trained in the school of Johan. I repeat, brother, van Baerle does not know either the nature or the value of the packet that I entrusted to him.'

'Quickly, then!' Johan cried. 'Since we still have time, let's order him to burn it.'

'How can we get such an order to him?'

'Through my servant, Craeke, who was to have accompanied us on horseback and who came into the prison with me so that he could help you to get down the stairs.'

'Think before you burn these precious documents, Johan.'

'What I am thinking most of all, my good Cornelius, is that the de Witt brothers must save their lives to save their fame. When we are dead, who shall defend us? Who will even understand us?'

'Do you think they would kill us if they found those papers?'

Without answering, Johan pointed towards the Buitenhof, from where at that moment bursts of savage shouting could be heard.

'Yes, yes,' said Cornelius. 'I can indeed hear the shouting, but what are the cries saying?'

Johan opened the window.

'Death to the traitors!' yelled the mob.

'Now do you hear it, Cornelius?'

'And are we the traitors?' the prisoner said, looking up towards heaven and shrugging his shoulders.

'We are,' said Johan de Witt.

'Where is Craeke?'

'At the door of your cell, I assume.'

'Then bring him in.'

Johan opened the door. The faithful servant was indeed waiting on the threshold.

'Come here, Craeke, and listen carefully to what my brother tells you.'

'No, no, telling will not be enough, Johan. I have to write it down.'

'Why?'

'Because van Baerle will not hand over the package or burn it without a specific order.'

'But will you be able to write, my dear friend?' Johan asked, looking at his brother's poor burnt and twisted hands.

'If I had pen and ink, you should see,' said Cornelius.

'Here is a pencil at least.'

'Do you have any paper? They allowed me nothing here.'

'This Bible. Tear out the first page.'

'Very well.'

'But will your handwriting be legible?'

'Come, come,' said Cornelius, looking at his brother. 'These hands resisted the torturer's firebrands, and will overcame the pain he inflicted; they will unite in a common effort and, rest assured, brother, the line will be written without a single quaver.'

Cornelius took the pencil and wrote. As he did so, one could see the drops of blood drawn out of the open wounds by the pressure of the fingers on the pencil, staining the white linen bandage. Sweat was running from the temples of the Grand Pensionary.

Cornelius wrote:

Dear Godson,

Burn the parcel that I entrusted to you, burn it without looking at it, without opening it, so that it remains a mystery to you. Secrets of the kind that it contains kill those who know them. Burn it and you will have saved Johan and Cornelius.

Farewell.

Your affectionate,

Cornelius de Witt

20th August, 1672

Johan, with tears in his eyes, wiped away a drop of the noble blood that had stained the page, which he gave to Craeke with one final instruction before returning to Cornelius. The latter was paler still from his effort and seemed about to faint.

'Now, when that good Craeke sounds his old boatswain's whistle,' Johan said, 'that means he will be away from the crowds, on the far side of the pond. Then we can leave in our turn.'

Not five minutes had passed when the prolonged vigorous call of a mariner's whistle pierced the black leafy domes of the ash trees, rising above the noise on the Buitenhof. Johan raised his eyes in thanks to heaven and said, 'Now, Cornelius, let us be gone.'

CHAPTER 3

Johan de Witt's Pupil

While the shouts of the crowd assembled on the Buitenhof were growing ever more terrifying as they rose up towards the two brothers (making Johan de Witt determined to speed the departure of his brother Cornelius), a deputation of citizens had gone to the town hall, as we mentioned, to demand the expulsion of Tilly and his corps of cavalry.

It was not far from the Buitenhof to the Hoogstraat,[1] and one might have observed a stranger, who had been following the details of these events with curiosity from the start, going along with the rest – or, rather, behind the rest – towards the town hall, in order to find out at once what would occur there.

This stranger was a very young man, barely twenty-two or twenty-three years old, and not sturdy in appearance. He must have had some reason to avoid recognition, because he was hiding his long, pale face behind a fine kerchief of Frisian linen, with which he constantly wiped the perspiration off his brow or dabbed his burning lips.

With his piercing eyes, like those of a bird of prey, his long, aquiline nose and his straight, thin-lipped mouth that was open – or rather, split like the edges of a wound – he would have offered Lavater[2] (had Lavater been living at that time) the subject of a physiological study that would not have been entirely flattering.

What difference, they said in Antiquity,[3] between the face of the conqueror and that of the pirate? The same as between the eagle and the vulture: serenity or anxiety. So this livid face, this frail and suffering body, as it went with uneasy steps in pursuit of the howling crowd from the Buitenhof to the Hoogstraat, was the very picture of a suspicious master or an anxious thief; and a police constable would undoubtedly have opted for the latter, because of the care that the man in question was taking to conceal himself.

Apart from that he was plainly dressed, and with no visible weapon; his arm was slender but nervous, and his dry, white hand, finely made and aristocratic, rested not on the arm, but on the shoulder of an officer, who, with his own hand on his sword, had been looking at all the events in the Buitenhof with understandable interest until the moment when his companion had set out, taking him along as he went.

Once they had arrived at the square of the Hoogstraat, the man with the pale face drew the other into the shelter of a window shutter and fixed his attention on the town hall.

In response to the frenzied clamour of the mob, the window looking over the Hoogstraat opened and a man came forward to address them.

'Who is that on the balcony?' the young man asked the officer, with only a nod towards the speaker, who seemed quite disturbed and was supporting himself on the balustrade rather than just leaning on it.

'That is the deputy Bowelt,' the officer replied.

'And what kind of a man is this Deputy Bowelt? Do you know him?'

'A fine, upstanding man, at least, as far as I know, sire.'

When the young man heard this assessment of Bowelt's character from the officer, he gave such an odd shrug of disappointment and such evident signs of displeasure that the officer noticed it and hastened to add, 'At least, that is what they say, sire. For my part, I cannot swear to anything, as I'm not personally acquainted with Mijnheer Bowelt.'

'A fine, upstanding man,' repeated the one he had addressed as 'sire'. 'By upstanding, do you mean one who is likely to stand up to them?'

'Sire will excuse me, I cannot make such a judgement about a man who, I repeat, is known to me only by sight.'

'As you say,' the young man muttered. 'Then let's wait and see.'

The officer nodded and said nothing.

'If this Bowelt is a fine, upstanding man,' the royal personage continued, 'he will give short shrift to the request that these fanatics have come to make.'

The nervous, involuntary movement of his hand against his companion's shoulder, like the tapping of a musician's fingers on a keyboard, betrayed the extent of his impatience, which at times – and now especially – he had trouble concealing behind a dark and icy exterior.

At this point, they heard the leader of the townsfolk calling on the deputy to ask him where were his colleagues, the other deputies.

'Gentlemen,' Bowelt said, a second time. 'I am telling you that at this moment I am alone with Mijnheer d'Asperen, and I cannot take a decision by myself.'

'The order! The order!' cried several thousand voices.

Bowelt tried to speak, but his words were drowned out by the noise and all one could see were his arms making various desperate gestures. Then, seeing that he would not make himself heard, he turned back towards the open window and called d'Asperen.

D'Asperen in his turn appeared on the balcony where he was greeted with still more forceful cries than those which ten minutes earlier had greeted Bowelt. Even so, he did try to address the crowd, but the mob preferred breaking through the guard of the States – which offered no resistance to the sovereign people – to hearing d'Asperen's speech.

'Come on,' the young man said coolly as the people were pouring in through the main door of the Hoogstraat. 'It seems that the discussion will take place indoors, colonel. Let's go and hear it.'

'Be careful, sire!'

'Why should I?'

'Among the deputies, there are many who have had dealings with you. It would be enough for just one to recognize Your Highness.'

'Enough for me to be accused of instigating all this. You are right,' the young man said, his cheeks reddening for an instant with regret at having shown so much haste in his desires. 'Yes, you are right, let's stay here. From here, we shall see them return with or without the authorization and be able to judge from that whether Mijnheer Bowelt will be a fine, upstanding man, or one brave enough to stand up to them. I should like to know.'

The officer looked in astonishment at the man he called 'sire', and said, 'But Your Highness surely does not imagine for a moment that the deputies will order Tilly's men to leave?'

'Why not?' the young man asked coldly.

'Because if they were to order that, it would quite simply be signing the death warrants of Johan and Cornelius de Witt.'

'We shall see,' the royal personage replied calmly. 'God alone can know what goes on in the hearts of men.'

The officer looked askance at the impassive face of his companion, and the colour drained from his face. This officer was both a decent and a brave man.

From the place where they had stopped, the royal personage and his companion could hear the sound of voices and the tramping of feet on the staircase of the town hall. Then they heard this sound come out and spread across the square from the open windows of the room on the balcony of which Bowelt and d'Asperen had appeared. The two men themselves stayed inside, fearing, no doubt, that the crowd might press against them and push them over the balustrade.

Then shadows, turning noisily, could be seen passing across the windows. The council chamber was filling up.

Suddenly the noise ceased. Then, just as suddenly, it doubled in volume, reaching such a pitch that the old building shook from top to bottom. And finally the stream once again started to roll through the galleries and stairways down to the door, before emerging from it like a torrent.

At the head of the first group, a man, his face hideously distorted by joy, flew rather than ran. It was the barber Tyckelaer.

'We've got it! We've got it!' he cried, waving a sheet of paper in the air.

'They have the order,' the officer muttered in amazement.

'Well, now my mind is settled on the matter,' said the royal personage calmly. 'You could not tell me, dear Colonel, whether Mijnheer Bowelt was an upright man or a courageous one. He is neither.' And, unblinking, he watched the crowd surging past him.

'Now, Colonel,' he said, 'come to the Buitenhof. I think we shall see an odd spectacle.'

The officer bowed and followed his master without a word.

The crowd on the square and around the prison was immense. But Tilly's horsemen were still as successful – and as firm – in containing it.

Soon, the Count heard the mounting roar of the stream of men as they approached and saw the first waves pressing forward with the speed of a rushing waterfall. At the same time, he noticed the sheet of paper fluttering in the air above the clutching hands and shining weapons.

'Ah!' he exclaimed, rising in his stirrups and touching his lieutenant with the pommel of his sword. 'I think these wretches have their order.'

'The cowardly rogues!' said the lieutenant.

It was indeed the order, which the townspeople's militia received with roars of joy. They set off at once, marching forward towards Count Tilly and his men with loud cries. But the Count was not the sort of man to let them approach too close.

'Halt!' he cried. 'Halt! And keep back from my horses or I shall give the order to advance.'

'Here is the order!' replied a hundred insolent voices.

Incredulous, he took it, quickly glanced over it and said in a loud voice, 'Those who signed this order are the true murderers of Cornelius de Witt. As for me, I should rather lose both my hands than have written a single letter of this disgraceful order.'

Then, using the pommel of his sword to push back a man who was trying to take the paper from him, he said, 'One moment! A piece of paper such as this is important and should be kept.'

He folded it and carefully put it in the pocket of his jerkin. Then, turning back to his troop, he called: 'Tilly's horse, by the right, march!' And, in an undertone (but so that some could hear it), he exclaimed, 'And now, cut-throats, do your work!'

A furious shout, composed of all the eager hatreds and savage joys grumbling on the Buitenhof, greeted their departure.

The horsemen slowly walked off in line. The Count stayed at the back, confronting the intoxicated populace till the last moment, as it took over the ground relinquished by the captain's horse. As one can see, Johan de Witt had not exaggerated the danger when, helping his brother to get up, he urged him to depart. So Cornelius was coming down the staircase leading into the courtyard, supported by the arm of the former Grand Pensionary when, at the foot of the stairs, he met the lovely Rosa, shaking with fright.

'Oh, Mijnheer Johan,' she said. 'What a disaster!'

'What is it, child?' asked de Witt.

'It's that they have gone to the Hoogstraat to fetch the order for Count Tilly's horse to leave.'

'Ha!' said Johan. 'If as you say, my girl, the troop has left, then things are indeed looking bad for us.'

'So I have some advice to give you,' the girl said, trembling.

'Give it to me, child. What is remarkable about the fact that God might speak to me through your lips?'

'Well, Mijnheer Johan, I should not go out through the main street.'

'Why not, since Tilly's men are still at their post?'

'They may be, but until the order is countermanded, it is to stay in front of the prison.'

'Of course.'

'Do you have an order for them to accompany you outside the town?'

'No.'

'Well, as soon as you have stepped beyond the first row of horse, you will fall into the hands of the mob.'

'What about the town militia?'

'Huh! The militia is the most inflamed of all.'

'So what can we do?'

'In your place, Mijnheer Johan,' the young woman went on shyly, 'I should go out through the postern, which opens on an empty street, because everyone is in the main street waiting at

the main gate. I would then proceed to the town gate through
which you wish to depart.'

'But my brother cannot walk,' said Johan.

'I shall try,' Cornelius replied, with an expression of sublime
resolve.

'But don't you have your carriage?' the young woman asked.

'It is there, at the main gate.'

'No, it isn't,' she replied. 'I thought that your coachman must
be a faithful servant, so I told him to go and wait at the postern
gate.'

The two brothers looked at one another with feeling and then
both pairs of eyes, full of gratitude, turned to the young woman.

'Now,' said the Grand Pensionary, 'all that remains is to see
if Gryphus will open that gate for us.'

'Oh, no,' Rosa said. 'He won't.'

'So what are we to do, then?'

'Well, I guessed that he would refuse and just now, while he
was talking with a prisoner through the jail window, I took the
key off his bunch.'

'And do you have this key?'

'Here it is, Mijnheer Johan.'

'My child,' Cornelius said, 'I have nothing to give you in
exchange for the service you have done me, except the Bible
that you will find in my room. It will be the last present of an
honourable man and I hope it will bring you happiness.'

'Thank you, Mijnheer Cornelius, it will never leave me,' the
young woman replied. Then, with a sigh, to herself, she added,
'What a pity I cannot read!'

'The noise is getting louder, my child,' Johan said. 'I think we
have not a moment to lose.'

'Come on,' the lovely Frisian girl said, and she led the two
brothers by an inner corridor to the opposite side of the prison.

Still guided by Rosa, they went down a flight of some dozen
stairs, crossed a small yard with crenellated ramparts and, when
the arched door had been opened, they found themselves on the
other side of the prison in a deserted street, and in front of them
the carriage with its running board lowered.

'Quickly, quickly, masters, can you hear them?' the coachman cried in terror.

But after putting Cornelius in first, the Grand Pensionary turned to the young woman.

'Goodbye, my child,' he said. 'Whatever I say will be too feeble to express our gratitude. We entrust you to God, who will, I hope, remember that you have just saved the lives of two men.'

Rosa took the hand that the Grand Pensionary held out to her and kissed it respectfully.

'Go,' she said. 'Go now. It sounds as though they are breaking down the gate.'

Johan de Witt got in hurriedly, sat down beside his brother and drew the apron across the carriage, shouting, 'To the Tol-Hek!'

The Tol-Hek was the iron barrier across the gate leading to the little port of Schweningen, where a small boat was waiting for the brothers. The carriage set off at a gallop, carrying the fugitives and pulled by its two sturdy Flemish horses. Rosa looked after it, until it had turned the corner of the street. Then she went back inside, shutting the door behind her and throwing the key into a well.

The noise that told Rosa that the mob was breaking down the gate was indeed that of the mob dashing against the gate after the prison square had been emptied of Tilly's men. Though it was solid, and though the jailer, Gryphus – it must be said, in all fairness to him – was obstinately refusing to open it, one could tell that it would soon give way, and Gryphus, who had gone very pale, was wondering if it might not be better to open it than to have it broken down when he felt someone gently tugging at his coat.

He turned round and saw Rosa.

'Can you hear those fanatics?' he said.

'I can hear them so well, father, that if I were you . . .'

'You would open to them, wouldn't you?'

'No, I should let them break down the gate.'

'But they will kill me.'

'Yes, if they see you.'

'How do you expect them not to see me?'

'Hide.'

'Where?'

'In the secret dungeon.'

'What about you, child?'

'I shall come down into it with you. We shall close the door behind us and when they have left the prison, we shall come out.'

'By heavens, you're right,' exclaimed Gryphus, adding, 'It's astonishing how much good sense there is in that little head.'

Then, as the gate was collapsing, to the great delight of the mob, Rosa said, 'Come, come, father,' as she opened a small trapdoor.

'But what about our prisoners?' Gryphus asked.

'God will look after them, father,' the young woman said. 'Let me look after you.'

Gryphus followed his daughter and the trapdoor fell back above their heads, just as the broken gate was giving way to the people.

However, the dungeon into which Rosa took her father, known as the 'secret dungeon', offered a sure hiding place to these two characters, and we shall be obliged to leave them there for a while. Their hiding place was known only to the authorities, who sometimes used it to shut up one of those great criminals on whose behalf they feared some rebellion or attempt at abduction.

The mob burst into the prison, shouting, 'Death to the traitors! Cornelius de Witt to the gallows! Death! Death!'

CHAPTER 4

The Butchers[1]

The young man, with his head still covered by a large hat, still leaning on the officer's arm, and still wiping his forehead and his lips with his handkerchief, stood motionless in a corner of the Buitenhof, hidden in the shadow of an awning above a closed shop and watching the spectacle provided by this enraged mob which appeared to be reaching its climax.

'Ah!' he said to the officer. 'I think you are right, van Deken: the order that the deputies have signed is Mr Cornelius's death warrant. Just listen to those people. They certainly have a considerable grudge against the de Witts!'

'Yes, indeed,' said the officer. 'I've never heard such cries.'

'I assume that they have found our man's cell. Look! Wasn't that window the one of the room where Cornelius was held?'

A man had grasped the iron lattice over the window of Cornelius's cell, which the latter had left barely ten minutes earlier, and was holding it with both hands and shaking it violently.

'Hey!' the man was yelling. 'Hey! He's gone!'

'What do you mean? Isn't he there?' asked those late arrivals in the street who were unable to get inside the prison, because it was now so full.

'No! No!' the man repeated, furiously. 'He must have escaped.'

'What did that man say?' asked the royal personage, colour draining from his face.

'Sire, he says something that would be most fortunate if it were true.'

'Yes, it would be fortunate if it were true,' said the young man. 'Unfortunately, it can't be.'

'But look now,' said the officer.

More angry faces, twisted in fury, appeared at the windows, shouting, 'Gone! Escaped! They've got him away!'

The mob in the street repeated with ghastly oaths, 'Gone! Escaped! After them, follow them!'

'Sire, it does appear that Mijnheer Cornelius de Witt really has escaped,' said the officer.

'Yes, from the prison, perhaps,' the other man replied. 'But not from the town. You will see, van Deken, that the poor man will find the gate closed that he expected to find open.'

'Has the order to shut the town gates been given, sire?'

'No, I don't think so. Who might have given that order?'

'So, what makes you think . . . ?'

'There are turns of fate,' the royal personage replied casually. 'And the greatest men are sometimes subject to such turns of fate.'

Hearing these words, the officer felt a shudder run through his veins because he realized that, one way or another, the prisoner was lost. At that moment, the roar of the crowd burst out like thunder, because it was now clear that Cornelius de Witt was no longer in the prison.

In fact, Cornelius and Johan, after going round the pond, had taken the great street that leads to the Tol-Hek, while advising the coachman to slow the pace of his horses so that the carriage would not arouse any suspicion. But once he got halfway down the street and saw the barrier from a distance, once he felt that he was leaving behind the prison and death, and heading towards life and freedom, the coachman forgot every precaution and set off at a gallop.

Suddenly, he stopped.

'What's wrong?' Johan asked, putting his head out of the window.

'Oh, masters,' the coachman exclaimed. 'It's that . . .'

The good man's voice was suffocated with fear.

'Come on, tell us,' said the Grand Pensionary.

'The barrier is closed.'

'What do you mean: the barrier is closed? It's not usual to close the barrier in daytime.'

'See for yourself.'

Johan de Witt leant out of the carriage and saw that the barrier was indeed closed.

'Go on anyway,' said Johan. 'I have the commutation order, the guard will open the gate.'

The carriage went on, but one could see that the coachman was not driving his horses with the same confidence as before. Then, as he was leaning out of the window, Johan de Witt was seen and recognized by a brewer who, having fallen behind his comrades, was hurriedly closing his door before going to join them on the Buitenhof. He gave a cry of surprise and ran after two other men who were going on ahead of him. After a hundred yards, he caught up with them. They spoke and all three stopped, watching the carriage as it drove away, but still not too sure about who was in it.

Meanwhile, the carriage had arrived at the Tol-Hek.

'Open up!' the coachman cried.

'Open up?' said the gatekeeper, appearing at the door of his house. 'With what, may I ask?'

'For heaven's sake – with the key,' said the coachman.

'With the key. Right. But in that case, I should need to have the key.'

'What! Don't you have the key to the gate?' the coachman asked.

'No.'

'What have you done with it?'

'Why! Someone took it off me.'

'Who?'

'Probably someone who wanted to stop anyone leaving town.'

'My friend,' said the Grand Pensionary, thinking it worth putting his head out of the carriage window again, despite the risk. 'My friend, it is I, Johan de Witt, and my brother Cornelius, whom I am taking into exile.'

'Ah, Mr de Witt, I'm terribly sorry,' the gatekeeper said. 'But I swear to you, someone took the key away from me.'

'When did this happen?'

'This morning.'

'And who did it?'

'A young man of twenty-two, a pale, thin one.'

'Why did you give it up to him?'

'Because he had an order, signed and sealed.'

'From whom?'

'From the gentlemen in the town hall.'

'Well, then,' said Cornelius, calmly. 'It seems that we are well and truly done for.'

'Do you know if the same measure was taken everywhere?'

'I cannot say.'

'Come on,' said Johan to the coachman. 'God orders a man to do all he can to save his life. Go to another gate.'

Then, while the coachman was turning the carriage round, he said to the gatekeeper, 'Thank you for your good intentions, friend. The will may be counted for the deed. You meant to save us and, in the eyes of the Lord, it is as though you had done so.'

'Oh, look over there,' said the gatekeeper.

'Drive straight through that group at a gallop,' Johan shouted to the coachman. 'Then take the road to the left. It's our only hope.'

At the centre of the group that Johan indicated were the three men whom we saw looking after the carriage as it passed, who in the meantime, while Johan was talking to the gatekeeper, had been joined by seven or eight others. The new arrivals clearly meant the coach some harm. When they saw the horses galloping towards them, they spread out across the road, waving and brandishing sticks, yelling, 'Stop! Stop!' Meanwhile, the coachman leant over and whipped his horses.

Finally, the carriage and the men collided.

The de Witt brothers could not see anything, being shut up in the coach, but they felt the horses rear and then a violent shudder. There was a momentary pause and a shock went through the whole vehicle before it continued on its way, passing over something round and soft, apparently the body of a fallen man, and drove on, followed by a volley of oaths.

'Oh, dear!' said Cornelius. 'I'm afraid we have done something dreadful.'

'Press on, press on!' Johan shouted.

But despite the order, the coachman suddenly stopped.

'What is it?' Johan asked.

'Look there,' said the coachman.

Johan looked. The whole population of the Buitenhof had appeared at the far end of the street, and came forward with as much speed and noise as a hurricane.

'Stop the carriage and run,' Johan said to the coachman. 'There is no point in going further, we are done for.'

'There they are! There they are!' cried five hundred voices together.

'Yes, there they are, the traitors, the murderers, the assassins!' the men running after the carriage replied to those coming towards it. They were carrying the battered body of one of their number, who had tried to catch the harness of the horses and had fallen under the wheels. This was the man whose body the two brothers had felt the carriage pass over.

The coachman stopped, but however much his master insisted, he refused to run away.

In an instant, the carriage was caught between those running after it and those coming towards it. In another instant, it was rising above this raging mob like a floating island. Suddenly, the floating island stopped. A blacksmith had just struck down one of the horses with a hammer and it fell between the shafts.

At that moment, a window was partly opened and the pale face and dark eyes of the young man appeared, staring at the spectacle below. Behind him was the face of the officer, almost as pale as his own.

'Oh, my God, sire! My God! What is going to happen?' murmured the officer.

'Something frightful, surely,' the young man replied.

'Look, sire, they are dragging the Grand Pensionary out of the carriage. They are beating him, they are tearing him apart.'

'These people must truly be driven by very powerful feelings of indignation,' said the young man in the same impassive tone that he had adopted throughout.

'And now they're taking Cornelius from the carriage, Cornelius who has already been broken and injured on the rack. Oh, look! Look at that!'

'Indeed, yes, it is Cornelius.'

The officer gave a faint cry and turned away. He had just seen, on the bottom step of the running board, even before his foot touched the ground, the *Ruaart* being struck by a blow from an iron rod, which had broken his skull. Even so, he got up, then fell back at once. After that, some men took his feet and dragged him into the crowd, in the midst of which one could follow the bloody trail he left behind as the people closed behind him with great shouts of joy.

The young man became still paler, which one might have thought impossible, and for a moment his eyes were veiled behind their lids. The officer noticed this sign of compassion, the first that his companion had allowed himself, and said, hoping to take advantage of this more gentle frame of mind, 'Come away, sire, come away. They are going to kill the Grand Pensionary, too.'

But the young man had already reopened his eyes.

'Yes, indeed,' he said. 'This is a ruthless people. It is not a good idea to betray them.'

'Sire,' said the officer. 'Is there no chance that we might save this poor man, who was Your Highness's tutor? If there is any way, tell me, and even if it means losing my own life . . .'

William of Orange (for he was the royal personage) gave a dark frown and repressed the glimmer of brooding fury shining in his eyes, before replying, 'Colonel van Deken, I beg you to go and join your troops, ensuring that they are armed against any eventuality.'

'But should I leave Your Highness alone here, with these assassins?'

'Don't worry about me any more than I do myself,' the Prince said brusquely. 'Go!'

The officer left with a haste that said far less about his eagerness to obey his sovereign than his joy at no longer having to witness the awful murder of the second brother.

No sooner had he closed the door of the room than Johan, who by a supreme effort had reached the steps of a house situated almost directly opposite the one where his pupil was hiding, staggered under the blows that were raining down on him from all sides at once, crying out, 'My brother! Where is my brother?'

One of the mob knocked his hat off with a blow. Another showed him the blood dripping from his hands. He had just disembowelled Cornelius and had run over hoping that he might not miss the opportunity to do the same to the Grand Pensionary, while others were dragging the body of his brother, already dead, towards the gibbet.

Johan gave a pitiful cry and put one hand in front of his eyes.

'So! Shut your eyes, would you?' said one of the soldiers of the town militia. 'Well, I'll pluck them out for you!'

And he thrust his pike into Johan's face, drawing blood.

'My brother!' de Witt cried, trying to see what had happened to Cornelius through the stream of blood that was blinding him. 'My brother!'

'Go and join him!' yelled another murderer, placing the muzzle of his musket against Johan's temple and pulling the trigger. But the gun did not go off. At this, the killer turned his weapon around and, seizing it with both hands by the barrel, struck Johan de Witt with the butt.

De Witt staggered and fell at the man's feet. Then, straight away, with one final effort, he rose up and cried out, 'My brother!' in such a piteous voice that the young man drew the shutter on the scene.

In any case, there was little left to see, because a third assassin fired a pistol at point-blank range. This time, the gun did go off and blew out Johan's brains. This time he fell and did not get up. At that, each of the wretches, emboldened by his fall, tried to fire his weapon into the body. And everyone wanted to strike a blow with a hammer, a sword or a knife, everyone wanted to have his drop of blood and tear off his scrap of clothing.

When the two bodies were thoroughly beaten, thoroughly dismembered, and thoroughly stripped, the mob dragged them, naked and bleeding, to an improvised gibbet, where amateur executioners hung them up by the feet.

At this point, the most cowardly of all arrived and, not having dared to strike the living flesh, cut the dead flesh to pieces and went round the town selling small fragments of Johan and Cornelius at ten *sous*[2] each.

We cannot say whether the young man saw the end of this dreadful scene through the almost imperceptible opening in the shutter, but at the very moment when the two martyrs were being hung up on the gibbet, he was walking through the crowd – which was too engaged in its merry work to bother about him – and heading for the Tol-Hek, which was still closed.

'Sir,' the gatekeeper exclaimed. 'Are you bringing me back the key?'

'Yes, friend, here it is,' said the young man.

'It's a great pity you did not bring this key to me just half an hour earlier,' the gatekeeper said with a sigh.

'Why is that?' asked the young man.

'Because I could have opened the gate for the de Witts. Instead of which, finding the door shut, they had to turn round and fell into the hands of those who were pursuing them.'

'The gate! The gate!' cried the voice of a man who seemed to be in a hurry.

The Prince turned round and recognized Colonel van Deken.

'Is that you, Colonel?' he said. 'Have you not yet left the Hague? You are taking a long time to carry out my orders.'

'Sire,' the Colonel replied. 'This is the third gate I have come to, and I found both of the others shut.'

'Well, this good man here will open this one for us. Open up, my friend,' the Prince said to the gatekeeper, who had been left speechless by the title of 'sire' that Colonel van Deken had just given to the pale young man, to whom he had recently spoken with such familiarity. So, to make up for his error, he hurriedly opened the Tol-Hek, which rolled back with a creaking of hinges.

'Would Your Majesty like my horse?' the Colonel asked William.

'Thank you, Colonel, but I should have a mount waiting for me a short distance away.'

Taking a golden whistle out of his pocket, of a kind that was in those days used to call domestic servants, he drew a long, high-pitched sound out of it, at which an equerry rode quickly up, leading a second horse by the bridle.

William leapt into the saddle without using the stirrup and, spurring the horse on with both heels, headed for the Leyden road. When he reached it, he turned round. The Colonel was following, a horse's length behind. The Prince signalled for him to ride alongside.

'Do you know,' he said, 'that those scoundrels killed Johan de Witt just as they had killed Cornelius?'

'Ah, sire,' the Colonel said sadly. 'I should rather for your sake that those two obstacles were still to be overcome before you could be made Stadhouder of Holland.'

'It would certainly have been better,' the young man said, 'if what has just happened had not happened, but what is done is done, and we are not the cause of it. Let's hurry, Colonel, so that we reach Alphen before the messenger whom the States will certainly send to me in the camp.'

The Colonel bowed and let his Prince go on ahead, returning to the place where he had been before he was called forward.

'Now, what I should really like,' William of Orange muttered, with a malicious note in his voice, as he raised one eyebrow, tightened his mouth and drove the spurs into his horse's belly, 'what I should like is to see the look on the face of Louis, the Sun-King, when he learns how his good friends, the de Witts, have been treated! Oh, Sun, Sun – as I am called William the Silent, Sun, take care of your rays.'

The young Prince hurried forward on his fine horse, a bitter rival of the great king and a Stadhouder who, only the day before, had been so uncertain of his new powers, but for whom the townsfolk of the Hague had provided a more solid platform in the bodies of Johan and Cornelius, themselves two noble princes before man and before God.

CHAPTER 5

The Tulip Fancier and his Neighbour

While the townsfolk of the Hague were dismembering the bodies of Johan and Cornelius, and while William of Orange, after assuring himself that his two enemies were indeed dead, was galloping along the Leyden road followed by Colonel van Deken (a man whom he was finding a trifle too compassionate to deserve the confidence that he had placed in him up to then), Craeke, the faithful servant, who was also mounted on a fine horse, and knew nothing about the dreadful events that had taken place since his departure, rode along the tree-lined avenues until he was out of the town and the neighbouring villages.

Once he was safe, to avoid arousing suspicion, he left his horse at a stable and calmly continued his journey by boat, arriving by relay in Dordrecht after skilfully passing along the shortest routes, through the winding meanders of the river which, with moist embrace, enfold its charming islands, fringed with willows, rushes and flowering grasses where fat flocks idly graze under the bright sun.[1]

From a distance, Craeke recognized Dordrecht, the smiling town, under its hill dotted with windmills. He saw the lovely red houses trimmed in white, bathing their brick feet in the water, with silk carpets mottled with golden flowers, the wonderful work of India and China, hanging from their balconies, which opened on the river; and near the carpets, those long fishing lines, permanent traps to catch the hungry eels attracted to the houses by the daily distribution of largesse thrown on the water from the kitchen windows.

From the deck of the boat, through all the mills with their turning sails, Craeke saw the pink and white house for which he was bound on the slope of the hill. The crest of the roof was hidden in the yellowing leaves of a curtain of poplars and stood out against the dark background of a wood of huge elms. It was placed in such a way that the sun, falling on it as if into a funnel, dried up, warmed and even made fertile the last mists that the wind off the river brought up there every morning and every evening, despite the barrier of greenery.

Arriving in the midst of the ordinary bustle of the town, Craeke at once set off for the house, an indispensable description of which we shall now give our readers.

White, tidy, polished and more clean-washed and carefully waxed in the places one could not see than in those one could, this house contained a happy man. This happy being – a *rara avis*, as Juvenal[2] says – was Doctor van Baerle, Cornelius de Witt's godson. He had lived in the house that we have just described since childhood; it was the birthplace of his father and grandfather, former noble merchants of the noble city of Dordrecht.

Mijnheer van Baerle senior had amassed in the Indies trade some three to four hundred thousand florins, which Mijnheer van Baerle junior had found brand new in 1668, on the death of his dear, good parents, even though these florins were struck with dates – some of 1640, the rest of 1610 – which proved that they were florins of the father van Baerle and of the grandfather van Baerle. Let us hasten to add that these four hundred thousand florins were only small change, a sort of pocket money for Cornelius van Baerle, the hero of this story, since his properties in the province brought him an income of around ten thousand florins a year.

When that worthy citizen, Cornelius's father, died, three months after the funeral of his wife, who seemed to have gone on ahead to make the road of death easier for him, just as she had made easier the road of life, he embraced his son for the last time and said, 'Eat, drink and spend money, if you want to live in more than name, because it is not living to work all day on a wooden chair or a leather armchair, in a laboratory or in a shop. Your turn will come to die, and if you do not have the good fortune to have a son, our name will vanish and my florins will be amazed to find they have a new master – those new florins which no one has weighed except my father, myself and the founder at the mint. Above all, do not follow the example of your godfather, Cornelius de Witt, who has thrown himself into politics, the most unrewarding of careers: he will undoubtedly come to a bad end.'

Then the worthy Mijnheer van Baerle died, leaving his son Cornelius quite inconsolable, because he had very little love for florins and a great deal for his father.

So Cornelius remained alone in the big house.

In vain did his godfather Cornelius offer him a post in the public service and in vain did he wish to give him a taste of glory, when the younger Cornelius, in obedience to his godfather, set sail with de Ruyter[3] on the vessel the *Seven Provinces*, commanding a hundred and thirty-nine ships with which the famous admiral was single-handedly about to take on the combined fleets of England and France. When, guided by the pilot Léger, Cornelius had reached a point within musket range of the vessel the *Prince*, on which was the Duke of York, brother of the King of England; and when de Ruyter, his commander, had made so sudden and so skilful an attack that the Duke of York, feeling his ship about to be overwhelmed, just had time to escape on board the *Saint-Michel*; and when he had seen the *Saint-Michel*, broken and battered beneath the Dutch cannon, leave the line; when he had seen another vessel, the *Count of Sandwich*,[4] blow up so that four hundred sailors perished in the waves or in the fire; when he had observed that after all this – after twenty ships shattered to pieces, after three thousand dead, after five thousand wounded – nothing had been settled either for or against, but that each side claimed victory, that everything had to be done all over again and that another name, that of Southwold Bay,[5] had simply been added to the catalogue of battles; and when, finally, he had calculated how much time is lost in blocking his ears and eyes by a man who wishes even to think while his fellows are letting off cannons at one another, Cornelius said goodbye to de Ruyter, to the *Ruaart* of Putten and to glory, kissed the knees of the Grand Pensionary, whom he profoundly venerated, and returned home to his house in

Dordrecht, the richer for his retirement from the fray, for his twenty-eight years, his iron constitution, his sharp eyesight and, more than his four hundred thousand florins of capital and his ten thousand florins of income, richer for the conviction that a man has always received from heaven too much to be happy and enough not to be so.

Consequently, in order to find his own happiness in life, Cornelius began to study plants and insects, collected and classified all the flora of the islands, pinned up all the entomology of the province, writing a manuscript treatise about it with plates drawn by his own hand, and finally, not knowing what to do with his time – and, especially, with his money, which was increasing at a terrifying rate – he decided to choose one of the most elegant and costly of all the follies of his country and his time.

He fell in love with tulips.

As we know, this was a period when the Flemish and the Portuguese, vying with one another in this branch of horticulture, had reached the point where they accorded the tulip the status of a divinity and made of this flower from the East what no naturalist had ever dared make of the human race, for fear of exciting the envy of God. Very soon, from Dordrecht to Mons, no one spoke of anything except Mijnheer van Baerle's tulips, and his flowerbeds, his pits, his drying rooms and his trays of offsets[6] were visited as once famous Roman travellers would visit the galleries and libraries of Alexandria.

Van Baerle began by spending his income for the year in setting up his collection, then he depleted the stock of his new florins in perfecting it. As a result, his work was rewarded with fabulous success: he discovered five different varieties, which he named the Jeanne, for his mother, the Baerle for his father and the Cornelius for his godfather. The other names escape us, but connoisseurs can surely look them up in the catalogues of the time.

In 1672, early in the year, Cornelius de Witt came to Dordrecht to live for three months in the old family house; for not only was Cornelius himself born in Dordrecht, but the de Witts originated in the town.

This was the time when, as William of Orange said, Cornelius was starting to enjoy the deepest unpopularity. However, for his fellow citizens, the good townsfolk of Dordrecht, he was not yet a scoundrel fit for hanging, and they, while not entirely satisfied with his over-pure republicanism, were proud of his personal qualities and his valour, and happy to offer him a cup of honour when he entered the town.

Cornelius thanked his fellow citizens and went to see the old family home, ordering a few repairs to be made before Mrs de Witt, his wife, came to live there with the children. Then the *Ruaart* made for the house of his godson, perhaps the only person in Dordrecht who was still unaware that the *Ruaart* had arrived in his birthplace.

Just as Cornelius de Witt had aroused hatred by sowing those malevolent seeds that are called political passions, so van Baerle had acquired sympathy by neglecting to cultivate politics, being so much absorbed in the cultivation of tulips. He was loved by his servants and his labourers, to the extent that he could not imagine that there was in the world any man who wished ill to another.

And yet, let it be said to the shame of mankind, Cornelius van Baerle had without knowing it an enemy more ferocious, more determined and more implacable than even the *Ruaart* and his brother had up to then acquired among the Orangeists most hostile to that admirable pair of brothers, whose devotion to one another, untroubled in life, was destined to extend beyond death.

When Cornelius first conceived his passion for tulips, he dedicated his income for the year and his father's florins to his hobby. In Dordrecht, living right next door to him, there was a gentleman called Isaac Boxtel, who, since reaching the age of reason, had felt the same passion and used to swoon at the very mention of the word *tulban* – which the best-informed historian of the flower, in the *Floriste français*, assures us was the first word used in the Sinhalese language to designate that master-piece of creation called the tulip.[7]

Boxtel did not have the good luck to be as rich as van Baerle. It was thus with some difficulty, and with much care and patience, that he had made a garden in his house in Dordrecht suitable for growing the flowers and prepared the ground according to instructions, giving his beds the precise amount of heat and cold laid down by the gardeners' rule book.

Isaac knew the temperature of his frames to the twentieth of a degree. He knew the speed of the air current and adjusted it to suit the waving of the stems of his flowers. As a result, his products began to find favour: they were beautiful, even quite refined. Some tulip lovers came to visit Boxtel's tulips. Eventually, he launched a tulip bearing his own name on the world of Linnaeus and Tournefort.[8] This tulip had made its way in the world, crossed France, entered Spain and penetrated as far as Portugal, where the king, Don Alfonso VI, having been driven out of Lisbon, had taken refuge on the island of Terceira,[9] and amused himself not, like the great Condé,[10] in watering carnations, but in cultivating tulips, and pronounced 'Not bad' on seeing the aforementioned Boxtel tulip.

Suddenly, at the end of all the studies he had undertaken, Cornelius van Baerle was seized by a passion for tulips. He altered his house in Dordrecht, which, as we said, was next to that of Boxtel, and had a particular building in his courtyard raised by the height of a storey. This deprived Boxtel's garden of about half a degree of heat and in exchange gave it half a degree of cold, apart from which it broke the wind, upsetting all his neighbour's calculations and horticultural economy.

In the end, this misfortune was not great in Boxtel's eyes. Van Baerle was only a painter, that is to say a kind of madman who tries to reproduce the wonders of Nature on canvas, disfiguring them. The painter had raised his studio by one storey to improve the light, and had a right to do so. Mijnheer van Baerle was a painter as Mijnheer Boxtel was a tulip grower; he wanted sunlight for his paintings and had taken half a degree from Boxtel's tulips.

The law was on van Baerle's side. *Bene sit.*[11]

In any case, Boxtel had discovered that too much sun is harmful to tulips, and that the flower grows better and has an improved colour when given the warm sun of morning and evening, rather than the burning sun of noon. So he was almost grateful to Cornelius for having built him a free sunshade – though perhaps this was not entirely true and what Boxtel said about his neighbour van Baerle did not completely express his feelings. However, great minds, in the midst of great catastrophes, find astonishing consolations in philosophy.

But, alas, what was to become of the unfortunate Boxtel when he saw the windows of the newly built storey fill with bulbs, offsets, tulips in earth and tulips in pots – in short, everything to do with the hobby of a fanatical tulip grower? Cornelius had the packets of labels, the boxes, the cupboards with drawers and the iron gratings which surrounded these cupboards and allowed the air to reach them while keeping out mice, weevils, dormice, field mice and rats, those rare connoisseurs of tulips costing two thousand florins a bulb.

Boxtel was quite amazed when he saw all this equipment, but he still did not grasp the full extent of his misfortune. Van Baerle was known to be keen on everything that pleases the eye. He made a profound study of nature for his paintings, which were as polished as those of Gerrit Dow, his master, and Mieris,[12] his friend. Wasn't it conceivable that he had to paint the interior of a tulip grower's, that he had collected all the objects necessary for this décor in his new studio?

However, though he was somewhat placated by this misleading notion, Boxtel could not resist being devoured by burning curiosity. When evening came, he put a ladder up against the wall between the two houses and, looking into his neighbour's garden, he observed that a huge area, formerly occupied by a variety of plants, had been dug up and arranged in beds of leaf-mould with river mud, a mixture particularly favourable to tulips, and the whole reinforced with grass borders to prevent the soil slipping. Apart from that, there was morning and evening sunshine, with shade arranged to moderate the midday sun; abundant supplies of water close by; and a south-south-west aspect – in short, the very conditions needed to ensure not only success, but progress. There was no doubt about it: van Baerle had become a tulip grower.

At once, Boxtel envisaged this learned man, with his capital of four hundred thousand florins and his income of ten thousand florins, devoting all his intellectual and physical resources to the large-scale cultivation of tulips. In some vague but near future, he imagined his success and felt, in advance, such envy of it that his hands fell to his sides, his knees buckled and he slid in desperation to the foot of his ladder.

So, it was not for tulips in paint, but for real tulips that van Baerle had taken half a degree of heat from him. So, van Baerle was going to have the finest of exposures to the sun and, in addition, a huge room in which to keep his bulbs and offsets, a room that was well-lit, aired and ventilated, a luxury not known to Boxtel, who had had to give up his bedroom for this purpose and who, to avoid harming his own offsets and tubers through the effects of an animal presence, had been forced to sleep in the attic.

So, right next door, just beyond the wall, Boxtel was going to have a rival, an imitator, perhaps a victor, and this rival, far from being some obscure, unknown gardener, was the godson of Mijnheer Cornelius de Witt – in short, a celebrity!

Boxtel, as we see, was not so wise as Porus, who found consolation for his defeat by Alexander in the celebrity of his conqueror.[13]

And then, what would happen if van Baerle were to discover a new tulip and named it the Johan de Witt – having named another the Cornelius! He would suffocate with fury.

So Boxtel, in his envious imagination, prophesying misfortune for himself, guessed what was going to happen. And, having made his discovery, spent the most atrocious night anyone can imagine.

CHAPTER 6

A Tulip Grower's Hatred

From that moment on, what Boxtel felt was not anxiety but fear. Boxtel lost the thing that gives energy and nobility to the efforts of the body and the mind, which is the cultivation of an idea, and he lost it in thinking about the harm that his neighbour's idea would cause him.

As one might imagine, once he had applied the superb intellect that nature had given him to this end, van Baerle managed to grow the most beautiful tulips. Better than anyone in Haarlem or Leyden, towns which provide the best soil and climate, Cornelius succeeded in varying the colours, moulding the forms and multiplying the types of his flowers.

He belonged to that naive and ingenious school which took as its motto from the seventh century onwards the aphorism (which one of its number would embellish) 'Contempt for flowers is an offence against God'; which premiss the school of tulip fanciers, the most exclusive of all schools, in 1653 developed into the following syllogism: 'Contempt for flowers is an offence against God. The lovelier the flower, the greater the offence in despising it. The tulip is the loveliest of all flowers. So whoever despises the tulip offends God immeasurably.' By which reasoning, as one may see, had they so wished, the four or five thousand tulip growers of Holland, France and Portugal – not to mention those of Ceylon, India and China – would have outlawed the rest of the world and declared several hundred million men who were unmoved by the flower to be schismatics, heretics and punishable by death.

Undoubtedly, Boxtel, though he was the mortal enemy of van

Baerle, would have marched under the same banner beside him
in such a cause.

Thus, van Baerle had great success and became well-known,
while Boxtel vanished for ever from the list of leading tulip
growers in Holland, and tulip-growing in Dordrecht was rep-
resented by Cornelius van Baerle, that humble and harmless
scholar, in the same way as a graft makes the proudest shoots
grow from the most modest branch and the dog rose, with its
four odourless petals, gives rise to the huge, sweet-smelling rose.
Similarly, royal houses have sometimes had their roots in a
woodcutter's cottage or a fisherman's hut.

Van Baerle was entirely occupied in his tasks of sowing,
planting and picking. And van Baerle, honoured by all the
tulip lovers of Europe, did not even suspect that there was an
unfortunate man next door to him whose throne he had usurped.
He continued with his experiments – and so with his triumphs
– and in two years had covered his flowerbeds with such wonderful productions as no one, except perhaps Shakespeare and
Rubens, had created after God.

To have a notion of one of the damned not mentioned in
Dante's Hell, one would need to see Boxtel at this time. While
van Baerle would weed and hoe, fertilize and sprinkle his
flowerbeds, while, kneeling on the grassy verge, he would study
every vein in the flowering tulip and consider what alterations
might be made to it, the unions of colours that might be tried,
Boxtel, hidden behind a little sycamore tree that he had planted
beside the wall, which he used as a screen, would follow every
step and every gesture that his neighbour made with bulging
eyes and foaming lips. And when he thought that van Baerle
seemed pleased, when he glimpsed a smile on his lips or a flash
of happiness in his eyes, then he spat out so many curses and
angry threats that it was difficult to imagine why these breaths
laden with envy and rage did not spread among the stems of the
flowers and blight them with the seeds of disease and death.

Evil, once it has taken over a human soul, rapidly extends
through it and soon Boxtel was not content with watching van
Baerle; he also wanted to see his flowers – for, underneath it all,
he was an artist and his rival's masterpiece meant a lot to him.

He bought a telescope, with the help of which he could follow every development in the flower as well as the grower himself, from the moment in the first year when its pale shoot pushes through the earth to the one when, after it has completed its period of five years, the noble and graceful cylinder swells and the first vague hint of its colour appears as the petals of the flower develop: only then are the secret treasures of its calix revealed.

Ah, how many times had the unfortunate man, perched on his ladder, seen in van Baerle's flowerbeds tulips which dazzled him with their beauty and left him speechless at their perfection!

So, after this period of admiration, which he was powerless to overcome, he suffered the fever of envy, that sickness which gnaws away at the breast and changes the heart into myriad little serpents that devour one another and cause the most frightful suffering.

How many times, in the midst of these torments – which no words can convey – had Boxtel not been tempted to leap into the garden by night and ravage the plants, devouring the bulbs with his teeth and even sacrificing the owner himself to his fury if the man should dare to defend his tulips!

But to kill a tulip, in the eyes of a true gardener, is such a ghastly crime (while to kill a man – well, perhaps . . .). Yet, thanks to the progress that van Baerle was making daily in an art that he seemed to be acquiring by instinct, Boxtel was driven to such a paroxysm of rage that he considered throwing sticks and stones into his neighbour's tulip beds.

Then it would occur to him that the next day, on seeing the damage, van Baerle would inform the authorities, that it would be observed that the street was a long way away and that sticks and stones do not fall out of the sky in the seventeenth century as they did in the days of the Amalekites,[1] and consequently the author of the crime, even though he might have committed it under cover of darkness, would be discovered and not only punished, but also dishonoured for ever in the eyes of tulip-growing Europe; so Boxtel sharpened his hatred on the whetstone of cunning and decided to adopt a scheme that would not compromise him.

He had to search for a long time, admittedly, but at last he found the answer.

One evening, he tied two cats together, each by one of its hind legs, using a cord ten feet long, and he threw them from the top of the wall into the middle of the main flowerbed – the princely flowerbed, the royal flowerbed – which contained not only the Cornelius de Witt, but also the Lady of Brabant, milk white, purple and red; the Marbled of Rotterdam, flax grey, red and brilliant scarlet; and the tulips Marvel of Haarlem, Dark Columbine and Tarnished Clear Columbine.

The frightened animals, falling from the top of the wall to the bottom, first plunged into the flowerbed, each trying to run away in its own direction, until the cord attaching them to one another was pulled tight. Then, realizing that they could go no further, they wandered here and there, making horrible mewing sounds, their cord knocking down the flowers among which they floundered until finally, after a quarter of an hour of frantic struggle, they managed to break the string in which they were entangled and disappeared.

Boxtel, hiding behind his sycamore tree, could see nothing because of the darkness of the night, but from the furious cries of the two cats, he imagined everything and his heart, emptying its bile, was filled with joy. His desire to assure himself of the damage was so great that he stayed there until daylight for his eyes to enjoy the sight of the chaos that the struggle of the two cats had left in his neighbour's flowerbed. He was chilled by the morning mists, but he did not feel the cold; he was kept warm by the hope of revenge. His rival's suffering would recompense him for all his trouble.

At the first rays of the sun, the door of the white house opened and van Baerle appeared. He went over to his flowers, smiling like a man who has spent the night in his bed and enjoyed pleasant dreams.

All at once, he saw furrows and little mounds on ground which the day before had been as smooth as a mirror; then, suddenly, he noticed that the even ranks of his tulips were as disordered as the pikes of a battalion in the midst of which a bomb has landed. He ran over, the colour draining from his face.

Boxtel shuddered with joy. Fifteen or twenty torn and battered tulips were lying, bent over or entirely broken and already going pale. The sap was running from their wounds, the sap, that precious blood that van Baerle would have replaced at the cost of his own.

But, surprise, surprise! What was the joy of van Baerle! What was the inexpressible agony of Boxtel! Not one of the four tulips that he had intended to harm had been touched. Proudly, they raised their noble heads above the corpses of their companions. This was enough to console van Baerle and enough to poison the murderer with fury as he tore out his hair at the sight of the crime he had committed, and committed to no avail.

Van Baerle, while he regretted the misfortune that had struck him – although, by the grace of God, it was less serious than it might have been – still could not guess what had caused it. So he made enquiries and learned that the night had been disturbed by dreadful miaowing. Indeed, he could see where the cats had been by the marks of their claws and by the fur left behind on the battlefield, on which the drops of dew shuddered, unconcerned, as they did nearby on the leaves of a broken flower. So, to avoid a recurrence of such a disaster in future, he ordered one of the gardener's boys to sleep every night in the garden, in a sort of sentry box near the flowerbeds.

Boxtel heard him give the order. The very same day, he saw the box being put up and, happy at not having been suspected, but simply feeling more hostile than ever towards the fortunate grower, he waited for a better opportunity.

It was at about this time that the Haarlem Tulip Society offered a prize for the discovery (we dare not say the 'manufacture') of a great black tulip without a spot of colour, something that had never been done and was considered impossible, in view of the fact that at the time there was not even a flower of the species of a dark brown colour to be found in nature. Some remarked, in fact, that the founders of the prize might as well have offered two million florins as a hundred thousand: the thing was impossible.

None the less, the world of tulip-growing was shaken by it from top to bottom.

Some fanciers took up the idea, but without believing it achievable; and such is the power of the imagination among flower growers that, even while considering their notion a failure from the start, they thought of nothing except this great black tulip, reputed to be as much a chimera as Horace's black swan[2] or the white blackbird of French legend.

Van Baerle was among the tulip growers who took up the idea and Boxtel was one of those who considered the prize. As soon as van Baerle had settled this task into his far-sighted and ingenious head, he gradually set about sowing the plants and the other operations needed to transform the tulips that he had grown so far from red to brown and from brown to darker brown.

The following year he obtained flowers of a perfect dark brown colour and Boxtel saw them in his flowerbed. He himself had achieved only a light brown.

It might perhaps be important to explain to the readers those fine theories which prove that the tulip takes its colours from the elements. Perhaps the same reader would be grateful to us for explaining that nothing is impossible to the grower who, with patience and art, takes advantage of the sun's warmth, the clarity of water, the juices of the earth and the breath of the air. But what we have decided to write is not a treatise on tulips in general, but the story of one tulip in particular, and we shall stick to that, however alluring may be the attractions of that other subject, and close though it may be to our own.

Boxtel, who had once more been defeated by the superiority of his foe, grew tired of growing flowers and, becoming halfway mad, devoted himself entirely to observation.

His rival's house was open to view. The garden was exposed to the sunlight, the cabinets were glazed, and with a telescope the eye could easily see through the windows to pigeon-holes, cupboards, boxes and labels. Boxtel allowed his own bulbs to rot on their shelves, the seedlings to dry in their cases and the tulips to die in their beds. From now on, wearing away his life and his eyesight, he paid attention only to what was happening in van Baerle's, he breathed through the stems of his tulips, slaked his thirst at the water which van Baerle sprinkled on them, and fed on the soft, fine mould that his neighbour scattered on his cherished bulbs. But the most interesting part of the work did not take place in the garden.

The clocks might be striking one in the morning when van Baerle went up to his laboratory in the glazed study into which Boxtel's telescope could so easily penetrate, so that as soon as the lights of science, replacing the rays of the sun, had lit up the walls and the windows, Boxtel could see the inventive genius of his rival at work.

He watched him sorting his seeds and watering them with substances intended to alter or to colour them. He guessed that when van Baerle warmed certain of these seeds, then dampened them, then combined them with others by a kind of grafting – a minute and wonderfully skilled operation – he would shut up in darkness those that were to produce the colour black, expose to sunlight or to a lamp those that would give a red colour, and expose those that were to provide the colour white – a pure, hermetic representation of the liquid element – to the endless reflection of water.[3]

This innocent magic, the result of childish dreams and manly genius together, this patient, endless work that Boxtel knew he himself was incapable of performing, would make the whole life of the jealous man – all his thoughts and all his hopes – revolve around his telescope.

How strange it was! All his interest in growing and pride in his art had not extinguished Isaac's savage envy and thirst for revenge. Sometimes, when he had van Baerle in the sights of his telescope, he imagined that he was taking aim at him with an infallible musket and his finger would search for the trigger to fire the shot that would kill him. But it is time for us to connect this period of one man's work and the other's spying to the visit that Cornelius de Witt, *Ruaart* of Putten, was planning to make to his native town.

CHAPTER 7

The Happy Man Learns About Misfortune

Cornelius, after attending to his family affairs, came to the house of his godson, Cornelius van Baerle, in January 1672.

Night was falling.

Cornelius, although not much of a gardener and not much of an artist, visited the whole house from the study to the green-house and from the paintings to the tulips. He thanked his nephew for having joined him on the deck of the flagship the *Seven Provinces* during the battle of Southwold Bay and for having given his name to a splendid tulip; and he did so with the kindness and affability of a father talking to his son. While he was inspecting van Baerle's treasures, a crowd stood in front of the fortunate man's door, with signs of curiosity and even respect.

The noise attracted the attention of Boxtel, who was taking a light meal at his fireside. He asked what was going on and, when he was told, climbed up to his laboratory. There, despite the cold, he settled down, with his telescope to his eye.

The telescope had not been of much use to him since the autumn of 1671. Tulips feel the cold (like the daughters of the Orient that they are) and cannot be grown outside in winter. They need the inside of the house, the soft bed of a drawer and the gentle caress of the stove. So Cornelius spent the whole winter in his laboratory among his books and his paintings. Only seldom did he go into the room with the bulbs, except to let in a few rays of sunlight which he had glimpsed in the sky and which, by opening a skylight, he persuaded willy-nilly to shine into his house.

On the evening that we mentioned, after the younger and

elder Corneliuses had visited the apartments together, followed by a few servants, Cornelius the elder softly said to van Baerle, 'My son, send your people away and let's try to have a few moments on our own.'

Cornelius bowed obediently, then said aloud, 'Sir, would you now please to visit my tulip-drier?'

The drying room, that *pandaemonium* of tulip-growing, that tabernacle, that *sanctum sanctorum*, like ancient Delphi,[1] was forbidden to the uninitiated.

No servant ever dared his foot to set therein – as the great Racine,[2] who was flourishing at the time, would have put it. Cornelius would allow only the harmless broom of an old Frisian woman, his former nurse, to enter the place; and now that Cornelius had dedicated himself to the worship of the tulip, she no longer dared even to put an onion in his stew, for fear that she might inadvertently peel and season her nursling's god.

So when they heard the word 'drier', the valets carrying the torches stepped respectfully aside. Cornelius took the candles from the nearest one and led his godfather into the room.

We should add that this drying room was the same study with the large glass windows on which Boxtel fixed his telescope. The jealous man was more than ever at his post.

First of all, he saw the walls and windows light up, then two shadows appeared. One of them, tall, majestic, stern, sat down beside the table on which Cornelius had placed the light. In this figure, Boxtel recognized the pale face of Cornelius de Witt, whose long black hair, parted on the forehead, fell down across his shoulders.

The *Ruaart* of Putten, after saying a few words to Cornelius which the envious man could not interpret from the movement of his lips, took a carefully sealed white packet from inside his coat and handed it to his godson. From the way that Cornelius received it and placed it in a cupboard, Boxtel assumed that this packet contained papers of the greatest importance.

At first, he thought that this precious packet might contain some offsets newly brought in from Bengal or Ceylon, but it soon struck him that Cornelius de Witt did not have much to do with growing tulips, being more concerned with men, plants which are a good deal less pleasing to see and, in particular, much harder to bring to flower.

So he came round to the idea that the packet quite simply contained papers, and that these papers contained something political. But why give papers concerning politics to Cornelius, who boasted of being quite ignorant of that science, which he found much more obscure than chemistry or even alchemy?

No doubt, then, it must be something that de Witt, already threatened by the unpopularity with which his compatriots were starting to honour him, was entrusting for safekeeping to his godson van Baerle, and the move by the *Ruaart* was all the more clever since the younger Cornelius, untainted by any kind of intrigue, would certainly not be the first person in whose house one would look for such a thing. Apart from which, if the parcel had contained bulbs, Boxtel knew his neighbour: Cornelius would not have waited, but would have immediately assessed the value of the present he was given by studying them as an expert. Yet on the contrary, Cornelius had respectfully received the packet from the hands of the *Ruaart* and with the same respect put it into a drawer, pushing it to the back, firstly no doubt so that it could not be seen, and secondly so that it would not take up too much of the space reserved for his bulbs.

Once the packet was in the drawer, de Witt got up, shook his godson's hand and made for the door. Cornelius quickly took the lamp and hurried ahead to show his godfather the way, as was right and proper.

So the light faded in the study with the large windows, only to reappear on the staircase, then in the hallway and finally in the street, which was still full of people eager to see the *Ruaart* get back into his coach.

The envious neighbour had not been mistaken in his assumptions. The packet that the *Ruaart* had given his godson, which the latter had carefully put away, was Johan's correspondence with Monsieur de Louvois.

However, the packet had been entrusted to him, as Cornelius would tell his brother, without the slightest hint to his godson of its political importance. The only instruction that he had given him was to return the packet to no one but himself, at his request, whoever came to ask for it. And, as we have seen, Cornelius shut the packet up in the cupboard for rare bulbs.

Then, after the *Ruaart* had left, and the noise and lights had faded, he ceased to think about the said packet, while Boxtel, on the other hand, thought about it a great deal. Like a skilful seaman, he saw this packet as the distant and barely visible cloud which gets bigger as it approaches, heralding a storm.

Now all the ground for our story is marked out – in that rich soil that extends from Dordrecht to the Hague. Whoever wishes may follow it into the future of the chapters to come. Meanwhile, we have kept our word and proved that never had Cornelius or Johan de Witt had such savage enemies in the whole of Holland as the one that van Baerle possessed in the person of his neighbour, Mijnheer Isaac Boxtel.

However, blissful in his ignorance, the tulip grower had continued on his path towards the goal suggested by the Society of Haarlem, progressing from the dark brown tulip to a burnt coffee colour. And, returning to him on the same day that the great event which we have described took place in the Hague, we find him at about one o'clock in the afternoon, taking some bulbs out of his flowerbed, bulbs which had not yet produced flowers and had been grown from a seedling of burnt-coffee-coloured tulips, the flowering of which had so far been held back, being fixed for the spring of the year 1673, when they would surely produce the great black tulip demanded by the Haarlem Society.

So, on 20 August 1672, at one o'clock in the afternoon, Cornelius was in his drying room, his feet on the footrest beneath the table and his elbows on the rug draped over it, delightedly contemplating the three offsets which he had just detached from his bulb: they were pure, perfect and whole, the inestimable first causes of one of the most wonderful products of science and nature, united in an entity that when realized would make the name of Cornelius van Baerle illustrious for all time.

'I shall discover the great black tulip,' Cornelius said to himself, while he detached the offsets. 'I shall win the hundred thousand florins offered as the prize. I shall give the money to

the poor of Dordrecht, and in that way the hatred aroused by
any rich man during a civil war will be appeased and I shall have
nothing to fear from either Republicans or Orangemen as I
continue to keep my flowerbeds in a magnificent condition. Nor
shall I have to fear that one day there will be an uprising when
the shopkeepers of Dordrecht and the seamen of the port shall
come and seize my bulbs to feed their families, as they sometimes
threaten to do under their breath when they learn that I have
bought a single bulb for two or three hundred florins. So, that's
decided: I shall give the hundred-thousand-florin prize from
Haarlem to the poor.'

And yet . . .

At this, 'and yet', van Baerle paused and sighed.

'And yet,' he went on, 'it would have been sweet indeed
to spend those hundred thousand florins on expanding my
flowerbeds or even on a journey to the Orient, the home of
beautiful flowers.

'But, alas no, there is no time to think about all that. Muskets,
flags, drums and proclamations are what rules at the moment.'

Van Baerle looked upwards and gave a sigh. Then, turning
his gaze back towards his bulbs, which in his mind were far more
significant than those muskets, drums, flags and proclamations –
all of them things good for nothing except to trouble the mind
of decent folk – he said, 'What lovely bulbs these are, all the
same. How smooth they are, how finely shaped. And what a
melancholy aspect they have, promising me a tulip of ebony
black! The veins on them are invisible to the naked eye. Ah,
surely, there will not be a single blemish on the widow's weeds
of the flower that I shall have made . . .

'What will they call this daughter of my sleepless nights, my
work, my thoughts? *Tulipa nigra Barlænsis*.

'Yes, *Barlænsis* – a fine name. All of tulip-growing Europe,
that is, the whole intelligent part of the continent, would shudder
when the word was spread on the four winds to the corners of
the earth.

'The great black tulip has been found! What is it called?
connoisseurs will ask. *Tulipa nigra Barlænsis*. Why *Barlænsis*?
After the man who discovered it, van Baerle, they will be told.

Who is this van Baerle? He's the man who previously discovered five new species: the Jeanne, the Johan de Witt, the Cornelius, etc. Well, that's my ambition. It will cause no harm to anyone and they will still speak of *Tulipa nigra Barlænsis* when my godfather, that admirable statesman, may no longer be remembered except by the tulip to which I gave his name.

'Ah, what delightful little bulbs they are! When the tulip flowers,' Cornelius went on, 'and if peace has returned to Holland, I want to give the poor only fifty thousand florins. When all's said and done, that is a good deal for a man who is under absolutely no obligation. Then I shall devote the remaining fifty thousand florins to my experiments. With those fifty thousand florins, I want to give a scent to the tulip. Now, if I could give the tulip the scent of a rose or a carnation, or even a completely new scent, which would be even better . . . If I could give this queen of flowers the natural, generic scent that she lost on leaving her Oriental throne for a European one, the scent that she must have in the Indian subcontinent or in Goa, in Bombay, in Madras, and most of all in that island which was once, so they say, the earthly paradise, and which is called Ceylon . . . What glory! I tell you, I should rather in that case be Cornelius van Baerle than Alexander, Caesar or Maximilian.[3]

'What wonderful little bulbs!'

And Cornelius revelled in contemplating them, Cornelius abandoned himself to the sweetest of dreams.

Suddenly, the bell on his study door was rung with more than usual force. Cornelius shuddered, reached out his hand to cover his bulbs and turned round.

'Who goes there?' he asked.

'Sir,' his servant said, 'it is a messenger from the Hague.'

'A messenger from the Hague . . . What does he want?'

'It's Craeke, sir.'

'Craeke? Johan de Witt's personal valet? Very well, tell him to wait.'

'I cannot wait,' said a voice in the corridor.

This almost violent irruption was such a breach in the usual routine of Cornelius van Baerle's household that, seeing Craeke burst into the drying room, he made an almost convulsive movement with the hand covering the bulbs, which sent two of the precious objects rolling, one under a small table near the large one, the other into the fireplace.

'Devil take it!' Cornelius exclaimed, dashing after his offsets. 'What on earth is it, Craeke?'

'What it is, sir,' said Craeke, putting down a sheet of paper on the large table, where the third bulb had stayed in its place, 'what it is, sir, is that you are asked to read this paper without losing a single moment.'

At which Craeke, who thought he had seen the signs of a riot in the streets of Dordrecht like the one which he had just left in the Hague, fled without looking round.

'Very well, very well, my good Craeke,' Cornelius said, reaching under the table to retrieve the precious bulb, 'we'll read your paper.'

Then he picked up the bulb and held it in the palm of his hand to examine it.

'Good,' he said. 'That's one of them which is unharmed. That confounded Craeke, what! Rushing into my drying room like that! Now let's have a look at the other one.'

Without putting down the bulb that he had recovered, van Baerle went over to the fireplace, knelt down and started to feel around in the ashes, which luckily were cold. After a moment, he felt the second offset.

'Good,' he said, 'here it is.' And, looking at it with almost paternal concern, he added, 'Unharmed, like the first one.'

At the same moment, while Cornelius, still on his knees, was examining the second bulb, the door of the drying room was shaken so roughly and opened in such a manner after this shaking that Cornelius felt rising to his cheeks and ears the heat of that unwise counsellor called anger.

'Now what is it?' he asked. 'Is everyone going mad around here?'

'Sir, sir!' cried a servant, dashing into the drying room with a paler face and more terrified look than Craeke had worn.

'Well, then?' asked Cornelius, guessing at some disaster from this double breach of all the rules of the house.

'Sir, sir! Run, quickly, run!' cried the servant.

'Run away? Why?'

'Sir, the house is full of guards of the States.'

'What do they want?'

'They are looking for you.'

'For what reason?'

'They want to arrest you.'

'Arrest me?'

'Yes, sir, and they have a magistrate coming ahead of them.'

'What does all this mean?' van Baerle asked, holding his two bulbs tightly in his hand and casting a terrified look towards the staircase.

'They are coming up, they are coming up!' said the servant.

'Ah, my dear child, my worthy master,' said his old nurse, also making her appearance in the drying room. 'Take your gold and your jewels and flee! Flee!'

'Where do you expect me to flee, nanny?' van Baerle asked.

'Jump out of the window.'

'It's twenty-five feet high.'

'You will fall into six feet of soft earth.'

'Yes, and I'll fall on to my tulips.'

'Never mind that, jump!'

Cornelius took the third offset, went over to the window and opened it, but at the idea of the damage that he would cause in the beds, far more than the sight of the distance that he would have to fall, he said, 'Never!' and took a step back.

At that moment the halberds of the soldiers could be seen rising between the balusters of the staircase. The nurse raised her arms towards heaven. As for Cornelius van Baerle – it must be said to the credit of the tulip grower, rather than the man – his only consideration was for his invaluable bulbs.

He looked around for a paper to wrap them, saw the page from the Bible which Craeke had put down on the table. He picked it up, in such a state of anxiety that he did not recall where it came from, wrapped the three offsets in it, hid them in his shirt and waited.

At that moment, the soldiers, preceded by a magistrate, came into the room.

'Are you Doctor Cornelius van Baerle?' the magistrate asked, even though he knew the young man perfectly well; but he was following the procedures laid down by law, which, as one can see, added greatly to the gravity of the occasion.

'Yes, I am, Master van Spennen,' Cornelius replied, graciously bowing to his judge. 'As you very well know.'

'Then deliver to us the seditious papers which you are hiding in your house.'

'Seditious papers?' Cornelius repeated, quite astonished by the adjective.

'Don't pretend to be surprised.'

'I swear to you, Master van Spennen,' Cornelius continued, 'that I have absolutely no idea of what you mean.'

'Let me help you then, doctor,' said the magistrate. 'Hand over to us the papers that the traitor Cornelius de Witt left in your house last January.'

A light shone in Cornelius's memory.

'Ah, ha!' said van Spennen. 'Now you are starting to remember, aren't you?'

'Yes, indeed. But you spoke of seditious papers and I have none of that kind.'

'So you deny it?'

'Indeed I do.'

The magistrate turned round to survey the whole of the study.

'Which room in your house is the one called the drying room?' he asked.

'This one where we are, Master van Spennen.'

The magistrate examined a small note which was on top of the papers he was carrying.

'Very well,' he said, like a man sure of his ground. Then, turning back to Cornelius, he said, 'Will you give me those papers?'

'I can't do that, Master van Spennen. Those papers are not mine: they were given in trust to me and such a trust is sacred.'

'Doctor Cornelius,' the magistrate said, 'in the name of the States, I order you to open this drawer and to hand over to me the papers which are inside it.'

The magistrate pointed to the third drawer of a chest standing by the fireplace. And it was there, in the third drawer down, that the papers were which the *Ruaart* of Putten had given to his godson, proving that the information received by the police had been accurate.

'So, you don't want to?' said van Spennen, seeing Cornelius was struck dumb with amazement. 'In that case, I shall open it myself.'

Pulling out the drawer to its full extent, the magistrate first of all uncovered some twenty bulbs, carefully arranged and labelled, then the packet of papers which had remained precisely as it was when the unfortunate Cornelius de Witt had given it to his godson.

The magistrate broke the seals, tore the envelope open and looked eagerly at the top pages, then cried in a fearful voice, 'Ah, ha! So the law was not wrongly informed!'

'What!' said Cornelius. 'What is this?'

'Oh, you can stop pretending that you don't know anything, Mijnheer van Baerle,' the magistrate replied. 'And you can come with me.'

'What! Come with you!' the doctor exclaimed.

'Yes, because I am arresting you in the name of the States.'

People were not yet arrested in the name of William of Orange. He had not been Stadhouder long enough for that.

'Arrest me!' Cornelius exclaimed. 'But what have I done?'

'That's none of my business, doctor. You can have that out with your judges.'

'Where?'

'In the Hague.'

Cornelius, dumbstruck, kissed his nurse, who passed out, shook hands with his servants, who burst into tears, and followed the magistrate, who shut him up in a closed coach as a prisoner of state, and had him taken at the gallop to the Hague.

CHAPTER 8

An Invasion

As you may guess, what had just happened was the diabolical work of Mijnheer Isaac Boxtel.

Remember, with the help of his telescope he had not missed a single detail of the interview between Cornelius de Witt and his godson. Remember, he heard nothing, but he saw everything. And remember, he guessed how important the papers were that the *Ruaart* of Putten entrusted to his godson when he saw the latter carefully putting away the packet he was given in the drawer where he kept his most precious bulbs.

As a result, when Boxtel, who followed political affairs much more closely than his neighbour Cornelius, learned that Cornelius de Witt had been arrested and charged with high treason against the States, he privately thought that he would surely need to say no more than a word to have the godson arrested at the same time as the godfather.

However, much though Boxtel rejoiced at this, he shuddered at first at the idea of denouncing a man who might, through this denunciation, go to the gallows. But the dreadful thing about wicked ideas is that bit by bit wicked minds can become accustomed to them.

In any event, Mijnheer Isaac Boxtel put his mind at rest with the following sophistical argument:

Cornelius de Witt is a bad citizen, since he has been charged with high treason and arrested. I, on the other hand, am a good citizen, because I have not been charged with any crime at all and I am as free as air. Now since Cornelius de Witt is a bad citizen – which he must be, because he has been charged and arrested – his accomplice, Cornelius van Baerle, must be no less a bad citizen than he is. And so, since I, Isaac Boxtel, am a good citizen and it is the duty of good citizens to denounce bad ones, then it is my duty to denounce Cornelius van Baerle.

However, specious as it was, this argument might not have won over Boxtel so completely, and the jealous man might not have given in to the simple desire for revenge that was eating away at his heart, were it not that the demon of cupidity had risen up there at the same time as the demon of envy.

Boxtel was fully aware of how far advanced van Baerle was in his search for the great black tulip.

Modest though Doctor Cornelius was, he had not been able to hide from his closest friends the fact that he was almost certain to win the prize of a hundred thousand florins offered by the Haarlem Horticultural Society in that year of grace, 1673. And the fever that ravaged Isaac Boxtel was this near-certainty of Cornelius van Baerle.

If Cornelius was arrested, that would certainly cause a great disturbance in the household. The night after his arrest, no one would think to watch over the tulips in the garden. And that very night, Boxtel would clamber over the wall. As he knew precisely where to find the bulb for the great black tulip, he would steal it. Instead of flowering in Cornelius's garden, the tulip would flower in his. He, not Cornelius, would be the one to win the prize of a hundred thousand florins, not to mention the supreme honour of calling the new flower *Tulipa nigra Boxtellensis*. This outcome would satisfy his greed just as much as his desire for vengeance.

When awake, he thought only of the great black tulip; when asleep, he dreamed of nothing else.

Finally, on 19 August, at around two o'clock in the afternoon, the temptation proved so great that Mijnheer Isaac Boxtel could resist it no longer. He composed an anonymous denunciation, in which precision replaced authenticity, and put this letter of denunciation in the post.

No poisonous paper slipped into the mouths of the bronze lions in Venice[1] ever produced a swifter and more terrible result.

That same evening, the chief magistrate received the paper and called together his colleagues for the following morning.

The next day, they met, decided on the arrest and gave the order for it to be carried out to Master van Spennen, who, as we have seen, fulfilled his duty as a worthy Dutchman, arresting Cornelius van Baerle just as the Orangeists of the Hague were roasting the pieces of the bodies of Cornelius and Johan de Witt.

Either from shame or weakness in pursuing his crime to its end, Isaac Boxtel did not have the strength to turn his telescope that day on the garden or the study or the drying room. He knew only too well what was to happen in the house of poor Doctor Cornelius; he had no need to watch. He did not even get up when his one serving man, who envied the life of Cornelius's servants no less bitterly than Boxtel envied their master, came into his room. Boxtel told him, 'I shall not get up today. I am sick.'

At around nine o'clock, he heard a lot of noise in the street and shuddered at it. At that moment, he was paler than someone truly ill and shook more than a man with a genuine fever.

His valet came in and Boxtel hid beneath the blanket.

'Oh, sir!' cried the valet, not entirely unaware that, even as he deplored the misfortune that had befallen van Baerle, he would be announcing a piece of good news to his master. 'Oh, sir! You don't know what is going on at the moment!'

'How do you expect me to know?' Boxtel replied, in a barely comprehensible voice.

'Well, at this very moment, Mijnheer Boxtel, your neighbour Cornelius van Baerle is being arrested on a charge of high treason.'

'Puh!' Boxtel muttered weakly. 'Impossible!'

'Why, that's what they are saying, anyway. What's more, I have just seen Judge van Spennen and some archers go into his house.'

'Well, if you've seen it,' said Boxtel, 'that's another matter.'

'In any event, I shall get more news,' said the valet. 'And don't worry, sir, I shall keep you informed.'

Isaac merely made a gesture to encourage his servant's zeal. The man went out and returned a quarter of an hour later.

'Oh, sir!' he said. 'Everything I told you was the plain truth.'

'How do you mean?'

'Mijnheer van Baerle has been arrested and put in a carriage to be taken to the Hague.'

'To the Hague?'

'Yes, and there, if what they are saying is true, it will be a poor look-out for him.'

'And what are they saying?'

'What they are saying, sir, though by God it's not certain, is that the townsfolk are even now murdering Mijnheer Cornelius and Mijnheer Johan de Witt.'

'Ah!' Boxtel muttered – or, rather, moaned, closing his eyes so as not to see the dreadful picture that doubtless rose up in front of them.

'Dammit!' said the valet as he went out. 'Mijnheer Isaac Boxtel must be very sick indeed not to have jumped up and down on the bed at such a piece of news.'

Isaac Boxtel was indeed quite sick, sick as a man who has just killed another. But he had killed the man for two ends; he had achieved the first. Now there remained the second.

Night came. Boxtel had been waiting for dark. As soon as it came, he got out of bed. Then he climbed up into his sycamore.

His calculation had been right: no one was thinking about keeping an eye on the garden; the house and servants were in a state of confusion.

He listened as ten o'clock struck, then eleven and then midnight. At midnight, pale-faced, with beating heart and trembling hands, he got down from his tree, took a ladder, placed it against the wall, climbed up to the second but last rung, and listened.

All was quiet. Not a sound broke the silence of night. There was a light in just one window of the whole house, which was the window of the old nurse's room.

Boxtel was emboldened by the silence and the dark. He climbed on to the wall, paused for a moment on top of it and then, quite certain that he had nothing to fear, brought the ladder across from his garden into that of Cornelius and climbed down.

Then, since he knew to the nearest inch the place where the offsets of the future black tulip were buried, he ran towards them, though being careful to follow the paths so that he would not be given away by the prints of his feet, and, when he had reached the exact place, plunged his hands into the soft earth with tigerish joy.

He found nothing. He thought he must have made a mistake. None the less, sweat broke out on his brow.

He felt to one side. Nothing. He felt to the right and to the left. Nothing. He felt in front and behind. Nothing.

Finally, he noticed that the soil had been turned over that very morning. He almost lost his head.

As it happened, while Boxtel was in bed, Cornelius had come down into the garden, dug up the bulb and, as we saw, divided it into three offsets.

Boxtel could not make up his mind to leave the spot. He had dug over more than ten square feet with his hands. At last, he could be in no doubt about his misfortune. Mad with rage, he returned to his ladder, climbed the wall, took the ladder across from Cornelius's side to his own, threw it into the garden and jumped down after it.

Suddenly, he saw a last glimmer of hope. It was that the offsets might be in the drying room. It was simply a matter of getting into the drying room as he had got into the garden, and then he would find them there. In any case, it would not be any more difficult. The windows of the drying room could be lifted up like those of a hothouse. Cornelius van Baerle had raised them that very morning and no one had thought to close them. All that was needed was a long enough ladder, a twenty-foot one instead of a twelve-foot one. In the street where he lived, Boxtel had noticed a house being repaired and, beside that house, a huge ladder was standing. It was just what he needed, if the workmen had not taken it away with them.

He ran to the house. The ladder was there.

Boxtel took it and carried it with much difficulty into his garden. With still greater effort, he raised it against the wall of Cornelius's house. The ladder reached as far as the fanlight.

With a ready-lit dark lantern in his pocket, he climbed up the ladder and let himself into the drying room.

Once he was in this temple, he stopped, leaning against the

table. His legs were giving way and his heart beating fit to burst. It was much worse here than in the garden: it was as though ownership commanded less respect in the open air. The same person who might leap over a hedge or clamber over a wall will halt at the door or window leading into a room.

In the garden, Boxtel was simply a trespasser; in the room, he was a thief.

However, his courage returned. He had not come so far to go home empty-handed.

But much though he looked, opening and closing all the drawers, including even the special drawer where Cornelius had put the packet that had just been so disastrous for him, finding the *Joannis*, the *Witt*, the hazel tulip and the coffee-coloured tulip all marked as though in a botanical garden, there was no trace of the black tulip – or, rather, of the offsets in which it was still sleeping, locked in limbo, waiting to flower.

Yet on the double-entry register of seeds and offsets which was kept by van Baerle with greater care and precision than the books of the leading commercial houses in Amsterdam, Boxtel read as follows:

'Today, 20 August 1672, I unearthed the bulb of the great black tulip, which I separated into three offsets.'

'Those offsets! Those offsets!' Boxtel cried, hunting through everything in the drawer. 'Where can he have hidden them?'

Then suddenly he struck his forehead a blow that might have flattened his brains.

'Ah, wretch that I am!' he exclaimed. 'Ah, three times damned, Boxtel: does a man leave behind his bulbs, does he abandon them in Dordrecht when he is bound for the Hague? Can one live without one's bulbs, when they are those of the great black tulip? He would have had time to take them, the villain! He has them with him, he has taken them to the Hague.'

In a flash, Boxtel was looking down the abyss of a pointless crime. He slumped down against the table, at the very same place where a few hours earlier the unfortunate Baerle had for so long and with such delight contemplated the offsets of the black tulip.

'Well, after all,' said the jealous man, raising his ashen face, 'if he has them, he can only keep them for as long as he is alive, and . . .'

The rest of his dreadful idea was taken up in a frightful smile.

'The bulbs are in the Hague,' he said, 'so I can no longer stay in Dordrecht.'

To the Hague for the bulbs! To the Hague!

And Boxtel, without paying attention to the enormous riches he was leaving behind, so preoccupied was he with this one inestimable jewel, left through the fanlight, slid down the ladder, carried back this accessory to theft to the place where he had found it and, like a beast of prey, returned roaring into his house.

CHAPTER 9

The Family Room

It was around midnight when poor van Baerle was locked up in the Buitenhof prison.

It had turned out as Rosa predicted. Finding Cornelius's room empty, the mob had become very angry, and if old Gryphus had been there within reach of its fury he would certainly have paid for his prisoner. But the mob had quite enough to satisfy its rage in the persons of the two brothers, who had been caught by the killers thanks to William, a man of foresight, having taken the precaution of shutting the town gates.

So the time came when the prison emptied and the frightful thunder of shouting that echoed along the staircases gave way to silence.

Rosa took advantage of the opportunity to come out of her hiding place and to take her father with her. The prison was completely deserted: why should anyone want to stay there when throats were being cut at the Tol-Hek?

Gryphus emerged, trembling all over, behind the brave young woman. They went to shut the great gate, as best they could: we say 'as best they could' because the gate was half shattered. It was clear that a powerful flood of anger had passed through it.

At around four o'clock, they heard the noise coming back, but it was not a noise that held any terror for Gryphus and his daughter. The noise was that of the bodies being dragged along and taken to be hung up at the usual place of execution.

Rosa hid once more, but only to avoid witnessing this dreadful spectacle.

At midnight, there was a knock on the gate of the Buitenhof;

or, rather, on the barricade which had replaced it. They were bringing Cornelius van Baerle. As the jailer Gryphus was welcoming this new guest, he saw the prisoner's name on the warrant, and muttered with a jailer's smile, 'Godson of Cornelius de Witt ... Well, young man, we happen to have the family cell here, so we'll give you that one.'

Delighted by the joke, the fanatical Orangeist took his lantern and the keys to conduct Cornelius into the cell that the other Cornelius had left only that morning for 'exile' – as those great moralists, in times of revolution, understand the word when they proclaim it as an axiom of high policy: 'Only the dead do not come back.'

So Gryphus prepared to conduct the godson to the godfather's room.

On the way there, the despairing flower lover heard nothing but the barking of a dog and saw nothing but the face of a young woman. The dog was coming out of a niche in the wall, rattling a great chain, and sniffed at Cornelius so as to be sure to recognize him, in case it might be necessary to devour him some day.

As the rail of the staircase creaked under the prisoner's heavy hand, the girl half opened the small door of a room which she inhabited in the very wall of the staircase. Holding a lamp in her right hand, she at the same time lit up her delightful pink face, framed in splendid locks of thick blond hair, while with her left hand she drew her white nightdress across her breast, having been woken up by the unexpected arrival of Cornelius shortly after falling asleep.

It would have made a fine picture, worthy of Master Rembrandt: the black spiral of the staircase, lit by the reddish glow of Gryphus's lamp, together with the jailer's dark features; at the top, the sorrowful figure of Cornelius, leaning against the rail as he looked down, and below him, framed in the light from the door, Rosa's smooth face and her modest gesture, perhaps a little put out at Cornelius being above her, at a place on the stairs from where he cast a vague, sad glance over the round, white shoulders of the young woman.

Then, lower down, entirely in shadow, at the point on the

stairway where details were obscured by the darkness, the car-
buncle eyes of the mastiff shaking his chain, the links of which
glittered brilliantly in the double light from the lamps held by
Rosa and Gryphus.

What the sublime master could not have rendered in his
painting was the pained expression that appeared on Rosa's
face when she saw this pale, handsome young man slowly
climbing the stairs and she was able to attach to him the sinister
words spoken by her father, 'You shall have the family room.'

This vision lasted an instant, much less time than we have
taken to describe it. Then Gryphus continued on his way, Cornelius was forced to follow him, and five minutes later he was
inside the dungeon (which we do not need to describe, because
the reader knows it already).

After pointing the prisoner to the bed on which the martyr
had suffered, who that very same day had given up his soul to
God, Gryphus picked up his lamp and went out.

Left alone, Cornelius threw himself down on the bed, but
could not sleep. He kept his eye fixed on the narrow window
with its iron grating, which let in the light from the Buitenhof,
so that he saw the first pale rays of the sun shining over the trees
like a white cloak that the sky had lowered across the earth.

From time to time during the night, a few swift horses had
galloped across the Buitenhof, the heavy steps of patrolling
soldiers had struck the round cobbles of the square, and the
slow matches of their arquebuses, flaring up in the west wind,
had cast intermittent flashes as far as the prison windows. But
when the new day decked with silver the coping on the roofs of
the houses, impatient to see whether anything was alive about
him, Cornelius went over to the window and looked sadly
around.

At the far end of the square rose a blackish mass tinted with
dark blue by the morning mist, its irregular outline silhouetted
against the houses.

Cornelius recognized the gibbet.

Two shapeless scraps hung from the gibbet, still bleeding, but
no more than skeletons.

The good people of the Hague had torn the flesh of their

victims, but conscientiously taken the remains to the gibbet as the excuse for an inscription on a huge placard. With his twenty-eight-year-old's eyes, Cornelius managed to read on this placard the following lines, written with some sign painter's coarse brush:

Here hang that great scoundrel Johan de Witt and the little rogue Cornelius de Witt, his brother, two enemies of the people, but great friends of the King of France

Cornelius gave a cry of horror and in a fit of frantic delirium he beat his hands and feet against the door, so hard and so violently that Gryphus ran up furiously, holding his enormous bunch of keys.

He opened the door with a volley of dreadful curses against the prisoner who was troubling him outside the hours when he was used to being troubled.

'No, no, it's too much!' he said. 'Is this other de Witt a maniac?' he cried. 'But these de Witts must have the devil in them!'

'Sir, sir!' said Cornelius, grasping the jailer by the arm and dragging him across to the window. 'Tell me, what is written over there?'

'Where – over there?'

'On that placard.'

Trembling, pale and gasping for breath, he pointed to the far end of the square, at the gibbet with the mocking inscription on it.

Gryphus began to laugh.

'Well, now,' he answered. 'So you've read it. That, my dear sir, is where you end up if you have dealings with the enemies of the Prince of Orange.'

'The de Witts have been assassinated,' Cornelius murmured, his forehead sweating as he slumped down on his bed with his arms dangling and eyes shut.

'The de Witts have suffered the people's justice,' said Gryphus. 'Do you call that being assassinated? I'd rather say executed.'

Seeing that the prisoner had not only been calmed but

prostrated, he left the cell, slamming the door and noisily turning the keys in the locks.

When he regained his senses, Cornelius found himself alone and saw the room where he was, the 'family room' as Gryphus had called it, as the inevitable passage to a sad death. And, being a philosopher, and above all a Christian, he began by praying for the soul of his godfather, then for that of the Grand Pensionary, and finally he resigned himself to all the ills that God might be pleased to inflict upon him.

Then, after returning from heaven to earth and from the earth to his dungeon, he made sure that that dungeon was empty and took out of his coat the three offsets of the black tulip, which he hid behind a block of sandstone where the traditional water jug stood, in the darkest corner of the cell.

Wasted labour of so many years! Destruction of such sweet hopes! Was his discovery then going to end in nothingness, as he would in death? In this prison there was not a blade of grass, not a fragment of earth and not a ray of sunshine.

At that thought, Cornelius lapsed into a fit of black despair from which he was roused only by an extraordinary occurrence.

What occurrence was that?

We shall tell the reader in the next chapter.

CHAPTER 10

The Jailer's Daughter

That same evening, as he was bringing the prisoner his rations, Gryphus opened the door of the cell, slipped on the damp floor and fell, trying to save himself; but his hand turned awkwardly and he broke his arm above the wrist.

Cornelius took a step towards him, but, not suspecting the seriousness of the injury, Gryphus said, 'It's nothing, don't move.'

He tried to get up, putting his weight on his arm, but the bone gave way. Only then did Gryphus cry out in pain. He realized that his arm was broken; and this man, who was so hard on others, fell back swooning in the doorway, where he remained cold and motionless, as if dead. Meanwhile the door of the cell remained open and Cornelius was almost free.

However, the idea never occurred to him that he should take advantage of the accident. From the way that the arm had bent and the sound that it had made in doing so, he could tell that there was a fracture and that there was pain. He thought of nothing except bringing help to the wounded man, unfriendly though the wounded man had seemed towards him in the only conversation that had taken place between them.

At the noise of Gryphus falling and the groan that he had given, a hurried step could be heard on the staircase, and, seeing the apparition that immediately followed the footstep, Cornelius gave a little exclamation of surprise, which was answered by the cry of a young woman.

The person who had responded to Cornelius's cry was the beautiful Frisian girl who, when she saw her father stretched out on the ground with the prisoner bent over him, thought at first that Gryphus (whose rough manner she knew) had fallen in a struggle between himself and the prisoner.

Cornelius realized what the young woman was thinking at the very moment when the suspicion entered her heart. But another glance told her the truth and, ashamed of what she had thought, she turned her lovely, moist eyes on the young man and said, 'Forgive me and thank you, sir. Forgive me for what I thought and thank you for what you are doing.'

Cornelius blushed.

'I am only doing my Christian duty,' he said, 'by helping my neighbour.'

'Yes, and by helping him this evening, you have forgotten how he swore at you this morning. Sir, this is more than humane, it is more than Christian.'

Cornelius looked up at the beautiful girl, astonished to hear a statement so noble and compassionate on the lips of a child of the people. But he did not have time to express his surprise because Gryphus, regaining consciousness, opened his eyes. His usual brutality returned to him with his senses.

'There!' he said. 'That's how it is. You hurry to bring the prisoner his supper, you fall because you are hurrying, as you fall you break your arm and they leave you there on the floor.'

'Be quiet, father,' said Rosa. 'You are being unfair towards this young gentleman. I found him trying to help you.'

'Him?' said Gryphus, with a dubious look.

'It's true, sir, and I am even prepared to help you further.'

'You?' said Gryphus. 'Are you a doctor, then?'

'That was my first profession.'

'Which means you can set my arm?'

'Precisely.'

'So what do you need to do that, tell me?'

'Two wooden splints and some linen bandages.'

'Do you hear, Rosa?' said Gryphus. 'The prisoner is going to set my arm. Don't you see, it's a saving. Help me up, I feel like lead.'

Rosa offered the wounded man her shoulder; he put his good arm round her neck and, with an effort, got on his feet, while

Cornelius, to save him having to walk, pushed a chair over for him.

Gryphus sat down in the chair, then turned back to his daughter and said, 'Well, didn't you hear? Go and fetch what you were asked for.'

Rosa went down and came back a moment later with two staves from a cask and a large strip of linen cloth. In the meantime, Cornelius had taken off the jailer's jacket and rolled up his sleeves.

'Is this what you need, sir?' Rosa asked.

'Yes, miss,' said Cornelius glancing at the things she had brought. 'Yes, that's just right. Now can you push that table over while I support your father's arm?'

Rosa brought the table. Cornelius put the broken arm on it so that it was flat and, with great skill, set the fracture, adjusted the splints and fastened the bandages.

As the last fastening was attached, the jailer fainted again.

'Go and fetch some vinegar, please,' said Cornelius. 'We'll rub his temples with it and he'll come back to himself.'

But instead of carrying out the task she had been given, Rosa made sure that her father was really unconscious and came over to Cornelius.

'Sir,' she said, 'one good turn deserves another.'

'What do you mean, dear child?' Cornelius asked.

'What I mean, sir, is that the judge who will question you tomorrow came this morning to find out which cell you were in. He was told that you had been put in the room of Mijnheer Cornelius de Witt, and at that he laughed in a sinister way that suggests to me that he means you no good.'

'But what can be done to me?' Cornelius asked.

'You see that gibbet.'

'But I am not guilty,' said Cornelius.

'And were they guilty, those men over there, hanged, mutilated and torn apart?'

'That's true,' said Cornelius, his brow clouding.

'In any case,' Rosa went on, 'public opinion wants you to be guilty. And, guilty or not, you will be tried tomorrow. The day after tomorrow you will be sentenced. Nowadays these things are done quickly.'

'So what do you conclude from all that?'

'I conclude that I am alone and weak, that my father has fainted, that the dog is muzzled and that consequently nothing is stopping you from escaping. So escape – that's what I conclude.'

'What are you saying?'

'I am saying that I was unable to save Mijnheer Cornelius and Mijnheer Johan de Witt, alas, and that I would dearly like to save you. But you must act quickly. My father has started to breathe again; in a minute he may reopen his eyes and it will be too late. Aren't you going?'

Cornelius had indeed remained motionless, looking at Rosa, but looking at her as though he did not hear what she was saying.

'Don't you understand?' the girl said, impatiently.

'Yes, indeed, I understand,' said Cornelius. 'But . . .'

'But what?'

'I will not do it. You would be accused.'

'What does that matter?' Rosa said, blushing.

'Thank you, my child,' Cornelius went on. 'But I shall stay here.'

'Stay here! My God, my God! Don't you realize that you will be sentenced, condemned to death, executed on a scaffold and perhaps torn to bits, as Mijnheer Johan and Mijnheer Cornelius were assassinated and torn to bits! In heaven's name, don't worry about me. Get away from this room, beware of it, it brings misfortune on the de Witts.'

'What's that?' cried the jailer, coming back to life. 'Who mentioned those scoundrels, those rogues, those wretches, the de Witts?'

'Don't excite yourself, my good man,' said Cornelius, with a gentle smile. 'The worst thing for a fracture is to heat the blood.'

Then, under his breath, to Rosa, he added, 'My child, I am innocent; I shall confront my judges with the calm and easy mind of an innocent man.'

'Hush!' said Rosa.

'Why?'

'My father must not suspect that we have spoken to one another.'

'What harm would there be in that?'

'What harm? It would mean that he would prevent me from ever returning here,' the girl said.

Cornelius received this confidence with a smile; it seemed to him that a glimmer of happiness was shining in his misfortune.

'Well, what are you two muttering about?' asked Gryphus, getting up and supporting his right arm on his left.

'Nothing,' Rosa replied. 'The gentleman is just telling me what he prescribes for you.'

'Prescribes! Prescribes! Well, I've got a prescription for you, my beauty!'

'What is that, father?'

'Not to come into the prisoners' rooms, or if you do, to leave as soon as you can. So walk ahead of me, and make it quick!'

Rosa and Cornelius exchanged glances. Rosa's look said, 'Do you see what I mean?' And Cornelius's look implied, 'Let the Lord's will be done.'

CHAPTER II

The Testament of Cornelius van Baerle

Rosa had not been wrong. The judges came to the Buitenhof the next day and interrogated Cornelius van Baerle. Moreover, the interrogation was not long; it was established that Cornelius had kept the fatal correspondence between the de Witts and the French in his house.

He did not deny it.

All that remained in doubt in the eyes of the judges was whether the letters had been handed over to him in person by his godfather, Cornelius de Witt. But since, after the death of the two martyrs, Cornelius van Baerle no longer had anyone else to consider, he not only did not deny that the package was entrusted to him by Cornelius in person, but even described how, in what manner and what circumstances the package was entrusted to him.

This admission implicated the godson in the godfather's crime. There was evident complicity between the two Corneliuses.

Cornelius was not content with this confession. He told the whole truth about his sympathies, his habits and his acquaintances. He spoke of his indifference in political matters, his love of study, the arts, the sciences and flowers. He stated that not once, since the day when Cornelius came to Dordrecht and entrusted the parcel to him, had this parcel been touched or even noticed by the person to whom it was entrusted.

To this, the objection was made that he could not possibly be speaking the truth, since the papers were enclosed in a cupboard which he reached and looked into every day.

Cornelius replied that this was true, but that he put his hand into the drawer only to make sure that his bulbs were dry, and looked into it only to find out if his bulbs were beginning to sprout.

They objected that his pretended indifference to the package did not stand up to reasonable scrutiny, because it was not possible that he should not realize the importance of the package when he had been given it from the hand of his godfather.

To this, he replied that his godfather, Cornelius, loved him too well, and above all was too wise a man, for him to have said anything about the content of the papers, because the information would only have tormented the person entrusted with them.

At this, they replied that if Mijnheer de Witt had acted in that way, he would have attached a certificate to the package, in case of accident, stating that his godson was entirely foreign to this correspondence, or otherwise, during his trial, would have written a letter which could serve to exonerate him.

Cornelius replied that his godfather had doubtless never considered that his packet was in any danger, being hidden in a chest of drawers that, for everyone in the van Baerle household, was considered as sacred as the Ark, and that consequently he would think a certificate unnecessary. As for a letter, he did vaguely remember that a moment before he was arrested, while he was absorbed in contemplating one of the rarest of bulbs, Johan de Witt's servant had come into his drying room and handed him a piece of paper. But he recalled no more of all this than one does of a vision. The servant had vanished and, as for the paper, it might be found if they looked for it carefully.

It was impossible to find Craeke, because he had left Holland. As for the paper, it was so unlikely that it would be found that they did not even bother to look for it.

Cornelius himself did not insist greatly on it, because, even if the paper were to be found, it might have nothing to do with the correspondence that formed the grounds for the accusation.

The judges tried to look as though they were encouraging Cornelius to defend himself better than he was. They adopted the attitude of benign patience that indicates either a magistrate who is favourable to the accused, or a victor who has floored his adversary and, having him entirely at his mercy, does not need to press him further to defeat him.

Cornelius did not accept this hypocritical benevolence and said, in a final defence that he delivered with the nobility and calm of a just man, 'Gentlemen, you ask me things to which I cannot reply other than with the exact truth. And the exact truth is as follows. The package came into my house by the means I said. I swear before God that I was and remain unaware of what it contained, and that it was only on the day of my arrest that I knew that what had been entrusted to me was the correspondence of the Grand Pensionary with the Marquis de Louvois. Finally, I swear that I have no idea either how anyone knew that the package was in my house, or how I can be considered guilty for having accepted what was brought to me by my illustrious and unfortunate godfather.'

This was Cornelius's entire plea. The judges retired to consider their verdict.

They concluded that any offshoot of civil discord is harmful, since it revives the war that it is in everyone's interest to snuff out.

One among them, considered to be a keen observer, stated that this young man, who seemed so devoid of emotion, was in reality very dangerous, since behind this icy exterior he must be concealing his burning desire to avenge his friends, the de Witts.

Another pointed out that a love of tulips was perfectly compatible with politics, history having demonstrated that many very dangerous men tended their gardens with no more or less assiduity than if it had been their vocation, even though underneath they were engaged in something entirely different. Look at Tarquin the Elder,[1] who cultivated poppies at Gabii, and the great Condé, who watered his carnations in the dungeon of Vincennes, even at the very moment when the former was considering a return to Rome and the latter an escape from prison.

The judge summed up the problem as follows:

Either Cornelius van Baerle is very fond of tulips or he is very fond of politics. In either event, he has lied to us, firstly because it has been proved, through the letters that were found in his house, that he was involved in politics, and then because it has been shown that he was involved with growing tulips. We have the offsets to prove it. Finally – and here lies the enormity of the case – since the accused, Cornelius van Baerle, was involved both with tulips and with politics, he is hybrid by nature, amphibious in constitution, working with equal ardour for the ends of politics and of tulips, which would give him all the characteristics of the kind of man most dangerous to the public order, and a mind quite, or rather completely, analogous to the type exemplified earlier by Tarquin the Elder and Condé.

The outcome of all this debate was that the Prince Stadhouder of Holland would without any doubt be infinitely grateful to the magistrates of the Hague if they were to make it easier for him to administer the Seven Provinces by eradicating the least seed of a conspiracy against his authority.

This argument outweighed all others and, in order the more effectively to eradicate the seeds of conspiracy, the death sentence was pronounced against Cornelius van Baerle, accused and convicted of having, under the innocent guise of a tulip lover, taken part in the abominable intrigues and foul plots of the de Witts against the Dutch nation, and in their secret dealings with the French enemy.

The sentence additionally provided for the aforementioned Cornelius van Baerle to be taken from the prison of Buitenhof to the scaffold on the square of the same name where the public executioner would cut off his head.

Since the matter had been a serious one, their deliberations lasted for half an hour and, during that half-hour, the prisoner was taken back to his prison. It was there that the Recorder of the States came to read the sentence to him.

Master Gryphus was confined to his bed by the fever occasioned by the break in his arm. His keys had passed to one of his assistant warders and, behind this man, who had admitted the Recorder, Rosa, the lovely Frisian girl, had stationed herself beside the door, holding a handkerchief over her mouth to stifle her sighs and sobs.

Cornelius listened to the sentence with a look that expressed more astonishment than sadness. When it had been read to him, the Recorder asked whether he had anything to say.

'My goodness, no,' he replied. 'Though I will confess that of all the causes of death against which a cautious man might guard himself, this is one that I should never have expected.'

At this answer, the Recorder bowed to Cornelius with all the respect that such officials are inclined to show to great criminals of every sort. As he was about to leave, Cornelius asked him, 'By the way, sir, on what day is the . . . thing, if you please?'

'Why! Today,' said the Recorder, a little put out by the condemned man's self-control.

A sob could be heard from behind the door.

Cornelius leant forward to see who had sobbed, but Rosa anticipated him and shrank back.

'And at what time is the execution?' Cornelius added.

'At midday, sir.'

'The devil it is!' said Cornelius. 'I think I heard ten o'clock strike at least twenty minutes ago. I have no time to lose.'

'Yes, sir, to make your peace with God,' said the Recorder, bowing down to the ground. 'You can ask for a minister of whatever religion you please.'

While he spoke, he was backing out of the cell and the assistant jailer was about to follow him, shutting the door on Cornelius, when a trembling white hand came between him and the heavy door.

Cornelius could only see the cap of golden brocade trimmed with white lace which the beautiful Frisian women wear. He could hear nothing but someone whispering in the turnkey's ear, but the man handed his heavy keys over to the white hand reaching towards him and, going down a few steps, sat in the middle of the stairway, which was thus guarded upwards by him and downwards by the dog.

The gold cap swung around and Cornelius recognized the face of the lovely Rosa, streaked with tears, and her big blue eyes, brimming with them. She went over to Cornelius, clasping her two hands on her sorrowful breast.

'Sir, oh, sir!' she said, unable to go any further.

'My sweet child,' Cornelius replied, very moved. 'What do you want of me? I no longer have any great influence on this earth, I must warn you.'

'Sir, I've come to ask a favour of you,' Rosa said, holding her hands half towards Cornelius and half towards heaven.

'Don't cry like that, Rosa,' the prisoner said. 'Your tears move me far more than the idea of my coming death. And, you know, the more innocent a prisoner is, the more calmly and even joyfully he should die, because he dies a martyr. So, come now, stop crying and tell me what you want, my dear Rosa.'

The young woman fell to her knees.

'Forgive my father,' she said.

'Your father!' Cornelius exclaimed in astonishment.

'Yes, he was so unkind to you. But he is like that by nature, he is like that towards everyone, and he was not being particularly cruel to you.'

'My dear Rosa, he has been punished, and more than punished, by the accident that happened to him, and I forgive him.'

'Thank you,' Rosa said. 'Now, tell me, is there anything I can do for you in return?'

'You can dry your pretty eyes, my dear child,' said Cornelius with a gentle smile.

'But anything for you . . . for you . . .'

'A man with only an hour left to live is a sybarite² indeed if he wants for anything.'

'What about the minister that they offered you?'

'I have loved God all my life, Rosa. I have worshipped Him in His works and blessed Him in His will. God can have nothing against me. So I shall not ask you for a minister. The last thought that concerns me, Rosa, has to do with the glorification of God and I beg you, my dear, to help me in carrying out this last idea.'

'Oh, Mijnheer Cornelius, tell me, tell me!' said the young woman, in floods of tears.

'Give me your pretty hand, and promise not to laugh, my child.'

'Laugh!' Rosa exclaimed, in despair. 'Laugh – at a moment such as this! Just look at me, Mijnheer Cornelius!'

'I am looking at you, Rosa, with the eyes of the body and

those of the soul. Never have I contemplated a more lovely woman and a more beautiful soul. And if I do not look at you any more from this moment onwards, it is because, in preparing to leave this life, I would rather not have any regrets at what I am leaving behind.'

Rosa shuddered. As the prisoner was speaking these words, eleven o'clock struck in the belfry of the Buitenhof. Cornelius knew what her shudder meant.

'Yes, yes, we must hurry,' he said. 'You are right, Rosa.'

At this he took the sheet of paper containing the three offsets out of his shirt, where he had again hidden it when he was no longer afraid that he would be searched.

'My dear friend,' he said, 'I have been very fond of flowers. That was at a time when I was unaware that there were other things to be fond of . . . Oh, don't blush, Rosa, don't turn away, even if I were to make you a declaration of love, it would amount to nothing: down there, on the Buitenhof, there is a certain piece of steel which in sixty minutes will put an end to my temerity. But, as I said, I loved flowers, Rosa, and I discovered – at least, I think I did – the secret of the great black tulip that people think is impossible to grow and which, as you may or may not know, is the subject of a prize of a hundred thousand florins offered by the Horticultural Society of Haarlem. I have those hundred thousand florins in this piece of paper – and, God knows, they are not what I regret. They will be won with the three bulbs in here, and you can take them, Rosa; I am giving them to you.'

'Mijnheer Cornelius!'

'Oh, you can take them, Rosa; you are not wronging anyone, child. I am alone in the world, my father and mother are dead, I have never had either a brother or a sister, I have never fallen in love with anyone, and if it ever occurred to someone to love me, I knew nothing about it. In any case, you can quite well see that I am abandoned, Rosa, because at this moment you alone are here in my dungeon, to help and comfort me.'

'But, sir, a hundred thousand florins . . .'

'Ah, now, let's be serious, my good child,' said Cornelius. 'A hundred thousand florins will make a fine dowry to go with your beauty – and you will have those hundred thousand florins, because I am sure of my bulbs. So you will have them and in exchange, Rosa, I ask for nothing except the promise that you will marry a fine young lad, one whom you will love and who will love you as much as I loved flowers. Don't interrupt me, Rosa, I have only a few minutes left.'

The poor girl was choking on her sobs.

Cornelius took her hand. 'Listen,' he continued, 'here is what you will do. You will take some soil from my garden in Dordrecht. Ask my gardener, Butruysheim, for some leaf-mould from my number six bed. Then plant these three offshoots in it, in a deep box. They will flower next May, that is, seven months from now, and when you see the flower appear on the stem, devote your nights to protecting it from wind and your days in shielding it from the sun. It will flower black, I am certain of it. At that, you will inform the President of the Haarlem Society. He will get the committee to confirm the colour of the flower and they will pay you the hundred thousand florins.'

Rosa gave a great sigh.

'Now,' Cornelius went on, wiping a tear that quivered on his eye and fell much more for the wonderful black tulip that he would never see than for the life that he was leaving, 'I want nothing more except that the tulip should be called *Rosa Barlænsis*, so that it will simultaneously recall your name and mine; and since, as you are surely not acquainted with Latin, you might forget the word, try to find me a pencil and some paper so that I can write it down.'

Rosa burst into tears and held out a leather-bound book, bearing the initials C.W.

'What's this?' the prisoner asked.

'Alas!' Rosa replied. 'This is the Bible belonging to your poor godfather, Cornelius de Witt. This is where he found the strength to undergo torture and to hear his sentence without flinching. I found it in this room after the martyr's death and I have kept it as a relic. I brought it for you today, because it seemed to me that this book has a divine power in it. You did not need that strength because God has placed it in you, thank heavens! Write on it what you have to write, Mijnheer Cornelius, and though

I am unfortunately unable to read, I shall carry out whatever you write.'

Cornelius took the Bible and kissed it respectfully.

'What can I write with?' he asked.

'There is a pencil in the Bible,' said Rosa. 'It was there and I left it.'

The pencil was the one that Johan de Witt had lent his brother and not thought to take back.

Cornelius took it and on the second page – because, as you will recall, the first had been torn out – about to follow his godfather into eternity, he wrote in no less firm a hand:

This 23rd August 1672, being about to give my soul to God on the scaffold, though innocent, I bequeath to Rosa Gryphus the only thing that is left to me out of all my goods in this world, the rest having been confiscated; therefore, as I say, I bequeath to Rosa Gryphus three offsets which, as I firmly believe, should produce in the month of May next the great black tulip for which the Society of Haarlem has offered a prize of one hundred thousand florins, desiring that she should receive these hundred thousand florins in my stead as my sole heiress, with the one provision that she should marry a young man of around my age who will love her and whom she will love, and that she should give the great black tulip, which will create a new species, the name of *Rosa Barlænsis*, that is, a combination of her name and my own.

May God give me grace, and, to her, health!

Cornelius van Baerle.

Then, giving the Bible to Rosa, he said, 'Read it.'

'Alas!' the young woman replied. 'As I already told you, I cannot read.'

So Cornelius read Rosa the will that he had just made. The poor girl's tears flowed twice as fast.

'Do you accept my conditions?' the prisoner asked, giving a melancholy smile and kissing the lovely Frisian's trembling fingers.

'No, I cannot, sir,' she stammered.

'You cannot, my child? Why is that?'

'Because there is one of those conditions that I could not keep.'

'Which one? I thought we had settled it all by our agreement.'

'You are giving me the hundred thousand florins as a dowry?'

'Yes.'

'To marry a young man that I love?'

'Indeed!'

'Well, sir, I cannot have the money. I shall never love anyone and I shall never marry.'

After managing, with much difficulty, to speak these words, Rosa's knees began to give way and she almost fainted with grief.

Cornelius, terrified at seeing her so overcome and so pale, was about to take her in his arms when a heavy step, followed by other sinister sounds, echoed along the stairway, together with the barking of a dog.

'They are coming to fetch you!' Rosa cried, wringing her hands. 'My God, my God, sir, do you have anything more to say to me?'

She fell to her knees, her head buried in his arms, choking with sobs and tears.

'I have to say to you only that you must carefully hide away your three bulbs and look after them in the way that I told you, for my sake. Farewell, Rosa.'

'Oh, yes,' she said, without looking up. 'Oh, yes, I shall do everything that you said.' Then she added softly, 'Except to get married, because that, I swear, that is something I cannot do.'

And she pressed Cornelius's precious treasure to her breast.

The sound that Cornelius and Rosa had heard was made by the Recorder coming to fetch the condemned man, followed by the executioner, the soldiers who were to provide the guard around the scaffold, and some inquisitive frequenters of the prison.

Cornelius, showing neither weakness nor bravado, greeted them as friends rather than as persecutors, and agreed to whatever these gentlemen required to carry out their functions.

Then, with a glance across the square through the little barred window, he saw the scaffold and, twenty yards further on, the gibbet, from which the ill-treated remains of the two de Witt brothers had been taken down on the order of the Stadhouder.

When he had to go down after the guards, Cornelius turned round for a last look from Rosa's angelic eyes, but all he could see behind the swords and halberds was a body lying near a wooden bench and a livid face half hidden by long hair. But even as she fell senseless to the ground, Rosa had done as her friend said and pressed her hand on her velvet bodice; and even as consciousness left her, she managed instinctively to hold on to the precious gift that Cornelius had confided to her.

As he was leaving the dungeon, the young man could see, partly hidden by Rosa's clenched hands, the yellowish leaf of the Bible on which Cornelius de Witt had so slowly and painfully written the few lines that, had Cornelius read them, would certainly have saved the man and his tulip.

CHAPTER 12

The Execution

Cornelius had less than three hundred yards of ground to cross outside the prison before arriving at the foot of his scaffold.

At the bottom of the stairs, the dog watched him go past calmly. Cornelius even thought he saw a certain mild look in the mastiff's eyes that was close to compassion. Perhaps the dog recognized when a prisoner was condemned, and bit only those who left as free men.

As one may imagine, the shorter the distance between the door of the prison and the foot of the scaffold, the more it was filled with onlookers. And these were the same onlookers who, their thirst not slaked from the blood they had drunk already three days earlier, were now waiting for a new victim.

So, hardly had Cornelius appeared before a great howl coursed along the street, spread across the whole of the square and extended in different directions down the streets leading to the scaffold, which were full of the mob. The scaffold was like an island beaten by the flood of four or five rivers.

In the midst of these threats, curses and cries – and, no doubt, so as not to hear them – Cornelius retreated into himself.

What did this just man think of as he was about to die? Not of his enemies, not of his judges, not of his executioners.

He thought about the fine tulips that he would see from heaven, either in Ceylon or in Bengal or elsewhere, when, seated with all the other innocents at the right hand of God, he could look with pity on this earth where the throats of Johan and Cornelius de Witt had been cut because they thought too much about politics, and where Cornelius van Baerle was to have his throat cut for thinking too much about tulips.

The cut of a blade, said our philosopher to himself, and my fine dream will begin.

All that remained was to see whether, as with Monsieur de Chalais or Monsieur de Thou,[1] and other poorly executed people, the headsman was not about to inflict more than one blow, that is more than one martyrdom, on the poor tulip grower.

None of this weakened van Baerle's resolve as he mounted the scaffold.

He was proud to mount it, in spite of everything, proud to have been the friend of the illustrious Johan de Witt and godson of the noble Cornelius, whom the ruffians now crowding to see him die had torn to pieces and burnt three days earlier.

He knelt down, said his prayer, and noticed with a great sensation of joy that if he put his head on the block and kept his eyes open, he would see the barred window of the Buitenhof right up to the final moment.

Finally, the time for that awful passage came. Cornelius put his chin on the cold, damp block, and in that instant, despite himself, closed his eyes, so as to endure more resolutely the frightful avalanche that was about to descend on his head and sweep away his life.

A flash of light shone on the planks of the scaffold. The executioner was raising his sword.

Van Baerle said farewell to the great black tulip, certain that he would awake to greet God in a world lit by a different light and different colours.

Three times he felt the cold draught of the sword pass above his shivering neck. But what was this? He felt no pain or shock. He saw no change in anything about him.

Then suddenly, without knowing by whom, van Baerle felt himself lifted up by quite gentle hands and was soon standing on his rather unsteady feet.

He reopened his eyes.

Someone close by him was reading something from a great parchment sealed with a great seal of red wax.

The same sun, yellow and pale as a Dutch sun should be, was glowing in the sky, the same window was staring at him from the top of the Buitenhof, and the same ruffians, no longer yelling but struck dumb, were looking at him from the square.

By opening his eyes, looking and listening, van Baerle began to understand it all.

The fact was that William, Prince of Orange, doubtless fearing that the seventeen pounds of blood, give or take an ounce, that van Baerle had in his body might make the cup of celestial justice overflow, had been moved to pity by his character and his appearance of innocence. As a result, His Highness had granted him his life. And this is why the sword, rising with that sinister flash of light, had swung three times around his head like the fatal bird around that of Turnus,[2] and had not fallen on his neck, but left his vertebrae intact.

This is why there had been no pain or shock. This is why the sun continued to smile against the admittedly commonplace but still very acceptable blue of the celestial vault.

Cornelius, who had hoped for God and the tulipic expanses of the universe, was slightly disappointed, but consoled himself by exercising that part of the body which the Greeks called *trachelos* and which we modestly designate the neck.

Then Cornelius began to hope that his pardon was complete and that he would be restored to freedom and to his flowerbeds in Dordrecht. But Cornelius was wrong: as Madame de Sévigné[3] remarked at about this time, there was a *post scriptum* to the letter and the most important part of it was in that postscript.

In the postscript, William, Stadhouder of Holland, condemned Cornelius van Baerle to imprisonment for life. He was not guilty enough for death, but he was too guilty to be set free.

So Cornelius listened to his postscript; then, after the first moment of annoyance that the postscript caused him, he thought, 'Huh! All is not lost. There are some good things about life imprisonment. Rosa will be there, in life imprisonment. And I still have my three offsets of the black tulip.' But Cornelius was forgetting that the Seven Provinces might have seven prisons, one for each province, and that a prisoner's bread is cheaper outside the Hague, which is a capital city.

His Highness William, who apparently did not have the means to feed van Baerle in the Hague, was sending him to serve his life imprisonment in the fortress of Loevestein,[4] which is quite close to Dordrecht, but, still, alas, quite far away. For Loevestein, geographers tell us, is situated on the point of the island formed by the Waal and the Meuse, opposite Gorcum.

Van Baerle knew enough about the history of his country for him not to be unaware that the famous Grotius[5] had been shut up in this castle after the death of Barneveldt[6] and that the States, in their generosity towards the celebrated publicist, jurisconsult, historian, poet and theologian, had awarded him the sum of twenty-four Dutch *sous*[7] a day for his food.

'I am very far from being worth as much as Grotius,' van Baerle said to himself. 'They will give me twelve *sous*, if that, and I shall live rather poorly – but I shall live.'

Then, suddenly struck by a dreadful thought, Cornelius exclaimed, 'Oh! That part of the country is so damp and cloudy! And the soil is not good for tulips!'

Then there was Rosa, he murmured, Rosa, who would not be in Loevestein.

He let his head fall on his chest, the same head that had just very nearly fallen lower still.

CHAPTER 13

What was Going On Meanwhile in the Heart of One Spectator

While Cornelius was reflecting on those things, a carriage came up to the scaffold. The carriage was for the prisoner. He was asked to get into it and did so.

He cast a final glance over the Buitenhof. He was hoping to see Rosa's face, with a look of consolation on it, at the window, but the carriage was harnessed to good horses, which rapidly carried van Baerle away from the shouts of the mob in honour of the most magnanimous Stadhouder, mixed with a certain number of curses directed against the de Witts and their godson who had been saved from death.

This made the onlookers exclaim, 'It's just as well that we didn't hesitate to see justice done to that great villain Johan and that little rogue Cornelius, or His Highness's clemency would surely have deprived us of them as it has just deprived us of this one!'

Among the spectators whom the execution of van Baerle had attracted to the Buitenhof, and whom the outcome of events had in any way disappointed, the most disappointed of all was certainly a well-dressed gentleman who since daybreak had made such good use of his feet and his hands that he had managed to be separated from the scaffold only by the line of soldiers surrounding the instrument of death.

Many people had shown their eagerness to see the shedding of the 'perfidious' blood of that guilty man Cornelius, but none of them had been so unrelenting in his expression of that grim wish than the gentleman in question.

The most fanatical had come at dawn to the Buitenhof to

keep the best places, but he, ahead of the most fanatical, had spent the night at the prison gates and from the prison had reached the first row, as we said, *unguibus et rostro*,[1] by stroking some and hitting others.

And when the executioner brought the condemned man to the scaffold, the gentleman, who had climbed on to a corner of the fountain, the better to see and be seen, had made a sign to the executioner which meant 'It's a deal, isn't it?' And the executioner replied with another sign that meant 'Don't worry.'

So who was this gentleman, who seemed so well acquainted with the executioner? And what did this sign language mean?

Nothing could be more obvious. The gentleman was Mijnheer Isaac Boxtel, who, after Cornelius's arrest, as we have seen, had come to the Hague in an attempt to obtain the three offsets of the black tulip.

First of all, Boxtel had tried to win over Gryphus, but the jailer had something of the bulldog about him in his loyalty, his aggression and his ability to bite. Consequently, his hackles had risen at Boxtel's hatred, and he had assumed him to be a close friend making enquiries about trifles in order, no doubt, to contrive some means of escape for the prisoner.

So to Boxtel's first suggestion that Gryphus should purloin the offsets which Cornelius van Baerle must be hiding, if not about his person, at least in some corner of his cell, Gryphus had responded only by throwing him out, with some blandishments from the mastiff on the stairs.

Boxtel had not been put off just because he had left the seat of his trousers in the creature's jaws. He tried again, but this time Gryphus was in bed with a fever and a broken arm, so he did not even admit the man; so Boxtel turned to Rosa, offering her a headdress of pure gold in exchange for the three bulbs. At this, the noble young woman, though she did not yet realize the value of what she was being invited to steal and for which she was being offered so much, told the tempter to go to the executioner, as he was not only the last judge but also the last heir of the prisoner.

This reply gave Boxtel an idea.

Meanwhile, though, the sentence had been pronounced – and

was to be swiftly carried out, as we saw. Isaac did not have the time to corrupt anyone, so he fixed on the idea that Rosa had suggested to him and went to look for the executioner.

Isaac had no doubt that Cornelius would die with his tulips beside his heart. But there were two things that he could not have anticipated. One was Rosa, that is to say, love; the other was William, that is to say, clemency.

Without taking Rosa and William into account, the jealous man had judged correctly. Without William, Cornelius would have died. Without Rosa, Cornelius would have died with his bulbs at his heart.

Mijnheer Boxtel therefore went to the executioner, announced himself to the man as a great friend of the condemned prisoner and – apart from the gold and silver jewels which he left to the executioner – he bought all the clothes of the dead-man-to-be for the somewhat exorbitant amount of a hundred florins; though what was a payment of a hundred florins to a man who was more or less certain that he was buying the prize offered by the Haarlem Society? It was like lending it out at a thousand per cent interest, which, you must agree, is quite a good investment.

For his part, the executioner had nothing or almost nothing to do to earn his hundred florins. All that was needed was that, when the execution was over, he should allow Mijnheer Boxtel to come on to the scaffold with his servants to collect the inanimate remains of his friend. Actually, this was quite common practice among faithful admirers when a political leader died publicly on the Buitenhof. A fanatic like Cornelius could very well know another fanatic ready to give a hundred florins for his remains.

So the executioner agreed to the proposition. He had only one condition, which was that he should be paid in advance. Boxtel, like people who go inside a tent at a fair, might not be happy on coming out, and consequently unwilling to pay.

Boxtel paid in advance, and waited.

After that, one may imagine how worried Boxtel was, and how he watched the guards, the Recorder and the executioner, and how concerned he was about van Baerle's movements. How would he position himself at the block? How would he fall? As he fell, might he not crush the invaluable bulbs? Had he at least thought to shut them up in a box – of gold, for example, gold being the hardest of all metals?[2]

We will not try to describe the effect on this worthy man of the delays to the carrying out of the sentence. Why was the executioner wasting his time by flashing his sword over Cornelius's head instead of striking it off? But when he saw the Recorder take the condemned man's hand and help him up, while pulling a parchment out of his pocket, and when he heard the public announcement of the pardon that the Stadhouder had granted him, Boxtel was a man no longer. The fury of the tiger, the hyena and the serpent flashed out in his eyes, in his cry, in his gestures. Had he been within reach of van Baerle, he would have pounced on him and assassinated him.

So Cornelius would live, Cornelius would go to Loevestein. He would take his bulbs there and, in his prison, he might perhaps find a garden where he could manage to bring the black tulip to flower.

There are some catastrophes that a poor writer's pen cannot describe and which he is obliged to leave to the imagination of his readers with a bald statement of the facts.

Boxtel, quite overcome, fell from his place on the fountain on to some Orangeists, who, like himself, were unhappy at the turn of events. These fellows, thinking that Mijnheer Boxtel's cries were cries of joy, punched him with blows that would surely not have been better delivered on the far side of the Channel.[3]

But what could a few punches add to the pain that Boxtel felt!

He tried to run after the carriage taking away Cornelius and his bulbs. But in his haste he tripped over a paving stone, lost his balance, rolled over ten yards and was unable to get up until he had been kicked and trampled, the whole muddy population of the Hague having passed over him. Once again, Boxtel, who was having a run of bad luck, had his coat torn, his back bruised and his hands scraped. You might think that that would be enough for him. But you would be wrong. Getting back on his feet, he pulled out as much of his hair as he could and threw it as a sacrifice to the fierce and hard-hearted goddess called Envy. No doubt the offering was agreeable to one who, according to myth, has snakes in place of her own hair.[4]

CHAPTER 14

The Pigeons of Dordrecht

It was undoubtedly a great honour for Cornelius van Baerle to be shut up in the very same prison that had housed the learned Mijnheer Grotius. But once he reached the prison, a much greater honour awaited him. It so happened that the very room in Loevestein once inhabited by Barneveldt's illustrious friend[1] was vacant at the time when the Prince of Orange's clemency sent the tulip fancier van Baerle there.

The cell had enjoyed a bad reputation in the castle since Grotius, thanks to his wife's ingenuity, had escaped in the famous book chest which the warders forgot to search. On the other hand, it seemed like a good omen to van Baerle that he had been given this room to stay in, because in his opinion a jailer should not have given a second pigeon the cage from which the first had flown with such ease.

The room is a historic monument, so we shall not spend time here in describing it, except to mention an alcove which had been put there for Mrs Grotius. It was a prison cell like any other, perhaps with higher ceilings and, through its barred window, a delightful view.

In any case, the interest of our story consists in more than a certain number of descriptions of interiors. For van Baerle, life was more than merely being able to breathe. There were two things that the poor prisoner loved far more than his lungs, two things that only thought, that free traveller, could deceive him into believing that he possessed: a flower and a woman, both now for ever lost to him.

Fortunately, the good van Baerle was mistaken. God, who had looked down upon him with the smile of a father at the moment when he mounted the scaffold, destined for him, in the very heart of his prison, in Grotius's cell, the most adventurous life that ever a tulip fancier was fortunate enough to enjoy.

One morning, at his window, while he was sniffing the fresh air that rose up from the Waal and admiring, in the distance, behind a forest of chimneys, the windmills of his home town of Dordrecht, he noticed some pigeons flocking from that point on the horizon to perch, fluttering in the sunlight, on the sharp gables of Loevestein.

Now, van Baerle told himself, these pigeons come from Dordrecht, so they can go back there. If a person were to attach a note to the wing of one of these pigeons, he would have a chance of getting news to Dordrecht, where there are those who regret his absence. Then, after a moment's thought, he added: I shall be that person.

A man is patient when he is twenty-eight years old and condemned to life imprisonment, that is to say, something of the order of twenty-two or twenty-three thousand days.

Van Baerle, even while thinking about his three bulbs (because this thought beat constantly in the depths of his memory as the heart beats in the breast), van Baerle, I say, even as he thought about his three bulbs, made a pigeon trap. He tempted the creatures with all the resources of his kitchen (eighteen Dutch *sous* a day, or twelve French); and after a month of fruitless efforts, he captured a female.

It took him a further two months to catch a male. He then shut them up together and, around the beginning of the year 1673, when he had obtained some eggs, he released the female, who, confident that the male would hatch them in her place, set off joyfully towards Dordrecht with a letter under her wing.

She returned the same evening. The letter was still there.

She kept it for a fortnight, to the great disappointment, then the great despair of van Baerle. Finally, on the sixteenth day, she came back without it.

Van Baerle had addressed the letter to his nurse, the old Frisian woman, begging any charitable soul who found it to deliver it as safely and swiftly as possible. In the letter addressed to his nurse, there was a little note for Rosa.

God, whose breath carries the seeds of wallflowers to the walls of ancient castles and brings them to flower with a little rain, allowed van Baerle's nurse to get this letter.

Here is how:

When he had left Dordrecht for the Hague and the Hague for Gorcum, Mijnheer Isaac Boxtel had not only left behind his house, and his servant, and his observatory, and his telescopes, but also his pigeons. The servant, who had been abandoned without wages, started by devouring the small savings that he owned and afterwards started to devour the pigeons. When the pigeons noticed this, they emigrated from Isaac Boxtel's roof to that of van Baerle.

The nurse was a good-hearted woman who needed to love something. She conceived an affection for the pigeons which had come to beg her hospitality and, when Isaac's servant requested the dozen or so remaining ones, so that he could eat them as he had eaten the other dozen, she offered to buy them from him at six Dutch *sous* apiece. As this was twice what the pigeons were worth, the servant only too gladly accepted, and the nurse found herself the legitimate owner of the envious neighbour's pigeons.

The pigeons, together with others, visited the Hague, Loevestein and Rotterdam in their travels, no doubt searching for a new kind of corn or a different flavour of hemp. And chance – or rather God, whose hand we see behind everything – arranged for Cornelius van Baerle to capture one of these very pigeons.

Hence it happened that, if the envious man had not left Dordrecht to follow his rival firstly to the Hague, then afterwards to Gorcum or Loevestein (as you wish, the two places being separated only by the meeting of the Waal and the Meuse), it would have been into his hands and not those of the nurse that van Baerle's letter would have fallen, so that the poor prisoner, like the Roman cobbler's raven,[2] would have wasted his time and efforts, and instead of having the varied events to

tell that are about to unfold beneath our pen like a carpet of a
thousand colours, we would have had nothing to describe except
a long series of days, each as pale, as sad and as gloomy as the
cloak of night.

But the letter fell into the hands of van Baerle's nurse.

So it was that in the first days of February, at the time when
the first hours of evening fall across the sky and leave upon it
the first glimmering of the stars, Cornelius heard a voice on the
stairway of his turret that sent a shudder through him.

He put a hand on his heart and listened. It was the sweet,
harmonious voice of Rosa.

We must admit that Cornelius was not so astonished or so
overwhelmed with joy as he would have been were it not for the
matter of the pigeon. In exchange for his letter, the pigeon had
brought him hope under its empty wing and, knowing Rosa, he
was every day expecting, if the note had been forwarded to her,
to hear from his love and about his bulbs.

He got up and strained his ear, leaning towards the door. Yes,
those were indeed the sounds that had so sweetly moved him in
the Hague. But now would Rosa, who had made the journey
from the Hague to Loevestein . . . would Rosa, who had succeeded, Cornelius did not know how, in getting inside the prison,
have equal success in reaching the prisoner himself?

While Cornelius was turning this idea over in his mind, hope
pulling against anxiety, the shutter in the door of his cell opened
and Rosa, shining with joy, beautifully dressed and made lovely,
most of all, by the sorrow that had added pallor to her cheeks
over the preceding five months, pressed her face to the bars and
said to Cornelius, 'Oh, sir, sir! Here I am!'

Cornelius spread his arms, looked towards heaven and gave
a cry of joy.

'Oh, Rosa, Rosa!' he exclaimed.

'Hush! Don't speak too loudly. My father is coming up behind
me,' the young woman said.

'Your father?'

'Yes, he is in the courtyard at the bottom of the stairs, getting
his instructions from the governor. He is coming up.'

'Instructions from the governor?'

'Listen, I shall try to tell you everything as briefly as I can. The Stadhouder has a country house a league³ outside Leyden, a large dairy more than anything else. My aunt, who was his nurse, is in charge of all the animals that are kept on this farm. As soon as I got your letter – a letter that I was unable to read, alas, but which your nurse read to me – I hurried to see my aunt and stayed there until the Prince came to the dairy, and when he did so, I asked him if my father could exchange his post as chief warder at the prison in the Hague for that of jailer at the fortress of Loevestein. He did not suspect my reason for the request; had he done so, he might have refused. But in fact, he granted my wish.'

'And here you are.'

'As you see.'

'And I shall see you every day?'

'As often as I can.'

'Oh, Rosa! My lovely madonna, Rosa!' said Cornelius. 'Do you love me a little, then?'

'A little!' she said. 'Ah, you expect too little, Mijnheer Cornelius.'

Cornelius held his hands out to her with a passionate gesture, but only their fingers could touch through the bars.

'My father's coming!' Rosa said. She quickly stepped back from the door and ran towards old Gryphus, who had appeared at the top of the staircase.

CHAPTER 15

The Grating

Gryphus was followed by the mastiff. He was taking him on his rounds so that the dog would recognize the prisoners.

'Father,' said Rosa, 'here is the famous cell from which Mijnheer Grotius escaped. You know, Mijnheer Grotius?'

'Yes, yes, that rascal Grotius, a friend of that scoundrel Barneveldt, whom I saw executed when I was a child. Grotius! Ah, so this is the room that he escaped from. Well, I guarantee no one will escape from here after him.'

He opened the door and started to address the prisoner in the darkness. Meanwhile, the dog went to sniff around the prisoner's heels, as if wondering what right he had to be alive, after he had seen him go out between the jailer and the executioner.

But the lovely Rosa called him and the mastiff went over to her.

'Sir,' Gryphus said, raising his lantern in order to throw a little light around him, 'you see in me your new jailer. I am the head turnkey and I have the rooms under my supervision. I am not a bad man, but I am a stickler for every sort of discipline.'

'But I know you perfectly well, my dear Master Gryphus,' the prisoner said, stepping into the circle of light thrown by the lantern.

'Well, I never, it's you, Mijnheer van Baerle,' said Gryphus. 'Yes, indeed, it's you! Well, well, that's a turn up for the books!'

'Yes, Master Gryphus, and I am very pleased to see that your arm is perfectly mended, since you are holding that lantern in it.'

Gryphus frowned. 'That's how it is,' he said. 'Politicians are always making mistakes. His Highness gave you your life, which I wouldn't have done, in his place.'

'Ah?' Cornelius asked. 'Why not?'

'Because you are the sort of chap to start conspiring all over again. You scholars, you're in communication with the devil.'

'Now, now, Master Gryphus, are you unhappy at the way I set your arm or the fee that I asked for it?' Cornelius said, with a laugh.

'On the contrary, by God, on the contrary!' the jailer growled. 'You set it for me only too well. There's some witchcraft in it: after six weeks, I was using it again as though nothing had happened – so much so that the doctor at the Buitenhof, who knows his business, wanted to break it for me again and set it properly, promising that, this time, I'd be three months without the use of it.'

'Did you refuse, then?'

'I did. I said, "No, as long as I can make the sign of the cross with this one" (Gryphus was a Catholic) "as long as I can make the sign of the cross with this one, I don't give a damn about the devil."'

'But if the devil doesn't bother you, Master Gryphus, you have all the less reason to be bothered by scholars.'

'Oh, scholars! Scholars!' Gryphus cried, without responding to the suggestion. 'Scholars! I'd rather have ten soldiers to guard than a single scholar. Soldiers smoke, drink and get drunk; they are mild as lambs when you give them some brandy or wine from the Meuse. But a scholar – drinking, smoking, getting drunk? Huh, I should think! They stay sober, spend nothing and keep their heads clear for plotting. Well, I'm telling you straight away that you won't find it easy to plot. Firstly, no books, no paper, no book of spells or mumbo jumbo. It was books that helped Mijnheer Grotius to escape.'

'I assure you, Master Gryphus,' van Baerle replied, 'that while I may for a moment have considered the idea of escape, I am certainly not doing so any longer.'

'Good, very good!' said Gryphus. 'You look after yourself, and I'll do likewise. But, all the same, His Highness made a big mistake.'

'By not having my head chopped off? Thank you very much, Master Gryphus.'

'Of course he did. Just look how quiet those de Witt gentlemen are keeping nowadays.'

'That's a dreadful thing to say, Master Gryphus,' van Baerle said, turning away to hide his disgust. 'You forget that one of those unfortunate men was my friend, and the other . . . the other was a second father to me.'

'Yes, and I also recall that both of them were conspirators. And I'm saying this out of the kindness of my heart.'

'Really? Tell me why that is, dear Master Gryphus, because I can't quite understand it.'

'Yes, because if your head had stayed on Master Harbruck's block . . .'

'What then?'

'Why, then you would not be suffering any longer. Whereas, I shall not disguise from you that I am going to make life very hard for you here.'

'Thank you for the promise, Master Gryphus.'

While the prisoner was smiling ironically at the old jailer, Rosa answered him from behind the door with a smile full of angelic consolation.

Gryphus walked over to the window. It was still light enough for the vast horizon indistinctly to be made out, vanishing into a greyish mist.

'What view do you get from here?' asked the jailer.

'Very beautiful,' said Cornelius, looking at Rosa.

'Yes, yes, there's too much view, too much view.'

At that moment the two pigeons, startled by the sight and still more by the voice of this stranger, left their nest and flew off in alarm into the fog.

'Now, now! What's this?' the jailer asked.

'My pigeons,' said Cornelius.

'My pigeons!' the jailer cried. 'My pigeons! Does a prisoner have anything that belongs to him?'

'Well, then,' said Cornelius, 'the pigeons that the good Lord has lent me?'

'Even that is an infringement,' Gryphus replied. 'Pigeons! Oh, young man, young man, I warn you of one thing, which is that tomorrow at the latest, those birds will be boiling in my pot.'

'You'll have to catch them first, Master Gryphus,' said van Baerle. 'You won't agree that they are my pigeons, but they are still less yours, I promise you, than they are mine.'

'Later is not never,' the jailer growled. 'And by tomorrow, I'll wring their necks.'

Even as he was making this unkind promise to Cornelius, Gryphus leant out of the window to study the structure of the nest, which gave van Baerle time to run over to the door and press Rosa's hand. She whispered, 'Until nine o'clock this evening.'

Gryphus who was completely taken up with his determination to catch the pigeons the next day, as he had promised, saw nothing and heard nothing. When he had closed the window, he took his daughter by the arm and went out, giving a double turn to the key and shooting the bolts before going to make the same promises to another prisoner.

Hardly had he disappeared than Cornelius went across to the door to listen to the sound of his footsteps fading, then, when the steps had ceased, ran back to the window and utterly destroyed the pigeons' nest. He preferred to drive them away for ever than to expose these kind messengers to death, after they had brought him the happiness of seeing Rosa again.

Nothing, not the jailer's visit, his brutal threats or the gloomy prospect of being under his supervision, knowing what that meant, could distract Cornelius from pleasant thoughts, and above all the sweet hope that the presence of Rosa had reawakened in his heart. He waited impatiently for nine o'clock to strike on the tower of Loevestein.

Rosa had told him: expect me at nine o'clock.

The last note of the bronze bell was still ringing in the air when Cornelius heard her light footsteps and the rustling of the lovely Frisian's dress, and soon there was a light behind the bars of the door on which Cornelius's eager gaze was fixed.

The shutter of the little window had been opened from outside.

'Here I am,' said Rosa, still breathless from climbing the stairs. 'Here I am!'

'Oh, my dear Rosa!'

'Are you pleased to see me, then?'

'How can you ask? But how did you manage to come? Tell me.'

'Listen, then. Every evening, almost as soon as he has finished supper, my father falls asleep, so I put him to bed, somewhat the worse for gin. Don't say a word of this to anyone, because thanks to his sleeping, I'll be able to come and talk to you for about an hour every evening.'

'Oh, thank you, Rosa, dear Rosa!'

As he spoke, Cornelius brought his face so close to the bars that Rosa drew away.

'I've brought you back your tulip bulbs,' she said.

Cornelius's heart leapt. He had not yet dared to ask Rosa what she had done with the precious treasure that he had given her.

'So you did keep them?'

'Didn't you entrust them to me as something dear to you?'

'Yes, but since I gave them to you, I felt that they were yours.'

'They were mine after your death and you are alive, thank heavens. Oh, how I blessed His Highness. If God should grant Prince William all the good fortune I wished for him, King William will certainly be not only the happiest man in his kingdom, but on all the earth. But, as I said, you were alive and, while I kept the Bible of your godfather Cornelius, I was determined to bring you back your bulbs, but I didn't know how to do it. In fact, I had just decided to go and ask the Stadhouder to give the post of jailer in Gorcum to my father when your nurse brought me your letter. Oh, the two of us wept together, believe me. But your letter made me all the more determined. So I left for Leyden; you know the rest.'

'What, my dear Rosa!' said Cornelius. 'Were you thinking of coming to join me even before you received my letter?'

'Did I think about it!' said Rosa, her love taking precedence over modesty. 'I thought of nothing else!'

As she said this, Rosa became so beautiful that, once more, Cornelius pressed his forehead and his lips to the bars, no doubt with the idea of thanking her. As before, Rosa shrank back.

'Truly,' she said, with that coquetry that lies in the heart of every young woman, 'truly, I have often regretted not being able to read, but never so much and in the same manner as when your nurse brought me your letter, for then I was holding in my hand a letter that could speak to others but was dumb for me, poor fool that I am.'

'You have often regretted not being able to read?' said Cornelius. 'On what occasion?'

'Why?' Rosa said with a laugh. 'So that I could read all the letters that were written to me.'

'Did you get letters, Rosa?'

'Hundreds of them.'

'And who wrote to you?'

'Who wrote to me? Why, firstly, all the students who went by on the Buitenhof, all the officers who went to the parade ground, all the clerks and even the tradesmen who saw me in my little window.'

'And what did you do with these letters, dear Rosa?'

'At one time,' Rosa replied, 'I got a friend to read them to me, which amused me very much. But for some time now, what point has there been in listening to all that foolishness, so recently, I've been burning them.'

'For some time now.' Cornelius exclaimed, with a look that expressed both love and happiness.

Rosa blushed and lowered her eyes, the consequence of which was that she did not see Cornelius's lips approaching hers and encountering, alas, only the iron bars; though, despite this obstacle, they transmitted to the lips of the young woman the warm breath of the tenderest of kisses.

When this flame burnt her lips, Rosa became as pale, or even more so, than she had been at the Buitenhof on the day of the execution. She gave a plaintive moan, closed her lovely eyes and fled, trying in vain to stifle the beating of her heart. Cornelius, left alone, could do no more than breathe in the sweet scent of Rosa's hair, which lingered like a captive between the bars.

Rosa had left in such haste that she had forgotten to give Cornelius the three bulbs of the black tulip.

CHAPTER 16

Master and Pupil

That fine fellow Gryphus, as we have seen, was not much inclined to share his daughter's goodwill towards the godson of Cornelius de Witt.

There were only five prisoners in Loevestein, so the warder's job was not a hard one and the jail was a kind of sinecure given to him because of his age.

But, in his ardour, the worthy jailer had exaggerated the task entrusted to him with all the power of his imagination. In his mind, Cornelius took on the vast proportions of a leading criminal and had consequently become the most dangerous of his prisoners. He watched every move that he made, always approached him with a look of furious anger, and made him bear the punishment for what he called his dreadful rebellion against the merciful Stadhouder.

Three times a day, he would come into van Baerle's room, hoping to catch him in some misdemeanour; but Cornelius had given up letter-writing now that he had his correspondent to hand. It was even probable that, had Cornelius been granted total freedom and permission to retire to any place that he chose, this home in the prison with Rosa and the offsets of his bulbs would have seemed to him preferable to any other home without his bulbs and without Rosa.

This was because Rosa had promised to come and talk to the dear prisoner every evening at nine o'clock, and, as we have seen, she kept her word from the first evening.

The next day, she came up as she had done on the previous one, with the same mysterious air, taking the same precautions. Only this time she had promised herself that she would not put her face too near the bars. In any event, so that she could talk immediately about something that would seriously engage van Baerle's attention, she began by handing his three bulbs to him through the bars, wrapped in the same piece of paper.

However, to Rosa's great astonishment, van Baerle gently pushed away her white hand with his fingers. He had been thinking.

'Listen,' he said. 'We would be risking too much, I think, if we were to put all our eggs in one basket. Just consider, dear Rosa, that this is about an achievement which has so far been considered impossible. It is about producing a flower from the great black tulip. So let's take every precaution so that if we should fail we shall have no reason to reproach ourselves. Here is how I think we shall be able to accomplish our aim.'

Rosa directed all her attention to what the prisoner was about to tell her, more because of the importance that the unfortunate tulip grower himself attached to it than for any significance that it might have for her.

'Here,' Cornelius went on, 'is how I have worked out our joint cooperation in this great matter.'

'I am listening,' said Rosa.

'You must have in this fortress a little garden or, if not, then some kind of courtyard, or failing that a terrace.'

'We have a very fine garden,' said Rosa. 'It extends along the banks of the Waal and is full of fine old trees.'

'Dear Rosa, can you bring me a little soil from this garden so that I can see what it is like?'

'I shall do so tomorrow.'

'Take it from a sunlit place and from a sheltered one, so that I can judge its two qualities in the two conditions of dryness and humidity.'

'Rest assured, I shall.'

'When I have chosen the soil and altered it if necessary, we shall separate our three offsets. You will take one and plant it the day that I tell you to do so in the soil I have chosen. It will surely flower if you care for it according to my directions.'

'I shall stay by it at every moment.'

'You will give me another offset, which I shall try to grow

here in my room, which will help me to pass these long days during which I do not see you. I confess, I have little hope for that one and consider it in advance as a sacrifice to my selfishness. And yet the sun does shine in here from time to time. I shall use all my ingenuity to make use of everything, even the warmth and ash from my pipe. Finally, we shall keep – or rather, you shall keep – the third bulb in reserve, as our last resort should our first two experiments fail. In this way, dear Rosa, it is unthinkable that we should not win the hundred thousand florins for your dowry and enjoy the supreme happiness of seeing our work crowned with success.'

'I understand,' said Rosa. 'Tomorrow, I shall bring you some earth so you can choose mine and yours. As far as yours is concerned, I shall have to make several trips because I can only bring you a little at a time.'

'Oh, we're not in any hurry, dear Rosa. Our tulips don't need to be planted for a full month at least. So you see we have lots of time. But when it comes to planting your bulb, you will follow all my instructions, won't you?'

'I promise.'

'And once you have planted it, you will keep me informed of everything that might affect our little protégé, such as changes in the atmosphere, or marks on the paths and marks on the flowerbeds. Listen at night to make sure that our garden is not frequented by cats. Two of those miserable creatures destroyed two of my beds in Dordrecht.'

'I shall listen.'

'On moonlit nights – do you have a view over the garden, my child?'

'My bedroom window overlooks it.'

'Good. On moonlit nights, watch whether any rats come out of holes in the walls. Rats are rodents with fearful teeth, and I know unfortunate tulip growers who have cursed Noah for putting a pair of them in the ark.'

'I'll keep a look-out for cats and rats.'

'Good, keep me informed. And then,' said van Baerle, who had become suspicious since being in prison, 'then there is an animal still more to be feared than cats or rats!'

'What animal is that?'

'Man! You see, dear Rosa, a man steals a florin and will risk jail for such a trifle, so how much more might he steal a tulip bulb worth a hundred thousand florins.'

'No one will go into the garden.'

'Do you promise?'

'I swear it.'

'Very good, Rosa. Thank you, my dear Rosa. Ah, you will be the source of all joy to me.'

And, as van Baerle's lips came towards the bars with the same ardour as on the previous day, and as in any case the time had come for her to go, Rosa put her head back and reached out her hand. In this pretty hand, to which the young woman paid particular care, being concerned about her appearance, was the bulb.

Cornelius kissed the tips of her fingers passionately. Was this because the hand held one of the offsets of the great black tulip? Was it because the hand was Rosa's hand? Those wiser than ourselves must find the answer.

Meanwhile, Rosa left with the two other offsets, pressing them to her breast. Did she press them to her breast because they were the offsets of the great black tulip, or because they came from Cornelius van Baerle? We believe that this question will be easier to answer than the other.

However it may be, from then on life became sweet and full for the prisoner.

As we said, Rosa had given him one of the offsets. Every evening she brought him, handful by handful, soil from the part of the garden that he had judged the best (and which, indeed, was excellent). A wide jug, which Cornelius had skilfully broken, gave him a reasonably good pot and he filled it halfway, mixing the soil that Rosa had brought him with a little river mud, which he dried out to make mould. Then, at the beginning of April, he planted the first offset.

It is beyond our powers to describe the care, the ruses and the subtlety that Cornelius employed to disguise his joy in his work from Gryphus's watchful eye. Half an hour is a century of thoughts and feelings for a prisoner of philosophical bent.

No day passed without Rosa coming to talk to Cornelius.

Rosa took a complete course on the subject of tulips and this provided the bulk of their conversation; but, interesting though they are, one cannot talk constantly of tulips. So they talked about other things and, to his great astonishment, the tulip lover realized how much there was in the world to talk about.

However, Rosa had a habit of keeping her lovely face constantly six inches away from the little window, because the beautiful Frisian was no doubt wary of herself since she had felt through the bars how much the breath of a prisoner can burn the heart of a young woman.

There was one thing above all others that now worried the tulip grower almost as much as his bulbs, a subject to which he continually returned. It was the extent to which Rosa was dependent on her father. Thus the life of van Baerle, the wise doctor, the talented painter, the superior human being, van Baerle who was in all probability the first to have discovered that masterpiece of creation which (the matter being already decided in advance) was to be called *Rosa Barlænsis*, the life and, even more than the life, the happiness of this man depended on the simple whim of another, a man of inferior mind and infinite baseness: this man was a jailer, somewhat less intelligent than the locks that he shut and harder than the bolts that he slammed. He was something like Caliban in *The Tempest*, halfway between man and beast.

Yet Cornelius's happiness depended on this man. One fine morning, this man might become bored with Loevestein, find that the air was bad there or that the gin was not good, and leave the castle, taking his daughter with him – and once more Rosa and Cornelius would be separated. Then God, who tires of doing too much for his creatures, might perhaps decide not to reunite them again.

'And then, what use would carrier pigeons be,' Cornelius asked the young woman, 'since, dear Rosa, you would not be able to read what I wrote to you or to write down your own thoughts?'

'Well, then,' said Rosa, who in her heart dreaded separation as much as Cornelius did, 'we have an hour every evening. Let's use it well.'

'It seems to me,' said Cornelius, 'that we are not using it badly.'

'Let's use it better still,' said Rosa with a smile. 'Show me how to read and write. I shall make the most of your lessons, believe me, and in this way we shall no longer be separated except by our own will.'

'In that case,' Cornelius exclaimed, 'we have eternity ahead of us!'

Rosa smiled again and gently shrugged her shoulders.

'Will you remain in prison for ever?' she asked. 'After having given you your life, will not His Highness give you your freedom? And then, will you not recover your fortune? Won't you be rich? And once you are free and rich, when you ride by on horseback or in a carriage, will you deign to look at little Rosa, jailer's daughter, almost an executioner's child?'

Cornelius was about to protest, and would certainly have done so with all his heart and in the sincerity of a heart full of love. But the girl interrupted him.

'How is your tulip?' she asked with a smile.

Talking to Cornelius about his tulip was Rosa's way of making him forget everything, even Rosa.

'Quite well,' he said. 'The skin is darkening, the work of fermentation has begun, the veins of the offset are warming up and swelling. In a week's time, or perhaps even sooner, we shall be able to make out the first signs of germination. What about yours, Rosa?'

'Oh, I'm doing it all on a grand scale and according to your instructions.'

'Come, now, Rosa, what have you done?' asked Cornelius, his eyes shining with perhaps as much fervour and his breath as short as on the evening when those eyes burnt into Rosa's face and that breath singed her heart.

The young woman smiled, because in her heart of hearts she could not prevent herself from studying the prisoner's double love for her and for his black tulip. 'I've done everything on a large scale,' she said. 'I have prepared a bare patch for myself, far from any trees or walls, in a slightly sandy soil, more damp than dry, without a single stone or pebble. I have set out a bed as you described to me.'

'Good, Rosa, good.'

'The ground that I have prepared in this way is only waiting for your word. On the first fine day, tell me to plant my bulb and I shall do so. You know I must follow behind you, having all the advantages of good air, sunshine and an abundance of earthly moisture.'

'That's right, that's right,' Cornelius exclaimed, clapping his hands for joy. 'You are a good pupil, Rosa, and you will certainly win your hundred thousand florins.'

'Don't forget,' Rosa said with a laugh, 'that your pupil, since you call me that, has other things to learn apart from how to grow tulips.'

'Yes, yes, and I am as interested as you are, my lovely Rosa, in teaching you to read.'

'When shall we start?'

'At once.'

'No, tomorrow.'

'Why tomorrow?'

'Because today our hour is over and I must leave you.'

'Already! But what shall we read?'

'Oh, I have a book,' said Rosa, 'a book that, I hope, will bring us luck.'

'So . . . until tomorrow?'

'Tomorrow.'

On the following day, Rosa came back with the Bible that had belonged to Cornelius de Witt.

CHAPTER 17

The First Bulb

On the following day, as we said, Rosa came back with Cornelius de Witt's Bible.

Then, between master and pupil began one of those charming scenes that bring joy to a novelist's heart when he has the good fortune to find it beneath his pen.

The window, the only opening through which the two lovers could communicate, was too high to read the book that Rosa had brought conveniently for people who, until then, had been content to read what they had to say on one another's faces.

As a result, the young woman had to lean against the opening, her head bent and the book level with the light which she held in her right hand and which, to relieve her a little of it, Cornelius had thought to attach with a handkerchief to the iron grating. In that way, Rosa could follow with a finger on the book the letters and syllables that Cornelius asked her to spell out, while Cornelius, using a straw as a pointer, guided his attentive pupil through the bars.

The light from the lamp brought out Rosa's rich colouring, her deep blue eyes and her blond locks under the gold brocade headdress which, as we said, Frisian women wear. The blood drained from her raised fingers, which took on the pale pink tone that glows in the light and shows the mysterious life circulating beneath the flesh.

Rosa's intelligence quickly developed in contact with Cornelius's invigorating mind, and when the difficulties seemed too great, these eyes gazing into one another, these eyelashes brushing against one another and their mingling hair emitted electric sparks that would even have lit the darkness of idiocy.

And Rosa, going back down to her room, went over the reading lessons alone in her mind, at the same time rehearsing the unconfessed lessons of love in her soul.

One evening she arrived half an hour later than usual.

Half an hour's lateness was too serious an event for Cornelius not to enquire before anything else what had caused it.

'Oh, don't be cross with me,' said the girl. 'It's not my fault. My father has once more made the acquaintance in Loevestein of a man who often came to ask him if he could see the prison in the Hague. He was a jolly fellow, who liked a drink and told funny stories, as well as being generous with his money and ready to pay for a round.'

'Don't you know any more than that about him?' Cornelius asked in surprise.

'No,' the girl replied. 'It's about a fortnight now that my father has been so taken with this new arrival, who visits him regularly.'

'Ah!' said Cornelius, shaking his head anxiously, seeing any unusual event as the prelude to a catastrophe. 'He is some spy of the kind they send into prisons to keep an eye on both the prisoners and their warders.'

'I don't think so,' said Rosa with a smile. 'If this fellow is spying on someone, it isn't my father.'

'Who is it, then?'

'Well, me, perhaps.'

'You?'

'Why not?' Rosa asked with a laugh.

'Oh, it's true,' Cornelius said with a sigh. 'You will not always have suitors who court you in vain, Rosa. This man may become your husband.'

'I'm not denying it.'

'What grounds do you have for believing in this happy prospect?'

'You should say, this dreaded one, Mijnheer Cornelius.'

'Thank you, Rosa, you are right: this dreaded prospect.'

'I base it on the following . . .'

'I am listening.'

'This man came several times to the Buitenhof in the Hague

– why, just around the time that you were a prisoner there. When I left, he also left, and when I came here, he came too. His excuse, in the Hague, was that he wanted to see you.'

'To see me?'

'Oh, it must certainly have been an excuse because now that he could still offer the same reason – seeing that you are once more my father's prisoner, or rather that my father is once more your jailer – he no longer mentions you, quite the contrary. I heard him tell my father yesterday that he did not know you.'

'Carry on, Rosa, please. I am trying to guess who this man is and what he wants.'

'Are you sure, Mijnheer Cornelius, that none of your friends is taking an interest in your fate?'

'I have no friends, Rosa, I only had my nurse, whom you know and who knows you. Alas, poor Zug, she would come herself quite openly and say, weeping, to your father and you, "Dear sir, or dear young lady, my child is here, look how desperate I am, let me see him if only for an hour, and I shall pray to God all my life for you." Oh, no!' Cornelius went on. 'No, apart from my dear Zug, no, I have no friends.'

'Which brings me back to my first idea, all the more so since yesterday evening, at sunset, when I was tidying the flowerbed where I will be planting your bulb, I saw a figure slipping out of the half-open gate between the elders and the aspens. I pretended not to have seen him, but it was our man. He hid and watched me turning over the soil. I was definitely the one he had followed and on whom he was spying. I did not rake an inch or touch an atom of earth without him observing it.'

'Ah, yes, yes, he's in love with you,' said Cornelius. 'Is he young and handsome?'

He looked attentively at Rosa, impatient to hear her reply.

'Young? Handsome?' said Rosa, bursting out laughing. 'His face is horrible, his body is bent, he is nearly fifty and he doesn't dare look me in the face or speak loudly.'

'What is his name?'

'Jacob Gisels.'

'I don't know him.'

'So you see now, he can't have come about you.'

'In any case, if he does love you, Rosa, which he most probably does, because to see you is to love you, you don't love him, do you?'

'Oh, no! Definitely not!'

'So I should set my mind at rest?'

'I am asking you to do so.'

'Well, now that you are starting to know how to read, Rosa, you will read everything I write for you, about the torments of jealousy and those of separation, won't you?'

'I shall if you write in large letters.'

Then, as the turn that the conversation was taking had started to cause Rosa concern, she said, 'By the way, how is your tulip growing?'

'Rosa, just imagine how happy I am: this morning, I looked at it in the sunlight and, after gently moving away the layer of soil covering the offset, I saw the shaft of the first sprout peeping through. Oh, Rosa, my heart melted with joy. That minuscule whitish bud which would be grazed if a fly's wing were to touch it – that imperceptible evidence revealing the merest presence of life – caused me more emotion than the reading of His Highness's order when it restored me life and stayed the executioner's axe on the scaffold at the Buitenhof.'

'So you have hope?' said Rosa, with a smile.

'Oh, yes, I have hope!'

'So when shall I plant my bulb?'

'On the first propitious day, I shall tell you. But most of all, ask no one to help you, and especially do not entrust your secret to anyone in the world. You see, a trained eye could recognize the value of this bulb just by looking at it. And above all, above all, my sweetest Rosa, cherish the third bulb that you still have.'

'It is still in the same piece of paper and just as you gave it to me, Mijnheer Cornelius. I have put it at the bottom of my wardrobe, underneath my lace, which keeps it dry without weighing on it. And now, goodbye, poor prisoner.'

'What! Already?'

'I must.'

'You come so late and leave so early!'

'My father may become impatient if I do not return. Or the lover may guess that he has a rival.'

She listened anxiously.

'What's wrong?' van Baerle asked.

'I thought I heard something.'

'What?'

'Something like the creak of a footstep on the stairs.'

'For one thing,' the prisoner said, 'it can't be Gryphus. You can hear him a long way off.'

'No, it's not my father, I'm sure, but . . .'

'But?'

'But it could be Mijnheer Jacob.'

Rosa ran down the stairs and someone could be heard quickly closing a door before the young woman had descended the first ten steps.

Cornelius was left feeling very worried, but this was only the start.

When Fate decides to carry out an unpleasant job of work, it is rare for her not to offer due warning to her victim, as a duellist does to his adversary, to give him time to draw his weapon.

In almost every case, these warnings – which derive from the instinct of mankind or the complicity of inanimate objects (often less inanimate than is generally supposed) – these warnings, I say, are almost always neglected. The blow whistles through the air and falls on a head which should have been warned by this whistling and, being forewarned, be forearmed.

The following day passed without anything unusual taking place. Gryphus paid his three visits. He found nothing. When he heard his jailer coming – and, in the hope of surprising his prisoner's secrets, Gryphus never came at the same times – van Baerle had devised a mechanism of his own invention like the pulley used to haul sacks of corn up and down in a farm, with which he lowered his jug, firstly below the ledge of tiles, then below the ledge of stone below his window. Our inventor had found a means to hide the strings by which the pulley was operated in the moss growing on the tiles and in the recesses of the stone.

Gryphus guessed nothing.

The device worked for a week. Then one morning, when Cornelius was absorbed in contemplating his bulb, out of which a tiny shoot was already rising, he did not hear old Gryphus coming up the stairs; there was a high wind that day and everything in the tower was creaking. The door suddenly opened, and Cornelius was caught with his jar between his knees.

Seeing something that was unfamiliar to him, and consequently forbidden, in his prisoner's hands, Gryphus descended on the object with greater speed than a falcon on its prey. Chance, or the dread skill that ill-will sometimes gives to evildoers, guided his heavy hand to the very middle of the jar, on the patch of soil that bore the precious bulb – the very hand that had been broken above the wrist, which Cornelius van Baerle had set so well for him.

'What have you got there?' he shouted. 'Ah, I've caught you!'

He plunged his hand into the soil.

'Me? Nothing, nothing!' Cornelius cried, trembling.

'Ha! I've got you! A jar! Some earth! There's some guilty secret hidden under there!'

'My dear Master Gryphus,' van Baerle pleaded, as anxious as a partridge whose chicks have just been snatched by a reaper at harvest-time.

Gryphus had started to dig in the soil with his crooked fingers.

'Please, sir, be careful!' Cornelius said, the colour draining from his face.

'Careful of what?' shouted the jailer. 'Of what?'

'Take care, I tell you. You will scratch it.'

In a flash, near to desperation, he seized the jar out of the jailer's hands and hid it like a treasure behind the rampart of his two arms.

But that stubborn old man Gryphus, increasingly convinced that he had just uncovered a conspiracy against the Prince of Orange, ran towards his prisoner with his stick raised and, when he saw the man's invincible determination to protect his flowerpot, realized that Cornelius was a lot less fearful for his own head than for his jug, and tried to take it from him by force.

'Ah!' the jailer said, in fury. 'Now you see: you are a rebel.'

'Let me have my tulip!' van Baerle cried.

'Yes, yes, your tulip,' the old man retorted. 'I know all about you prisoners and your tricks.'

'But I swear . . .'

'Let go,' Gryphus said, kicking him. 'Let go or I'll call the guard.'

'Call whoever you like, but you will only have this poor flower at the cost of my life.'

In exasperation, Gryphus plunged his fingers once more into the soil and this time pulled out the offset, which was quite black; and, while van Baerle, happy at having saved the container, did not imagine that his adversary had got hold of the contents, Gryphus flung the crushed bulb against the stone floor, where it broke and almost immediately vanished, crushed to atoms under the jailer's wide boot.

Van Baerle saw the murder, glimpsed the damp fragments, felt Gryphus's savage joy and gave a cry of despair that would have softened the heart of the murderous jailer who, a few years earlier, had killed Pellisson's spider.[1]

The idea of thumping this wicked man passed like a flash through the tulip fancier's mind. Blood and fire rushed to his head and blinded him. With both hands he raised the jar, heavy with all the useless earth that remained in it. A moment more and he would have let it fall on old Gryphus's bald pate.

A cry stopped him, a cry full of tears and anguish, poor Rosa's cry, which she gave, pale and trembling, from behind the barred window before, raising her arms to heaven, she intervened between her father and her friend.

Cornelius dropped the jug, which smashed into a thousand pieces with a frightful noise. At this, Gryphus realized the danger that he had narrowly escaped and let out a stream of fearful threats.

'Ah!' said Cornelius. 'You must be a very cowardly and churlish man to deprive a poor prisoner of the tulip bulb that was his only consolation.'

'Shame on you, father!' Rosa added. 'That was a crime that you just committed.'

'Oh, so you're there, are you, scatterbrain?' the old man cried, turning to look at his daughter and seething with rage. 'You mind your own business and go back downstairs this very minute!'

'Wretch! Wretch!' Cornelius shouted in despair.

'After all, it was only a tulip,' Gryphus went on, somewhat ashamed. 'I'll give you as many tulips as you like. I've got three hundred in my loft.'

'To hell with your tulips!' Cornelius shouted. 'They are worth as much as you are, and vice versa. Oh, a hundred thousand million! That's what I'd give, if I had it, for the bulb that you have just crushed here.'

'There!' said Gryphus triumphantly. 'You see: it's not the tulip that was important to you. It's quite clear there was some sorcery in that false bulb, perhaps some means of corresponding with the enemies of His Highness, who spared your life. I said so at the time: they were wrong not to take your head off.'

'Father! Father!' Rosa cried.

'Well, so much the better! So much the better!' Gryphus went on, warming to his subject. 'I destroyed it, so I destroyed it. And the same will happen every time you do this. Oh, I did warn you, my fine friend, that I would make life hard for you!'

'Accursed wretch! Accursed wretch!' Cornelius yelled, from the depth of his despair, as his trembling fingers turned over the last remains of the bulb, the corpse of so many hopes and joys.

'We shall plant the other one tomorrow, dear Mijnheer Cornelius,' Rosa whispered, understanding the extent of the tulip grower's grief as, with her pure heart, she spread these sweet words like a drop of balm on Cornelius's bleeding wound.

CHAPTER 18

Rosa's Lover

Rosa had barely spoken these words of consolation to Cornelius than they heard a voice on the stairs asking Gryphus what was going on.

'Father,' said Rosa. 'Can you hear?'

'What?'

'Mijnheer Jacob is calling you, he is worried.'

'There was so much noise,' said Gryphus. 'You might have thought he was murdering me, this scholar. Oh, what trouble one always has with the clever ones!'

Then, pointing Rosa towards the stairs, he said, 'You go first, miss!' And, closing the door, he added, 'I am coming, Jacob, my friend!'

And Gryphus went out, taking Rosa with him, and leaving poor Cornelius to solitude and bitter sorrow, murmuring, 'Oh, you are the one who has murdered me, you old tormentor. I shall not survive it!'

The unfortunate prisoner would indeed have fallen ill had it not been for the counterweight, called Rosa, that Providence had placed in his life.

That evening, the young woman returned. Her first word was to tell Cornelius that from now on her father would not object to his cultivating his flowers.

'How can you tell?' the prisoner asked her with a doleful look.

'I know because he told me so.'

'Perhaps he was trying to deceive me?'

'No, he regrets what he did.'

'Really? It's too late.'

'His repentance did not come by itself.'

'So how did it come?'

'If only you could have heard how his friend told him off!'

'Ah, Mijnheer Jacob! So he's still with you, this Mijnheer Jacob?'

'He is with us as much as possible.'

And she smiled in such a way that the little cloud of jealousy that had passed across Cornelius's brow melted away.

'How did it happen?' he asked.

'Well, when his friend questioned him over supper, my father told the story of the tulip – or, rather, the offset – and the mighty deed he had performed in crushing it.'

Cornelius gave a sigh that might have been a moan.

'If you could have seen Master Jacob at that moment!' Rosa went on. 'I truly believed that he was about to set fire to the fortress. His eyes were two blazing torches, his hair stood on end and he clenched his fists; for a moment I thought he was about to strangle my father. "Did you do that?" he cried. "Did you crush the bulb?" "Certainly I did," said my father. "It's outrageous, it's hateful!" Jacob went on, shouting, "What you did there was a crime!" My father was dumbstruck. "Are you mad, too?" he asked his friend.'

'Ah, what a fine fellow that Jacob is,' Cornelius murmured. 'A heart of gold, a pure soul.'

'The fact is that it would be impossible to tell a man off more severely than he did my father,' Rosa said. 'He showed real despair and kept on repeating, "Crushed, the offset crushed! Oh, God! Crushed!" Then he turned to me and asked, "But it was not the only one he had, surely?"'

'Did he ask you that?' said Cornelius, pricking his ears.

'"You think it's not the only one?" said my father. "Fine! We'll look for the others."'

'"You'll look for the others," Jacob cried, grabbing my father by the scruff of his neck, but at once letting him go.

'Then, turning to me, he asked, "And what did the poor young man say?"'

'I didn't know what to answer, as you instructed me never to let anyone suspect the importance that you attached to that bulb. Fortunately, my father helped me out of my predicament: "What did he say? He was foaming at the mouth!"

'I interrupted him, "Of course he was furious," I said, "when you were so cruel and unjust."

' "What! Are you mad?" my father exclaimed in his turn. "A fine misfortune it is, crushing a tulip bulb. You can buy hundreds of them for a florin at the market in Gorcum."

' "But they may be less precious than that one," I replied, without thinking.'

'And what did Jacob say to that?' asked Cornelius.

'When I said it, I must admit, I thought I saw a spark of interest in his eyes.'

'Yes,' said Cornelius. 'But that's not all. Did he say anything?'

' "So, dear Rosa," he said in a honeyed voice, "you think this was a precious bulb?"

'I saw that I had made a mistake.

' "How can I tell?" I replied, nonchalantly. "What do I know about bulbs? All I know, alas, since we are forced to live with these prisoners, is that for a prisoner any hobby is valuable. Poor Mijnheer van Baerle was amused by that bulb, so I think that it's cruel to deprive him of his amusement."

' "But first of all," said my father, "how did he get hold of the bulb? That's what we want to know, I think."

'I turned away to avoid my father's gaze, but I found myself looking at Jacob. You would have thought he was trying to read the very bottom of my heart.

'A show of irritation can often take the place of an answer. I shrugged my shoulders, turned my back and went towards the door. But I was stopped by a remark that I heard, even though it was whispered. Jacob was saying to my father, "It's not hard to find out, now, is it?"

' "We can search him and if he has the other offsets, we shall find them."

' "Yes, usually there are three." '

'There are three!' Cornelius exclaimed. 'He said that I had three offsets!'

'You know, I was as struck by that as you are. I turned round. But they were both so preoccupied that they did not notice that

I moved. My father said, "But perhaps he does not have them on him, these bulbs."

'"Then get him down here under some pretext or other and meanwhile I can search his room."'

'Oh, oh!' Cornelius said. 'But your Mijnheer Jacob is a scoundrel!'

'I'm afraid he is.'

'Tell me, Rosa,' Cornelius said, deep in thought.

'What?'

'Did you not tell me that, on the day when you were preparing your flowerbed, this man followed you?'

'Yes.'

'And that he passed like a shadow behind the elders?'

'Indeed, he did.'

'That he did not miss a single one of your passes with the rake?'

'Not one.'

'Rosa,' Cornelius said, going pale.

'Well?'

'You are not the one he was following.'

'So who was he following?'

'It is not you that he loves.'

'So who does he love, then?'

'He was following my offset, he was in love with my tulip.'

'My word! It could well be,' Rosa exclaimed.

'Do you want to make sure?'

'How can I?'

'Oh, it's very easy.'

'Tell me how.'

'Tomorrow, go to the garden. Make sure that Jacob knows you are going, as he did the first time. And, like the first time, try to make sure that he follows you. Pretend to plant the offset and leave the garden, but look behind you through the gate and see what he does.'

'And then what?'

'Then, we shall act according to how he acts.'

'Ah!' Rosa said with a sigh. 'You love your bulbs very much, Mijnheer Cornelius.'

'The fact is,' the prisoner said with a sigh, 'that since your father crushed that poor bulb, I feel that part of my life has been paralysed.'

'Come, now!' said Rosa. 'Would you like to try something else?'

'What?'

'Would you like to accept my father's suggestion?'

'What suggestion?'

'He offered you tulip bulbs by the hundred.'

'So he did.'

'Accept two or three of them and, among these two or three bulbs, you can cultivate the third offset.'

'Yes, that would be good,' said Cornelius, frowning, 'if your father was alone. But this other one, this Jacob, who is spying on us . . .'

'Yes, that's true. But think about it. I can see that you are depriving yourself of a very great pleasure.'

She said this with a smile that was not entirely without irony.

Cornelius did, indeed, reflect for a moment and it was plain to see that he was struggling against a very strong impulse.

'And yet, no!' he exclaimed, with Roman stoicism. 'No! It would be a weakness, a folly; it would be cowardly! If I were to hand over the last resource that remains to us in this way to all the misfortunes of anger and envy, I should be a man unworthy of forgiveness. No, Rosa, no! Tomorrow we shall come to a decision about your tulip, which you must cultivate according to my instructions. As for the third offset' (here, Cornelius gave a great sigh) 'as for the third, keep it in your wardrobe! Keep it as the miser keeps his first or his last gold piece, as the mother keeps her son, as the wounded man keeps the last drop of blood in his veins. Keep it, Rosa! Something tells me that our salvation lies there, that it is our wealth! Keep it! And if the fire of heaven were to fall upon Loevestein, swear to me, Rosa, that instead of your rings, instead of your jewels, instead of that lovely golden hair that so beautifully frames your face, swear to me, Rosa, that you would carry out the last offset that contains my black tulip.'

'Have no fear, Mijnheer Cornelius,' said Rosa, with a sweet

blend of sadness and solemnity. 'Have no fear, your wishes are orders for me.'

'And even if,' said the young man, increasingly excited, 'even if you were to notice that you were being followed, that your every move was watched and your conversations aroused the suspicions of your father and that frightful Jacob, whom I hate . . . Well, Rosa! Sacrifice me at once, I who live only through you, I who have only you in the world, sacrifice me – do not see me any more.'

Rosa felt her heart squeezed within her breast and tears rose to her eyes.

'Alas!' she said.

'What?' Cornelius asked.

'I can see one thing.'

'What can you see?'

'I see,' said the young woman, bursting into tears, 'I see that you love tulips so much that there is no longer any room in your heart for any other affection.'

At which, she fled.

After the young woman had left, Cornelius spent one of the worst nights of his life.

Rosa was angry with him, and she was right. Perhaps she would not come back again to see the prisoner, and he would have no further news, either of Rosa or of his tulips.

Now, how can we explain this odd character to those perfect tulip growers, who still exist in this world? We must confess, to the shame of our hero and of horticulture, that, of his two loves, the one that Cornelius felt most inclined to regret was the love of Rosa. And when, at around three o'clock in the morning, he fell asleep, overcome by tiredness, pursued by fears and beaten down by remorse, the great black tulip gave way in his dreams to the sweet blue eyes of the blonde Frisian girl.

CHAPTER 19

Woman and Flower

Poor Rosa, shut up in her room, could not know what or about whom Cornelius was dreaming. As a result, judging by what he had told her, she was far more inclined to believe that he was dreaming about his tulip than about her; and yet Rosa was mistaken.

But since no one was there to tell her that she was mistaken and since Cornelius's rash words had fallen upon her soul like drops of poison, Rosa was not dreaming, but weeping.

Indeed, since she was a noble-minded being, of deep and clear perceptions, Rosa judged herself not on her moral and physical qualities, but on her social position.

Cornelius was learned, Cornelius was rich – or, at least, he had been until the confiscation of his possessions. Cornelius belonged to that commercial bourgeoisie prouder of its shop signs, shaped and contoured like coats of arms, than ever any hereditary nobility has been of its family escutcheon. So Cornelius might find Rosa good to while away the time, but, undoubtedly, when he came to give his heart, it would be on a tulip, that is to say, to the noblest and proudest of flowers, that he would bestow it, rather than on Rosa, the humble jailer's daughter.

Thus, Rosa understood Cornelius's preference for the black tulip over herself, but was none the less desperate for having understood it. And, during that terrible night, that night of insomnia, she made a resolution. It was not to go back to the cell door again.

However, she knew how ardently Cornelius wanted to have news of his tulip; and since she did not wish to lay herself open to seeing once again a man for whom she felt her sympathy

growing until, having gone beyond fellow feeling, it was proceeding directly by leaps and bounds towards love, and as she
did not want to drive the man to desperation, she resolved to
continue by herself the lessons in reading and writing that they
had started together. Fortunately, she had reached a point in
her learning where a teacher was no longer a necessity for her –
unless the teacher was called Cornelius.

So Rosa set to reading assiduously in the Bible that had
belonged to poor Cornelius de Witt, on the second leaf of which
(now the first, since the preceding one had been torn out) was
written the last will and testament of Cornelius van Baerle.

'Ah!' she sighed, rereading this will, which she never completed without a tear, a pearl of love, emerging from her clear
eyes and rolling down her pale cheeks. 'Ah! At that time I
thought for a moment that he loved me.'

Poor Rosa! She was mistaken. Never had the prisoner's love
been truer than at the moment in our story which we have now
reached, because, as we were ashamed to admit, in the struggle
between the great black tulip and Rosa, it was the great black
tulip that had to give way. But Rosa, as we said, did not know
about the defeat of the great black tulip.

So, having finished her reading – a task in which she had
made great progress – Rosa took the pen and set herself with no
less admirable zeal to the still harder task of writing. And
as Rosa could already write almost legibly on the day when
Cornelius so incautiously declared himself to her, she did not
despair of making enough progress in a week at the latest to be
able to give the prisoner news of his tulip.

She had not forgotten one word of the instructions that
Cornelius had given her. As it happens, Rosa never forgot one
word of anything that Cornelius said to her, even when what he
was saying did not take the form of instructions.

Cornelius, for his part, woke up more in love than ever. The
tulip was still bright and radiant to his mind, but he no longer
saw it as a treasure for which everything, including Rosa,
should be sacrificed, but rather as a precious flower, a wonderful
combination of nature and art that God had granted him to
decorate his mistress's bosom.

All day, however, a vague sense of unease oppressed him. He was like those men whose spirit is strong enough to forget that a great danger is threatening them, that evening or the next day. Once they have overcome their anxiety, they carry on with their lives; except that, from time to time, the forgotten danger gnaws away at their hearts with its sharp teeth. They shudder and ask themselves why they have shuddered; then, remembering what it was they had forgotten, they sigh and say, 'Ah, yes, that's what it was!'

That, for Cornelius, was the fear that Rosa would not come that evening as she usually did. And as the evening fell, the concern became more real and more immediate, until finally this concern took over the whole of Cornelius's body and became the only living thing in him.

So it was with a rapid beating of the heart that he greeted darkness, and, as it came, the words that he had spoken to Rosa the day before, and which had caused the young woman so much pain, returned increasingly to his mind. He wondered how he could have said to this woman, who was such a consolation to him, that she should give him up for the sake of his tulip, in other words, that she should not see him if need be, when the sight of Rosa had become a vital necessity for him.

From Cornelius's room one could hear the hours strike on the castle clock. Seven o'clock, eight o'clock and then nine o'clock struck. Never had any bronze bell resounded more profoundly in the depths of any heart than the hammer striking the ninth blow as it marked the ninth hour.

Then everything returned to silence. Cornelius pressed his hand to his heart to stifle its beating, and listened.

The sound of Rosa's footsteps and that of her dress brushing against the stairs were so familiar to him that, as soon as she climbed the first step, he would say, 'Ah! Here's Rosa!'

But this evening no sound broke the silence of the corridor. The clock struck quarter past nine. Then, on two different notes, half past. Then a quarter to ten, before finally, with its deep voice, proclaiming not only to the guests in the fortress, but also the inhabitants of Loevestein, that it was ten o'clock.

This was the time when Rosa would usually leave Cornelius. The hour had struck and Rosa had not yet come.

So his forebodings had not been mistaken. Rosa was annoyed, she was staying in her room and abandoning him.

'Oh, I have fully deserved what is happening to me,' said Cornelius. 'Oh, she will not come and she will be right not to come. In her place, I should surely do the same.'

Yet despite this, Cornelius listened, waited and continued to hope. He listened and waited in this way until midnight, but at midnight he ceased to hope and, still dressed, threw himself on his bed.

The night was long and sad. The day broke. But the new day brought no hope to the prisoner.

At eight in the morning, his door opened. But Cornelius did not even turn round. He had heard Gryphus's heavy steps in the corridor and he had realized that these steps were approaching alone. He did not even look towards the jailer.

Despite that, he would dearly have loved to question him, to ask for news of Rosa. He was on the point of putting the question, however strange it would have seemed to her father. The egotist was hoping that Gryphus would reply that his daughter was ill.

Except in the event of something extraordinary happening, Rosa never came during the day. Cornelius, as long as the day-light lasted, did not really expect her. However, from the way that he would shudder suddenly, from the way that he listened to the door and from the way that he would glance across at the barred window, one could see that the prisoner had a vague hope that Rosa would make an exception to her usual practice.

On Gryphus's second visit, Cornelius, against all precedent, had asked after the old jailer's health – and had done so in the sweetest tone of voice. But Gryphus, laconic as a Spartan, merely replied, 'It's fine.'

On the third visit, Cornelius varied the form of the question:
'Is anyone ill in Loevestein?' he asked.

'No one!' Gryphus replied, more abruptly even than before, shutting the door in his prisoner's face.

Gryphus, who was unaccustomed to such courtesies from Cornelius, saw in them the start of an attempt by his prisoner to corrupt him.

Cornelius was left alone. It was seven o'clock in the evening. The feeling of anguish that we have tried to describe returned with even greater intensity than before. But, as on the previous day, the hours went past without bringing the sweet vision which used to light up Cornelius's dungeon through the wicket, and which, when it went, left behind enough light to last throughout its absence.

Van Baerle spent the night in a state of real despair. The next day, Gryphus seemed even uglier, more brutish and more depressing than usual. In Cornelius's mind (or, rather, in his heart) there was the hope that it was Gryphus who had prevented Rosa from visiting him. He felt a strong desire to strangle him. But if Gryphus should be strangled by Cornelius, all the laws of God and man would prevent Rosa from ever seeing him again.

So, without realizing it, the jailer was saved from one of the greatest dangers that had ever threatened his life.

Evening came and despair turned to melancholy. The melancholy was all the more profound since, despite van Baerle's efforts, the memory of his poor tulip mingled with the pain that he felt. It was just that time in April which the most expert gardeners designated as the precise moment for the planting of tulips. He had told Rosa, I shall let you know the day when you must put the offset in the ground. The day after, he had planned to fix the planting for the following evening. The weather was good, the atmosphere, although a little humid, was starting to be tempered by the pale rays of the April sun, which seem so gentle, despite their pallor, because they are the first to arrive. What if Rosa were to let the moment for planting pass? What if, to the pain of not seeing the young woman, was to be added that of seeing the offset fail, for having been planted too late, or even for not having been planted at all?

With these two anxieties together, there was certainly enough to take away one's appetite.

That is what happened on the fourth day.

It was pitiful to see Cornelius, struck dumb with pain and

pale from lack of food, leaning out of the barred window (at the risk of not being able to get his head back through the bars), in an attempt to see the little garden on the left which Rosa had mentioned to him, saying that its parapet was beside the river; and all this in the hope of glimpsing either the young woman in the first rays of this April sun, or the tulip – his two broken loves.

In the evening, Gryphus took away Cornelius's lunch and dinner. He had hardly touched them.

The next day, he did not touch them at all, and Gryphus took back the food intended for these two meals just as he had brought it.

Cornelius did not get out of bed all day.

'Good,' said Gryphus, coming down from his most recent visit. 'I think we're going to be rid of the scholar.'

Rosa shuddered.

'Huh!' said Jacob. 'And why is that?'

'He's not eating, he's not drinking, he doesn't get up,' said Gryphus. 'Like Mijnheer Grotius, he will leave here in a chest, except that this time the chest will be a coffin.'

Rosa went as pale as death.

'Oh!' she murmured. 'I understand. He is worried about his tulip.' And, getting up with a heavy heart, she went into her room, where she took a pen and paper, and spent the whole night trying to form letters.

The next day, Cornelius was getting up to drag himself towards the window when he saw a sheet of paper that someone had slipped under the door. He pounced on it, opened it and, in handwriting that he could hardly recognize as Rosa's, so greatly had it improved during this seven-day absence, he read:

Have no fear, your tulip is well

Although this brief word from Rosa calmed one of Cornelius's anxieties, he was still aware of the irony in her words. So that was it: Rosa was not ill, Rosa was upset. It was not that she was prevented from coming, but that, of her own free will, she was staying away from Cornelius.

So, free though she was, Rosa had enough strength of will not to come to the man who was dying of grief at not seeing her.

Cornelius had paper and a pencil that Rosa had brought him. He realized that the young woman was expecting a reply, but that she would not come to fetch this reply until night-time. So he wrote on a sheet of paper like the one she had sent him:

It is not anxiety about my tulip that is making me ill. It is the pain I feel at not seeing you.

Then, when Gryphus had left and evening had come, he slipped the paper under the door and listened. But however hard he strained his ears, he could not hear either her step or the rustling of her dress.

He heard only a voice as low as a breath and soft as a caress which murmured the single word, through the bars of the door, 'Tomorrow.'

Tomorrow was the eighth day. For eight whole days, Cornelius and Rosa had not seen one another.

CHAPTER 20

What Had Happened in Those Eight Days

The next day, at the usual time, van Baerle heard a scratching on his door like the one that Rosa used to make in the best days of their friendship. As one might expect, Cornelius was not far from the door, through the bars of which he would at last see the delightful face that he had been parted from for too long.

Rosa, who was waiting with her lamp in her hand, could not repress a shudder when she saw how sad and pale the prisoner was.

'Are you ill, Mijnheer Cornelius?' she asked.

'Yes,' Cornelius replied. 'I am sick in mind and in body.'

'I saw that you were no longer eating, sir,' said Rosa. 'My father said that you had stopped getting up. So I wrote to reassure you about the precious object of your concern.'

'And I replied,' said Cornelius. 'Seeing you here, I thought, dear Rosa, that you had received my letter.'

'Yes, I did receive it.'

'You can no longer pretend that you cannot read. Not only do you read fluently, but you have advanced tremendously in your writing.'

'Indeed, I not only received, but also read your note. That is why I came to see if there was not some way of restoring you to health.'

'Restoring me to health!' Cornelius exclaimed. 'But does that mean you have some good news for me?' As he spoke, the young man stared at Rosa, his eyes burning with hope.

Either not understanding this look or not wishing to understand it, the young woman replied gravely, 'I have come to

speak only about your tulip, which, I know, is the thing that
worries you most.'

Rosa spoke these few words in an icy tone that made Cornelius shiver. The zealous tulip fancier did not understand all
that the poor child was hiding behind her mask of indifference,
as she struggled with her rival, the black tulip.

'Ah!' Cornelius sighed. 'Again, again! Good Lord, Rosa,
haven't I told you that I was thinking only of you, that it was
you alone that I missed, you alone that concerned me, you
alone who, through your absence, deprived me of air, sunshine,
warmth, light and life?'

Rosa smiled wistfully.

'And yet,' she said, 'your tulip was in such great danger.'

Cornelius shuddered despite himself and fell into the trap (if,
indeed, it was one).

'Such great danger!' he exclaimed, trembling all over. 'My
God! What was it?'

Rosa looked at him with gentle compassion, sensing that
what she wanted was beyond the power of this man, and that
she had to take him with his weakness.

'Yes,' she said. 'You were right. The suitor, the lover, that
Jacob, was not interested in me.'

'So what was he interested in?' Cornelius asked anxiously.

'He came because of the tulip.'

'Ah!' said Cornelius, going more pale at this news than he
had done when Rosa, mistakenly, had announced a fortnight
before that Jacob was coming to see her.

Rosa saw his terror and, from the expression on her face,
Cornelius realized that she was thinking what we have just said.

'Ah, forgive me, Rosa!' he said. 'I know you, I know the
honest goodness of your heart. But God has given you a mind,
judgement, strength and movement to defend yourself, but He
has given none of these to my poor threatened tulip.'

Rosa gave no answer to the prisoner's excuse, but went on,
'While you were uneasy about this man, who had followed me
into the garden and whom I recognized as Jacob, I was still more
uneasy about him. So I did as you told me, the day after I saw
you last, when you said to me . . .'

Cornelius interrupted her.

'Forgive me once more, Rosa,' he cried. 'I was wrong to say what I did. I have already begged you to forgive me for speaking those fatal words. I beg you again. Must I always beg in vain?'

'The day after that,' Rosa continued, ignoring him, 'remembering what you told me . . . about the trick that I was to use to determine whether it was me or the tulip that that hateful man was after . . .'

'Yes, hateful,' he said. 'It's true, isn't it? You hate that man?'

'Yes, I do hate him,' said Rosa, 'because it is his fault that I have suffered so much in the past eight days.'

'Oh, did you suffer too, Rosa? Thank you for saying that.'

'So, the day following that unhappy day,' Rosa continued, 'I went down into the garden and walked towards the flowerbed where I was to plant the tulip, looking behind me to see if on that occasion I was being followed, as I had been before.'

'Well?' Cornelius asked.

'Well, the same shadow crept between the gate and the garden wall, and once more vanished behind the elderberry trees.'

'But you pretended not to have seen it, didn't you?' Cornelius asked, recalling every detail of the advice that he had given Rosa.

'Yes, and I leant over the flowerbed, digging it with a trowel, as though I was planting the offset.'

'And what . . . what was he doing meanwhile?'

'I could see his eyes burning like a tiger's through the branches of the trees.'

'You see? You see?' said Cornelius.

'Then, after I had finished this pretended planting, I went away.'

'But you only went behind the garden gate, didn't you? So that you could see what he was doing after you had gone through the gaps or through the keyhole.'

'He waited for a short while, no doubt to be sure that I was not coming back. Then he crept out of his hiding place on tiptoe, went over to the flowerbed by a very roundabout way and, when he had reached his goal, that is a place opposite the one where the earth had been freshly turned, he stopped, with an air of indifference, looked all around him, searching every corner of the garden, searching every window of the neighbouring houses, searching the earth, the sky, the air, and when he thought that he was quite alone, altogether on his own and quite unobserved by anyone, he threw himself on the flowerbed, dug both his hands into the soft earth, took some of it out and gently rubbed it between his fingers to see if the offset was there, going through the same procedure three times, each time more eagerly than the last, until finally, starting to realize that he might be the victim of some trick, he managed to conceal the anxiety that was eating him up, took the rake, smoothed out the earth so as to leave it in the same state when he left as before he had disturbed it, and all shamefaced and contrite, walked back towards the gate, assuming the innocent air of an ordinary man out for a stroll.'

'Oh, the wretch,' Cornelius muttered, wiping away the drops of sweat that were pouring down his forehead. 'Oh, the wretch! I guessed as much. But, Rosa, what did you do with the offset? Alas, it's already a little late to plant it.'

'The offset has been in the ground for six days.'

'Where? How?' Cornelius exclaimed. 'Oh, good heavens, how rash of you! Where is it? In what soil? Does it have good or bad sunlight? Is there no risk that it will be stolen from us by that ghastly Jacob?'

'There is no risk of it being stolen, unless Jacob forces the door of my room.'

'Ah, so it's in your room, is it?' said Cornelius, with some relief. 'But in what soil, in what kind of receptacle? You're not germinating it in water, like the good women of Haarlem and Dordrecht, who persist in believing that water can replace soil, as if water, which is composed of thirty-three parts of oxygen and sixty-six parts of hydrogen, could replace . . . But what am I telling you, Rosa?'

'Yes, all that is a little learned for me,' the girl replied with a smile. 'So, to set your mind at rest, I shall simply reply that your offset is not in water.'

'Ah, I can breathe again.'

'It's in a good earthenware pot of the same width as the one in which you planted yours. It is in earth made up of three-quarters of ordinary soil taken from the best part of the garden, and a quarter of earth from the street. I've often heard you and that infamous Jacob, as you call him, talking about the kind of soil in which tulips should grow, so I know it as well as the best gardener in Haarlem!'

'But then there is the matter of sunlight. What light does it get, Rosa?'

'Now it is getting the sun all day, on the days when it is shining. But when it will come up and the sun is warmer, I shall do as you did here, Mijnheer Cornelius. I shall expose it at my morning window from eight o'clock to eleven o'clock and at my evening window from three in the afternoon until five.'

'That's right, that's right!' Cornelius cried. 'You are a perfect gardener, my lovely Rosa. But I've just thought: growing my tulip will take up all your time.'

'That's true,' said Rosa. 'But what does it matter? Your tulip is my daughter. I shall give her the time that I should give to my child, if I were a mother. It is only by becoming her mother,' Rosa said with a smile, 'that I can cease to be her rival.'

'My dear, good Rosa,' Cornelius sighed, giving the young woman a look in which there was more of the lover than the gardener, which consoled Rosa a little. Then, after a moment's silence, during which Cornelius reached through the opening between the bars to find Rosa's hand, he went on, 'So, the bulb has been in the ground for six days?'

'Yes, Mijnheer Cornelius, for six days,' she replied.

'And it has still not appeared?'

'No, but I think that it will tomorrow.'

'Tomorrow, then, and you will give me news of it when you give me news of yourself, won't you, Rosa? I am anxious for the daughter, as you called her just now, but I am far more interested in the mother.'

'Tomorrow,' Rosa said, giving Cornelius a sidelong glance, 'I am not sure that I can.'

'For heaven's sake!' said Cornelius. 'Why might you not be able to tomorrow?'

'But, Mijnheer Cornelius, I have a thousand things to do.'

'While I have only one,' he said softly.

'Yes,' Rosa replied. 'To love your tulip.'

'To love you, Rosa.'

She shook her head.

There was a further silence.

'Ah, well,' said van Baerle, breaking the silence. 'Everything in nature changes. New flowers replace the flowers of spring and we see the bees, which tenderly caressed the violet and the stock, settle with the same love on honeysuckle, rose, jasmine, chrysanthemum and geranium.'

'What do you mean by that?' Rosa asked.

'What I mean, Miss Rosa, is that at first you loved to hear the story of my joys and sorrows. You caressed the flower of our shared youth, but mine has faded in the gloom. The garden of hopes and pleasures of a prisoner lasts but a season. It is not like a lovely garden under the sun and in the open air. Once the May harvest is done, once the booty has been gathered, bees like yourself, Rosa, bees with fine waists and golden antennae and diaphanous wings, fly between the bars, abandon cold, solitude and sadness to seek sweet scents and warm breath elsewhere . . . in short, happiness!'

Rosa was looking at Cornelius with a smile which he could not see; his eyes were turned towards heaven. With a sigh, he continued, 'You have abandoned me, Rosa, to enjoy your season in the sun. You were right to do so, I am not complaining. What right did I have to demand fidelity from you?'

'Fidelity!' Rosa cried, weeping and not trying any longer to hide the pearly dew that ran across her cheeks. 'Fidelity! Haven't I been faithful to you?'

'Alas, was it fidelity,' he cried, 'to leave me, to abandon me to die here?'

'But, Mijnheer Cornelius,' said Rosa, 'aren't I doing everything to please you? Aren't I looking after your tulip?'

'What bitterness, Rosa! You reproach me for the one unmixed joy that I have had in this world.'

'I am not reproaching you with anything, Mijnheer Cornelius, except the one deep sorrow that I have felt since the day in the Buitenhof when they came to tell me that you were to be executed.'

'But you are unhappy, Rosa, my sweet Rosa, unhappy because I love flowers.'

'I am not unhappy because you love them, Mijnheer Cornelius; I am just sad that you love them more than you love me.'

'Oh, my dear, my dear beloved,' Cornelius cried. 'Look how my hands are trembling, look how pale my brow is, listen, listen to my beating heart. Well, this is not at all because my black tulip is smiling and calling to me. No, it is because you are smiling at me, you! And because you are leaning towards me. It is because – though I do not know whether this is true or not – it is because it seems to me that, even as you pull away from them, your hands are seeking mine, and that I can feel the warmth of your lovely cheeks behind the cold grating. Rosa, my love, break the offset of the black tulip, destroy my hope in that flower, extinguish the light of that pure, charming dream to which I have become accustomed every day! Yes! Let there be no more flowers in their rich livery, with their elegant charms and their divine whims. Take all that away from me, flower that you are, jealous of those others, take it from me . . . But do not deprive me of your voice, your gestures and the sound of your steps on the heavy staircase, do not deprive me of the fire of your eyes in the dark corridor, or the certainty of your love which used constantly to caress my heart. Love me, Rosa, because I truly feel that I love only you.'

'After the black tulip,' the young woman sighed, at last allowing his lips to touch her warm, soothing hands through the iron grating.

'Before everything, Rosa . . .'

'Should I believe you?'

'As you believe in God.'

'Very well, but loving me does not commit you to very much.'

'Unfortunately, no: to too little, dear Rosa. But it does commit you.'

'Me?' asked Rosa. 'To what does it commit me?'

'First of all, not to get married.'

She smiled.

'Ah, that's how you tyrants are,' she said. 'You love a beauty, you think only of her, you dream only of her; you are condemned to death and, as you are going to the scaffold, you devote your last sigh to her; and yet you ask me, poor girl that I am, to sacrifice my dreams and my ambition.'

'But what beauty are you talking about, Rosa?' said Cornelius, seeking in vain through his memory for the woman to whom Rosa might be referring.

'But the black beauty, sir, the black beauty with the supple waist, the slender feet and the head full of nobility. I am speaking about your flower, sir.'

Cornelius smiled.

'An imaginary beauty, my good Rosa, while you, without counting your lover – or, rather, my lover Jacob – you are surrounded by gallants who court you. Do you remember what you told me, Rosa, about the students, the officers and the clerks of the Hague? Are there no clerks, no officers and no students here in Loevestein?'

'Yes, indeed there are, and quite a lot of them,' said Rosa.

'And they write?'

'They write.'

'And now that you can read . . .'

Cornelius sighed, poor prisoner that he was, thinking that he was the one to whom Rosa owed the privilege of being able to read the *billets doux* that she received.

'Well, now,' said Rosa. 'It seems to me, Mijnheer Cornelius, sir, that by reading the notes that they send me and by taking a good look at the young men who present themselves, I am only following your instructions.'

'How do you mean, my instructions?'

'Yes, your instructions. Have you forgotten,' Rosa went on, sighing in her turn, 'have you forgotten the will that you wrote on the Bible belonging to Mijnheer Cornelius de Witt? I shall not forget it, because, now that I know how to read, I reread it every day and more often twice than once. And in this will you order me to love and marry a handsome young man of between twenty-six and twenty-eight years old. I am still looking for this young man, and since my whole day is devoted to your tulip, you must at least leave me the evening to find him.'

'Ah, Rosa, that will was made in the event of my death and, thank God, I am still alive.'

'Very well, then. I shall not look for this handsome young fellow of twenty-six to twenty-eight years old, and instead I shall come and see you.'

'Oh, Rosa, come, please come!'

'But on one condition.'

'I accept it in advance.'

'Which is that for three days we shall not speak about the tulip.'

'We shall never again speak about it, if you insist, Rosa.'

'Oh, no,' the girl said. 'One must not ask the impossible.'

And, as though by accident, she brought her fresh cheek so close to the grating that Cornelius could touch it with his lips.

Rosa gave a little cry full of love, and ran off.

CHAPTER 21

The Second Offset

The night was good and the next day better still. On the previous days, the prison had grown heavier, darker and lower. It pressed down with all its weight upon the poor prisoner. Its walls were black, its air was cold, and the bars were set so close that the daylight could hardly pass between them.

But when Cornelius woke, a ray of morning sunlight was playing across the bars, and some pigeons were spreading their wings against the air, while others cooed amorously on the roof beside the not-yet-open window.

Cornelius ran to this window and flung it wide. He felt as though life, joy and maybe even freedom were pouring into the dark room with this ray of sunshine.

The reason was that love was flourishing inside and making everything blossom around it – love, that flower of heaven which is far more radiant and more sweetly scented than all the flowers on earth.

When Gryphus entered the prisoner's cell, instead of finding him lying disconsolate on his bed as he had done on previous days, he found him up and about, singing a little aria from an opera.

Gryphus gave him a suspicious look.

'Huh!' he said.

'And how are we this morning?'

Gryphus was still looking suspicious.

'And how is the dog, and Mijnheer Jacob, and our lovely Rosa, and all the rest?'

Gryphus ground his teeth.

'Here's your breakfast,' he said.

'Thank you, my good Cerberus,'[1] said the prisoner. 'It's about time, because I'm very hungry.'

'Huh! You're hungry, are you?' said Gryphus.

'Well, yes. Why not?' asked van Baerle.

'It seems that the conspiracy is going well,' said Gryphus.

'What conspiracy is that?' asked Cornelius.

'As you like! I know what I know, but I've got my eye on you, Master Scholar, don't worry, I've got my eye on you.'

'Keep your eye there, friend Gryphus,' said van Baerle. 'Keep watching. My conspiracy, like my person, is entirely at your disposal.'

'We'll see about that at midday,' said Gryphus. And he left.

'At midday?' Cornelius repeated to himself. 'What does he mean? Very well, let's wait for midday, then we shall see.'

It was easy for Cornelius to wait for midday: Cornelius was waiting for nine o'clock in the evening.

The clock struck twelve and he heard on the staircase not only the footsteps of Gryphus, but those of three or four soldiers coming up with him. The door opened, Gryphus entered, showed the men in and shut the door behind them.

'Here we are! Now, search!'

They went through Cornelius's pockets, searched between his jacket and his waistcoat, between his waistcoat and his shirt, between his shirt and his flesh, and found nothing.

They hunted through the sheets, the mattress and the straw pallet on his bed, but found nothing.

This was when Cornelius congratulated himself on not having taken the third offset. Gryphus would surely have found it in the course of this search, however well it was hidden, and treated it like the first. As it was, no prisoner ever watched his premises being searched with a more tranquil expression.

Gryphus left with the pencil and the three or four sheets of white paper that Rosa had given Cornelius. This was the only prize that he took away from his expedition.

At six o'clock, Gryphus came back, this time alone. Cornelius tried to placate him, but Gryphus growled, showed him a tooth which he had in the corner of his mouth and went out backwards like a man afraid that he will be violated.

Cornelius burst out laughing, the result of which was Gryphus, who knew his literature, shouting through the grating, 'Very well, then, we'll see who has the last laugh.'

The one who was to laugh last, at least that evening, was Cornelius, because Cornelius was expecting Rosa.

She came at nine, but she came without a lantern. She did not need a light any longer, because she had learnt to read. And then, a light might betray her, because she was being watched more than ever by Jacob. And finally, when there was a light, one could see Rosa's blushes too clearly, when Rosa blushed.

What did the young people speak about that evening? About the things that lovers speak of on the threshold of a door in France, across a Spanish balcony or an Oriental terrace.

They spoke of those things that put wings on the feet of the hours and add feathers to the wings of time.

They spoke of everything except the black tulip.

Then at ten o'clock, as usual, they parted. Cornelius was happy – as utterly happy as a tulip fancier can be when he has not spoken about his tulip. He thought Rosa as pretty as all the loved ones in the world: he thought her good, gracious and enchanting.

But why did Rosa forbid him to speak about the tulip? This was a serious defect in Rosa's character. Cornelius told himself, with a sigh, that woman is not perfect.

He meditated on this imperfection for part of the night – which is to say that as long as he was awake, he thought of Rosa. And once asleep, he dreamed of her.

But the Rosa of his dreams was far more perfect than the Rosa of reality. Not only did this other Rosa speak about tulips, but she brought Cornelius a magnificent black tulip growing from a Chinese vase. He woke up shuddering with joy and murmuring, 'Rosa, Rosa, I love you.' And since it was already daylight, Cornelius did not consider it appropriate to go back to sleep, so he remained the whole day with the idea which he had had on awakening.

Now, if Rosa had spoken about tulips, Cornelius would have preferred Rosa to Queen Semiramis, Queen Cleopatra, Queen Elizabeth or Queen Anne of Austria,[2] in other words, to the greatest and most beautiful queens in the world. But Rosa, under threat of not returning to see him, had forbidden him for three days to speak about tulips. True, this meant seventy-two hours for the lover, but it also meant seventy-two hours taken away from the gardener. It was also true that, of these seventy-two hours, thirty-six had already gone.

The thirty-six hours would pass very quickly: eighteen in waiting and eighteen in remembering.

Rosa came back at the same time and Cornelius bore his penance heroically. He was a very remarkable Pythagorean,[3] Cornelius, and, provided he was allowed to ask once a day for news of his tulip, he would have remained bound for five years by the statutes of the order without speaking of anything else.

However, his lovely visitor knew that if one insists on one point, one must give way on another. Rosa allowed Cornelius to touch her fingers through the grating and allowed Cornelius to kiss her hair through the bars.

Poor child! All these games of love were far more dangerous to her than talking about tulips.

She realized this when she returned home, with her heart beating, her cheeks aflame, her lips dry and her eyes moist. So the following evening, after the first words and the first caresses had been exchanged, she looked through the grating at Cornelius and, in the darkness, with one of those looks that one can feel even though one does not see it, she said, 'Well! It's up!'

'It's up? Who is? What?' Cornelius asked, not daring to believe that Rosa herself would shorten the period of his test.

'The tulip,' said Rosa.

'What!' Cornelius exclaimed. 'So, do you permit me . . . ?'

'Yes, yes,' said Rosa in the tones of a gentle mother allowing her child some indulgence.

'Oh, Rosa!' said Cornelius, extending his lips through the grating in the hope of touching a cheek, a hand, a forehead . . . or something, at least.

He did better than all that. He found two half-open lips.

Rosa gave a little cry.

Cornelius saw that he must quickly resume the conversation;

he could feel that this unexpected contact had quite frightened Rosa.

'Is it growing straight upright?' he asked.

'Straight as a Frisian spindle,' said Rosa.

'And is it quite high?'

'At least two inches.'

'Oh, Rosa, take good care of it and you will see how quickly it grows.'

'How can I take better care of it than I do?' said Rosa. 'I think of nothing else.'

'Of nothing else? Be careful, Rosa, or I shall be the one to be jealous.'

'You know that to think about the tulip is to think about you. I never lose sight of it. I can see it from my bed; when I wake up it is the first thing I look at, and when I go to sleep the last thing I see. By day, I sit and work near it, because since it has been in my room, I have not left there.'

'You are right, Rosa. It is your dowry, you know.'

'Yes, and thanks to it I shall be able to marry a young man of twenty-six or twenty-eight with whom I shall fall in love.'

'Hush, you naughty girl!'

Cornelius managed to grasp the young woman's fingers – which, though it did not change the subject of conversation, at least brought a little silence after the dialogue.

That evening, Cornelius was the happiest of men. Rosa let him hold her hand as long as he liked and he could speak of tulips as much as he wished.

Every day from then on brought some progress in the growth of the tulip and in the love between the two young people. One day, the leaves had opened; then the flower itself was forming.

At that news, Cornelius was overjoyed and fired off questions with a rapidity which showed the importance he attached to them.

'Formed!' Cornelius cried. 'It is formed!'

'It is formed,' said Rosa.

Cornelius staggered back with joy and had to support himself on the bars.

'Oh, my God!' he exclaimed. Then, turning back to Rosa,

he asked, 'Is the oval regular, the cylinder full and the points quite green?'

'The oval is nearly an inch and tapered like a needle, the cylinder swells at the sides and the points are ready to start opening.'

That night, Cornelius slept little. The moment when the points began to open was a crucial one.

Two days later, Rosa announced that they were partly open.

'Partly opened, Rosa!' Cornelius exclaimed. 'The involucrum is partly open! But then, one can see ... one can already detect ...'

The prisoner stopped, panting for breath.

'Yes,' Rosa replied. 'One can detect a line of different colour, thin as a hair.'

'And what colour is it?' Cornelius asked, trembling.

'Oh,' said Rosa, 'it is very dark.'

'Brown?'

'Oh, no, darker than that.'

'Darker, dear Rosa, darker. Thank you. Dark as ebony, dark as ...'

'As dark as the ink with which I wrote to you.'

Cornelius gave a cry of wild joy. Then, suddenly, he stopped.

'Oh!' he said, clasping his hands. 'Oh, there is no angel comparable to you, Rosa.'

'Really?' said Rosa, smiling at this exaltation.

'Rosa, you have worked so hard, you have done so much for me. Rosa, my tulip will flower and it will flower black, dear Rosa, you who are the most perfect thing that God has created.'

'After the tulip, I suppose?'

'Oh, be quiet, wicked girl. Be quiet, for pity's sake, and do not spoil my joy. But, tell me, Rosa, if the tulip has reached this stage, in two or three days at the latest it will flower?'

'Tomorrow or the day after, yes.'

'I shall not see it,' Cornelius moaned, leaning backwards. 'I shall not kiss it as a God-given wonder that deserves to be worshipped, as I kiss your hands, Rosa, as I kiss your hair, and as I kiss your cheeks when by chance they come within reach of the grating.'

Rosa brought her cheek closer, not by chance, but intention-
ally. The young man's lips clung to it eagerly.

'Good Lord, I'll pick it for you, if you like,' said Rosa.

'No, no! As soon as it opens, Rosa, put it in the shade and
immediately, but immediately, send to Haarlem to inform the
President of the Horticultural Society that the great black tulip
has flowered. I know it is a long way, Haarlem, but with a little
money you should find a messenger. Do you have some money,
Rosa?'

She smiled.

'Oh, yes,' she said.

'Enough?' Cornelius asked.

'I have three hundred florins.'

'Well, if you have three hundred florins, you should not send
a messenger, but go yourself. You yourself, Rosa, must go to
Haarlem.'

'But meanwhile, the flower . . .'

'Oh, you will take the flower with you. You understand? You
must not be parted from it for a moment.'

'But if I am not parted from it, Mijnheer Cornelius, I shall be
parted from you,' Rosa said sadly.

'Oh, that's true, my sweet, my dearest Rosa. My God! How
wicked men are! What have I done to them that they should
deprive me of my freedom? You are right, Rosa, I shall not be
able to live without you. Well, you must send someone to
Haarlem, that's all there is for it. By heaven, the miracle is great
enough for the President to take some trouble. He must come
to Loevestein himself to fetch the tulip.'

Then, stopping suddenly, he murmured in a trembling voice,
'Rosa! But, oh, Rosa! Suppose it is not black!'

'Why you'll know tomorrow evening, or the one after.'

'How can I wait until the evening to find out! Rosa, I'll die of
impatience. Couldn't we agree a signal?'

'I shall do better than that.'

'What will you do?'

'If it starts to open at night, I'll come, I'll come and tell you
myself. If it is in the day, I shall slip you a note as I pass by the

door, either underneath it or through the grating, between my father's first and second inspections.'

'Oh, yes, Rosa, that's right. A note from you announcing this news to me will be a double happiness.'

'It is ten o'clock,' Rosa said. 'I must go.'

'Yes, yes!' said Cornelius. 'Go, Rosa, you must go.'

She went off feeling almost sad. It was almost as though Cornelius had sent her away. Of course, he did so in order that she could watch over the black tulip.

CHAPTER 22

In Bloom[1]

The night passed very sweetly for Cornelius, yet at the same time in some agitation. At every moment, he thought he heard Rosa's voice softly calling to him. He would wake up with a start, go over to the door and press his face to the grating. There was nothing at the grating and the corridor was empty.

Rosa was no doubt also awake, but more fortunate than he was, because she could watch over the tulip, having the wonderful flower under her eyes, that marvel of marvels, not only unknown until then, but considered impossible.

What would the world say when it learnt that the black tulip had been found, that it existed and that the prisoner van Baerle was the one who had discovered it?

How Cornelius would have spurned any man who might have offered him freedom in exchange for his tulip!

The day arrived with no news. The tulip had still not flowered. The day passed like the night. Then night came and with the night came Rosa, joyful and light as a bird.

'Well?' Cornelius asked.

'Well, everything is going perfectly. Tonight without fail our tulip will flower.'

'And will it flower black?'

'Black as jet.'

'Without a single spot of any other colour?'

'Without a single spot.'

'Heaven be praised, Rosa! I spent the whole night dreaming, of you first of all . . .'

Rosa made a small sign of incredulity.

'Then of what we should do.'

'Well?'

'Well, here is what I decided. Once the tulip has flowered, when it is fully established that it is black and perfectly black, you will have to find a messenger.'

'If that is all, I have the messenger already.'

'A reliable messenger?'

'I can answer for him, he is one of my suitors.'

'Not Jacob, I hope?'

'No, no, don't worry. It's the Loevestein ferryman, a quick-witted lad of twenty-five or twenty-six.'

'The devil he is!'

'Calm down,' said Rosa, laughing. 'He's not yet old enough, because you yourself set the age at between twenty-six and twenty-eight.'

'So you think you can count on this young man?'

'As I can on myself. He would throw himself out of his boat into the Waal or the Meuse, whichever I asked him.'

'Very well, Rosa. In ten hours, this boy can be in Haarlem. Give me a pencil and paper, or better still a pen and ink, and I shall write, or rather you will write yourself. Since I am a poor prisoner, perhaps like your father they would see a conspiracy behind it. You will write to the President of the Horticultural Society and I am sure that the President will come.'

'What if he takes a long time?'

'Suppose he waits for a day, or even two . . . But that's impossible. A tulip lover like him will not delay an hour, a minute, or even a second before setting out to see the eighth wonder of the world. But, as I was saying, even if he should delay a day or two, the tulip will still be in all its splendour. Once the tulip has been seen by the President and he has drafted his report, everything will have been done. You will keep a copy of the report, Rosa, and entrust the tulip to him. Ah, if only we could have taken it ourselves, it would not have left my hands except to go into yours. But this is a dream that we cannot allow ourselves,' Cornelius continued, with a sigh. 'Other eyes will see the flower fade. And, most important of all, Rosa, before the President sees it, do not show it to anyone else. The black tulip! Good heavens, if anyone were to see the black tulip, he would steal it!'

'Oh, no!'

'Didn't you tell me yourself what you feared from your suitor, Jacob? A person can steal one florin, so why not a hundred thousand of them?'

'I shall keep watch over it, have no fear.'

'And what if it were to open while you are here?'

'The capricious little beauty is quite capable of that,' said Rosa.

'And suppose you were to find it open when you got back?'

'What then?'

'Then, Rosa, remember that as soon as it opens, not a minute must be lost in informing the President.'

'And informing you. Yes, I see.'

Rosa sighed, but without bitterness, as a woman who is starting to understand a weakness, or even to become accustomed to it.

'I shall go back to the tulip, Mr van Baerle, and as soon as it is open, you shall be informed. And as soon as you are informed, the messenger will leave.'

'Rosa, Rosa, I cannot think what marvel of heaven or earth I can compare you to.'

'Compare me to the black tulip, Mijnheer Cornelius, and I shall be most flattered, I promise. So, let's say goodbye, Mijnheer Cornelius.'

'Please say: goodbye, my friend.'

'Goodbye, my friend,' said Rosa, a little consoled.

'Say: my dearest friend.'

'Oh, my friend . . .'

'My dearest friend, please Rosa. My dearest, no?'

'Dearest, yes, dearest,' said Rosa, trembling, intoxicated, mad with joy.

'Then, Rosa, since you have said "dearest", say also "happiest", say "happy as no one has been happy and blessed under heaven". I need only one thing, Rosa.'

'What is that?'

'Your cheek, your fresh cheek, your pink, your downy cheek. Oh, Rosa, of your own free will, not any more by surprise or by accident, Rosa . . . Ah!'

The prisoner ended this prayer with a sigh. He had just found the lips of the young woman, not this time by accident or by surprise, but as, a hundred years later, Saint-Preux would find the lips of Julie.[2]

Rosa fled.

Cornelius stayed there, with his soul hanging on his lips, his face pressed to the grating.

He was overcome with happiness. He opened his window and looked out for a long time, with a heart swelling with joy, at the cloudless expanse of the sky and the moon throwing a silver light on the double river as it flowed past beyond the hills. He filled his lungs with pure, generous air, his mind with pleasant thoughts and his soul with pious gratitude and admiration.

'Ah, You are still up there, God,' he exclaimed, half kneeling, his eyes eagerly turned towards the stars. 'Forgive me for having almost doubted You these last few days; You were hidden behind Your clouds and for a moment I could not see You, good Lord, eternal and merciful God. But now, this evening, this night, now I can see You whole in the mirror of Your heavens and still more in the mirror of my heart.'

The poor sick man was cured, the poor prisoner was free!

For part of the night, Cornelius stayed there, holding the bars on his window and listening, his five senses concentrated into one – or rather two, since he was watching as he listened.

He watched the sky and listened to the earth.

Then, from time to time, turning towards the corridor, he said, 'Down there is Rosa, Rosa who is watching as I do and waiting from minute to minute. Down there, before Rosa's eyes, is the mysterious flower, which is alive, half-opening, then fully opened. Perhaps at this moment, Rosa is holding the stem of the tulip between her warm, delicate fingers. Touch it gently, that stem, Rosa. Perhaps her lips are touching the half-open calyx – but be careful how you kiss it, Rosa, with your burning lips. Perhaps at this moment, under the eyes of God, my two loves are kissing . . .'

At that moment, a star blazed in the south, crossed the whole space between the horizon and the fortress, and fell in Loevestein. Cornelius shuddered.

'That was God, sending a soul down to my flower.'

And, as though he had guessed correctly, almost at the same instant, the prisoner heard light steps like those of a sylph in the corridor and the brush of a dress that seemed like wings beating, as a well-known voice said, 'Cornelius, my friend, my dearest and most fortunate friend, come, come quickly.'

Cornelius crossed from the window to the grating in a single bound. Once more his lips found the murmuring lips of Rosa, who said to him as they were kissing, 'It has opened, it is black, here it is.'

'What do you mean, here it is!' Cornelius exclaimed, tearing his lips from those of the young woman.

'Yes, yes, my friend, one must take a slight risk to give such a great joy. Here it is, look.'

And with one hand she raised a little dark lantern, which she had just turned up, and brought it to the level of the grating, while with the other she raised the miraculous tulip to the same height.

Cornelius gave a cry and thought he would faint.

'Ah,' he sighed. 'My God, my God! You have compensated me for my innocence and my captivity, since you have made these two flowers grow beside the bars of my prison.'

'Kiss it,' said Rosa, 'as I kissed it a moment ago.'

Cornelius, with bated breath, touched the tip of the flower with his lips, and never had any kiss he had given the lips of a woman, even Rosa's, reached so deep into his heart.

The tulip was beautiful, splendid, magnificent; its stem was more than eighteen inches high and rose out of four green leaves, smooth and straight as a javelin, while its flower was entirely black and shone like jet.

'Rosa,' Cornelius said, gasping for breath. 'Rosa, there is not an instant to lose. You must write the letter.'

'I have written it, my dearest Cornelius,' said Rosa.

'Really!'

'While the tulip was opening, I was writing, because I did not want a single instant to be lost. Look at the letter and tell me what you think of it.'

Cornelius took the letter and read, in handwriting that had improved still further since the little note that Rosa had sent him:

Mr President,
The black tulip may perhaps open in ten minutes. As soon as it is open, I shall send a messenger to ask you to come in person to get it at the fortress of Loevestein. I am the daughter of the jailer Gryphus and almost as much a prisoner as the prisoners guarded by my father. This is why I cannot bring this wonder to you and why I beg you to come and fetch it yourself.
I want it to be called *Rosa Barlænsis*.
It has just opened. It is perfectly black. Come, President, please come.
I have the honour to be,
Your humble servant,
Rosa Gryphus

'That's it, that's it, dear Rosa! This letter is perfect. I could not have put it so simply myself. When the committee meets you, you will give them all the information they ask for. They will know how the tulip was made, how much trouble and many sleepless nights and fears it has caused. But, for the moment, Rosa, there is not an instant to lose. The messenger, the messenger!'

'What is the President's name?'

'Give me the letter and I shall write the address. Oh, he is well-known. It is Mijnheer van Systens, the burgomaster of Haarlem. Give it to me, Rosa, give it to me.'

And, his hand trembling, Cornelius wrote on the letter:

To Mijnheer Peters van Systens, burgomaster and President of the Horticultural Society of Haarlem.

'And now, Rosa, go, go,' said Cornelius. 'And let us put ourselves under God's protection, since He has protected us so well up to now.'

CHAPTER 23

The Envious Man

In point of fact, the young people had great need of the Lord's protection, for never had they been so close to despair than at this very moment, when they felt so certain of their success.

We shall not question the reader's intelligence to the extent of believing that he has not recognized in Jacob our old friend – or, rather, our old enemy – Isaac Boxtel. Thus the reader will have guessed that Boxtel had come from the Buitenhof to Loevestein in pursuit of the object of his love and the object of his hatred, namely the black tulip and Cornelius van Baerle.

Envy had allowed Boxtel, if not to discover, at least to guess, what anyone who was not a tulip fancier, and still more an envious one, could never have imagined, which is the existence of the offsets and the aspirations of the prisoner.

We have seen him, more at ease with the name of Jacob than of Isaac, befriending Gryphus, whose gratitude and hospitality he cultivated for several months, watering it with the best gin that has ever been made from Texel to Antwerp.

He put the jailer's suspicions to rest – because, as we have seen, old Gryphus was mistrustful; but he put this mistrust to rest, as we said, by flattering Gryphus with the prospect that he might marry Rosa. Moreover, after thus appealing to his fatherly pride, he played on his instincts as a jailer, describing the learned prisoner that Gryphus was holding under lock and key in the most lurid colours and claiming that he had entered into a pact with Satan to harm His Highness the Prince of Orange.

At first, he succeeded quite well with Rosa, not by inspiring any sympathy in her, Rosa having always rather disliked

Mijnheer Jacob, but by allaying any suspicions that she might have with his talk of marriage and mad passion.

We have seen how his rashness in following Rosa to the garden betrayed him to the young woman and how Cornelius's instinctive misgivings warned them both against him. And the reader must recall that what chiefly inspired these anxieties in the prisoner was Jacob's great fury against Gryphus on the subject of the broken bulb. At that time, Boxtel's anger was all the greater since he suspected Cornelius of having a second offset, but was not sure about it. This was when he started to spy on Rosa and follow her not only in the garden, but also inside the fortress. However, since he was following her barefoot and in darkness, he was neither seen nor heard, except on the one occasion when Rosa thought she saw something like a shadow passing down the staircase.

It was already too late: Boxtel had learnt of the existence of the second offset from the prisoner's own lips.

Fooled by Rosa's trick, when she pretended to plant it in the flowerbed, and not doubting that this little drama was acted out in order to force him to betray himself, he took still greater precautions and used all the ingenuity at his disposal so that he could continue to spy on the lovers without being spied on himself.

He saw Rosa transporting a large earthenware pot from her father's kitchen into her own room. He saw Rosa with buckets of water washing her hands that were covered in the earth she had kneaded when preparing the best possible bed for the tulip.

Finally, he rented a little room in an attic just opposite Rosa's window, far enough for him to avoid recognition with the naked eye, but close enough for him to follow with the aid of his telescope everything that was happening in Loevestein in the young woman's bedroom, as he had followed everything that happened in Dordrecht in Cornelius's drying room.

He had not been three days in his attic before his suspicions were confirmed.

As soon as the sun rose, the earthenware pot was at the window, and Rosa, like those delightful women of Mieris and

Metsù,[1] appeared at the same window, framed in the first green shoots of the honeysuckle and wild vine.

Rosa was giving the earthenware pot a look that indicated to Boxtel the real value of the object it contained. What was in that pot, then, was the second offset, that is to say, the prisoner's chief hope.

When the nights threatened to be too cold, Rosa brought the earthenware pot inside. So she was following Cornelius's instructions: he was afraid that the offset might suffer frostbite.

When the sun got hotter, Rosa brought the pot indoors from eleven o'clock in the morning until two o'clock in the afternoon. Once again, Cornelius was afraid that the soil might dry out.

But when the shoot of the flower emerged from the earth, Boxtel was entirely convinced, and before it was an inch high, thanks to his telescope, the envious man was in no further doubt.

Cornelius had two offsets and the second of them had been entrusted to the love and care of Rosa. For, as one might imagine, the love between the two young people had not escaped the notice of Boxtel. So it was this second bulb that he must manage to remove from Rosa's care and Cornelius's love.

However, this was no easy task. Rosa watched over her tulip as a mother over her child; or even as a dove hatching its eggs. She did not leave her room during the day; and, stranger still, she no longer left her room in the evening. For a whole week, Boxtel spied in vain on Rosa: she did not leave her room. These were the seven days of the quarrel which made Cornelius so unhappy, since it deprived him of any news either of Rosa or of his tulip.

Was Rosa going to stay away from Cornelius for ever? This would make the theft far more difficult than Mijnheer Isaac had at first imagined.

We say 'theft', because Isaac had quite simply made up his mind to steal the tulip; and since it was growing in the most utter secrecy; since the two young people were hiding its existence from everyone; since he, a recognized tulip grower, was more likely to be believed than a young woman who knew nothing about horticulture and a prisoner sentenced for the crime of high treason who was under guard, supervised and closely watched, and who in any case would have difficulty in making any claim from the depths of his dungeon; and since, finally, he would be in possession of the tulip and, in the case of furniture and other movable assets, possession is evidence of ownership, so he would most surely win the prize, most surely be crowned in Cornelius's place, and the tulip, instead of being named *Tulipa nigra Barlænsis* would be called *Tulipa nigra Boxtellensis* or *Boxtellea*.

Mijnheer Isaac had not yet decided which of these two names he would give the black tulip, but since each of them meant the same thing, that was not the most important point.

The important thing was to steal the tulip.

But if Boxtel was to steal the tulip, Rosa would have to leave the room. So it was with real joy that Jacob – or Isaac, as you wish – saw the usual evening meetings resume.

He began by taking advantage of Rosa's absence to study her door. The door shut well and was double-locked, with a simple lock, but one to which only Rosa had a key.

Boxtel considered stealing Rosa's key. However, quite apart from the fact that it would be no easy matter to rummage in the young woman's pockets, when Rosa realized that she had lost her key, she would have the lock changed and not leave the room until it was changed, so Boxtel would have committed a pointless crime.

Better, then, to employ some other method.

Boxtel collected all the keys that he could find, and while Rosa and Cornelius were spending one of their pleasant hours at the grating, he tried all of them out. Two of them would go into the lock; one would turn once, but stuck on the second turn.

So there was not much that had to be done to this latter key.

Boxtel put a thin layer of wax on it and tried again. The obstacle that the key met on the second turn left its mark on the wax. Boxtel had only to follow this mark with the rough edge of a file as fine as a knife. After two days' work, he had brought his key to perfection. Rosa's door opened noiselessly, effort-lessly, and Boxtel was in the young woman's room, alone with the tulip.

His first criminal act had been to climb over a wall to unearth the tulip. The second had been to go into Cornelius's drying room through an open window. The third was to enter Rosa's room with a forged key. As we can see, envy and desire were leading Boxtel further and further along the path of crime.

He was alone with the tulip.

Any ordinary thief would have put the pot under his arm and made off with it. But Boxtel was no ordinary thief. He paused to think.

He thought, as he looked at the tulip, by his dark lantern, that it was not far enough advanced for him to be certain that it would flower black, even though appearances made it seem probable that it would.

He thought that if it did not flower black, or if it were to flower with some kind of blemish, then he would have carried out a pointless theft. He considered, too, that the rumour of the theft would spread and the thief would be suspected, in view of what had happened in the garden; a search would be made and, however well he might hide the tulip, it would be possible to find it. He thought that, if he were to hide the tulip so that it could not be found, it might be damaged in all the comings and goings that it would have to suffer.

Finally, he thought that, since he had a key to Rosa's room and could go in and out of it as he wished, it would be better to wait for the tulip to flower, to take it one hour before it opened, or one hour after it had opened, and to leave at the same moment without delay for Haarlem, where the tulip could be in front of the judges even before it had been reported as missing. In that way, Boxtel would be able to accuse whoever made the report of theft.

It was a well-conceived plan and in every way worthy of the planner.

So, each evening during the sweet hour that the two lovers spent at the grating in the prisoner's door, Boxtel went into the young woman's room, not to violate the sanctuary of her virginity, but to follow the progress that the black tulip had made on its way to flowering.

On the evening at which we have arrived, he was going to

enter as usual; but, as we saw, the two lovers had only exchanged
a few words when Cornelius sent Rosa to keep watch on the
tulip. Seeing Rosa return to her room only ten minutes after
leaving it, Boxtel realized that the tulip had flowered or was
about to do so.

This, then, was the night when all would be decided. So Boxtel
arrived at Gryphus's with twice as much gin as usual; that is,
with a bottle in each pocket. With Gryphus drunk, Boxtel would
be more or less master of the house.

At eleven o'clock, Gryphus was dead drunk. At two o'clock
in the morning, Boxtel saw Rosa come out of her room, clearly
holding an object in her arms and carrying it with great care.
This object was doubtless the black tulip, which had just
flowered.

But what was she going to do with it? Would she set out
immediately for Haarlem? It was not possible that a young
woman would undertake such a journey alone and at night.

So did she just intend to show the tulip to Cornelius? That
was likely.

Barefoot and on tiptoe, he followed Rosa. He saw her go up
to the grating.

He heard her call Cornelius. By the light of the dark lantern,
he saw the open tulip, black as the night in which he was hiding.

He heard the plan that Cornelius and Rosa made to send a
messenger to Haarlem.

He saw the lips of the two young people touch, then he heard
Cornelius telling Rosa to go.

He saw Rosa put out the dark lantern and make her way to
her room.

He saw her go back into her room.

Then, ten minutes later, he saw her leave her room and close
its door carefully, double-locking it behind her.

The reason that she locked the door with such care was that
she was closing the door on the black tulip.

Boxtel, who saw all this while hiding on the landing of the
floor above Rosa's room, came down one step from his floor
when Rosa went down one step from hers, so that when Rosa
was touching the last step of the staircase with her light foot,

Boxtel, with a still lighter hand, was touching the lock of Rosa's room.

And in his hand, as you will realize, was the counterfeit key that could open the door of Rosa's room no less easily than the original one.

This is why, at the start of this chapter, we said that the unfortunate young people badly needed to be under the direct protection of the Lord.

CHAPTER 24

In Which the Tulip Changes Hands

Cornelius stayed in the place where Rosa had left him, seeking almost in vain within himself the strength to bear the double burden of his happiness.

Half an hour passed.

Already the first rays of the morning sun were shining, bluish and fresh, through the bars of the window in Cornelius's prison, when he shuddered suddenly to hear steps coming up the stairs and cries getting closer. Almost at the same moment, his face was looking at the pale and contorted features of Rosa.

He shrank back, startled, the colour draining from his own face.

'Cornelius! Cornelius!' she cried, panting.

'My God! What is it?' the prisoner asked.

'Cornelius, the tulip!'

'What about the tulip?'

'How can I tell you?'

'Tell me, Rosa, tell me . . .'

'It's been taken, it's been stolen from us.'

'It's been taken! It's been stolen from us!' Cornelius repeated.

'Yes,' Rosa said, supporting herself against the door so as not to fall. 'Yes, taken, stolen.'

Despite her efforts, her legs gave way, she slipped and fell to her knees.

'But how did it happen?' Cornelius asked. 'Tell me, explain to me . . .'

'Oh, it is not my fault, my friend.'

Poor Rosa! She did not dare say: my dearest friend.

'You left it alone!' said Cornelius in a pitiful tone.

'Just for a moment, to go and inform our messenger, who lives barely fifty yards away on the banks of the Waal.'

'And during that time, despite my instructions, you left the key in the door, you unhappy child!'

'No! no! no! This is what I cannot understand. The key did not leave me, I held it constantly in my hand, grasping it as though I were afraid it might run away.'

'But in that case, how did it happen?'

'How can I tell? I gave the letter to my messenger and I watched him leave. I went home, the door was locked, everything was in its place in my room, except for the tulip, which had vanished. Someone must have obtained a key to my room or had a duplicate made.'

She was choking, left speechless by her tears.

Cornelius stood there, his face contorted, listening almost without understanding and simply muttering.

'Stolen! Stolen! Stolen! I am lost!'

'Oh, Mijnheer Cornelius, forgive me! Forgive me!' cried Rosa. 'It will kill me.'

At this threat, Cornelius grasped the bars and pressed them furiously.

'Rosa!' he cried. 'We have been robbed, certainly, but should we let that defeat us? No, great though our misfortune is, we may be able to repair it. We know the thief, Rosa.'

'Alas, how can I tell you for sure?'

'No? I shall tell you, then. It's that scoundrel Jacob. Are we to let him take the fruit of our efforts to Haarlem, the fruit of our sleepless nights and the child of our love? No, Rosa, you must follow him and catch up with him.'

'But how can I do all that, my friend, without revealing to my father that we have been communicating with one another? How could I, a woman who has so little freedom and so few talents, accomplish this, when it is something that even you might not accomplish?'

'Open this door for me, Rosa, and you will see if I cannot do it. See if I cannot discover the thief and make him confess his crime. See if I cannot make him beg for forgiveness.'

'Alas!' Rosa said, bursting into tears. 'Can I let you out? Do

I have the keys on me? If I did have them, would you not have been freed long ago?'

'Your father has them, your vile father, the torturer who has already smashed the first offset of my tulip. Ah, the wretch! The wretch! He is Jacob's accomplice.'

'Quieter, quieter, in heaven's name!'

'And if you do not open this door for me, Rosa,' Cornelius shouted, in a paroxysm of rage, 'I shall break through the grating and massacre everyone in the prison.'

'My friend, I beg you.'

'I am telling you, Rosa, I shall demolish this dungeon stone by stone.'

And the unfortunate man, his strength multiplied by anger, seized the door in both hands and shook it loudly, hardly caring that the sound of his voice was echoing down the sonorous spiral of the staircase.

Rosa, terrified, tried quite in vain to calm this frightful storm.

'I tell you, I shall kill the wretched Gryphus,' van Baerle shouted. 'I tell you, I shall shed his blood as he shed the blood of my black tulip.'

The poor man was starting to go mad.

'Very well, then, yes,' said Rosa, trembling. 'Yes, yes, but please be calm. Yes, I shall take his keys, I shall open the door to you, yes, but please be calm, my Cornelius.'

She could not finish. A howl from beside her interrupted what she was saying.

'Father!' Rosa cried.

'Gryphus!' van Baerle roared. 'Ah, you scoundrel!'

Old Gryphus, in the midst of all this noise, had come up the stairs without anyone hearing him. He roughly grasped his daughter by the wrist.

'So! You would take my keys,' he said, in a voice stifled by rage. 'Oh, that vile wretch! That monster! That conspirator fit for the gallows is "your Cornelius". You are in league with a prisoner of the State! That's good!'

Rosa beat her two hands in despair.

'Well, now!' Gryphus went on, his voice changing from the feverish tone of wrath to the cold irony of a victor. 'Well, my innocent tulip fancier, my gentle scholar! So you will murder me, will you? You will drink my blood? Very well! Is that all? And in complicity with my daughter! By Jesus, I am in the midst of a cave of brigands, a nest of thieves! Very well, the governor will know all about it in the morning and the Stadhouder the day after that! We know the law: whoever rebels in prison comes under Article 6. We are going to give you a second edition of the Buitenhof, Master Scholar, and this time it will be the right one. Yes, yes, you can gnaw your paws like a bear in a cage. And you, my lovely, take a good eyeful of your Cornelius, because I warn you, you two lambs, that you will not have this freedom to conspire together any more. Now, you come downstairs, you unnatural child. And you, Master Scholar, goodbye – or rather, *au revoir*. Believe me, we shall meet again.'

Rosa, mad with terror and despair, threw Cornelius a kiss and then, an idea no doubt passing suddenly across her mind, she ran down the stairs saying, 'All is not yet lost, trust me, my Cornelius.'

Her father followed, shouting.

As for the poor tulip lover, he gradually prised his hands away from the bars, which he was grasping convulsively. His head felt oppressed, his eyes rolled in their sockets and he fell heavily to the floor of his room, muttering, 'Stolen! It has been stolen from me!'

Meanwhile, Boxtel, who had left the fortress by the gate which Rosa herself had opened, Boxtel, with the black tulip wrapped in a broad cloak, had jumped into a carriage that was waiting for him in Gorcum and vanished – as one might imagine, without informing his friend Gryphus of his sudden departure.

Now that we have seen him get into the carriage, we shall follow him, if the reader permits, to the end of his journey.

He proceeded slowly. One does not get away with carrying a black tulip post-haste. Even so, Boxtel, afraid he might not arrive quickly enough, had had a box manufactured in Delft and lined it all round with fresh moss, in which he encased his tulip. The flower was now gently held on all sides, and open to the air at the top, so the carriage could set off at a gallop without any risk of damaging it.

The following morning he arrived in Haarlem, exhausted but triumphant. He changed the tulip's pot and broke the earthenware one, flinging the shards into a canal, then wrote a letter to the President of the Horticultural Society, in which he announced that he had just arrived in Haarlem with a perfectly black tulip, before settling into a good hostelry with his flower intact.

And there he waited.

CHAPTER 25

President van Systens

Rosa, as she left Cornelius, made up her mind.

She decided that she would get back the tulip that Jacob had just stolen from him, or else never see him again.

She had witnessed the poor prisoner's despair, a profound and incurable despair. And for one thing, separation was inevitable, now that Gryphus had discovered the secret of their love and of their meetings. Another thing was the dashing of all Cornelius van Baerle's hopes, hopes which he had nourished for seven years.

Rosa was one of those women who can be dispirited by a trifle, but who are full of strength against a supreme misfortune, finding in misfortune itself the energy to overcome it or the strength to put it right.

The young woman returned to her room, cast one last glance around it, to make sure that she was not mistaken, that the tulip was not somewhere in a corner where it might have escaped her notice. But she searched in vain, the tulip was still absent, still stolen.

She made a small parcel of the clothes which she needed, took the three hundred florins in savings that were all her fortune, went through her lace, where she had hidden the third offset, carefully hid it in her breast, double-locked her door, to delay the moment when her flight was discovered by the time that it would take to open it, came down the stairs and out of the prison by the door through which one hour earlier Boxtel had left, went to a stables and asked to hire a carriage.

The stables had only one carriage, which happened to be the one that Boxtel had already hired on the previous evening and in which he was hurrying along the road to Delft. We say 'the road to Delft' because it was necessary to make a huge detour to travel from Loevestein to Haarlem; as the crow flies, the distance would have only been half as great. But only crows can travel as the crow flies in Holland, the country most cut up by rivers, streams, canals and lakes in the world.

Rosa was therefore obliged to take a horse, which was readily given her: the stable-keeper knew Rosa as the daughter of the warder at the fortress.

She had one hope, which was to catch up with her messenger, a fine, good lad, whom she could take with her to guide and support her. And indeed she had not gone one league before she saw him striding out on one of the verges of a delightful road that ran alongside the river. She urged her horse to a trot and joined him.

The good fellow had not been aware of the importance of his message, yet he was marching along as fast as if he had known it. In less than an hour, he had already gone a league and a half.

Rosa took the now pointless note from him and explained that she needed him. The ferryman put himself at her disposal, promising to go as fast as the horse, provided Rosa allowed him to rest one hand either on its rump or its withers. The young woman gave him permission to put his hand wherever he wanted, as long as he did not delay her.

The two travellers had been gone for five hours already and had covered more than eight leagues, and still old Gryphus did not suspect that the girl had left the fortress. In any case, the jailer, who was a very nasty man underneath, was enjoying the pleasure of having inspired such profound terror in his daughter. But while he was savouring the fact that he had a fine story to tell his friend Jacob, Jacob himself was on the road for Delft. The difference was that, thanks to his carriage, he already had four hours' advance on Rosa and the ferryman.

So, while Gryphus imagined Rosa trembling and sulking in her room, she was gaining ground. No one, except the prisoner, was where Gryphus thought that they were.

Rosa had appeared so rarely in her father's house since she had begun looking after the tulip that it was only at lunchtime, that is to say, at midday, that Gryphus noticed that his daughter had been sulking too long for the good of his appetite. He got one of the turnkeys to call her. And when the man came down saying that he had searched and called in vain, Gryphus resolved to search and call for her himself.

He started by going straight to her room, but, even though he knocked, Rosa did not answer.

He called for the prison locksmith, who opened the door. But Gryphus no more found Rosa behind it than Rosa had found the tulip.

Rosa at that moment had just entered Rotterdam – which is why Gryphus did not find her in the kitchen any more than in her room, and no more in the garden than in the kitchen.

One may imagine the jailer's anger when, having enquired in the neighbourhood, he learned that his daughter had hired a horse and, in the style of Bradamante or Clorinda,[1] had set off like an adventuress, without saying where she was going.

Gryphus stormed up to see van Baerle, cursed him, threatened him, kicked all his miserable furniture, and promised him the lowest dungeons, the oubliettes, hunger and the rod.

Cornelius did not even listen to what the jailer was saying, but let himself be mistreated, abused and threatened, staying sad, motionless, overwhelmed, devoid of any feeling and dead to fear.

After looking for Rosa everywhere, Gryphus sent for Jacob, and when he no more found him than he had found his daughter, he immediately began to suspect Jacob of having abducted her.

Meanwhile, the girl, after stopping for two hours in Rotterdam, resumed her journey. That same evening she slept in Delft and on the following day she arrived in Haarlem, four hours after Boxtel himself had arrived there.

Rosa immediately had herself taken to see the President of the Horticultural Society, Master van Systens. She found this worthy citizen in a situation that we must describe if we are not to fail in all our duties to describe and record. The President was writing a report to the committee of the Society. This report was a large piece of paper and in the President's finest handwriting.

Rosa had herself announced as plain Rosa Gryphus; but this name, however well it might strike the ear, was not known to the President, and Rosa was refused entry. It is hard to get past the door in Holland, a land of dykes and sluices.

But Rosa was not put off. She had given herself a task and sworn not to be discouraged by rebuffs, or by rejection, or by insults.

'Please tell the President,' she said, 'that I have come to speak to him about the black tulip.'

These words, no less magical than the famous 'Open Sesame' in the *Thousand and One Nights*, served as her passport. Thanks to them, she reached the study of President van Systens himself, and found him gallantly on his way to meet her.

He was a good little man with a spindly frame, looking almost precisely like the stem of a flower, his head forming the calix, two dangling arms representing the oblong double leaves of the tulip and a habit of swaying as he walked completing his resemblance to the flower when it is bending beneath the wind.

We mentioned before that he was called Mijnheer van Systens.

'My dear young lady,' he said. 'You say that you are coming on behalf of the black tulip?'

For the President of the Horticultural Society, *Tulipa nigra* was a power of the first order which could very well, as Queen of the Tulips, send him ambassadors.

'Yes, sir,' Rosa replied. 'Or at least I have come to talk to you about it.'

'Is she well?' van Systens asked, with a smile of tender adoration.

'Alas, sir, I do not know,' said Rosa.

'What! Has some misfortune befallen her?'

'A very great misfortune, sir. Not to her, but to me.'

'What is it?'

'She has been stolen from me.'

'Someone has stolen the black tulip from you?'

'Yes, sir.'

'Do you know who?'

'Ah, I suspect someone, but I dare not accuse him yet.'

'But the matter will be easy enough to confirm.'

'How?'

'Since it has been stolen from you, the thief cannot be far.'

'Why can't he be far?'

'Because I saw her not two hours ago.'

'You saw the black tulip!' said Rosa, rushing towards Mijnheer van Systens.

'As plain as I see you, young lady.'

'Where?'

'With your master, I suppose.'

'My master?'

'Yes. Aren't you in service with Mijnheer Isaac Boxtel?'

'Me?'

'Yes, of course: you.'

'Then who do you think I am, sir?'

'And who do you think I am, in that case?'

'I think, sir, and hope, that you are who you are, that is to say, the honourable Mijnheer van Systens, burgomaster of Haarlem and President of the Horticultural Society.'

'And what have you come to tell me?'

'I have come to tell you that my tulip has been stolen from me.'

'So your tulip must be the one belonging to Mijnheer Boxtel. In that case, you are explaining the matter badly, my child. It is from Mijnheer Boxtel, not from you, that the tulip has been stolen.'

'I repeat, sir, that I do not know who this Mijnheer Boxtel is. This is the first time I have ever heard his name.'

'You don't know who Mijnheer Boxtel is, yet you too had a black tulip?'

'What! Is there another one?' Rosa asked, trembling.

'Yes, there is Mijnheer Boxtel's.'

'What is it like?'

'Why, it's black.'

'Flawless?'

'Flawless, without a single blemish.'

'Do you have the tulip? Has it been deposited here?'

'No, but it will be, because I am due to show it to the committee before the prize is awarded.'

'Sir,' Rosa exclaimed, 'this Boxtel, this Isaac Boxtel, who claims to be the owner of the black tulip . . .'

'And who in fact is the owner . . .'

'Isn't he a thin man?'

'Yes.'

'Bald?'

'Yes.'

'With deep-set eyes?'

'I think so.'

'Restless, stooping, bow-legged?'

'Indeed, you have described Mijnheer Boxtel, feature by feature.'

'And tell me, sir, is the tulip in a blue and white earthenware pot with yellow flowers representing a basket on three sides of it?'

'As for that, I can't be sure. I was looking at the man rather than the pot.'

'Sir, this is my tulip, the one that was stolen from me. It's my property, sir, and I have come to claim it here, before you.'

'What's that?' said Mijnheer van Systens, looking at her. 'What! Have you come here to demand Mijnheer Boxtel's tulip? By heaven! You're a cheeky little minx, I must say.'

'But sir,' said Rosa, somewhat put out by this expression. 'I am not saying that I have come to claim Mijnheer Boxtel's tulip. I am saying that I have come to claim mine.'

'Yours?'

'Yes, the one I planted and cultivated myself.'

'Well, then, go and look for Mijnheer Boxtel at the hostelry of the White Swan and come to some arrangement with him. As far as I'm concerned, this case seems as hard to judge as the one brought before the late King Solomon. Since I do not pretend to be as wise as he was, I shall simply make my report, establish the existence of the black tulip, and order the hundred thousand florins to be paid to its discoverer. Good day, my child.'

'But, sir, please, sir!' Rosa insisted.

'The only thing I would say is this, my child,' van Systens went on. 'As you are pretty, as you are young and as you are not yet entirely corrupted, take my advice: be cautious in this matter, because we have courts and prisons in Haarlem – and, what's more, we are very sensitive when it comes to the honour of tulips. Off with you, my child, off with you. Mijnheer Isaac Boxtel, Hotel of the White Swan.'

And Mijnheer van Systens, taking up his beautiful pen again, went on with his interrupted report.

CHAPTER 26

A Member of the Horticultural Society

Rosa was in a dreadful state, almost mad with joy and fear at the idea that the black tulip had been found. She set out for the hostelry of the White Swan, still with her ferryman in tow, a sturdy Frisian lad who was capable of devouring ten Boxtels all by himself.

On the way, she told him everything and he was not alarmed at the idea of a fight, should there be one. Just one thing: in that event, he was under orders to mind the tulip.

But when they arrived in the Grote Markt,[1] Rosa stopped suddenly, a thought crossing her mind just like when, in Homer, Minerva[2] grasped Achilles by the hair, as he was about to fly into a rage.

'My God!' she exclaimed. 'I've made a terrible mistake. I may have ruined everything – for Cornelius, for the tulip and for myself! I have given the alarm, I have raised suspicions. I am a mere woman and those men might join forces against me, in which case I am done for. And if I am done for, that will not matter at all – but Cornelius! And the tulip!'

She paused for a moment to think.

'If I go to see this Boxtel and don't recognize him, if this Boxtel is not my Jacob, if he turns out to be another tulip fancier who has also discovered the black tulip, or if my tulip has been stolen by someone other than the person I suspect, or has already passed into other hands, if I do not recognize the man but only my tulip, then how can I prove that the tulip is mine? On the other hand, if I recognize Boxtel as the false Jacob, who knows what will happen? While we are disputing over it, the tulip will

die. Oh, Holy Virgin, inspire me! My whole life is at stake, like
the poor prisoner who may be dying even at this moment.'

Having made this prayer, Rosa waited piously for heaven to
supply the inspiration that she had requested.

Meanwhile, a great noise could be heard at the far end of the
Grote Markt. People were running, doors opening. Only Rosa
was unaware of this popular commotion.

'We must go back to the President,' she said quietly.

'Let's go,' said the ferryman.

They went down the little Rue de la Paille,[3] which took them
directly to the office of Mijnheer van Systens who, in his finest
handwriting and with his best pen, was still working on his
report.

Everywhere, as she went, Rosa could hear people talking
about nothing except the black tulip and the prize of a hundred
thousand florins. The news was already getting about.

Rosa had no little difficulty in once more obtaining an audience with Mijnheer van Systens, though as before he was moved
by the magic words 'black tulip'. But when he recognized Rosa,
who, he had decided by now, was mad, or worse, he was seized
with anger and wanted to have her expelled. But Rosa clasped
her hands and, with those tones of honest truth that strike
directly at the heart, she said, 'Oh, sir, in heaven's name, do not
reject me! Listen instead to what I have to tell you, and if you
cannot obtain justice for me, at least you will not one day
have to reproach yourself, before God, with having been the
accomplice in a wicked deed.'

Van Systens was shaking with impatience. This was the second
time that Rosa had interrupted him in the midst of a composition
that doubly involved his pride: as burgomaster and as President
of the Horticultural Society.

'But my report!' he exclaimed. 'What about my report on the
black tulip?'

'Sir,' Rosa continued, with the resolution of innocence and
truth, 'sir, if you do not hear me, your report on the black tulip
will be founded either on criminal facts or on inaccuracies. I beg
you, sir, to bring this Mijnheer Boxtel here, before you and
before me, because I claim that he is Mijnheer Jacob and I swear

to God that I shall leave him the ownership of his tulip if I do not recognize either the tulip or its owner.'

'Huh! That will be a great help!'

'What do you mean?'

'I mean: what will it prove if you do recognize them?'

'But, after all, sir,' said Rosa in desperation, 'you are an honest man. What would you think if you were to give the prize to a man not only for something that he had not done, but also for something that he had stolen from another?'

It may be that Rosa's tone of voice had gone some way to convincing van Systens, and he was about to answer the poor girl more kindly, when a great commotion was heard outside in the street, which sounded purely and simply like an increase in the noise that Rosa had already heard, without attaching any importance to it, in the Grote Markt, and which had not managed to distract her from her fervent prayer.

The house was shaken by deafening shouts and cries.

Van Systens turned to listen to these sounds, which Rosa hadn't at first noticed, and for whom they were now nothing out of the ordinary.

'What's that?' the burgomaster cried. 'What's that? Can I have heard correctly?'

He rushed into his antechamber, not bothering about Rosa, but leaving her behind in his study. He had barely arrived in the antechamber, when he gave a great cry, seeing his staircase invaded as far back as the entrance hall.

Accompanied, or rather followed, by the multitude, a young man, dressed simply, in a coat of plain, violet-coloured velvet embroidered with silver, was proceeding with lordly and un-hurried steps up the immaculately shining white stone stairs.

Behind him came two officers, one of the navy, the other of the cavalry.

Van Systens, edging his way past the crowd of awestruck servants, bowed, almost prostrating himself in front of the new arrival who was causing all this fuss.

'Monseigneur!' he exclaimed. 'Sire! Your Highness! In my house! This is an everlasting honour for my humble abode!'

'Dear Mijnheer van Systens,' said William of Orange, with a

serenity that took the place of a smile. 'I am a true Dutchman, you know. I love water, beer and flowers, and even, sometimes, the cheese that the French think so highly of. When it comes to flowers, the one I prefer is, of course, the tulip. I was informed in Leyden that the city of Haarlem possesses at last the black tulip; and, after making sure that the report was true, however incredible, I have come to ask for news of it from the President of the Horticultural Society.'

'Sire, sire!' van Systens exclaimed in delight. 'What an honour it will be for the Society if its work pleases Your Majesty!'

'Do you have the flower here?' asked the Prince, probably already regretting having said so much.

'Alas, no, sire, I do not.'

'So where is it?'

'With its owner.'

'And who is this owner?'

'A fine tulip grower of Dordrecht.'

'Of Dordrecht?'

'Yes.'

'And his name is . . . ?'

'Boxtel.'

'And he is staying . . . ?'

'At the White Swan. I am about to call for him. If meanwhile Your Highness would do me the honour of coming into my drawing room, knowing that Your Highness is here, he will make haste to bring sire his tulip.'

'Very well, call for him.'

'Yes, Your Highness. Except . . .'

'What?'

'Oh, nothing important, sire.'

'Everything in this world is important, Mijnheer van Systens.'

'Well, Your Highness, a difficulty has arisen.'

'Which is?'

'That the tulip is already being claimed by impostors. Of course, it is worth a hundred thousand florins.'

'Really?'

'Yes, Your Highness, by impostors, counterfeiters.'

'That's a crime, Mijnheer van Systens.'

'Yes, Your Highness.'

'Do you have proof of this crime?'

'No, sire. The guilty party . . .'

'The guilty party?'

'I mean, Your Highness, the young woman who is claiming the tulip, is here, in the room next door.'

'Here! And what do you think about it, Mijnheer van Systens?'

'I think, Your Highness, that the lure of a hundred thousand florins may have tempted her.'

'She claims the tulip?'

'Yes, sire.'

'And what does she offer as proof of her claim?'

'I was about to question her when Your Highness entered.'

'Let's hear her, Mijnheer van Systens, let's hear her. I am the highest justice in the land, so I shall hear the case and pronounce on it.'

'I have found my King Solomon,' said van Systens, bowing and showing the way. The Prince was about to go ahead of his host when he suddenly stopped and said, 'You go first – and call me Mijnheer.'

They went into the study.

Rosa was still at the same place, leaning against the window and looking out of it into the garden.

'Ah, a Frisian girl,' said the Prince, noticing Rosa's golden cap and red skirts.

At the sound of their entrance, she turned, but hardly saw the Prince, who sat down in the darkest corner of the room. As one might imagine, all her attention was directed to the important person who was named van Systens, not to the humble stranger who had come in after the master of the house, and might as well have no name at all.

The humble stranger took a book out of the bookcase and motioned to van Systens to start the enquiry.

Again at the invitation of the young man with the violet coat, van Systens sat down in his turn and said (delighted and proud of the importance being accorded to him), 'Young woman, do you promise to tell me the truth, the whole truth and nothing but the truth about this tulip?'

'I do.'

'Very well, tell us, in front of this gentleman. This gentleman is one of the members of the Horticultural Society.'

'But what can I tell you, sir' said Rosa, 'that I have not already told you?'

'Well, then, what is it?'

'I have come to repeat the request that I made to you just now.'

'Which is?'

'To have Mijnheer Boxtel brought here with his tulip. If I do not recognize it as mine, I shall say so openly. But if I do recognize it, I shall claim it. And I shall do so even if I should have to go before His Highness the Stadhouder himself, with my proof in my hand.'

'So you do have proof, my dear girl?'

'God, who knows that I have right on my side, will supply it.'

Van Systens exchanged a look with the Prince who, from the first words that Rosa had spoken, seemed to have been trying to remember something, as though this was not the first time that this sweet voice had struck his ears.

An officer left to fetch Boxtel. Van Systens continued his questioning.

'On what do you base this assertion that you are the owner of the black tulip?'

'But on a very simple thing, which is that I planted it and cultivated it in my own room.'

'In your room. And where is this room of yours?'

'In Loevestein.'

'You come from Loevestein?'

'I am the daughter of the jailer at the fortress.'

The Prince made a slight movement, implying, 'Ah, that's it! Now I remember.' And, still pretending to read, he watched Rosa more closely than before.

'And do you like flowers?' asked van Systens.

'Yes, sir.'

'So you are a skilled florist?'

Rosa hesitated for a second, then, in a voice that echoed the deepest feelings of her heart, she said, 'Gentlemen, I am speaking to honourable men, aren't I?'

The tone was so true that van Systens and the Prince both responded at once with a nod.

'Well, then, no. I am not the one who is the skilled florist. No, I am just a poor child of the people, a poor Frisian peasant girl who only three months ago did not know how to read or write. No, I did not discover the black tulip by myself.'

'So, who did discover it?'

'A poor prisoner in Loevestein.'

'A prisoner in Loevestein?' said the Prince.

This time, it was Rosa who shuddered at the sound of the voice.

'Then it must be a prisoner of the State,' the Prince continued. 'Because in Loevestein there are only prisoners of State.'

And he went back to his reading, or pretended to do so.

'Yes,' Rosa said, trembling. 'Yes, a prisoner of the State.'

Van Systens grew pale on hearing such a confession in front of such a witness.

'Carry on,' William said coldly to the President of the Horticultural Society.

'Oh, sir,' said Rosa, addressing the man whom she thought to be her real judge. 'I am going seriously to incriminate myself.'

'Yes, you are,' said van Systens. 'Prisoners of State should be in solitary confinement in Loevestein.'

'Alas, sir!'

'And according to what you are telling us, it seems that you took advantage of your position as the jailer's daughter and communicated with this prisoner to cultivate flowers?'

'Yes, sir,' Rosa murmured in dismay. 'Yes, I have to admit, I saw him every day.'

'You wretched girl,' said Mijnheer van Systens.

The Prince looked up, seeing how frightened Rosa was and how pale the President.

'That,' he said sharply, in his decisive voice, 'cannot concern the members of the Horticultural Society. They are to assess the black tulip and not to judge political crimes. Go on, young woman, go on.'

Van Systens, with an eloquent glance, thanked the new member of the Horticultural Society on behalf of all tulips.

Rosa, reassured by the sort of encouragement that the stranger had given her, described everything that had happened in the previous three months, everything that she had done and all that she had suffered. She spoke about Gryphus's harsh treatment; the destruction of the first offset; the prisoner's distress; the care taken so that the second offset would sprout; the prisoner's patience and his agonies during their separation; how he had tried to starve himself because he had no news of his tulip; the joy that he had felt at their reunion; and finally, the despair that they had both suffered when they saw that the tulip, which had just flowered, had been stolen from them an hour after flowering.

All this was told with a conviction that left the Prince, at least in appearance, unmoved, but which was not without its effect on Mijnheer van Systens.

'But you have not known this prisoner for long?' asked the Prince.

Rosa opened her eyes wide and looked at the stranger, who shrank back into the shadows, as though wanting to escape her gaze.

'Why do you ask, sir?' she said.

'Because the jailer Gryphus and his daughter have only been in Loevestein for four months.'

'That's right, sir.'

'And unless you asked for your father to be posted there in order to follow some prisoner who had been transported from the Hague to Loevestein . . .'

'Sir!' Rosa exclaimed, with a blush.

'Carry on,' said William.

'I admit, I did know the prisoner in the Hague.'

'What a happy prisoner he is!' said William, with a smile.

At that moment the officer who had been sent for Boxtel returned, announcing to the Prince that the person he had gone to fetch was following him, with his tulip.

CHAPTER 27

The Third Offset

No sooner had Boxtel been announced, than Boxtel himself entered Mijnheer van Systens's drawing room, followed by two men carrying the precious object in a box, which they put on a table.

The Prince, being informed of this, left the study and went into the drawing room, where he looked in silent admiration at the flower, then returned in silence to resume his place in the dark corner where he himself had placed his chair.

Rosa, shivering, pale and full of terror, was waiting to be invited to go and look in her turn. Then she heard the voice of Boxtel.

'That's him!' she said.

The Prince motioned to her to go and look through the half-open door into the drawing room.

'That's my tulip,' Rosa exclaimed. 'That's it, I recognize it. Oh, my poor Cornelius!' And she burst into tears.

The Prince got up and went over to the door, where he stayed for a moment in the light. Rosa looked carefully at him. She was more certain than ever that this was not the first time that she had seen this stranger.

'Mijnheer Boxtel,' the Prince said, 'would you come in here?'

Boxtel hurried over eagerly and found himself face to face with William of Orange.

'Your Highness!' he exclaimed, taking a step back.

'His Highness!' Rosa repeated in amazement.

Hearing this exclamation from his left, Boxtel turned and saw Rosa. And when he saw her, the envious man's body shuddered as though it had touched a Voltaic pile.[1]

'Ah!' the Prince said softly to himself. 'He is disturbed.'

But Boxtel had already managed to control himself by a powerful effort of will.

'Mijnheer Boxtel,' said William, 'it appears that you have discovered the secret of growing the black tulip?'

'Yes, sire,' Boxtel replied, in a slightly troubled voice. Of course, it could be that the unease came from the emotion felt by the tulip grower when he recognized William.

'But,' the Prince continued, 'we have here a young woman who also claims to have discovered it.'

Boxtel gave a contemptuous smile and shrugged his shoulders. William followed all of his movements with a remarkable degree of interest and curiosity.

'So, you do not know this young woman?' the Prince said.

'No, sire.'

'And you, miss, do you know Mijnheer Boxtel?'

'No, I do not know Mijnheer Boxtel, but I do know Mijnheer Jacob.'

'What do you mean by that?'

'I mean that, in Loevestein, the man who is calling himself Isaac Boxtel went under the name of Mijnheer Jacob.'

'What have you to say to that, Mijnheer Boxtel?'

'I say that the girl is lying, sire.'

'Do you deny ever having been in Loevestein?'

Boxtel hesitated. The stare of the Prince's imperiously penetrating eye kept him from lying.

'I cannot deny that I have been in Loevestein, sire, but I do deny having stolen the tulip.'

'You did steal it, from my room!' Rosa cried indignantly.

'I deny that.'

'Listen: do you deny having followed me into the garden on the day when I was preparing the bed where I was to plant it? Do you deny having followed me into the garden on the day when I pretended to plant it? Do you deny that, on that evening after I had gone out, you hurried to the spot where you hoped to find the offset? Didn't you go through the earth with your hands – in vain, thank God! – because it had only been a trick to discover your intentions? Tell me: do you deny all that?'

Boxtel did not think it appropriate to answer these various questions, but gave up the argument he had started with Rosa and turned towards the Prince.

'For twenty years, sire,' he said, 'I have grown tulips in Dordrecht, and I have even acquired a certain reputation in the art: one of my hybrids is in the catalogue under an illustrious name. I dedicated it to the King of Portugal. Now here is the truth. This young woman knew that I had found the black tulip and, in collusion with a lover that she has in the fortress of Loevestein, she plotted to ruin me by obtaining for herself the prize of a hundred thousand florins which I hope to win thanks to your justice.'

'Oh!' gasped Rosa, in outraged fury.

'Silence!' said the Prince. Then, turning back to Boxtel, 'And who is the prisoner who you say is the lover of this young woman?'

Rosa almost fainted, because the prisoner was considered by the Prince to be an arch criminal. But nothing could have pleased Boxtel more than the question.

'Who is the prisoner?' he repeated.

'Yes.'

'The prisoner, sire, is a man whose very name will prove to Your Highness how much he is to be trusted. This prisoner is a prisoner of State, once condemned to death.'

'And he is called?'

Rosa hid her head in both hands with a movement of despair.

'He is called Cornelius van Baerle,' said Boxtel. 'He is the godson of that scoundrel Cornelius de Witt.'

The Prince shuddered. A flaming glance shot from his usually calm eyes and a deathly impassivity once more spread across his cold features. He went over to Rosa and, with one finger, signed to her to take her hands away from her face. She obeyed like a woman obeying a magician's wand.

'So, it was in order to follow this man that you came to me in Leyden and asked for your father to be transferred?'

Rosa hung her head and her body sagged as if crushed, as she muttered, 'Yes, sire.'

'Carry on,' the Prince said to Boxtel.

'There is nothing more to say,' Boxtel continued. 'Your Highness knows everything. Now, here is what I did not want to mention, in order to spare this girl's blushes for her ingratitude. I went to Loevestein because I had business there. I met old Gryphus and fell in love with his daughter. I asked for her hand in marriage and, since I was not rich, I unwisely revealed my expectation of winning a hundred thousand florins. To justify this, I showed her the black tulip. So, since her lover had pretended to be a tulip grower while he was in Dordrecht as a cover for his subversion, the two of them plotted my downfall.

'On the day before the tulip flowered, it was stolen by the young woman and taken into her room, where I was fortunate enough to repossess it at the moment when she sent a messenger to announce to the members of the Horticultural Society that she had just discovered the great black tulip. But she did not stop there. No doubt, in the few hours that she had it in her room, she showed the flower to some people whom she will call as witnesses. But fortunately, sire, you have now been warned against this schemer and her witnesses.'

'Oh, my God! Oh, my God! The wretch!' Rosa groaned, weeping and throwing herself at the feet of the Stadhouder, who, even though he thought her guilty, was moved to pity by her dreadful agony.

'You have done wrong, young woman,' he said. 'And your lover will be punished for leading you on. But since you are so young and look so honest, I would like to think that the evil came from him and not from you.'

'Sire, sire!' Rosa cried. 'Cornelius is not guilty.'

William started.

'Not guilty of having led you on: that's what you mean, I suppose?'

'I mean, sire, that Cornelius is not guilty of the second crime with which he is charged any more than the first.'

'Of the first? Do you know what this first crime was? Do you know on what charge he was accused and convicted? That it was of having, as an accomplice of Cornelius de Witt, hidden the Grand Pensionary's correspondence with the Marquis de Louvois?'

'Sire, he was unaware that he had this correspondence; he

knew nothing about it. My goodness! He would have told me! Could that heart, pure as a diamond, have a secret and hide it from me? No, no, sire, I repeat, even at the risk of angering you, Cornelius is no more guilty of the first crime than of the second, or of the second than the first. Oh, sire! If only you knew my Cornelius!'

'One of the de Witts!' Boxtel exclaimed. 'Well, Your Highness knows him only too well, having already once spared his life.'

'Silence,' said the Prince. 'As I have already said, all these state affairs are not within the competence of the Haarlem Horticultural Society.' Then, frowning, he added, 'As far as the tulip is concerned, Mijnheer Boxtel, have no fear, justice will be done.'

Boxtel bowed, his heart full of joy, and was congratulated by the President.

'And you, young woman,' William of Orange continued, 'you almost committed a crime. I shall not punish you, but the true criminal will pay for both of you. A man with his name may conspire and even commit treachery . . . but he should not steal.'

'Steal!' Rosa cried. 'Steal! Cornelius! Sire, beware! He would die if he were to hear your words – your words would kill him more surely than the axe of the executioner on the Buitenhof. If there was a theft, sire, I swear, it is this man who committed it.'

'Prove it,' Boxtel said coldly.

'Very well, I shall. With God's help I shall prove it,' the Frisian girl said emphatically.

Then she turned back towards Boxtel.

'Is the tulip yours?'

'Yes.'

'How many offsets did it have?'

Boxtel hesitated for a moment, but he realized that the young woman would not be asking the question if the two offsets he knew about were the only ones in existence.

'Three,' he said.

'And what became of these offsets?' Rosa asked.

'What became of them? One failed to grow, the other produced the black tulip . . .'

'And the third?'

'The third?'

'The third, where is the third?'

'The third one is in my house,' said Boxtel, anxiously.

'In your house in Loevestein or in Dordrecht?'

'In Dordrecht,' said Boxtel.

'You are lying!' Rosa cried. Then, turning towards the Prince, she added, 'Sire, I shall tell you the true history of these three offsets. The first was crushed by my father in the prisoner's cell, and this man knows that very well, because he was hoping to get his hands on it, and when that hope was dashed with the bulb, he almost fell out with my father, who had deprived him of it. The second offset, which I cared for, produced the black tulip; and the third, the last one' – the young woman produced it from her breast – 'the third one is here, in the same paper that wrapped it with the two others when, as he was about to mount the scaffold, Cornelius van Baerle gave all three of them to me. Here, sire, take it.'

Rosa, extracting the bulb from the paper in which it was wrapped, handed it to the Prince, who took it in his hands and examined it.

'But, sire, could this young woman not have stolen it as she stole the tulip?' Boxtel stammered, alarmed at the care with which the Prince was examining the offset, and still more by that with which Rosa was reading a few lines written on the paper which she had kept in her hands.

Suddenly, the young woman's eyes blazed. She once again read over the mysterious sheet of paper and, with a cry, handed it to the Prince.

'Ah, read this, sire,' she said. 'In heaven's name, read it!'

William handed the third offset to the President, took the paper and read. But hardly had he glanced at the sheet than he swayed on his feet, his hand shook as though the paper was about to fall from it, and his eyes took on a frightful expression of sorrow and pity.

The sheet of paper that Rosa had just given him was the page from the Bible that Cornelius de Witt had sent to Dordrecht with Craecke, his brother Johan's messenger, begging Cornelius to burn the Grand Pensionary's correspondence with Louvois.

As the reader will recall, the letter was couched in the following terms:

Dear Godson,
Burn the parcel that I entrusted to you, burn it without looking at it, without opening it, so that it remains a mystery to you. Secrets of the kind that it contains kill those who know them. Burn it and you will have saved Johan and Cornelius.
Farewell.
Your affectionate,
Cornelius de Witt
20th August, 1672

This sheet of paper was at once the proof of van Baerle's innocence and of his right to ownership of the tulip bulbs.

Rosa and the Stadhouder exchanged a single glance.

Rosa's meant: There, you see!

The Stadhouder's signified: Be quiet and wait!

The Prince wiped a drop of cold sweat that was running down his forehead on to his cheek. Slowly, he folded the paper, his eyes gazing with his thoughts into that bottomless and helpless pit that is called repentence and regret for the past. Then, turning round with an effort, he said, 'Very well, Mijnheer Boxtel, justice shall be done, as I promised.' And, turning to the President, he added, 'Would you, my dear Mijnheer van Systens, take care of this young woman and of the tulip? Farewell.'

Everyone bowed and the Prince left, oppressed by the huge clamour of the cheering crowd.

Boxtel went back to the White Swan in a state of some anxiety. He was worried by that paper which William had been given by Rosa, which he had read and then put so carefully into his pocket.

Rosa went across to the tulip, reverently kissed one of its leaves and entrusted herself to God, murmuring, 'My Lord! Did you even know yourself for what purpose my Cornelius taught me to read?'

Yes, God knew, since He is the one who punishes and rewards men according to their deserts.

CHAPTER 28

The Song of the Flowers

While the events that we have just described were taking place, the unfortunate van Baerle was lying abandoned in his cell in the Loevestein fortress and suffering from Gryphus everything that a prisoner can suffer when his jailer has quite made up his mind to become his tormentor.

Since Gryphus had had no news of Rosa and none of Jacob, he persuaded himself that everything that had happened to him was the work of the devil and that Doctor Cornelius van Baerle was the devil's emissary on earth.

As a result, one fine morning, on the third day after the disappearance of Jacob and Rosa, he went up into Cornelius's cell still more furious than usual. Cornelius, with both elbows resting on the window sill and his head between his hands, was staring bleakly out towards the horizon, where the windmills of Dordrecht were beating the mist with their sails, while he breathed in the air in order to drive back his tears and to prevent the clouding of his philosophical frame of mind.

The pigeons were still there, but hope had gone and the future was blank.

Alas! Rosa would be under surveillance and no longer able to visit him. Would she even be able to write? And if she did write, would she be able to get her letters to him?

No, he had seen too much fury and malevolence in the eyes of old Gryphus on the previous day and the one before to think that his vigilance would relax for an instant; and then, apart from reclusion and absence, what worse torments might she have to suffer? Surely this brute, this rogue, this drunkard, would take his revenge like a father in a Greek tragedy? When the gin got into his brain, surely his arm – which Cornelius had set only too well – would acquire the strength of two arms and a stick?

The idea that Rosa might be mistreated drove Cornelius to distraction. He felt his own impotence, his uselessness, his nothingness. He wondered if God had been just in sending so many miseries to two innocent creatures. Certainly, at such time he doubted it. Misfortune does not help us to believe.

Van Baerle had decided to write to Rosa. But where was she? He had the notion of writing to the Hague to anticipate the new storms that Gryphus was no doubt planning to bring down on his head with a denunciation. But what could he write with? Gryphus had taken away his pencils and paper. In any case, even if he had had both of these things, Gryphus would certainly not be the one to deliver his letter. So Cornelius went over in his head all the sad schemes that prisoners devise.

He thought again of escape, something that did not occur to him when he could see Rosa every day. But the more he thought about it, the more impossible escape appeared. He was one of those exceptional beings who have a horror of everything that is common and who often miss the opportunities in life for not doing the obvious, that is to say, following the path of ordinary people that leads to everything.

'How could I possibly escape from Loevestein,' Cornelius thought, 'after Grotius has already got out of here? Since his escape, they have taken every conceivable precaution. The windows are guarded, the doors are double or triple in thickness, the sentries are ten times more vigilant. And then, apart from the guarded windows, the double doors and the ever-more vigilant sentries, don't I have an unassailable Argus?[1] An Argus who is still more dangerous since he has the eyes of hatred – Gryphus himself?

'Finally, there is one circumstance that prevents me: Rosa's absence. Were I to spend ten years of my life making a file to saw through my bars, plaiting ropes to let myself down through the window or sticking wings to my shoulders to fly like Daedalus[2] . . . But my luck is out at the moment: the file would lose its edge, the rope would break, my wings would melt in the sunlight and I should kill myself, but badly – they would pick me up lame, one-armed, legless. They would exhibit me in the museum in the Hague, between William the Silent's blood-stained doublet and the mermaid found at Stavesen,[3] and my attempt would have had no outcome except to bring me the honour of counting among the curiosities of Holland.

'No! This is better: one fine day Gryphus will subject me to some atrocity. Since I lost the joy and company of Rosa, and above all since I lost my tulips, I have also been losing my patience. One may be sure of it, one day or another, Gryphus will attack me in a way that involves my pride, my love or my personal safety. Since I have been shut in here, I have felt a sort of strange, aggressive and unbearable strength in me. I am itching for a fight, hungry for battle, inexplicably thirsting for fisticuffs. I shall leap at the old rascal's throat and strangle him!'

At these last words, Cornelius paused for a moment, staring ahead with pursed lips. Clearly, he was turning some agreeable idea over in his mind.

'Well, well!' he continued. 'Once Gryphus is strangled, why not take the keys off him? Why not go down the stairs as though I had just committed the most honest action? Why not go and fetch Rosa from her room? Why not explain what has happened and jump out of the window with her into the Waal? I can surely swim well enough for the two of us . . .

'Rosa! But, good heavens, that Gryphus is her father. What-ever affection she may have for me, she can never approve of my strangling her father, however brutal and wicked he may be. I shall need to talk it over with her, to persuade her with a speech in the course of which some assistant warder or turnkey is bound to arrive after finding Gryphus still in his death throes or completely strangled, and arrest me again. Then I shall once more see the Buitenhof and the flash of that ugly blade, which this time will not stop halfway, but become directly acquainted with my neck. So, none of that, Cornelius, my friend. That's not the way.'

But, in that case, what was to become of him? How was he to recover Rosa?

Such was the state of Cornelius's mind three days after the grim scene of separation with Rosa and her father, just at the moment when we showed him to the reader leaning on his window sill.

This was the moment when Gryphus came in.

In his hand, he held an enormous stick, his eyes were gleaming with wicked thoughts, a cruel smile twisted his lips, there was an unpleasant swing to his step and his whole silent being exuded evil intent.

Cornelius, beaten down as we have seen by the need for patience, a need which reason had forcibly impressed upon him, heard the man enter, guessed who it was, but did not even turn his head.

He knew that this time Rosa would not be there behind him.

Nothing is more annoying for a person who is brewing up a temper than the indifference of those against whom his anger is supposed to be directed. Having reached this point, one hates to waste one's spleen; one has got oneself worked up, one's blood is boiling, and it is all wasted unless the boiling expresses itself in a little outburst. Every honest rascal who has brought his ill-will to bursting point wants at least to give someone a bloody nose.

So Gryphus, seeing Cornelius stand there without moving, tried to attract his attention with a sharp 'Hum, hum!'

Cornelius was softly singing that sad but charming ditty, the Song of the Flowers:

> 'We are the daughters of the secret fire
> That courses through the veins of the earth,
> We are the daughters of dew and dawn,
> Of water and of air we're born,
> But above all, we are the daughters of heaven.'

This song, its melancholy intensified by its calm, sweet tune, drove Gryphus to distraction. He struck the stone floor with his stick and cried, 'Hey, Master Songster! Can't you hear me?'

Cornelius turned round.

'Good morning,' he said. Then he carried on with his song:

> *'Men defile and kill us with their love,*
> *A single thread binds us to earth,*
> *It is our root, it is our life,*
> *And we raise our hands to the sky above.'*

'Ah, you cursed wizard! You're making fun of me, I think!'
Cornelius continued:

> *'Our true home is the blue sky,*
> *Our true home, whence our souls are sent,*
> *And unto it our souls must fly,*
> *Our souls, that is to say, our scent.'*[4]

Gryphus went over to the prisoner. 'Can't you see that I have
taken the proper means to cow you and make you confess your
crimes?'

'Are you mad, my dear Master Gryphus?' Cornelius asked,
turning round. And as he did so, he saw the contorted face,
blazing eyes and foaming mouth of the old jailer.

'By God, you are!' he said. 'And more than mad, it seems to
me: raving mad!'

Gryphus swung his stick around, but van Baerle, crossing his
arms and not flinching, continued, 'Now, now, Master Gryphus:
you appear to be threatening me.'

'Yes, I am,' shouted the jailer. 'I am threatening you.'

'With what, may I ask?'

'First of all, look at what is in my hand.'

'I believe it's a stick,' Cornelius said calmly. 'And even quite
a thick stick. But I don't suppose that is what you are threatening
me with.'

'Oh, you don't suppose so! And why not?'

'Because any jailer who strikes a prisoner is liable to two
punishments. First of all, under Article 9 of the Loevestein
prison rules: "Any jailer, inspector or turnkey who lays a hand
on a prisoner of State will be dismissed."'

'A hand!' said Gryphus, mad with rage. 'But a stick, what
about a stick, huh! The rules don't mention that.'

'And secondly,' Cornelius continued, 'there's something that is not in the rules, but which is to be found in the Gospel: "All they that take the sword shall perish with the sword."[5] And all they that strike with the stick shall be beaten with the stick.'

Gryphus, growing more and more infuriated by Cornelius's calm and sententious tone, brandished his cudgel, but just as he was raising it, Cornelius dashed towards him, tore it from his hands and put it under his own arm.

Gryphus screamed with rage.

'Now, now, my good man,' Cornelius said. 'Don't risk losing your job.'

'Oh, you sorcerer, I'll get you in some other way, you'll see,' Gryphus roared.

'As you wish.'

'Can you see that my hands are empty?'

'Yes, I can, and I may even say I'm pleased by it.'

'You know that this is not usually the case when I come upstairs in the morning?'

'No, it isn't, very true. You usually bring me the worst soup and the most miserable meal that one can imagine. But this is not a punishment for me. I live only on bread, and the worse it tastes to you, the better it tastes to me.'

'The better it tastes to you?'

'Precisely.'

'How's that?'

'Very simple.'

'So tell me, then.'

'Gladly. I know that you think you are making me suffer when you give me bad bread.'

'Well, I certainly don't give it to you to please you, you brigand!'

'Well, since I am a sorcerer, as you know, I change your bad bread into excellent bread which is more delicious to me than your cakes. And in that way I have a double pleasure, which is firstly to eat as I like, and secondly to make you even more angry.'

Gryphus shouted, 'So you admit you're a sorcerer, do you?'

'My goodness, yes, indeed I am. I wouldn't say so in front of everyone, because that might send me to the stake like Gaufredy or Urbain Grandier,[6] but since we are alone together, I can see no reason to deny it.'

'Right, then,' Gryphus replied. 'But while a sorcerer can make white bread out of black, doesn't the same sorcerer die of starvation if he has no bread at all?'

'What?' said Cornelius.

'I shall not bring you any bread, and after a week we'll see.'

Cornelius went pale.

'And we'll start today,' Gryphus continued. 'From today onwards, then, since you're such a good sorcerer, you can change all the furniture in your room into bread. Meanwhile, I shall be making the eighteen *sous* a day that I am given to feed you.'

'But that's murder!' Cornelius exclaimed, seized with quite an understandable feeling of terror at the idea of this dreadful death.

'Good!' Gryphus said, railing at him. 'Good. Since you're a sorcerer, you will survive in spite of it.'

Cornelius recovered his mocking wit and shrugged his shoulders.

'Haven't you seen me summoning the pigeons of Dordrecht here?'

'Well?' said Gryphus.

'Pigeon makes a nice roast. A man who ate a pigeon every day would not starve to death, I think?'

'What about a fire?' said Gryphus.

'Fire? But you know I've made a pact with the devil. Do you think that the devil would leave me without fire, when that's his element?'

'However fit a man is, he couldn't eat a pigeon day after day. There have been bets made of that kind, and those who wagered eventually gave it up.'

'Maybe,' said Cornelius. 'But when I am tired of pigeons, I'll bring up the fish from the Waal and the Meuse.'

Gryphus's eyes opened wide with terror.

'I quite like fish,' Cornelius continued. 'You never give me any. Well, I'll take advantage of the fact that you are trying to starve me to death to have a feast of fish.'

Gryphus nearly fainted with anger and even fear. But he pulled himself together.

'Very well,' he said, putting a hand in his pocket. 'Since you leave me no option –' and he took out a clasp knife, which he opened.

'Ah, a knife!' said Cornelius, raising his stick in self-defence.

CHAPTER 29

In Which van Baerle, Before Leaving Loevestein, Settles his Score with Gryphus

Both of them remained motionless for an instant, Gryphus on the offensive, van Baerle on the defensive. Then, as the situation seemed likely to continue indefinitely, Cornelius enquired about the cause of this resumption of his antagonist's anger.

'So,' he said. 'What do you want now?'

'I'll tell you what I want,' Gryphus replied. 'I want you to give me back my daughter, Rosa.'

'Your daughter!' Cornelius exclaimed.

'Yes, Rosa – Rosa who you've taken from me with your devilish arts. Come on, will you tell me where she is?'

Gryphus's attitude became still more threatening.

'Is Rosa not in Loevestein?' asked Cornelius.

'You know very well that she's not. I ask again: will you give me back Rosa?'

'Very good,' said Cornelius. 'This is a trap you are setting me.'

'For the last time, will you tell me where my daughter is?'

'Well, you scoundrel, guess, then, if you don't know.'

'Just you wait,' Gryphus growled, going pale, his lips twisted by the madness that had started to invade his brain. 'You won't tell me? Well, I'll unlock your teeth for you.'

He took a step towards Cornelius, showing him the weapon in his hand.

'You see this knife?' he said. 'Huh? I've killed more than fifty black cocks with it. Just wait, I'll kill their master the devil with it just as I killed them, you'll see.'

'But, you rogue,' said Cornelius, 'do you seriously want to kill me?'

'I want to open your heart and look inside it to find the place where you are hiding my daughter.'

As he said these words, in the delirium of fever, Gryphus rushed at Cornelius, who just had time to step behind his table to avoid the first stab. Gryphus waved his big knife, shouting horrible threats.

Cornelius sensed that though he was beyond reach of Gryphus's hand, he was not beyond reach of the weapon: thrown from afar it could cross the space between them and sink into his chest; so he wasted no time and, with the stick which he had been careful not to drop, he struck a powerful blow on the wrist that was holding the knife.

The knife fell to the ground, and Cornelius put his foot on it. Then, since Gryphus seemed determined to continue a struggle that the pain in his wrist and the shame of twice having been disarmed would have made quite pitiless, Cornelius took an important decision. He rained blows down upon his jailer with the most heroic self-control, each time choosing precisely the place where the dreadful cudgel would land.

Gryphus was soon begging for mercy. But before he did so, he had cried out, and a great deal. His cries had been heard and had aroused all the staff of the prison. Two turnkeys, an inspector and three or four guards suddenly appeared and surprised Cornelius in full swing with the stick in his hand and the knife under his foot.

At the sight of all these witnesses to the misdemeanour that he had just committed – the extenuating circumstances (as we say today) being unknown – Cornelius felt that he was irredeemably lost. And, indeed, all appearances were against him.

In a second, he was disarmed and Gryphus, surrounded, lifted up and supported, roaring with rage, was able to count the bruises swelling on his shoulders and his spine like so many outcrops shimmering on the slopes of a mountain.

A statement of the violence perpetrated by the prisoner against his warder was immediately taken down – and the details whispered by Gryphus could not be accused of lacking in colour. They described nothing less than an attempted assassination, planned over a long period and carried out against the jailer with premeditation and open sedition.

The information supplied by Gryphus made it unnecessary for him to be present while the charge against Cornelius was being drawn up, so the two turnkeys took him downstairs to his apartment, groaning and covered in bruises.

Meanwhile, the guards who had seized hold of Cornelius were busy giving him generous instruction in the manners and customs of Loevestein, which as it happened he knew as well as they did, the rules having been read out to him when he had first arrived at the prison, and he recalled certain articles of the statutes perfectly well from that time.

Moreover, they told him how the rules had been applied in the case of a prisoner called Mathias, who, in 1668, that is to say five years earlier, had committed an act of rebellion rather more harmless than the one committed by Cornelius.

This Mathias had found his soup too hot and had thrown it at the head of the chief warder, who had had the discomfort, when wiping his face after this anointment, to take off some of his skin.

Within the next twelve hours Mathias had been taken out of his room. He had been conducted to the guardhouse, where he had been registered as leaving Loevestein. Then he was taken to the esplanade (from which one had a very fine view over eleven leagues of countryside). There his hands were tied, a blindfold was put over his eyes, three prayers were recited. After that he was invited to kneel down, and the guards of the fortress, twelve in number, on a sign from their sergeant, had each very skilfully placed a musket ball in his head.

From this, Mathias had expired directly.

Cornelius listened most attentively to this unpleasant story. Then, when he had heard it, he asked, 'Within the next twelve hours, you say?'

'Yes, the twelfth hour had not yet struck, to the best of my knowledge,' the storyteller said.

'Thank you,' said Cornelius.

The guard's face was still wearing the kindly smile with which he had accompanied his tale when a loud sound of footsteps echoed through the stairway. Spurs were ringing on the worn edges of the stairs. The guards stepped aside to let an officer come in.

The officer entered Cornelius's cell while the Loevestein scribe was still taking down the evidence.

'Is this Number 11?' he asked.

'Yes, Colonel,'[1] said a corporal.

'Then this is the cell of the prisoner Cornelius van Baerle?'

'Precisely, Colonel.'

'Where is the prisoner?'

'I am here, sir,' Cornelius replied, the blood draining from his face, despite his courage.

'You are Mijnheer Cornelius van Baerle?' the officer asked, this time addressing the prisoner himself.

'Yes, sir.'

'Then follow me.'

'Alas, alas!' Cornelius said, his heart sinking at the first pre-monitions of death. 'How quickly they do things here in the fortress of Loevestein, when this fellow talked about twelve hours!'

'There, what did I say?' the guard who had told the story whispered in the victim's ear.

'You lied.'

'What do you mean?'

'You promised me twelve hours.'

'Perhaps I did. But they've sent you an aide-de-camp to His Highness, and one of those closest to him, in fact, Mijnheer van Deken. Strewth! They didn't accord such an honour to poor Mathias.'

'Very well, then,' said Cornelius, puffing out his chest as far as it would go. 'Let's show these people that a burgher, the godson of Cornelius de Witt, can without flinching hold as many musket balls as any Mathias.'

And he passed proudly in front of the clerk, who, being interrupted in his work, ventured to say to the officer, 'But, Colonel van Deken, the drawing up of the report has not yet been completed.'

'Don't bother to finish it,' the officer replied.

'Very well,' said the clerk, resignedly putting away his papers and pen in a worn and dirty portfolio.

It is written, poor Cornelius thought, that I shall not in this world give my name to a child, to a flower or to a book, those three necessities of which God requires at least one, I am told, from every man who is at all organized, and whom He allows to enjoy the ownership of a soul and the tenancy of a body on this earth.

He followed the officer with a resolute heart, his head held high.

Cornelius counted the steps leading to the esplanade, regretting that he had not asked his guard how many there were – something that the guard, with his officious eagerness to oblige, would surely have told him.

The one thing that the prisoner was afraid of during this walk, which he was certain would finally take him to the end of life's great journey, was that he would see Gryphus and not see Rosa. What satisfaction there must be on the father's face! What grief on that of the daughter! How Gryphus would applaud this execution, the savage revenge for an entirely justified action that Cornelius felt he had had a duty to perform!

But Rosa, poor girl, suppose he did not see her, suppose he were to die without having given her a final kiss or at least a last farewell?

And finally, what if he were to die without having any news of his great black tulip and to awake in heaven without knowing which way he should turn to find it?

In truth, to restrain his tears at such a moment, the poor tulip lover must have had more *aes triplex* around his heart than Horace attributes to the voyager who first sailed into the infamous Acroceraunian reefs.[2]

Even though Cornelius searched to right and left, he reached the esplanade without seeing either Rosa or Gryphus. There was some consolation in that. And once on the esplanade, he bravely looked around for the guards who were to be his executioners, and saw a dozen soldiers chatting together in a group. But they were standing there without muskets, and not in a line. They were even whispering among themselves rather than chatting, and this behaviour seemed to Cornelius inappropriate in view of the gravity that is usually attached to such occasions.

Suddenly Gryphus, limping and swaying, leaning on a crutch, appeared outside his prison. He had stoked up all the fire in his old grey cat's eyes for a last look of hatred, and he began to spew out a torrent of abominable curses against Cornelius, so that Cornelius, turning to the officer, said, 'Sir, I do not think it proper for you to allow me to be insulted in this way by this man, particularly at such a moment.'

'Now, now,' the officer said with a laugh. 'Isn't it natural that this good fellow should have a bone to pick with you, since you apparently beat him black and blue?'

'But it was in self-defence, sir.'

'Huh!' the Captain said, shrugging his shoulders in a decidedly philosophical way. 'Huh! Let him shout. What does it matter to you now?'

A cold sweat broke out on Cornelius's brow at this reply, the irony of which he considered to be a bit brutal, especially from an officer who was said to be attached to the entourage of the Prince. The unfortunate man felt that he had nothing and no one to support him now, and resigned himself to his fate.

'Very well,' he said, bowing his head. 'Christ was worse treated and, innocent though I am, I cannot compare myself to Him. Christ would have allowed himself to be beaten by his jailer and would not have defended himself.'

Then, turning to the officer, who seemed calmly to be waiting for him to finish his meditation, he said, 'Come on, then, sir, where do I have to go?'

The officer showed him a carriage harnessed to four horses, which struck him as very like the carriage which in similar circumstances he had already seen on the Buitenhof.

'Get in,' the officer said.

'Ah, well,' Cornelius muttered. 'It appears that I am not to be given the honour of the esplanade.'

He said this loudly enough for it to be heard by the historian of the fortress, who seemed to be right behind him. No doubt thinking that it was his duty to supply Cornelius with further information, he came over to the door of the carriage and, while the officer was standing on the step, giving some orders, he whispered, 'It has been known for condemned men to be taken to their own towns, as it would make a better example to others, and executed in front of the door of their own homes. It all depends.'

Cornelius nodded his thanks; then, to himself, he said, 'Very well, then. And here is a lad who never misses the opportunity to utter a consoling word when he gets the chance. Farewell.'

The carriage set off.

'You rogue! You brigand!' Gryphus shouted, waving a fist at the victim who was escaping from him. 'And he's leaving without giving me back my daughter!'

'If they do take me to Dordrecht,' Cornelius said to himself, 'when we go past my house, I shall see if my poor flowerbeds have been badly damaged.'

CHAPTER 30

*In Which We Start to Guess What Suffering Awaited
Cornelius van Baerle*

All day the carriage went. It left Dordrecht on the left, crossed
Rotterdam and arrived at Delft. By five o'clock in the evening,
they had covered at least twenty leagues.

Cornelius made a few enquiries of the officer who was serving
as his guard and companion, but however carefully his questions
were framed, he was sorry to note that they remained un-
answered. He regretted not having beside him that obliging
guard who would speak without being asked to do so. No
doubt, he would have given him as much revealing detail and
precise explanation in this third part of his adventures as he had
in the first two.

They spent the night in the carriage. The next day, at daybreak, Cornelius found himself outside Leyden, with the North
Sea on his left and Zuyder Zee on his right. Three hours later,
he entered Haarlem.

Cornelius did not know what had happened in Haarlem, and
we shall leave him in this ignorance until events enlighten him.
But the same cannot be true for the reader, who has the right to
be told about things even before our hero.

We saw that Rosa and the tulip, like two sisters and two
orphans, had been left behind with President van Systens by
Prince William of Orange. Rosa had no news of the Stadhouder
until the evening of the day when she had met him face to face.

That evening, an officer arrived at van Systens's house, coming
on behalf of His Highness to invite Rosa to go to the town hall.
There, when she was shown into the great council chamber, she
found the Prince writing.

He was alone, with a large Frisian greyhound at his feet staring intently at him, as if the faithful beast were trying to read his master's thoughts – something that no man could do.

William went on writing for a moment, then, looking up and seeing Rosa standing near the door, he said, 'Come here, young lady,' without leaving what he was writing.

Rosa took a few steps towards the table.

'Sire,' she said, stopping.

'That's all right,' said the Prince. 'Sit down.'

Rosa obeyed, because the Prince was looking at her, but no sooner had the Prince returned to his paper than she stood up, quite abashed.

The Prince finished his letter. Meanwhile, the greyhound had gone up to Rosa and was looking at her and licking her.

'Ah, there!' William said to his dog. 'It's easy to see that she's a compatriot of yours: you recognize her.'

Then, turning to Rosa and staring at her with an expression which was at once enquiring and veiled, he said, 'Come now, my child.'

The Prince was barely twenty-three and Rosa was eighteen or twenty years old, so he could just as well have said 'my sister'.

'My child,' he said, in those strangely impressive tones that chilled the blood of all who came near him. 'We are alone here. Let's talk.'

Rosa began to tremble all over, yet there was nothing except benevolence in the Prince's face.

'Sire,' she stammered.

'You have your father in Loevestein?'

'Yes, sire.'

'Don't you love him?'

'I don't love him, sire, as a daughter should.'

'It is wrong not to love one's father, my child, but it is good not to lie to one's Prince.'

Rosa lowered her eyes.

'So why is it that you do not love your father?'

'He is a wicked man.'

'And how does his wickedness show itself?'

'My father mistreats the prisoners.'

'All of them?'

'Yes, all of them.'

'You are not reproaching him with having mistreated someone in particular?'

'My father did particularly mistreat Mijnheer van Baerle, who . . .'

'Who is your lover.'

Rosa stepped back.

'Whom I love, sire,' she replied, proudly.

'Since when?' asked the Prince.

'Since the moment I first saw him.'

'And when did you first see him?'

'The day after the Grand Pensionary Johan and his brother Cornelius were so horribly slaughtered.'

The Prince pursed his lips, furrowed his brow and lowered his eyelids in such a way that for an instant his eyes were hidden. After a moment's silence, he continued, 'But what sense is there for you in loving a man who is destined to live and die in prison?'

'The sense is, sire, if he lives and dies in prison, to help him to live and die.'

'And would you accept being the wife of a prisoner?'

'I should be the proudest and happiest of human beings if I were to be the wife of Mijnheer van Baerle. But . . .'

'But what?'

'I dare not say, sire.'

'There is a note of hope in your voice. What are you hoping for?'

She raised her lovely eyes to look at William, her limpid eyes, full of such penetrating intelligence that they found mercy in the depths of his dark heart, sleeping a sleep like that of death.

'Ah! Now I see.'

Rosa smiled, clasping her hands.

'You have put your hope in me,' said the Prince.

'Yes, sire.'

'Huh!'

The Prince sealed the letter that he had just written and called one of his officers.

'Mijnheer van Deken,' he said, take this message to

Loevestein. You will read the orders that I am giving to the governor and carry them out insofar as they concern yourself.'

The officer saluted, and the sound of a galloping horse was heard echoing under the cavernous archway of the house.

'My child,' the Prince continued, 'on Sunday it is the Festival of the Tulip, and Sunday is the day after tomorrow. Dress yourself up with these five hundred florins, because I want that day to be a day of great celebration for you.'

'How would Your Highness like me to dress?' asked Rosa.

'Wear the costume of a Frisian bride,' said William. 'It will suit you very well.'

CHAPTER 31

Haarlem

Haarlem, where we arrived three days ago with Rosa and where we have just returned with the prisoner and his entourage, is a pretty town, justly proud of being one of the most sheltered in Holland.

While others took pride in their arsenals and their factories, in their shops and markets, Haarlem invested its self-esteem in being the first among all the towns in the States for its fine, bushy elms, its tall poplars and most of all its shady avenues, with oaks, limes and chestnuts making a vault above them.

Seeing that its neighbour, Leyden, and its sovereign, Amsterdam, had taken, in the case of the first, the path of knowledge and, in that of the other, that of a city of trade,[1] Haarlem had decided to be an agricultural – or, rather, a horticultural – town. And being sheltered, yet well aired and warmed by the sun, it offered advantages to gardeners that no other town, with sea breezes or sunlit plains, could have done.

The consequence was that all those quiet souls who loved the earth and its riches came to settle in Haarlem, just as people of restless and energetic mind who loved travel and trade had settled in Rotterdam and Amsterdam, while politicians and society folk went to the Hague. Leyden, as we said, had been conquered by scholars, while Haarlem had acquired a taste for the gentle arts, for music, painting, orchards, walks, woods and flowerbeds.

Haarlem became mad about flowers; and, most of all among them, about tulips.

Haarlem offered prizes in honour of tulips, and this is how, quite naturally as you can see, we come to the prize that the town offered on 15 May 1673 for the great black tulip, a tulip without fault or blemish, which would bring a hundred thousand florins to the one who discovered it.

Now that Haarlem had brought to light its speciality, now that it had proclaimed its love of flowers in general and tulips in particular at a time when all was war and sedition, now that the town had had the signal joy of seeing the ideal to which it aspired flourish and the signal honour of seeing the ideal of tulips flower, Haarlem, that pretty little town so full of woods and sun, light and shade, wanted to make the ceremony for the inauguration of the prize a festival that would last for ever in the memory of mankind.

It was all the more entitled to do so since Holland is the land of festivals. Never has more natural laziness produced more eagerness in shouting, singing and dancing than that shown by the good republicans of the Seven Provinces on the occasion of a fête.

Just look at the paintings of the two Tenierses.[2]

It is certainly true that, of all men, a lazy one is the most willing to tire himself out, not in the course of work, but in the pursuit of pleasure.

Haarlem was thus thrice happy, because it had three solemn events to celebrate: the black tulip had been discovered; William of Orange, like the true Dutchman that he was, would be present at the ceremony; and finally it behoved the honour of the States, after a war as disastrous as that of 1672, to show the French that the foundations of the Batavian republic[3] were solid enough for the people to dance on them to the accompaniment of the cannons of the fleet.

The Horticultural Society of Haarlem had lived up to its reputation by giving a hundred thousand florins for a single tulip bulb.[4] The municipal authorities had not wanted to be less generous and had voted an equal sum which had been presented to the leading citizens to celebrate this national prize.

So it was that on the Sunday fixed for the ceremony there was such a crowd and so much popular enthusiasm that, even with the ironic smile of a Frenchman – who laughs at everything and everywhere – one could not help admiring the character of these good Dutch people, who are ready to empty their pockets to pay for a ship that is designed to fight against their enemies and sustain the honour of the nation, but no less to reward the invention of a new flower, destined to blossom for a day and, on that day, to please women, scholars and the inquisitive.

At the head of the leading citizens and of the horticultural committee was Mijnheer van Systens, adorned with his most expensive clothes.

This worthy man had made every effort to resemble his favourite flower, judging by the sombre and strict elegance of his dress, and in his honour we must observe straight away that he had perfectly succeeded.

Jet-black cloth, purple velvet and dark purple silk: this, with dazzlingly white linen, was the President's ceremonial costume as he marched at the head of his committee with a huge bouquet like the one that was to be carried a hundred and twenty-one years later by Monsieur de Robespierre at the Festival of the Supreme Being.[5] However, the good President, instead of the heart swollen with hatred and ambitious resentment that would beat in the breast of the French revolutionary orator, had in his own breast a flower no less innocent than the most innocent of those in his hands.

Behind the committee, shimmering like a lawn and scented like spring, came the learned men of the town, the magistrates, the soldiers, the nobles and the farmers. The common people, even among the republican gentlemen of the Seven Provinces, had no place in this procession; they formed a hedge on either side.

This is, as it happens, the best place of all to see – and to be. It is the place of the multitude who wait, philosophically, for the triumph to march past, so that they will know what they should say about it and sometimes what they should do.

But this time it was not a question of the triumph of Pompey or the triumph of Caesar; this time, they were celebrating neither the defeat of Mithridates nor the conquest of the Gauls.[6] The procession was as gentle as the passing of a flock of sheep across a field and as harmless as the flight of a flock of birds through the air.

No one triumphed in Haarlem except its gardeners; Haarlem worshipped flowers and deified florists.

In the midst of this peaceful, sweet-smelling procession, one could see the black tulip, carried on a litter covered with white velvet trimmed in gold. Four men carried the shafts of the litter and were relayed by others, just as the place of the litter bearers of the mother goddess Cybele in Rome was taken by others when she entered the eternal city, brought from Etruria to the sound of fanfares and the acclamations of a whole adoring people.[7]

This display of the tulip was the homage of an entire people with neither culture nor taste to the taste and culture of the famous and pious leaders whose blood it had succeeded in spilling on the muddy stones of the Buitenhof, although it would later write the names of its victims on the finest stone of the Dutch Pantheon.

It had been agreed that the Prince Stadhouder himself would definitely hand out the prize of a hundred thousand florins, which interested everyone in general, and that he would perhaps make a speech, something that interested particularly his friends and his enemies. Indeed, in the most banal speeches of politicians, their friends or enemies always try to find a ray of their real thoughts shining through, which they consequently think they can interpret – as if the hat of a politician was not a bushel designed to hide all light.

Finally, the great and long-awaited day of 15 May 1673 had come, and all the people of Haarlem, together with those from the outskirts, had spread out along the tree-lined avenues, with the firm intention of not for once applauding either conquerors in war or heroes of science, but quite simply those who had triumphed over Nature, forcing that inexhaustible mother to give birth to something up to then considered impossible: a black tulip.

But nothing is harder for a people to stick by than the resolve not to applaud a particular thing. Once a city has started applauding, it is the same as when it has started to hiss: it never knows when to stop.

First of all it applauded van Systens and his bouquet, it applauded its corporations, it applauded itself. And finally, justly this time, we must admit, it applauded the excellent music that the gentlemen of the town generously lavished upon it at every halt.

After the heroine of the festival, who was the black tulip, all eyes sought the hero who, naturally, was the author of the tulip. Had this hero appeared after the delivery of the speech which we have seen the good man Systens draft so conscientiously, he would surely have created a more sensational effect than the Stadhouder himself.

But, for us, the most interesting aspect of the day is not this venerable speech of our friend van Systens, however eloquent it may have been, nor the young aristocrats dressed up in their Sunday best and eating their stodgy cakes, or the poor little plebeians, half-naked, snacking on smoked eels like sticks of vanilla. It is not even the beautiful Dutch girls, with their rosy complexions and white breasts, or the plump, stocky gentlemen who have never left home, or the thin, yellow-complexioned travellers coming back from Ceylon or Java, or the thirsty populace swallowing cucumbers pickled in brine as refreshment. No, for us, the interest of the scene, the powerful and dramatic interest, lies elsewhere.

It lies in the radiant, lively features of the man marching among the members of the horticultural committee; it lies in this figure, with flowers down to his belt, his hair combed and smoothed, who is entirely dressed in scarlet, a colour that heightens his dark hair and sallow skin.

This radiant, intoxicated conqueror, this hero of the day, destined to have the signal honour of outshining van Systens's speech and the presence of the Stadhouder, is Isaac Boxtel, who sees carried before him on his right, on a velvet cushion, the black tulip, his pretended daughter, and on his left, in a huge purse, the hundred thousand florins sparkling in lovely glistening gold coins; Boxtel, who has decided to squint in public in order to lose neither of these things from sight.

From time to time he walks faster so that he can rub shoulders with van Systens. Boxtel takes a little merit from everyone to make up his own, just as he stole the tulip from Rosa to make his name and his fortune.

Another quarter of a hour, though, and the Prince will arrive, the procession will reach the final halt and, with the tulip on its throne, the Prince, giving way to this rival in the affections of the people, will take a splendidly illuminated parchment, on which is written the name of the discoverer, and proclaim that a marvel has been found, that Holland, by the intermediary of this man, Boxtel, has forced Nature to produce a black flower, and that this flower will henceforth be known as *Tulipa nigra Boxtellea*.

However, from time to time, Boxtel takes his eyes for a moment off the tulip and the purse, and casts a timorous glance into the crowd, fearing most of all that in this crowd he will see the pale face of the beautiful Frisian girl. This, you understand, would be a spectre that would disrupt the occasion quite as much as the spectre of Banquo disturbed Macbeth's feast.

And yet we must say at once that this wretch, who climbed over a wall that was not his wall, who clambered through a window to enter his neighbour's house, and who, with a counterfeit key, broke into Rosa's room, in short, this man, who has stolen another man's fame and a woman's dowry, does not consider himself a thief.

He has watched over this tulip for so long; he has followed it so ardently from the drawer in Cornelius's drying room to the scaffold on the Buitenhof, and from the scaffold on the Buitenhof to the prison in the fortress of Loevestein; he has seen it being born, he has seen it growing on Rosa's window sill and he has warmed the air around it so often with his breath that no one is more the author of it than he is. Whoever were now to take the tulip from him would be stealing it.

But he did not see Rosa. And, as a result, Boxtel's joy was untarnished.

The procession stopped in the centre of a roundabout where the magnificent trees were decorated with garlands and inscriptions. The procession stopped to the accompaniment of loud music, and the young women of Haarlem made their appearance to escort the tulip to the high seat that it was to occupy on the dais, beside the golden chair of His Highness the Stadhouder.

And the proud tulip, raised up on its pedestal, soon dominated the whole assembly, which was clapping and making Haarlem resound with the echoes of its applause.

CHAPTER 32

One Last Request

At this solemn moment, and while this applause could be heard, a carriage proceeded along the road beside the wood, driving carefully to avoid the children who had been pushed out of the avenue of trees by the crush of men and women.

The carriage, covered in dust, travel-worn, its axles creaking, contained the unfortunate van Baerle, who was staring through the open window in the door to witness the scene that we have just tried, no doubt imperfectly, to describe to our readers.

The prisoner was dazzled by the crowd, the noise and the glittering of all the splendours of mankind and Nature; it was as if a shaft of lightning had flashed into his dungeon.

Despite his companion's evident unwillingness to answer him when he asked about his own fate, he did venture to enquire one last time about all this commotion, which at first he could only imagine to be quite unconnected to him.

'What is that, if I may ask, Colonel?' he said to the officer escorting him.

'As you can see, sir,' the man replied, 'it is a festival.'

'Ah, a festival!' said Cornelius, in the lugubrious and indifferent tone of a man who has not for a long time enjoyed any of the pleasures of this world.

Then, after a moment's silence during which the carriage had advanced by a few steps, he asked, 'Is it that of the patron saint of Haarlem? I can see a lot of flowers.'

'Certainly, it's a festival in which flowers play the leading role, sir.'

'Oh, what lovely scents! What beautiful colours!' Cornelius exclaimed.

'Stop, so that the gentleman can see,' said the officer to the soldier who was acting as postilion, in one of those sympathetic gestures that one only finds among the military.

'Ah, thank you for your kindness, sir,' said van Baerle, in a melancholy voice. 'But the joy of other men is painful to me, so please spare me from it.'

'As you wish. Let's proceed, then. I ordered a halt because you asked for it and also because you are supposed to be someone who loves flowers, in particular those which are being celebrated today.'

'And what flowers are those, sir?'

'Tulips.'

'Tulips!' van Baerle exclaimed again. 'Is it a festival of tulips today?'

'Yes, sir, it is. But since the sight of it displeases you, let's carry on.'

The officer prepared to give an order to continue, but Cornelius stopped him, a painful doubt entering his mind.

'Tell me, sir,' he said in a trembling voice. 'Could it be today that they are awarding the prize?'

'The prize for the black tulip, yes.'

Cornelius's cheeks went purple, a shudder ran through his whole body and sweat burst out on his forehead. Then, considering that, without himself and his tulip, the festival would doubtless collapse for want of a man and a flower to crown, he said, 'Alas! All these good people will be as unhappy as I am, because they won't see the solemn event to which they have been invited, or at least they will only see an incomplete version of it.'

'What do you mean?'

'I mean,' said Cornelius, sinking back into the depths of the carriage, 'that the black tulip will never be found, except by someone that I know.'

'In that case, sir,' said the officer, 'the someone that you know has found it, because what all Haarlem is looking at now is the very flower that you consider undiscoverable.'

'The black tulip!' cried van Baerle, leaning half his body out of the carriage door. 'Where? Where?'

'Over there, on the throne. Can't you see it?'

'I can!'

'Now, then, sir,' said the officer. 'We must be going.'

'Oh, for pity's sake, I beg you, sir,' said van Baerle. 'Don't take me away! Let me look at it again! What! Is the black tulip that I can see over there truly black? Is it possible? Oh, sir, have you seen it? It must have some blemish, it must be imperfect, perhaps it has only been coloured black. Oh, if I was there, I would be able to tell. Let me out! Let me see it close to, I beg you.'

'Are you mad, sir? How can I?'

'I beseech you.'

'Have you forgotten that you are a prisoner?'

'I am a prisoner, I know, but I am also a man of honour, sir. I shall not escape, I shall not try to run away. Just let me look at the flower!'

The officer once more gestured to the soldier to get moving. But Cornelius stopped him again.

'Oh, please be patient, be generous. My whole life depends on a gesture of pity from you. Alas! My life will probably not be long now. But you cannot tell, sir, how much I am suffering; you cannot tell all that is struggling within my head and in my heart. Because,' Cornelius went on, 'suppose it were my tulip, the one that was stolen from Rosa. Do you realize, sir, what it is to have discovered the black tulip, to have seen it for a moment, to have recognized that it was perfect, that it was a masterpiece at once of Art and Nature, then to lose it, to lose it for ever? Oh, I must get down, I must go and see it. Kill me afterwards if you wish, but I shall see it, I shall . . .'

'Be quiet, unhappy wretch, and get back into your carriage quickly: here is the escort of His Highness the Stadhouder going past, and if the Prince notices a disturbance or hears a sound, it will be all up with both of us.'

Van Baerle, even more fearful for his companion than for himself, hurriedly threw himself back into the carriage; but he was unable to stay there half a minute and the first twenty horsemen had hardly gone past before he was back at the window, gesticulating beseechingly at the Stadhouder just as he went by.

William, plainly dressed and impassive as ever, was on his way to the square to carry out his presiding duties. In his hand, he was carrying a roll of parchment which, on this festive occasion, had become his commander's baton.

Seeing a man gesticulating imploringly, and also perhaps recognizing the officer who was with that man, the Prince Stadhouder gave the order to halt. At that moment his horses, shuddering on their powerful legs, drew up six yards from where van Baerle was encaged in his carriage.

'What's this?' the Prince asked the officer, who, at the Stadhouder's first order, had leapt down from the carriage and was respectfully going towards him.

'Sire,' he said, 'it is the prisoner of State whom I went to fetch from Loevestein, on your orders, and am bringing to you in Haarlem, as Your Highness requested.'

'What does he want?'

'He is entreating me to be allowed to stop here for a moment.'

'To see the black tulip, sire,' van Baerle cried, clasping his hands. 'And then, when I have seen it and know what I need to know, I shall die, if I must, but in dying I shall bless Your Highness's mercy for intervening between God and myself – I shall bless Your Highness, who will have allowed my work to achieve its end and its apotheosis.'

It certainly was a curious sight: these two men, each at the door of his carriage, surrounded by their guards, the one allpowerful, the other powerless, the one about to mount his throne, the other thinking that he was preparing to mount the scaffold.

William stared coldly at Cornelius and listened to his urgent prayer. Then, turning to the officer, he said, 'Is this man the rebellious prisoner who tried to kill his jailer in Loevestein?'

Cornelius sighed and bowed his head. His sweet and honest face went pale and blushed at the same time. These words from this all-powerful, omniscient Prince, this divinely infallible person, who, through some messenger unknown and invisible to the common run of men, already knew of his crime, made him anticipate not only a more certain punishment, but a refusal of his request.

He did not try to fight, he did not try to defend himself: he offered the Prince a touching spectacle of naive despair, which was both comprehensible and moving for a heart and mind as great as those that witnessed it.

'Let the prisoner get down,' said the Stadhouder. 'And let him go and see the black tulip, which is indeed worth seeing once at least.'

'Ah!' Cornelius cried, nearly fainting with joy and swaying as he stood on the steps of the carriage. 'Ah, sire!'

He could not catch his breath. Without the arm of the officer to support him, poor Cornelius would have thanked His Highness on his knees and with his face in the dust.

Permission having been granted, the Prince continued on his way through the park, amid a chorus of the most enthusiastic cheers.

He soon reached the platform, and the sound of cannon echoed across the furthest reaches of the horizon.

Conclusion

Led by four guards, who opened a way through the crowd, van Baerle was taken diagonally across the park towards the black tulip which he examined more and more eagerly as he approached.

At last he saw it, the unique flower that was destined, through unpredictable combinations of heat, cold, shade and light, to appear for a day, then vanish for ever. He saw it from six yards away, he savoured its perfection and beauty; he saw it behind the young women who formed a guard of honour for this queen of nobility and purity. And yet, the more his own eyes convinced him of the perfection of the flower, the more his heart was rent. He searched around him to find someone to whom he could put one question, one single question. But everywhere were unknown faces, everywhere attention was directed at the throne on which the Stadhouder had just sat down.

William, the focus of all eyes, got up and calmly contemplated the intoxicated crowd, and his keen gaze alighted in turn on the three points of a triangle formed in front of him by three interests and three very different dramas.

At one of the angles was Boxtel, shaking with impatience and staring eagerly at the Prince, the money, the black tulip and the assembled dignitaries.

At another angle was Cornelius, panting, speechless, with eyes, heart, life and love only for the black tulip, his daughter.

Finally, at the third angle of the triangle, standing on a platform among the maidens of Haarlem, was a beautiful Frisian girl dressed in a costume of fine red wool embroidered with silver and covered with lace that tumbled from her golden headdress. It was Rosa, who was leaning on the arm of one of William's officers, faint, with tears in her eyes.

The Prince, then, seeing all his audience in place, slowly unfolded the parchment and, in a clear and calm but low voice, not a note of which was lost because of the religious silence that had suddenly fallen over the fifty thousand spectators, who hung on his every word, he said, 'You know for what reason you are gathered here. A prize of a hundred thousand florins was promised to whoever should find the black tulip. The black tulip! This wonder of Holland is here, before your eyes. The black tulip has been found, and its discovery made according to all the conditions imposed by the rules of the Horticultural Society of Haarlem. The history of its birth and the name of its creator will be inscribed in the Book of Honour of the town. Let the person who is the owner of the black tulip approach.'

As he spoke these words, the Prince, in order to judge their effect, turned his sharp eyes on the three extremities of the triangle.

He saw Boxtel start up from his seat. He saw Cornelius make an involuntary movement. And finally he saw the officer who was keeping an eye on Rosa lead her, or rather push her, before the throne.

A double cry echoed at once to the right and to the left of the Prince: Boxtel thunderstruck, Cornelius frantic, had both cried: 'Rosa! Rosa!'

'This tulip is yours, is it not, young lady?' the Prince said.

'Yes, sire!' Rosa stammered, as a universal murmur acclaimed her touching beauty.

'Ah!' Cornelius sighed. 'She was lying, then, when she said that the flower had been stolen from her. So that is why she left Loevestein! Alas, I am forgotten and betrayed by her, by the one whom I thought to be my best friend!'

'Ah!' Boxtel cried to himself. 'I am lost!'

'This tulip,' the Prince continued, 'will therefore bear the name of its inventor and will be inscribed in the Catalogue of Flowers under the title *Tulipa nigra Rosa Barlænsis*, because of the name "van Baerle", which will henceforth be the married name of this young lady.'

At the same time, William took Rosa's hand and put it into that of a man who had just rushed forward and who, pale, amazed and overwhelmed with joy, was now at the foot of the throne, bowing alternately to his Prince, to his fiancée and to God, who from the depths of His azure heaven smiled as he looked down on these two happy hearts.

At the same time another man, overwhelmed by a quite different emotion, fell at the feet of President van Systens. Boxtel, crushed by the collapse of all his hopes, had just lost consciousness. He was lifted up and they felt for his pulse and his heart. He was dead.

The incident did not cause too much interruption to the festivities, since neither the President nor the Prince seemed to be greatly troubled by it. However, Cornelius shrank back in horror: in the thief, in the false Jacob, he had just recognized the real Isaac Boxtel, his neighbour, whom in the purity of his soul he had never suspected for a moment of such a wicked deed.

It was, however, a great stroke of luck for Boxtel that God had so conveniently sent him this attack of apoplexy, which prevented him from witnessing things that were so painful to his pride and greed any longer.

Then, to the sound of trumpets, the procession continued with no change to the ceremony, except that Boxtel was dead and Cornelius and Rosa, triumphant, walked side by side and hand in hand together.

When they returned to the town hall, the Prince pointed out the purse with the hundred thousand florins to Cornelius.

'We're not quite sure,' he said, 'who won this money, whether it was you or Rosa – because you discovered the black tulip and grew it and made it blossom, so it would be unfair for her to take it as her dowry. In any case, it is the gift of the city of Haarlem to the tulip.'

Cornelius waited to see where the Prince was leading. William continued, 'I am giving Rosa a hundred thousand florins, which she has justly earned and which she can give to you. She has gained them through her love, her courage and her honesty.

'As for you, sir, once more thanks to Rosa, who brought the

proof of your innocence' (and, at these words, the Prince handed Cornelius the famous leaf out of the Bible on which Cornelius de Witt's letter was written, and which had served to wrap up the third offset of the tulip) 'as for you, we have discovered that you were imprisoned for a crime that you did not commit.

'This means not only that you are free, but, as the possessions of an innocent man cannot be confiscated, that your possessions will therefore be returned to you.

'Mijhneer van Baerle, you are the godson of Cornelius de Witt and the friend of Johan de Witt. Remain worthy of the name that one of them gave you at the baptismal font and the friendship that the other felt for you. Uphold the tradition of their merit, because these de Witts, who were ill-judged and ill-punished in a moment of error by the people, were two great citizens of whom today Holland is proud.'

The Prince, after these few words, which he had spoken, unusually for him, in a voice touched by emotion, gave his two hands to the couple kneeling by his side for them to kiss.

Then with a sigh, he said, 'Alas! You two are very fortunate, for perhaps dreaming of the true glory of Holland, and above all of its true happiness, you seek to conquer only new colours of tulip.'

And, casting a glance in the direction of France, as though he could see fresh clouds gathering there, he got back into his carriage and left.

Cornelius departed the same day with Rosa for Dordrecht, while she informed her father of everything that had happened by the intermediary of old Zug, who had been sent to him as ambassador.

Those who have learnt to know the character of old Gryphus from what we have already written about him will realize that he had difficulty in coming to accept his son-in-law. He resented the blows he had received, which he had counted by the bruises that they left; he claimed that they numbered forty-one. But eventually he relented, so, as he said, as not to be less generous than His Highness the Stadhouder.

Having become a keeper of tulips after having been a jailer

of men, he proved to be the roughest jailer of flowers ever encountered in the whole of Flanders. He had to be seen, keeping an eye on dangerous butterflies, killing slugs and chasing away over-hungry bees.

Furious, having been told the truth about Boxtel, that he had been fooled by the false Jacob, he was the one who pulled down the observatory formerly set up by the envious man behind the sycamore tree – because Boxtel's garden, sold at auction, was now incorporated into Cornelius's, with the result that the flowerbeds were now protected from all the telescopes in Dordrecht.

Rosa, increasing in beauty, also increased in wisdom: after two years of marriage she could read and write so well that she took charge herself of educating her two lovely children, who had sprouted like two tulips in May 1674 and May 1675 – giving her much less trouble than the famous flower which was responsible for her having them.

It hardly needs to be said that one was a boy and the other a girl, the first called Cornelius and the second, Rosa.

Van Baerle remained as faithful to Rosa as he was to his tulips. Throughout his life, he dedicated himself to the happiness of his wife and the cultivation of his flowers. As a result of the latter, he discovered a great number of new varieties that are listed in the Dutch catalogue.

The two main ornaments of his sitting room were in two great gold frames: they were the two leaves from the Bible of Cornelius de Witt. On one of them, it will be recalled, his godfather had written to him to burn his correspondence with the Marquis de Louvois, while on the other Cornelius had bequeathed to Rosa the offsets of the black tulip, on condition that, with her dowry of a hundred thousand florins, she would marry a handsome lad of between twenty-six and twenty-eight years, who would love her and whom she would love.

The condition had been scrupulously fulfilled, even though Cornelius had not died – indeed, because he had not died.

Finally, to ward off any future envious neighbours whom Providence might not find time to dispose of as it had disposed of Mijnheer Isaac Boxtel, he wrote above his door these lines

that Grotius had carved on the wall of his prison, on the day of
his escape: 'Sometimes, one has suffered enough to have the
right never to say: *I am too happy*.'

Notes

CHAPTER I

A Grateful People

1. *seven United Provinces*: The Union of Utrecht (1579), between the seven northern provinces of the Spanish Netherlands (Holland, Utrecht, Zeeland, Gelderland, Friesland, Groningen, Overijssel), pledged them to political unity and military alliance. The ten southern provinces remained under the Hapsburgs (and would eventually form the modern kingdom of Belgium). Following the Treaty of Utrecht, the United Provinces combined in an eighty-year war for independence from Spain.

2. *Buitenhof*: In fact the open space in front of the Binnenhof, the seat of government at the Hague (though Dumas seems to confuse the two, also using the word to refer to the building, formerly a prison).

3. *Cornelius de Witt*: Cornelius (Cornelis) de Witt (1623–72) was *Ruaart* (steward) of Putten and the brother of Johan de Witt (1625–72), the Grand Pensionary of Holland (see note below). In 1670, Cornelius was arrested and charged with attempting to assassinate William of Orange. His accuser, William Tyckelaer, a barber, had been charged with an offence and asked Cornelius to abolish a fine against him. Cornelius allegedly replied that he would do so if Tyckelaer would assassinate the Prince. Cornelius was horribly tortured but refused to admit his guilt.

4. *Grand Pensionary of Holland*: This was the highest official in that one of the seven provinces and the most powerful person in the government of the United Provinces after the Prince of Orange (the Stadhouder).

5. *Ruaart of Putten*: The original text has 'Pulten' and Dumas seems to think that the title '*Ruaart* of Pulten' refers to an office ('keeper of the dykes') rather than to the steward or governor of the town of Putten.

6. *States of Holland*: The States-General (parliament) of the Seven United Provinces.

7. *Stadhouderat*: The office of Stadhouder.

8. *the Silent*: Dumas is confusing William of Orange (later William III of England) with William I, known as 'the Silent'.

9. *Louis XIV*: Known as the Sun King, Louis XIV (1638–1715) was King of France from 1643 until his death, a period regarded as a golden age for French culture. Married to Marie-Thérèse, daughter of King Philip IV of Spain, he pursued a claim on the Spanish Netherlands and campaigned against the Dutch in a series of wars that lasted until 1679.

10. *Comte de Guiche*: Guy-Armand de Gramont, Comte de Guiche (1638–73), was a colourful figure, famous for his debauchery, at the court of Louis XIV, who distinguished himself in service with the Dutch navy in the war against England (1665–7). He then joined Louis XIV's campaign against the Netherlands. He appears as a character in the novels of the Three Musketeers cycle and in Edmond Rostand's play *Cyrano de Bergerac*.

11. *Boileau*: Nicolas Boileau-Despréaux (1636–1711) was a theorist of Classicism and a leading satirical poet during the reign of Louis XIV. Among his works is a *Précis historique des campagnes de Louis XIV*.

12. *mocked . . . as best they could*: M. Capefigue, in his history of the age of Louis XIV (*Louis XIV*, Paris, 1844), describes the various ways in which the Protestant Dutch irritated Louis by, for example, mocking at his pretentions as the Sun-King, and gives these as one of the main motives behind Louis's decision to go to war.

13. *Mithridates of the Republic*: Mithridates, King of Pontus (c.132–63 BC), led his people against Rome in three successive wars and finally took his own life after being defeated by Pompey. He is the subject of a tragedy by Racine (1673).

14. *procurator fiscal*: The magistrate known in Scotland as a 'procurator fiscal', a public prosecutor and coroner, is a reasonably close equivalent to the official Dumas here calls a *procureur fiscal* (though some translations prefer 'attorney general').

15. *Horace's* Justum et tenacem: A reference to Horace, *Odes*, III, 3, l. 1, about the conduct of the 'strong and righteous man', whose will is not shaken by tyranny. It appears that Cornelius de Witt did in fact quote this line to his torturers.

16. *Aristides*: Aristides (c.530–468 BC) was an Athenian general who played an important part in the city-state's victory in the Persian wars. Though he was banished by his rival Themistocles, the Athenians did

recall him before the full term of banishment was complete. However, he died in poverty

17. *Marquis de Louvois*: Louis XIV's minister in the Dutch wars, during which he proved a particularly intractable enemy of the Netherlands. Johan de Witt was accused of complicity with him, but the charge was later dismissed.

18. *Schweningen*: There must be a confusion here between the German town and Schevening, the port near the Hague.

19. *in Frisian dress*: Rosa comes from Friesland, a region in the north-west of Holland.

CHAPTER 2

The Two Brothers

1. *magnetism*: The experiments of Luigi Galvani (1737–98), Alessandro Volta (1745–1827), François Arago (1786–1853) and André-Marie Ampère (1775–1836) had shown the relationship between electricity and magnetism and aroused great interest, particularly since the forces involved were invisible and so all the more mysterious. There was much speculation about the relation between electricity, magnetism and life.

2. *Tromp's fleet ... the Scheldt*: Admiral Maarten van Tromp (1597–1653) was the Dutch commander in the naval war against England. The Scheldt is a river that flows through France and Belgium into the North Sea via an estuary in the south-west Netherlands. Historically, it had considerable strategic importance because the Dutch could close the estuary and deny shipping entry to the port of Antwerp.

3. *the defeats of Rees, Orsay, Vesel and Rheinberg*: Towns in the Rhineland which were taken by the French early in the war with Holland.

CHAPTER 3

Johan de Witt's Pupil

1. *Hoogstraat*: The street that leads to the town hall.

2. *Lavater*: Johann Kaspar Lavater (1741–1801) put forward a 'scientific' method of reading character from the features of the face, which was very popular in the late eighteenth and early nineteenth centuries.

3. *they said in Antiquity*: A reference to the occasion when a pirate was brought to justice in front of Alexander the Great, and remarked that he saw no difference between the two of them, except that Alexander had more ships.

CHAPTER 4

The Butchers

1. *The Butchers*: This chapter, like Chapter 22, had no title in the 1865 edition of the novel, but titles such as the one given were attributed to it in some later editions.
2. *sous*: Dumas uses the French unit of currency. A *sou* was five centimes or one-twentieth of a franc, and the term was often used to describe a small amount of money.

CHAPTER 5

The Tulip Fancier and his Neighbour

1. *after skilfully . . . bright sun*: A piece of local colour, of the kind that nineteenth-century English translators used to cut out because they felt it held up the action, though it does suggest Dumas's use of Dutch painting as an inspiration for the novel. It has to be said, however, that the description of Dordrecht that follows bears little relation to contemporary views of the town in paintings by Cuyp or van Goyen.
2. *Juvenal*: The Roman poet, in his *Satires* (VI, 164), calls a happy man as rare a bird (*rara avis*) as a black swan; later (in *Satires*, VII, 202) he calls a happy man as 'rare as a white raven'.
3. *de Ruyter*: The admiral Michael de Ruyter (1607–75), who fought the French and English fleets at Southwold Bay on 7 June 1672. Dumas's account of the battle is broadly correct, but he distorts the chronology, saying later on that Cornelius retired to Dordrecht 'early in 1672', some time after his involvement in the battle.
4. *Count of Sandwich*: Dumas is confused here by his sources. The Count of Sandwich was one of the English commanders, not a ship.
5. *Southwold Bay*: The 1865 edition had Southwood.
6. *offsets*: The small growths, like extra bulbs, produced by the tulip bulb. They were especially important to growers because they allowed a prized tulip to be reproduced more quickly than if it was grown from seed.

7. *Floriste français . . . the tulip*: Published in 1654, *Le Floriste français*, by Charles Monstereul, was the standard work of reference. Dumas draws on it in the course of the novel, but in this case he is misinformed. Monstereul believed the tulip to have originated in Ceylon (Sri Lanka) – hence Dumas's reference to Sinhalese, the language of that country – whereas in reality the flower has its origin in the Near East, in Turkey or Persia. Monstereul proclaimed the tulip to be as much superior to other flowers as humans are to the animals or diamonds to other precious stones.

8. *Linnaeus and Tournefort*: Carl von Linné (1707–78), known as Carolus Linneus, was the Swedish naturalist whose *Sistema naturae* (1758) offered a reasoned classification of plants and animals. He was inspired by the work of his predecessor, the French botanist Joseph Pitton de Tournefort (1656–1708).

9. *Don Alfonso VI . . . Terceira*: Alfonso VI (1643–83), though physically weak and mentally retarded, succeeded to the throne of Portugal in 1656 and married the daughter of the Duc de Nemours. In 1667, his younger brother (later Peter II) deposed him in collusion with the Queen, whom he married after having her marriage to Alfonso annulled. Alfonso was exiled to Terceira in the Azores.

10. *the great Condé*: Louis de Bourbon, Prince de Condé (1621–86), who engaged in the pastime while briefly a prisoner in the Château de Vincennes. After being implicated in the civil insurrection known as the Fronde (1648–53), he retired to his home at Chantilly, where he was a noted patron of literature and the arts.

11. *Bene sit*: 'so be it' (Latin).

12. *Gerrit Dow . . . Mieris*: Gerrit Dow (or Dou) (1613–75), a genre painter, noted for his meticulous attention to detail. According to Houssaye, Dow had two 'characteristics of the Dutch genius: cleanliness and patience' (*Histoire de la peinture flamande et hollandaise*, II, p. 194). Franz van Mieris (1635–81), 'the prince of my pupils', according to Dow (Houssaye, p. 198), was also known for his genre paintings and portraits. However, a reference to Mieris in Chapter 23 suggests that Dumas may be thinking of Franz's son, Willem (1662–1747). See Chapter 23, note 1.

13. *Porus*: An Indian ruler, defeated by Alexander the Great. When Alexander asked how he expected to be treated, Porus replied 'like a king'.

CHAPTER 6

A Tulip Grower's Hatred

1. *Amalekites*: A people of the Sinai who clashed on several occasions with the Israelites (see, for instance, Exodus 17).
2. *Horace's black swan*: Dumas's attribution to Horace is wrong here. This may in fact be another reference to Juvenal (see Chapter 5, note 2).
3. *van Baerle . . . reflection of water*: Dumas makes the tulip grower's art sound like a kind of alchemy. Needless to say, the recipe for changing the colour of tulips has no basis in science.

CHAPTER 7

The Happy Man Learns About Misfortune

1. *pandaemonium . . . sanctum sanctorum . . . Ancient Delphi*: The reference to *pandaemonium* (the place in Hell, according to Milton, where the devils lived and chaos reigned) does not seem appropriate here. *Sanctum sanctorum* means 'Holy of Holies', the innermost part of the Jewish tabernacle, where the Ark of the Covenant is kept; Delphi was the site of the Greek oracle and a sacred city.
2. *the great Racine*: Jean Racine (1639–99), the dramatist, whose plays were written in the standard twelve-syllable French verse line, the alexandrine. The original French for 'No servant . . . therein' (*'Valet n'y avait mis un pied audacieux'*) is an alexandrine, though it is doubtful that Racine would have been especially proud of having written it.
3. *Maximilian*: Maximilian I (1449–1519), Emperor of Germany.

CHAPTER 8

An Invasion

1. *bronze lions in Venice*: Anonymous denunciations were placed in the mouths of these statues.

CHAPTER 11

The Testament of Cornelius van Baerle

1. *Tarquin the Elder*: In fact, Tarquin the Proud (534–510 BC), King of Rome. When Tarquin was besieging the town of Gabii during the Roman conquest of Italy, he sent his son Tarquinius Sextus to the inhabitants, covered in wounds. Convinced by the story that these had been inflicted during a quarrel with his father, the townspeople allowed Tarquinius inside. Then, by prior arrangement, Tarquinius sent a messenger to his father, who in response indicated how he wanted his son to treat the chief citizens of Gabii by knocking the heads off the tallest poppies in his garden.

2. *sybarite*: A person devoted to the pursuit of pleasure. From Sybaris, a Greek colony in southern Italy, whose inhabitants were notorious for their enjoyment of easy living.

CHAPTER 12

The Execution

1. *Monsieur de Chalais or Monsieur de Thou*: It took thirty blows of the axe, apparently, to behead the Comte de Chalais in 1626. François de Thou, executed in 1642, was also clumsily beheaded.

2. *Turnus*: King of the Rutuli, killed in single combat by Aeneas during a battle which was preceded by the appearance of an ominous bird, sent by Jupiter (see Virgil, *Aeneid*, Book XII).

3. *Madame de Sévigné*: Marie de Rabutin-Chantal, Marquise de Sévigné (1626–96), is celebrated for her letters, which give a vivid account of court life and politics under Louis XIV.

4. *Loevestein*: The castle of Loevestein is in the little town of Poederoyen, in Gelderland, not far from Rotterdam, on the junction of the Meuse and the Waal.

5. *the famous Grotius*: Hugo de Groot (1583–1645), usually known by the Latinized form of his name Grotius, was Loevestein's most famous prisoner. A lawyer, writer and scholar, he was imprisoned for his republican sympathies in 1618, but escaped with the help of his wife, hidden in a chest for carrying books, in 1620, and went to live in France. His cell in the castle can still be visited.

6. *Barneveldt*: Johan van Olden Barneveldt (1547–1619), Grotius's friend, was Grand Pensionary of Holland and concluded a truce with

Spain in 1609 during the Dutch wars of independence. However, he aroused the hostility of Calvinist and other anti-Spanish elements in the country and in 1619 was arrested by order of the States-General. Convicted of high treason, he was executed in 1619.

7. *Dutch sous*: According to Dumas in Chapter 14, the rate of exchange was three Dutch *sous* to two French.

CHAPTER 13

What was Going On Meanwhile in the Heart of One Spectator

1. *unguibus et rostro*: With fingernails and beak (Latin).
2. *the hardest of all metals*: An odd remark, since gold is notoriously soft.
3. *the far side of the Channel*: English boxers were famous in Dumas's day.
4. *Envy . . . in place of her own hair*: Dumas may be thinking of the Gorgon Medusa, who was punished, after Poseidon had seduced her in the temple of Athena, by having her hair replaced with snakes.

CHAPTER 14

The Pigeons of Dordrecht

1. *Barneveldt's illustrious friend*: That is, Grotius (see Chapter 12, note 5).
2. *the Roman cobbler's raven*: Refers to the story of a Roman cobbler who, on hearing that Emperor Augustus had given a large reward to a man who had taught a bird to greet him with his imperial title, bought a raven and tried to make it say the same phrase. However, the bird proved to be a slow learner, and the cobbler bemoaned its inability to remember. When it did eventually learn the trick, he presented it to Augustus, but instead of greeting him, it exclaimed: 'I've wasted my time and my money', the phrase it had often heard from its master. Dumas would have found this story in Abbé Lhomond's Latin reader, published with translation into French as *Sur les hommes illustres de la ville de Rome*.
3. *a league*: One league was about four kilometres.

CHAPTER 17

The First Bulb

1. *Pellisson's spider*: Paul Pellisson (1624–93), Protestant poet and a supporter of Louis XIV's minister of finance, Nicolas Fouquet. He stayed loyal to Fouquet after the latter's disgrace in 1661 and was imprisoned in the Bastille. Here, he tamed a spider to come when he called it on the flute. However, when he demonstrated this to the governor of the prison, the man inconsiderately crushed the spider with his foot.

CHAPTER 21

The Second Offset

1. *Cerberus*: In Greek mythology, the dog that guarded the entrance to Hell.
2. *Queen Semiramis ... Anne of Austria*: These are famous queens, though not all reputed for their beauty: Semiramis was Queen of Nineveh; Cleopatra, Queen of Egypt; Elizabeth I, Queen of England; and Anne of Austria, Queen of France and mother of Louis XIV.
3. *Pythagorean*: A follower of the Greek philosopher Pythagoras (c.580–c.500 BC), who subjected his disciples to a strict code of conduct that even regulated the subjects on which they could converse.

CHAPTER 22

In Bloom

1. *In Bloom*: Like Chapter 4, this chapter had no title in the 1865 edition of *The Black Tulip*.
2. *Saint-Preux ... Julie*: The lovers in Jean-Jacques Rousseau's *La Nouvelle Héloïse* (1761).

CHAPTER 23

The Envious Man

1. *Mieris and Metsù*: The Flemish painter Gabriel Metsù (or Metzu)
(1629–67) was known for his genre scenes and portraits, including
Woman Seated at a Window (c.1661), now in the Metropolitan
Museum of Art in New York, which shows the kind of scene that
Dumas has in mind. As far as Mieris is concerned, there are several
works in the Louvre by Willem van Mieris (1662–1747) where the
subjects are 'framed in the first green shoots of the honeysuckle and
wild vine', making it likely that he was the painter whom Dumas had
in mind, even though it was his father, Franz van Mieris (1635–81),
who lived and worked at the time of the events in the novel. See
Chapter 5, note 12.

CHAPTER 25

President van Systens

1. *Bradamante or Clorinda*: The heroine of Ariosto's *Orlando furioso*
(1516) and the heroine of Tasso's *Gerusalemme liberata* (1580–81),
respectively.

CHAPTER 26

A Member of the Horticultural Society

1. *Grote Markt*: The large market square in the centre of Haarlem.
2. *In Homer, Minerva*: The passage occurs in Book I of the *Iliad* (l.
197).
3. *Rue de la Paille*: In French in the text.

CHAPTER 27
The Third Offset

1. *Voltaic pile*: An early form of battery developed in 1800 by the Italian Count Alessandro Volta. The 'pile' was a stack of different metals (copper, zinc) separated by pads moistened with a conductive solution. See Chapter 2, note 1.

CHAPTER 28
The Song of the Flowers

1. *Argus*: In Greek mythology, the son of Arestor, who had a hundred eyes, of which two were always awake. He is associated with vigilance.
2. *Daedalus*: The legendary Athenian craftsman who constructed the labyrinth for King Minos and, for his pains, was shut up in it. In order to escape, with his son Icarus, he constructed wings of wax and feathers; but Icarus flew too close to the sun and the wax melted, plunging him to his death.
3. *bloodstained doublet . . . mermaid found at Stavesen*: Two curiosities of the time, the 'mermaid' probably being some kind of walrus. William the Silent was shot in Delft in 1584, by a French Catholic called Balthazar Gérard, after Philip of Spain had issued a reward for his life.
4. *'We are the daughters . . . our scent'*: The song appears to have been composed by Dumas.
5. *All they that take . . . with the sword*: From Matthew 26: 52.
6. *Gaufredy or Urbain Grandier*: Both men were burnt for witchcraft, the first in 1611, the second in 1635.

CHAPTER 29
In Which van Baerle . . . Settles his Score with Gryphus

1. *Colonel*: Although Dumas refers to van Deken as 'Colonel' at the beginning of the novel, in the 1865 edition he becomes 'Captain', and then 'Lieutenant' from this chapter onward.
2. *Acroceraunian reefs*: The reference is to Horace's *Odes*, I, 3, where he says (ll. 9–12) that 'oak and triple brass (*aes triplex*) bound the

heart of the man who first took a fragile boat on to the raging seas'
and wonders (ll. 19–20) how death could impress the man who had
faced the notorious Acroceraunian cliffs. The Acroceraunia are the
mountains in the Epirus separating the Ionian and Adriatic seas.
Because of their great height, they were said to attract lightning, making
them particularly fearsome to look at.

CHAPTER 31

Haarlem

1. *Leyden . . . Amsterdam . . . a city of trade*: The attribution of these
characteristics to the different towns is conventional. Leyden was
famous for its university, founded by William the Silent in 1575.
Amsterdam was the capital of the Netherlands and its main commercial
centre.

2. *the two Tenierses*: The painters David Teniers the Elder (1582–
1649) and his more famous son, David Teniers the Younger (1610–
90). There are several paintings of the sort described by Dumas in the
collections of the Louvre, for example those by the younger Teniers
known as *La Fête de village* and *Cabaret près d'une rivière*.

3. *Batavian republic*: Holland, after the tribe of the Batavi which
occupied roughly this area in classical times.

4. *a hundred thousand . . . a single tulip bulb*: At the height of 'tulipomania', even greater sums were paid for bulbs. See Introduction.

5. *Monsieur de Robespierre . . . Supreme Being*: In 1793, the French
revolutionary leader Maximilien Robespierre (1759–94) inaugurated
the cult of the Supreme Being as a rational alternative to existing
religions.

6. *triumph of Pompey . . . conquest of the Gauls*: Mithridates, King of
Pontus, was defeated by the Roman general Pompey in 64 BC (see
Chapter 1, note 13). Julius Caesar conquered Gaul in 50 BC.

7. *Cybele . . . a whole adoring people*: The festival of the goddess
Cybele took place in Rome during April and is described by Ovid in
the *Fasti* (Book IV, ll.179–372). The cult of Cybele was brought from
Greece to Italy, the goddess's statue first arriving at Ostia, the port of
Rome, according to Ovid. Etruria is the region north of Rome, roughly
between the rivers Tiber and Arno, formerly inhabited by the
Etruscans.

PENGUIN ⟨🐧⟩ CLASSICS

The Classics Publisher

'Penguin Classics, one of the world's greatest series' JOHN KEEGAN

'I have never been disappointed with the Penguin Classics. All I have read is a model of academic seriousness and provides the essential information to fully enjoy the master works that appear in its catalogue' MARIO VARGAS LLOSA

'Penguin and Classics are words that go together like horse and carriage or Mercedes and Benz. When I was a university teacher I always prescribed Penguin editions of classic novels for my courses: they have the best introductions, the most reliable notes, and the most carefully edited texts' DAVID LODGE

'Growing up in Bombay, expensive hardback books were beyond my means, but I could indulge my passion for reading at the roadside bookstalls that were well stocked with all the Penguin paperbacks . . . Sometimes I would choose a book just because I was attracted by the cover, but so reliable was the Penguin imprimatur that I was never once disappointed by the contents.

Such access certainly broadened the scope of my reading, and perhaps it's no coincidence that so many Merchant Ivory films have been adapted from great novels, or that those novels are published by Penguin' ISMAIL MERCHANT

'You can't write, read, or live fully in the present without knowing the literature of the past. Penguin Classics opens the door to a treasure house of pure pleasure, books that have never been bettered, which are read again and again with increased delight' JOHN MORTIMER

CLICK ON A CLASSIC
www.penguinclassics.com

The world's greatest literature at your fingertips

Constantly updated information on over 1600 titles, from
Icelandic sagas to ancient Indian epics, Russian drama to
Italian romance, American greats to African masterpieces

•

The latest news on recent additions to the list, updated
editions and specially commissioned translations

•

Original scholarly essays by leading writers: Elaine Showalter
on Zola, Laurie R. King on Arthur Conan Doyle, Frank
Kermode on Shakespeare, Lisa Appignanesi on Tolstoy

•

A wealth of background material, including biographies
of every classic author from Aristotle to Zamyatin, plot
synopses, readers' and teachers' guides, useful web links

•

Online desk and examination copy assistance for academics

•

Trivia quizzes, competitions, giveaways, news on
forthcoming screen adaptations

•

eBooks available to download

READ MORE IN PENGUIN

In every corner of the world, on every subject under the sun, Penguin represents quality and variety – the very best in publishing today.

For complete information about books available from Penguin – including Puffins and Penguin Classics – and how to order them, write to us at the appropriate address below. Please note that for copyright reasons the selection of books varies from country to country.

In the United Kingdom: *Please write to* Dept EP, Penguin Books Ltd, Bath Road, Harmondsworth, West Drayton, Middlesex UB7 0DA

In the United States: *Please write to* Consumer Services, Penguin Putnam Inc., 405 Murray Hill Parkway, East Rutherford, New Jersey 07073-2136. *VISA and MasterCard holders call 1-800-631-8571 to order Penguin titles*

In Canada: *Please write to* Penguin Books Canada Ltd, 10 Alcorn Avenue, Suite 300, Toronto, Ontario M4V 3B2

In Australia: *Please write to* Penguin Books Australia Ltd, 487 Maroondah Highway, Ringwood, Victoria 3134

In New Zealand: *Please write to* Penguin Books (NZ) Ltd, Private Bag 102902, North Shore Mail Centre, Auckland 10

In India: *Please write to* Penguin Books India Pvt Ltd, 11, Community Centre, Panchsheel Park, New Delhi 110017

In the Netherlands: *Please write to* Penguin Books Netherlands bv, Postbus 3507, NL-1001 AH Amsterdam

In Germany: *Please write to* Penguin Books Deutschland GmbH, Metzlerstrasse 26, 60594 Frankfurt am Main

In Spain: *Please write to* Penguin Books S. A., Bravo Murillo 19, 1°B, 28015 Madrid

In Italy: *Please write to* Penguin Italia s.r.l., Via Vittoria Emanuele 45ia, 20094 Corsico, Milano

In France: *Please write to* Penguin France, 12, Rue Prosper Ferradou, 31700 Blagnac

In Japan: *Please write to* Penguin Books Japan Ltd, Iidabashi KM-Bldg, 2-23-9 Koraku, Bunkyo-Ku, Tokyo 112-0004

In South Africa: *Please write to* Penguin Books South Africa (Pty) Ltd, P.O. Box 751093, Gardenview, 2047 Johannesburg

DUMAS

The Three Musketeers

'Now, gentlemen, it's one for all and all for one. That's our motto, and I think we should stick to it'

Dumas's tale of swashbuckling and heroism follows the fortunes of d'Artagnan, a headstrong country boy who travels to Paris to join the Musketeers – the bodyguard of King Louis XIII. Here he falls in with Athos, Porthos and Aramis, and the four friends soon find themselves caught up in court politics and intrigue. Together they must outwit Cardinal Richelieu and his plot to gain influence over the King, and thwart the beautiful spy Milady's scheme to disgrace the Queen. In *The Three Musketeers*, Dumas breathed fresh life into the genre of historical romance, creating a vividly realized cast of characters and a stirring dramatic narrative.

The introduction examines Dumas's historical sources, the balance between fact and fiction, and the figures from history that formed the basis for the central characters of *The Three Musketeers*.

Translated and with an introduction by LORD SUDLEY

DUMAS

The Count of Monte Cristo

'On what slender threads do life and fortune hang'

Thrown in prison for a crime he has not committed, Edmond Dantes is confined to the grim fortress of If. There he learns of a great hoard of treasure hidden on the Isle of Monte Cristo and he becomes determined not only to escape, but also to unearth the treasure and use it to plot the destruction of the three men responsible for his incarceration. Dumas's epic tale of suffering and retribution, inspired by a real-life case of wrongful imprisonment, was a huge popular success when it was first serialized in the 1840s.

Robin Buss's lively English translation remains faithful to the style of Dumas's original. This edition includes an introduction, explanatory notes and suggestions for further reading.

'Robin Buss broke new ground with a fresh version of *Monte Cristo* for Penguin' *Oxford Guide to Literature in English Translation*

Translated with an introduction by ROBIN BUSS

CHARLES DICKENS
A Tale of Two Cities

'Liberty, equality, fraternity, or death; – the last,
much the easiest to bestow, O Guillotine!'

After eighteen years as a political prisoner in the Bastille, the
ageing Doctor Manette is finally released and reunited with
his daughter in England. There the lives of two very different
men, Charles Darnay, an exiled French aristocrat, and Sydney
Carton, a disreputable but brilliant English lawyer, become
enmeshed through their love for Lucie Manette. From the tranquil roads of London, they are drawn against their will to the
vengeful, bloodstained streets of Paris at the height of the Reign
of Terror, and they soon fall under the lethal shadow of La
Guillotine.

This edition uses the text as it appeared in its first serial publication in 1859 to convey the full scope of Dickens's vision, and
includes the original illustrations by H. K. Browne ('Phiz').
Richard Maxwell's introduction discusses the intricate inter-
weaving of epic drama with personal tragedy.

Edited with an introduction and notes by
RICHARD MAXWELL

HUGO
Les Misérables

'He was no longer Jean Valjean, but No. 24601'

Victor Hugo's tale of injustice, heroism and love follows the fortunes of Jean Valjean, an escaped convict determined to put his criminal past behind him. But his attempts to become a respected member of the community are constantly put under threat: by his own conscience, when, owing to a case of mistaken identity, another man is arrested in his place; and by the relentless investigations of the dogged policeman Javert. It is not simply for himself that Valjean must stay free, however, for he has sworn to protect the baby daughter of Fantine, driven to prostitution by poverty. A compelling and compassionate view of the victims of early nineteenth-century French society, *Les Misérables* is a novel on an epic scale, moving inexorably from the eve of the battle of Waterloo to the July Revolution of 1830.

Norman Denny's introduction to his lively English translation discusses Hugo's political and artistic aims in writing *Les Misérables*.

'A great writer – inventive, witty, sly, innovatory' A. S. BYATT

Translated and with an introduction by NORMAN DENNY

CHARLES DICKENS

Bleak House

*'Jarndyce and Jarndyce has passed into a joke.
That is the only good that has ever come of it'*

As the interminable case of Jarndyce and Jarndyce grinds its
way through the Court of Chancery, it draws together a dis-
parate group of people: Ada and Richard Clare, whose in-
heritance is gradually being devoured by legal costs; Esther
Summerson, a ward of court, whose parentage is a source of
deepening mystery; the menacing lawyer Tulkinghorn; the
determined sleuth Inspector Bucket; and even Jo, a destitute
little crossing-sweeper. A savage but often comic indictment of
a society that is rotten to the core, *Bleak House* is one of
Dickens's most ambitious novels, with a range that extends
from the drawing-rooms of the aristocracy to the poorest of
London slums.

This edition follows the first book edition of 1853. Terry
Eagleton's preface examines characterization and considers
Bleak House as an early work of detective fiction.

'Perhaps his best novel ... when Dickens wrote *Bleak House* he
had grown up' G. K. CHESTERTON

'One of the finest of all English satires' TERRY EAGLETON

Edited with an introduction and notes by NICOLA BRADBURY
With a new preface by TERRY EAGLETON

ROBERT LOUIS STEVENSON

The Strange Case of Dr Jekyll and Mr Hyde and Other Tales of Terror

'He put the glass to his lips and drank at one gulp ... his face became suddenly black and the features seemed to melt and alter'

Published as a 'shilling shocker', Robert Louis Stevenson's dark psychological fantasy gave birth to the idea of the split personality. The story of respectable Dr Jekyll's strange association with 'damnable young man' Edward Hyde; the hunt through fog-bound London for a killer; and the final revelation of Hyde's true identity is a chilling exploration of humanity's basest capacity for evil. The other stories in this volume also testify to Stevenson's inventiveness within the Gothic tradition: 'Olalla', a tale of vampirism and tainted family blood, and 'The Body Snatcher', a gruesome fictionalization of the exploits of the notorious Burke and Hare.

This edition contains a critical introduction by Robert Mighall, which discusses class, criminality and the significance of the story's London setting. It also includes an essay on the scientific contexts of the novel and the development of the idea of the Jekyll-and-Hyde personality.

Edited with an introduction and notes by ROBERT MIGHALL

THOMAS DE QUINCEY
Confessions of an English Opium-Eater

'Thou hast the keys of Paradise, oh just, subtle, and mighty opium!'

Confessions is a remarkable account of the pleasures and pains of worshipping at the 'Church of Opium'. Thomas De Quincey consumed daily large quantities of laudanum (at the time a legal painkiller), and this autobiography of addiction hauntingly describes his surreal visions and hallucinatory nocturnal wanderings though London, along with the nightmares, despair and paranoia to which he became prey. The result is a work in which the effects of drugs and the nature of dreams, memory and imagination are seamlessly interwoven. *Confessions* forged a link between artistic self-expression and addiction, paving the way for later generations of literary drug-users from Baudelaire to Burroughs, and anticipating psychoanalysis with its insights into the subconscious.

This edition is based on the original serial version of 1821, and reproduces the two 'sequels', 'Suspiria De Profundis' (1845) and 'The English Mail-Coach' (1849). It also includes a critical introduction discussing the romantic figure of the addict and the tradition of confessional literature, and an appendix on opium in the nineteenth century.

Edited with an introduction by BARRY MILLIGAN